Schneid's
A Novel

TIMOTHY F. DEMPSEY

Copyright © 2015 Timothy F. Dempsey
All rights reserved.

ISBN: 1512330094
ISBN 13: 9781512330090
Library of Congress Control Number: 2015908830
CreateSpace Independent Publishing Platform
North Charleston, South Carolina

DEDICATION

To all of the Bellboys, Junior Bellboys, Navajos, Whelans, and all the other wannabe gang members from 1960s Queens. Bellerose forever!

1

I am paralyzed. I cannot move. I will not move. The moment is timeless, a defining moment, a moment from which the rest of my life will be measured. I stare through the encrusted panes of the kitchen window, glazed over with a fine translucent frosting. There is fresh, heavy snow on the ground, a typical winter day, but the clouds have moved on, and I can see the promise of the sun about to rise just beyond the ridge.

An observer might think I was mesmerized by the patterns of ice crystals, or maybe enthralled by a soundless bird flitting about from bush to bush, desperately seeking a seed or a berry. I watch, unblinking, as the physical world slips beyond me, and I crawl inside the darkness that I have avoided for years. The fears resurface faster than I could ever have imagined. In just a moment, they are back, as if they had never recessed. All of them. Encompassing my every thought, driving out hope. Almost denying who I had become and what I had accomplished.

It's not like the darkness slowly seeps into my consciousness, the way cobwebs form, starting as single, unsighted strands in a distant quiet corner of my mind. It was triggered by the briefest of glances, just a sidelong peek at the headline in the morning newspaper as I unfold it on the counter, ready to read as I brew a pot of coffee. The comfort of my morning ritual, so long taken for granted that it has become expected, has proven to be just an illusory, temporary safe harbor. I burrow into the darkness of the newsprint as the letters bleed together and redefine themselves as an abyss, a dark hole sucking me in, holding me, choking me, squeezing the very breath out of me. There is hazy realization that for the fears to so effortlessly repossess the top layers of my psyche, they must not have been very far removed.

I had certainly fooled myself. For a while, I was sure I had gotten over it. I had outgrown it. I had matured. Fear. Anxiety. Uncertainty. These feelings defined my past, not my now. This was not "I," not who I had become. Sure, they had helped shape me, mold me, but they no longer defined my essence. This depth of despair, this helplessness, hopelessness, this...nothingness had only been dormant. I had only buried it, and not very deeply. I had built such a thin shell. It was like pouring hot chocolate syrup on freezer-cold ice cream. It can diffuse itself, spread itself over the whole ball, darkening and hiding the vanilla. An inexperienced eye might think it was a ball of chocolate, solid, thick, and impenetrable. But the slightest tap of a spoon cracks the veneer, and the covering flakes away without resistance, exposing the hidden mass.

I am immobilized not just by the shock, not just by being suddenly startled, but also by a keen desire to understand the fears this time, to face them, to wrestle them to the ground and subdue them. If I cannot conquer or overcome them, then it is time to learn to live with them, to embrace them, to welcome them as part of who I am. I will examine them, explore their very depths, meditate and reflect upon them, and eventually possess them to prevent them from possessing me.

Had it only been four years since I last felt that I had no choice, no say in what happened to me? The sudden news of my mother's heart attack and death at sixty-one had unleashed the demons. I tried to grieve. I moaned and cried. I was devastated. Was it for her that I wept? For the loss of her life? Or was it because I had let her down, had failed to make her proud? Or was it because I was so desperately lonely and separate?

Cheryl had consoled me when I suggested that I might go to the funeral incognito, that I might take the risk of being able to return home. She had even goaded me, lovingly calling my bluff. "If it's going to haunt you for the rest of your life, confront it, take it on. What's the worst they can do? Times have changed. They probably won't even be there, won't even be looking for you. You flatter yourself to think you might be so important."

But I buckled then, backed all the way down, enabled by the fear, the darkness, to avoid the journey. "Jail," I told her. "They could send me to jail. I don't think I could handle going to jail." I had let the guilt direct my grieving, thus avoiding any deeper study of my other feelings. I must have sensed the fear but didn't consciously label it as such. No, guilt was easier to deal with. My unexamined assumptions, the longer they went unchallenged, began to take on the persona of truth. As my belief that I was a fugitive, that I would be arrested, hovered around for a while, it became a law, a fact, an inevitability. I wore it like a shroud shielding me from the light. I sought no reason to uncover the fallacy.

Not this time. This time I have to get beyond guilt. I have to get to responsibility, accountability. This time I have to focus on the fears. Was it my fault my best friend got killed? Was it my

4 TIMOTHY F. DEMPSEY

fault my mother died so young? Did I deserve to be scorned by my father? What might I have done differently, and what the hell am I supposed to do now?

I glanced again, less than a minute later, at the *Globe and Mail.* The word "pardon" reached out and grabbed my soul, the letters seeming to undulate and float from the page. A friendly, well-intentioned word. A friendly and well-intentioned act. "Pardon." "Reprieve." "Unconditional." But, President Carter, what about validation?

I looked again through the window. The first ray of the sun was firing like a laser, piercing the crystal formations, creating the illusion of color, a partial prism of hope, searing the molecules on the edge of the pane, imperceptibly burning the boundaries, beginning the long invisible process that will lead to melting.

2

It's hard to believe today, but Queens was seen as a utopia in the thirties and forties—at least to people struggling to get out of the streets of Brooklyn it was. Pop was the oldest of seven children. Five of them made it out of childhood, and there was not a lot of room in the family's cold-water flat. Whenever possible, he was outside, roaming the streets of Canarsie with his friends. Sure, Pop loved the romance of skinny-dipping in Sheepshead Bay or day trekking over to Ebbets Field in hopes of getting into the bleachers to see "dem bums." But in the Irish slums, those days of luxury were few and far between for the street urchins, who spent their afternoons scrounging for food, mostly finding trouble.

They went to the vegetable stands on Linden Boulevard. Two of them staged a brawl, distracting the owner, while Pop grabbed a few potatoes from the outside bin and ran like hell. They met behind some tenement, gathered some spilled coal from the cellar, and used trash from the street to start the fire. They warmed their hands while watching the coals burn to a white-hot ash. They threw the potatoes in with the coals and watched the vegetables turn as black as the coal had been before they ignited it. Poking the spuds with sticks and turning them for uniformity, they talked of baseball and girls and dreamed of faraway places. By the time they pulled the hot mickies out of the fire, they were salivating in anticipation. They split them open, burning their hands, releasing the hot, sweet steam that had been trapped in the hardened and burnt shells. Using their fingers to scoop the tender root into their mouths, they even ate the charred skin.

Bolstered by the energy from this bit of nourishment, they searched through the trash bins along the avenue, looking for empty soda and beer bottles. They collected the penny deposit on each one, gathering five cents each on a good day and blowing it all on a vanilla egg cream, mixed to perfection at the corner drugstore: an inch of sweet vanilla syrup at the bottom of the glass and several ounces of thick cream stirred in, topped off with a spritz of seltzer water and stirred vigorously until a tall, thick head overflowed the top of the glass. They passed it around, giggling and fighting, each wanting that first blast of carbon bubbles forcing open their constricted throats and floating through their sinuses. At night, they hung around outside the bars, where dads drowned their sorrows amid stories of the old country, pushing aside their fading memories of their wives as beautiful young lassies. The streets and bars were preferable to the tenements, which were filled with the cries of hungry babies and moaning mothers.

■ ■ ■

The struggle to both pay the rent and feed the family was an ongoing challenge for my paternal grandparents, second-generation

Irish-Catholic Americans. At sixteen, when his father died, Pop dropped out of high school for a job at a newsstand in Grand Central Station, hawking papers and selling nickel cigars.

He memorized the faces and the styles of his best customers— the ones who tipped—trying to anticipate their needs, readying their cigars and papers for them as they walked up. He served them with a deferential smile, looking up to them but knowing he could never be one of them. They came from upscale communities in faraway places with names like White Plains, Brewster, and New Haven. They were dressed in hundred-dollar suits and bought several cigars every day. Their trains ran on schedules, and he saw the same faces at the same times. They were headed for midtown office buildings or were jumping in taxis down to Wall Street.

Then there were the middle-class customers coming off the subways. He rode in with some of them from Brooklyn, but only the sleepy few who also started work before dawn. He needed to be there at five, even if the boss was late. The pretty young woman opening the coffee stand across from him gave him a free cup and a donut each morning, charmed by his warm smile and his self-deprecating sense of humor. The subways also arrived from the other outer boroughs, Queens and the Bronx. He dreamed of living in one of these distant places, where people lived in houses instead of apartments, where the common day laborer could own his own piece of property with a yard, a place for growing grass, flowers, and vegetables, all surrounded by a white picket fence.

My grandmother didn't have to ask Pop to drop out of school; he saw the situation, did it on his own, and just announced it. His mother was sad, wanting her firstborn to graduate from high school, but at the same time appreciative, needing to feed the younger children. Come Friday, Pop turned his whole paycheck over to her. He was making twenty-five dollars a week, and she would return to him fifty cents a day, enough for subway fare and a nutted-cheese sandwich at Chock full o'Nuts. Many days he would skip lunch and pocket the extra change, saving up to buy a new shirt or a pair of long pants. He wanted to dress like he belonged to a higher class, always dreaming that one day he'd be traveling through and would stop to buy a cigar.

■ ■ ■

Mom was born way out in the country, in Sag Harbor on the south fork of eastern Long Island, where her father grew potatoes. She remembered the vast open fields, dewy in the morning as the sun rose, chickens scattering as she went out to throw them some cracked corn. She remembered the flowers and the split-rail fences. She loved to recall her father singing Irish lullabies to her, lulling her to sleep at night. All the memories of her first six years of life were good and happy. But then she was haunted by the hushed conversations between her mother and the priest, the first time she heard the word: influenza. Her dad was feverish, speaking gibberish, not recognizing her. Then he was cold, rigid, laid out in the living room. All the neighbors in their Sunday best stood around, talking and eating a banquet of food spread out on the front porch.

She also remembered the dirt and the flowers and her mother dressed all in black: shoes, stockings, dress, hat, and a veil covering her face but unable to hide the tears and the swollen, red cheeks…and the pain. She could never forget the finality, the terrible, horrible voice that her mother used in answer to her questions. "Don't you understand? Da's not coming back—*ever*!"

Mom had two younger siblings, John and Millie, and one, Colin, who was a full ten years older.

Colin tried to comfort her, telling her that Brooklyn would be an exciting place to live. There would be streets and cars, buses and trains, stores, and more people than she ever imagined. Most important, there would be family, someone to help. "All Da left her was a mortgage that was behind on payments. She had nothing, only debts. She had to sell the farm to pay them off." As patient and understanding as he was, Colin could not get Mom to understand that she would have to grow up awful fast; her childhood was, in effect, already over.

■ ■ ■

They met at a church dance. Mom was a serious student, a good Catholic girl. She was a member of the Lourdesians, the teen club that sponsored the dances. Pop got in through the back door, but he dressed right, and he was not there to make trouble. He was there, as she was, to dance. From the moment of their first touch—when he picked her out of the crowd and asked her to waltz with him—they shared a special chemistry. They could make the cares of the world dissipate as they held each other and gracefully commanded the dance floor.

At seventeen, Pop had gotten a second job. He was bussing tables at the Roseland Ballroom. As he emptied the ashtrays and cleared the tables, he watched the diners dance, enthralled by the timeless moments that were created over and over again as the women, dressed in fancy red and made up like Broadway stars, moved to the dance floor in their high heels to join their partners in their shiny black wing-tip shoes. He marveled at how they melted into each other's arms when the lights dimmed and the strobe created the appearance of stars revolving around the night sky. After hours, as he swept the floor, he danced with his broom, imitating the steps and the manner of the gentlemen he so admired.

Mom's mother taught her how to dance in the tiny kitchen of the tenement they had moved to, often getting tears in her eyes as she held Mom a bit too close, reliving for a fleeting instant the joy and hope that she had shared as she danced with her husband, just a few years, but oh so long ago.

They dated, planning to wed, but patiently waiting until they could afford to live on their own. They were both desirous of escaping the slums but were unable to save, choosing instead to live for the moment, squandering any spare cash on dance halls and, for Pop, pool halls, where he was too often outhustled. They developed a taste for decent scotch and a habit for tobacco, Mom sucking on her cigarettes to relieve stress and repress anger, and Pop just enjoying the taste, settling for cigarettes when he had to, but preferring the fine taste of a good cigar on payday.

Lost in the daily grind of eking out a life in Brooklyn, the war in Europe seemed a distraction, the headlines telling a story that was hard to relate to. Pearl Harbor changed everything, and the wave of righteous indignation and patriotism swept Pop into the Army. When he enlisted, he volunteered to fly airplanes and go to Europe—whatever they needed to fight the Nazis. He was accepted into the Army Air Forces, but what they needed was a mechanic in Fort Benning, Georgia, and the closest Pop ever got to flying was when he would taxi a plane around the runway after working on the engine. Elevated to sergeant, he was beyond suspicion when the CO was trying to figure out who was smuggling beer across the border from Alabama into the dry state of Georgia.

It took Mom three days on the train to get there and visit him, and they finally threw away all restraint and made love underneath the mosquito netting. Inadequate, it was unable to keep out the dreaded palmetto bugs. Mom was terrified at the crackling sound they made when she stepped on them as they walked in the dark. She hid in his arms when she realized they were everywhere inside as well, the hot Georgia nights relentlessly sapping her will to resist.

When he got the letter announcing her pregnancy, Pop wrangled a three-day pass and hopped on a train. They were married in Our Lady of Lourdes on a crisp fall day, Pop proudly wearing his dress uniform and Mom radiant in her mother's wedding gown, updated only with a new veil. The money they received as gifts allowed them to honeymoon for two wonderful nights in Atlantic City, strolling on the nearly deserted boardwalk, dancing the night away on the Steel Pier, drinking Chivas Regal and smoking Du Mauriers.

By the end of the war, they had a three-year-old son, Brian, and Mom was pregnant with the second, who would be called Kevin. Pop parlayed his mechanical skills into a job with Consolidated Edison. He moved into her small bedroom, living for the first few years with her mother and the rest of her family. Pop worked as much as he could, grateful for the overtime, for the extra money as well as for the time out of the overcrowded tenement. There was no time for dancing, no time for each other. His mother released him from the duty of contributing to her household, freeing him up to care for his own.

When they made their big move to Queens, it was not the Queens of their dreams, but rather just over the border, down the elevated subway line. They rented a second-story apartment above a store on Liberty Avenue in Richmond Hill, barely more than ten feet from the El. The windows rattled and the shelves shook each time a train went by, but it was theirs, and for the first time in their lives, they shared a private apartment.

I was born nine months later, their third son. My parents were always totally exhausted, Pop from working seventy-hour weeks and Mom from having three sons under five years old. Tired of waiting for Pop to take the initiative, Mom went house hunting with her best friend from the Lourdesians, Libby, who had bought a house in Eastern Queens, a place called Bellerose, the last town in Queens before Nassau County began, close to the territory that people really meant when they talked about Long Island.

■ ■ ■

In 1906, Helen Marsh, a developer from Lynn, Massachusetts, raised $155,000 and purchased seventy-seven acres of gladiolus fields in western Nassau County. She carefully and meticulously drew up plans for a village, laying out streets, avenues, and houses around a series of circular flowerbeds. As each new house was built, she tried it out herself, living in the first twenty-two for weeks at a time to be assured that they met her standards. During periods of drought, she borrowed a wagon and a horse and watered the flowerbeds herself.

In 1911, she established a train station and called it Belle Rose. Standing on the railroad platform, facing north, one could throw a stone into the eastern part of Queens County. This area was part of the Jamaica land grant, first settled in 1656 by New Netherlands Governor Peter Stuyvesant. In 1664, the English defeated the Dutch, and the area became an English colony, formally annexed to Queens in 1683. It remained primarily farmland, known as the "little plains," until the early nineteen hundreds. A building boom began in the Roaring Twenties, and the town adopted the name of its sister village to the south, concatenated now to Bellerose. The incoming population was primarily second-generation immigrants, heavily Irish and Italian, with a handful of Jews.

To the people of Brooklyn, Bellerose became a promised land, an affordable place for families to grow and even to consider the idea of wealth. The definition of wealth was modest at midcentury: it was the absence of debt. If you could hold a mortgage-burning party before you died, you died rich. Bellerose was a good twenty-minute bus ride from 179th Street, the last subway station in Jamaica, and Pop at first objected to the extra commute time. But Mom insisted, and they rented a house on Commonwealth Boulevard.

My first memory is of the backyard of this house, where I had a sandbox to play in that I shared with the two-year-old girl who lived next door. Just a few months older than me, she was always babbling and pointing, taking control. She had short blond curls, bright blue eyes, and a precious innocent smile. She captured my heart, and I adoringly obeyed her every gesture. We filled pails with sand and dumped them on each other while our mothers gossiped, dreamed, and smoked cigarettes.

We made several trips back to Brooklyn. When I was four, I was invited to a birthday party. Mom and I set out early on a Saturday morning, and she held my hand as we walked about a mile to Jamaica Avenue. We took the Q36 bus to 169th Street. She handed the driver a dollar bill, and he gave her change from the coin holder on his belt. She dropped some coins into the glass chute, and he pushed on a lever that dropped them into a rotating fan until they disappeared. I thought it was some kind of magic. The bus was only about half full, and we sat near the front door, looking out of the windshield as we passed store after store, the pattern broken only by an occasional parking lot or apartment building. Each passenger dropped some coins into the magic fan, and I watched with renewed fascination over and over again.

We then took the El into Brooklyn. Going up the stairs to the platform, we rose above the stores and could see right into the apartments that were above them. I was entranced as the train passed through the business district, crossing into the tenements, unaware of the flood of memories that were distracting my mom, insensitive to the nature of the bittersweet smile on her face.

The party was a joyous, yet raucous affair. We played pin the tail on the donkey. Everyone laughed as I missed the poster completely and pinned the tail right into the wall. We ate cake and ice cream and watched the birthday girl open her presents, mostly five-and-dime dolls. We each got a tiny plastic basket with a piece of candy, a penny, and a plastic ring. We could keep these, and Mom told me they were called party favors. I guessed that we had done her a favor by coming to the party, and so she had to give us something back. We ran around and around the living room, bumping into the coffee table, falling, and getting up to run some more. Our mothers stayed in the kitchen, smoked cigarettes, and talked. I noticed only their occasional outbursts of unabashed laughter, choosing to ignore the serious and concerned demeanors that accompanied the muted voices.

On the train ride home, I sat on my basket and broke it. I cried, but Mom showed little sympathy, advising me to eat the candy—I would feel better. She salvaged the penny and the plastic ring, but threw the pieces of the blue plastic basket into the litter can on the subway platform. It was dark now, about five thirty in the evening on a cold winter day. She seemed very nervous walking to the bus stop and held me close. The streets were crowded with people, many of them carrying shopping bags and, much to my amazement, many of them colored.

3

When I turned five, Mom enrolled me in kindergarten. I had to take a bus to get to school. A school bus. A public-school bus. Both of my brothers went to Saint Gregory's, and all of my parents' education had been with Our Lady of Lourdes. But Saint Gregory's didn't start until first grade, and I guess Mom wanted me out of the house. I was to be the first to have a public-school experience. I was terrified, but I was not quite sure why.

As it turned out, there were good reasons. Mom and I were the only ones at the bus stop, and we waited for almost thirty minutes. We lived on the edge of PS 133's district, and the bus driver had trouble finding our stop. Mom chain-smoked and fretted that maybe we were not at the right corner. The bus finally came, but it was empty. This made us nervous, but the driver, a grizzled balding man with wrinkles cascading from his neck right into his shirt collar, assured Mom that he now knew where he was, but he had many other stops to make so he had to go. I slowly climbed the steps as the driver pulled the handle and closed the door behind me. I looked at the long rows of empty seats and wondered where I was supposed to sit. The driver turned ever so slightly toward me and growled, "Would'ya sit down, so I can go already?" I quickly slid into the front row and looked out the window. I saw the tears in my mother's eyes as I fought back my own.

Most of the other stops had multiple families waiting, and the kids who got on seemed to know each other. Most of the kids seemed much older than me. I spoke to no one on the bus, and no one spoke to me. I avoided eye contact and tried to look outside, through the window, not inside at the other kids. When we pulled up to the school and everyone filed off, it seemed like most of the kids knew where they were going, and they headed off into a few different directions. Chain-link fences surrounded the parking lot, and the walks led into the dark shadows cast by the imposing and aging red brick structure. There were bars on the windows, and I conjured up a prison rather than a school. I was silently shaking. I stood just a few short steps from the door of the bus. Where was I supposed to go? Should I follow someone? Who? I did not even see anyone walk up, but all of a sudden she was standing there right in front of me, looking down at me. "What's your name, hon?"

"Davey."

"Davey what, dear?"

"Davey O'Connor."

She looked at a bunch of papers and found my name. "Do you mean, David? Are you David H. O'Connor?"

"Yes," I whispered, barely audible.

"Come with me." She did not seem friendly. She was the skinniest woman I had ever seen.

When I was with Pop, I would boast that my name was Davey O'Connor, Superman Fireman Pal. It was our secret code, a symbol of the special bond between a father and his youngest son. When he called me that, I knew that I would have all the strength that I needed to heroically save people from certain peril and that I would always, always be my dad's best friend. My parents only called me by my full name, David, when they were angry with me, only when I had done something wrong.

I followed her through the dark and quiet hallways. The bus had arrived particularly late, so the morning bell had already rung, and classes had begun. Skinny Woman opened a classroom door without knocking, interrupting the teacher, who had all the kids sitting in a circle, Indian style. She told the teacher my name, and I was asked to join the circle. Two other kids had to be encouraged to make room for me as no one volunteered. I sat down, and the teacher, Miss Bailey, announced who I was, calling me "David." She let me know that I had missed the rest of the introductions, so I would have to meet the other children on my own.

Miss Bailey was taller than my mom, and she was awfully fat. She wore a bright-green cotton dress with white polka dots, and she was tottering around on black high-heeled shoes. Her arms looked like the salamis that I'd seen hanging in the window of Tom's Italian deli. Her face was round, and she wore lots of red makeup on her chubby cheeks. Her hair was all pulled up to the top of her head and sat there like a sleeping cat. She smelled a bit like stale bread, and I tried to lean back away from her, almost falling out of the circle.

She announced how the day would go. This, being the first day of school, would be a half day, ending at noon, and there would only be two activities, one for the whole class, followed by a "rest," and then an activity that we would "partake of" in smaller groups. I had very little idea of what she was talking about, but I kept my mouth shut and nodded along with everyone else as if I understood.

The whole-class activity started out fine. We were each assigned a desk, and on each desk was a picture that looked like it had been torn from a coloring book. Next to each picture were three crayons. I had red, green, and blue. We were instructed to color, using "whatever colors we wanted to." My picture was a simple bowl of fruit. I started by coloring the apple red, but then got stymied by not knowing what color to use for the banana or orange. I colored the bowl green. The teacher came by and quite coldly informed me that I was being sloppy; I was not supposed to color outside the lines. I stared at the miniscule crayon smudges that bled slightly over the thick black lines. I had not been coloring outside the lines, but I was way too scared to defend myself. I still did not know what color to use for the rest of the fruit, so I stopped coloring. The next time she came around, I tried to look busy. I kind of hunched my back over the work and covered up the fact that I was not progressing. She thrust her salami arm in front of me and grabbed my picture. "Sit up and take your arm off the picture so I can see it!" She held it in front of her and stared at it for a few seconds. "You haven't done anything since the last time I was here," she shouted

"I don't know what color to use."

"What?" she asked. I didn't know if she did not understand me because I was talking too low, or if she was just angry at my statement.

"Bananas are yellow," I stated matter-of-factly.

"Then borrow a yellow crayon from one of your classmates," she spat in disgust.

I had not noticed that the other kids had been trading back and forth, and when I looked up, a few of them giggled. I looked around my immediate area and didn't spy a yellow crayon, but a little boy a few desks away offered me one. I thanked him from the bottom of my heart, knowing he had just saved my life. I colored that banana for the rest of the exercise, absolutely assuring that I did not allow any of that yellow to escape outside the lines. Miss Bailey announced that coloring time was up and instructed us to pass our completed pictures to the front of the room. Indeed, most of the kids had finished coloring inside all the lines on their pictures, some elaborate and quite nice. I had not even gotten to the halfway point of the seven or eight large blocky items on my picture. When she looked at mine, she said, "Oh, no, those of you who have not finished this assignment take your pictures home and finish them there and bring them back tomorrow. This is your first homework assignment. Those of you have finished have no homework tonight." I could see all the smug smiles. Ashamed, I got my picture and held it, not knowing what to do with it. She offered me no help.

"Who has to go to the bathroom before rest period?"

A few kids raised their hands, but fortunately I felt no urges and was happy not to be in the situation of possibly messing up in that venue. Those who did have to go lined up and went out into the hallway together. We were then instructed to get out our blankets and pillows. Yet again, I was stunned; yet again, I was unprepared. Some of the other kids, obviously better informed, had brought blankets and pillows from home. Over half of us, though, had nothing, and we were directed to a closet at the back of the classroom, where we found a stack of straw-brown rolled-up pallets like the kind you might lay out on the sand at the beach. We each took one, and Miss Bailey instructed us to find a spot. All the good spots, those tucked in corners or up against a wall or bookcase, were already taken by the lucky prepared kids.

We had to unroll our pallets next to each other in the middle of the classroom.

We sat on them looking at each other, somewhat bewildered. "You *must* lie down," she instructed us, "no sitting up." I lay down as fast as if I had been shot. This still wasn't good enough. "Eyes closed," she yelled "No looking." I squeezed my eyes tight and held them shut, my mind racing, wondering what was next. Was I going to fail at rest period the way I had failed at coloring? "Okay, now rest," she barked. Everyone got so quiet that I could hear the clock tick the seconds away.

Unfortunately, the minute hand was moving in slow motion. It took a lifetime to go around once. I risked opening one of my eyes a crack and looked around. Some of the kids looked like they were actually going to sleep. Of course, they were comfortably snuggled in their own blankets; their heads nestled in their own pillows. Those of us on hard pallets with our heads on the floor were all peeking at each other; a few were even laughing. Much too terrified for that, I closed my eye again, wondering if I would survive the day.

Then it got really bad. After an interminable twenty minutes, during which I had opened my eyes at least ten times—successfully at least, without getting caught—Miss Bailey announced group activities, of which there would be five: coloring (I was wondering if I would be allowed to finish my homework), erector sets (I loved to build, so maybe this wouldn't be so bad after all), reading (I didn't know how yet), blocks (again, building) and house (oh my God, that must be for the girls). I was trying to decide whether I was going to choose blocks or an erector set when Miss Bailey announced that *she* was ready to make the assignments. She called out the name of the activity and then very quickly called out four or five names. She was reading out full names. I didn't hear my name as she went through the first four areas, and I was beginning to think maybe I was in the wrong classroom after all when she announced, "House...David H. O'Connor..." and then four other names, all of them girls! *There must be some mistake*, I thought. *She will realize that I am not a girl and reassign me.* I sat on my mat as the other children moved to their activity area. Activities started, and I just sat there. She came over to me and stood above me, glaring down. "Get up!" she commanded. I jumped out of my skin. I was trembling. I thought I was going to get hit. My brothers had told me about the hitting when you get in trouble and predicted that I would get hit almost every day. I was sure this was going to be hit number one, and I steeled myself. Instead, she miraculously lowered her voice, but said through slightly gritted teeth, "Why have you not moved to your activity?"

"I'm not a girl," I muttered.

"*What?*" Again did she not understand me?

"I'm not a girl."

"So?"

"So I don't want to play house." I was shocked at how brave I was, but I was soon to crumble.

"Did I ask you what you *wanted* to do?" She was growing livid.

"No."

"No, *what?*"

"No, you didn't ask me what I wanted." Had she forgotten what had gotten us this far?

"No, *ma'am!*"

All of a sudden we were formal. Did I join the army when I wasn't looking? "No, ma'am."

She managed to curl her left salami and set her fist on her hip in an impatient manner, and she held her right salami rigid, her index finger pointing straight out, straight at the miniature outside wall of a house with a front porch attached to it. "Get over to the house activity and...*play*." Oh, now I understood. I was supposed to go play house...with the girls. I shuffled over. I had died and gone to hell. There was a God, and I was being punished.

As I stood there, this pert little girl with curly black hair came over to me and, oh my God, took me by the hand. She pulled me into the area and ordered me to sit down. "You are going to be the daddy." Was this teacher spinning off clones? Women's liberation was at least a decade away. My mother didn't even drive a car. She took care of the house and did the cooking. Raised the kids. Pop worked two jobs. And here I was playing house. "You come home from work, and you're tired," she directed. Well, that sounded about right. I sat down, easily able to act that part. Like a good husband, I did what I was told. Mommy was clearly in charge, and I tried not to think; I certainly did not want to upset anybody and get Flailing Salamis on my case again. I was way too scared to have any fun, but at least I was busy. This turned out to be better than rest period.

After a while, Miss Bailey mercifully announced that it was time to get ready for the bus ride home. We were told to replace our blankets and pillows and collect our homework and anything else that we'd brought in. She reminded us that tomorrow would be our first "normal" day. In addition to our morning routine of class activity, rest, and group activity, we would have lunch, a second group activity, a second class activity, and a second rest period in between. "Tomorrow will be twice as much fun as today!"

We were led out in a line, and there were at least a dozen buses waiting, their motors running. Which one was I supposed to get on? Some kids seemed to know but many didn't. Other, luckier kids had their moms right there meeting them at school, either walking home with them, or in one or two cases, driving in a car. Mommies can drive? I was surprised. A kindly lady, with short bluish hair that seemed to be pasted onto her head in tight little knots, was going around telling the kids, "Take the same bus that you took to get here."

All the buses looked exactly alike. Was she kidding or what? Still, a few more kids got on buses. Others looked as perplexed and even as frightened as me. A brave soul asked, "How do we know which one we came on?"

"By the number on the side of course." Nobody moved. "Didn't you check your number this morning?" Apparently those who did were already on buses. Exasperated, she said, "Then look for the same driver." Relieved, I began to look for him. All the drivers were gray-haired, wrinkly men. The terror returned. A few more kids boarded buses, and we were down to the third of us who were completely hopeless. Flight or fight? I knew if I got on the wrong bus I would never see my parents again, so I thought about running back into the school and finding someone who would help me. My mother had written our phone number down on a small piece of paper, which I felt for and found in my pocket. Maybe I could call her, and she would somehow rescue me.

The blue-haired lady was reduced to dealing with us one by one, getting our names, looking up our addresses, matching the routes, and telling us which bus to get on. While I had some comfort that I had gotten the right grizzled, wrinkly man, I felt better when I was sure that I recognized some of the kids from the morning. I had a moment's respite. This *was* the right bus. I was going to live. I was even probably going to see my parents again.

Actually, I was comforted by the thought that I would be the first to be dropped off, given that I was the first to be picked up in the morning. Wrong. We went all over Bellerose, dropping kids off in the reverse order. The last one to be picked up was the first one to be dropped off. I envied him. I loathed his luck. After a while I was alone on the bus, just wrinkly old guy and me. "Come on up front," he told me. Now he wanted to chat. "How was your first day of school?"

"Fine," I lied. *Please take me home.*

He finally pulled up to the stop, and there was Mom, smoking away, looking just as scared as I was. She held my hand as we walked the two blocks home. She asked me how it went, but I couldn't speak. She seemed to understand and let it go. Cookies and milk were offered, but talking opened the floodgates: I sat down on the kitchen floor and dissolved into a puddle of tears. I was distraught, inconsolable. I don't know what she must have been thinking. She let me cry it out, though. When I was mostly spent, reduced to sobs, she tried again. "Was it that bad?"

"They made me play house...and hold hands with a girl. All she does is yell...I didn't have a blanket, I couldn't rest right, I couldn't color right." In the middle of this gibberish, I remembered that tomorrow was to be twice as much fun, and I wailed uncontrollably. "Don't make me go back," I pleaded. I begged.

Mom told me that the next day would be better. I told her about the endless bus ride. She asked me to give it another chance. I cried and cried. She put me off. "Wait till your father gets home."

This ruse always popped up when she couldn't deliver the hard news. I retreated to the bedroom. Oh my God, I was still carrying the coloring page! I ripped it up and threw the pieces on my bed, collapsed on top of them, and cried for the rest of the afternoon. Pop came home. I heard Mom telling him about my plight and my plea. I could not hear his response. "Davey, come on out here," she called.

I could not wait for the verdict. "Daddy, please don't make me go back, please."

"You have to, pal. Your mother thinks it's important that you get used to school."

I glared at her, but she was glaring at him. "But—"

"No 'buts,'" he said. "It's just kindergarten, Goddamn it. Now let me eat in peace!" I knew the finality of that tone and those words. I slithered through my brothers' laughing and taunting and slammed the door to the bedroom.

"I hate you!" I cried out. I looked in horror at the picture I had torn up. I threw the pieces on the floor and cried myself to sleep.

4

I survived kindergarten by keeping my mouth shut and doing what I was told, burying my daily fears deeper and deeper. The next fall, I started first grade at Saint Gregory's. I only had to cross Commonwealth Boulevard and walk up two blocks. I was excited to be going to the same school as my brothers, happy to be dressed in the same uniform. My green pants and white shirts were hand-me-downs from them, but my necktie was brand-new. Pop spent all weekend teaching me how to tie the knot and correctly predicted that the Windsor knot, as he called it, would be unique and would make me stand out.

Brian helped me find the first-grade line, and then he and Kevin went off to join their friends in the higher grades. The nuns demanded respect and discipline: follow the rules, obey them, and keep quiet. "Step out of line, and you are going to get smacked," Brian had warned, and this time he was right.

Returning in a line from the auditorium, I stopped at the water fountain to get a drink. As I turned from the fountain, she swung at me from the side. I didn't see her coming, could never have expected it. She caught me full in the face with her open palm and almost knocked my head into the wall. My cheek was on fire with pain. Tears welled in my eyes. "Who told you that you could get a drink of water?"

I stood there silently, trying not to cry. She hit me again, on the other side, so that both cheeks now stung equally. "Answer me."

"No one, Sister; I was thirsty." She raised her hand a third time but restrained herself, as I ducked for the blow. "You're in the first grade. You don't do *anything* without permission. You got that?"

"Yes, Sister."

"Get back to your classroom!"

■ ■ ■

When the lease ran out on the house, Mom announced, "It's time for us to buy!" She knew they could borrow money from Libby, whose husband, Ed, was doing very well managing the Bellerose branch of the Franklin American Savings Bank. Libby was willing to lend them the $300 they needed as a down payment out of her own savings account. No interest, just pay her back when they could. No paper work.

Although Mom proclaimed it with authority, she knew that she had to consider Pop's pride. He had some immediate resistance to the thought of borrowing money. As a veteran, he had no qualms about taking advantage of the GI Bill, but borrowing the down payment was taboo. Especially from his wife's friend. Especially from a woman.

Mom convinced Pop to at least look at a few houses and, sensing the inevitable, he agreed. He wanted to buy the first house he looked at, on 255th Street, because it was over a mile away from Libby. Aware that he was hurting from having to borrow the money, and allowing him the dignity of not having to bump into Libby on a regular basis, Mom agreed.

They paid the asking price of $13,500, with a fixed-rate, 30-year mortgage at five percent. When they came home from signing the papers and closing the deal, Pop commented, "I'll be in my seventies before this house is paid off. I sure hope I die before I get that old." He didn't notice me turning white, the comment sending chills to the marrow of my bones.

Toward the end of the summer, right before we moved, demolition crews came and began to tear up the railroad tracks and flatten the Commonwealth Boulevard hill. These tracks had served only one purpose. There was a single train that came every Wednesday, carrying coal to Creedmoor State Mental Hospital from the yards in Floral Park, a little farther out on Long Island. It did not go very fast, and it did not go very far. But it was loud, long, and reliable. The weekly passing of the train was an event.

Most of the time we were content to place a coin, usually a penny, but sometimes a nickel or a dime, on the tracks. We hid as the train passed, trying to watch the exact spot where we had placed the coin. A guard always rode on the caboose and yelled at us, threatening to have us arrested if he saw us doing anything to the tracks, so we learned to wait until the train was safely out of sight. We ran over to retrieve the now-flattened piece of metal, still hot, elongated, and almost welded to the track so that we often had to use the blade of a pocket knife to scrape it off. We marveled over and over again at how thin the coins became and how all traces of images or words were gone. The coins were reduced to thin pieces of scrap metal.

The hill came down because Creedmoor was transitioning to a new heating system, and the coal would no longer be needed. Something that had seemed so permanent was going to be ripped up, pulled out, and discarded. The road would be leveled. Saint Gregory's was going to expand where the tracks had been. It seemed as if everything was going to change. As I watched the demolition, I kept saying to myself, "It doesn't matter. We're moving anyway."

■ ■ ■

The new house, a bungalow, was enormous, almost eighteen hundred square feet. Between the sidewalk and the curb was a foot-wide strip of grass and a tall maple tree. The front yard was small and was divided by a sidewalk leading up to the front porch. On the right side of this walkway, about a third of the front yard, grass grew, seamlessly joining with the neighbor's lawn. The left two-thirds was scruffy dirt with a large crab apple tree shading almost the entire area. As you walked up to the porch, there was an established asparagus bed to the side, with a lot of tall plants beginning to go to seed. We picked some, but Mom said we were not allowed to eat them. "They might be poison." The concrete porch, about four feet by twelve, was cracked and broken and was surrounded by a rotting wooden railing overrun with flying ants.

Before the end of our first week in the new house, Brian called me over. "Watch this." He had a magnifying glass, one of Mom's tweezers, and a gleam in his eye. He grabbed a small stick and held an ant with it, ever so gently. Then he used the tweezers to pull out its wings and one of its legs. He had crippled but not killed it, so it hobbled around in circles, frantically trying to find its way to safety. Brian held the magnifying glass a few inches above it, focusing the enhanced and powerful sunbeam on its tiny body, burning a small hole in its flesh. It writhed, up and down, as if it were manically doing sit-ups. Brian relentlessly kept the glass in place until a thin plume of smoke rose from the dying insect, and we could actually smell its acrid cooked flesh. My stomach retched as I felt I could almost taste it.

This was not the first time I had witnessed Brian's wrath. Our last house had a cellar with access through a ground-level, horizontal, metal storm door like you see in *The Wizard of Oz* when the tornado is coming. When you lifted up the heavy metal doors and opened them, swinging one to the left and one to the right, you uncovered the steep concrete steps that descended straight down into what looked like a deep pit under the house.

One time after I had opened the storm door, I jumped back in fright and ran in to tell my mother, "There is a huge snail on the cellar steps!" It had a bulbous, elongated body, the signature antennae, and a small head that extended into a seamless and endless neck. I thought it was a snail without its shell.

"Just stay away from it," Mom said with little concern, "and close the cellar door. You are *not* supposed to be playing there."

But Brian had overheard me, and his eyes were electric as he grabbed the saltshaker off the kitchen table with a look of glee on his face, as if he had just gotten a new toy. "Watch this," he said as he ran out the front door and ran around the side of the house to the cellar steps. By the time I caught up with him, he was already sprinkling salt onto the back of the four-inch-long creature. For one nightmarish instant, I was afraid that he was going to eat it, just to gross me out, that he was flavoring it just the way he prepared his pizza or his corn on the cob.

It turned out to be the snail's nightmare, though. It contracted every cell in its body as the crystals sucked the life-force out of its fiber. The body shrank to about half of its original size, and its top layer of skin, which looked like a hard black pelt, curled back over itself, shrouding up like a vampire's cape, trying to shed itself from the rest of the body. Its antennae stretched to their limits, pulsating, searching, moving back and forth as if calling to the wind for relief. It squirmed and wiggled for minutes, silently trying to escape this sudden horror. I watched its movements intently, feeling sorry for it, afraid to let Brian know, curious why he would do such a thing.

He was fascinated at the effects of his torture. He sprinkled a second layer of salt on the snail, triggering a new round of accelerated squirming and peeling, and I imagined that on some plane beyond our senses, this creature was screaming and crying, begging to die. After a few more minutes, its resistance slowed; and its death throes became less dramatic, and Brian got bored. He dumped a lot more salt to finish it off. As we left, the snail was a singular mass of a sticky substance with the consistency of snot.

When Pop came home, I told him about the snail and finally learned that it was actually called a slug. Pop told me that we would deal with the "problem" after dinner. Later that evening, he grabbed one of Mom's pie pans. Off the kitchen, next to a closet, there was a door leading to a narrow stairway that led down to the cellar. It was always locked, though, and was supposed to be off-limits to our family. Pop got out his Con Ed toolbox and used the blade of a putty knife to release the lock in seconds, as if he were an expert cat burglar.

The cellar was dark, damp, and dank. It had the smell of rotten newspapers that had gotten wet and sat in a dark corner for too long. The smell was strong and pervasive. Pop placed the pie plate in the center of the room and poured some Schaefer out of the can that he had been drinking, filling the plate almost to the edge. "It might be a waste of good beer, but let's check it in the morning."

Pop woke me up early the next morning. He grabbed a flashlight and we went down the cellar stairs together. The plate was now filled with a bunch of slugs, piled on top of each other, intersecting and entwined like the ball of spaghettilike white worms our puppy had once coughed up. But this mass was not moving. Each slug was bloated to two or three times the size of the one I had seen yesterday. This group had died in some ecstatic frenzy, literally drinking themselves to death. Brian shrank them to death and Pop expanded them to death. Either way, they were just as dead.

"Must be Irish," Pop joked as he picked up the plate, went up the outside steps, still open from yesterday, and threw the whole mess on the ground near the back fence. There they lay, slowly shrinking, drying in the wind and the sun, until they became consumed by other insects and melded into the dirt over the next couple of days.

■ ■ ■

From the front porch, you entered the house directly into the living room, which was adorned on two sides with wooden cases around the steam radiators. There was also a wood-burning fireplace, complete with a mantel above it. Passing through the living room, you entered the tiny kitchen, which barely had room for a dinette table and four chairs. Mom lamented that the whole family would never be able to sit and have a meal together. The sink, gas stove, and small electric Norge refrigerator, all left for us by the previous owner, filled the rest of the kitchen, leaving less than a foot of space open to move around in.

The other living-room doorway, to the left, brought one to the two bedrooms, the bathroom, and the stairs up to the finished attic that had been converted into a bedroom for the older boys. The smaller bedroom was just big enough to hold the narrow, cot-size bed that was to be mine.

Off the kitchen were narrow stairs, leading down to the basement, two large rooms and two small. One of the large rooms was completely finished in knotty-pine and was going to be our playroom. The other, paneled in dark mahogany, was going to be theirs. It featured a bar, snug under the stairway, accessible only from the back washroom. They planned to offer elaborate parties for all their Brooklyn friends and relatives, with Pop tending bar. The washroom also had a mud sink, and Mom dreamed of the day she would be able to buy her own washing machine and dryer and end the tiresome trips to the Laundromat. Finally, there was an oil room with a noisy red-and-black burner and a tank to hold hundreds of gallons of oil that fed the furnace automatically. Many of the houses on the block still had coal furnaces, which had to be fed by shoveling the fuel. Mom and Pop took great pride in their central heating system. For summer ventilation, we had screens, one behind each window, all of which would remain open from May through September.

The kitchen door led to an enclosed breezeway, with separate steps going down to the back or front yards. The backyard was fully enclosed by three different types of fences, each belonging to a different neighbor. There was a beautiful Japanese red maple tree and a custom-made brick charcoal grill for barbecuing. On the side was a one-car garage, with two aging wooden doors hanging on rusted hinges that opened to the sides.

My brothers and I decided to play hide-and-seek while my parents were unpacking boxes. We discovered that we could circumnavigate the entire house without leaving our property. The most challenging part was the side breezeway when the doors were closed and locked. There was a small overhang of bricks that you could toe across, hanging on to the outside window ledge. Trying to do it fast, while someone was chasing you, became a favorite adventure that first night. If you slipped, although the fall was only about three feet, you fell into a neighbor's yard, a neighbor you hadn't met yet and who had a dog barking at you as it ran back and forth below, acting as if it was ferocious.

That first night in my new bedroom I slept on a bare mattress and woke up at dawn, as there were no curtains to block the sun. Pop was already up, and I joined him in the kitchen. Coffee was perking in the pot on the gas stove. I savored the aroma, and when it was ready Pop poured me a half cup. I added two teaspoons of sugar and filled the rest of the cup with milk. He'd also found the toaster and had it out on the table. I dropped in two slices of Wonder Bread and watched till they were just turning brown. I slathered on lots of butter, cut each slice in half and then dunked a piece into my coffee. I tried to quickly get the soggy mess to my mouth before it broke off and fell back into the cup or onto the table. Successful about half the time, I slurped down my breakfast and washed it all down with the coffee.

I still had a week off before I went back to school, but Pop had to go back to work. When he left at seven thirty, I hung around the porch for a while and then started climbing the crab apple tree. I saw the boy coming from the house across the street, watched him walk right up to the tree. Looking up at me, he yelled, "Do you live here now?"

"Yeah."

"Can I come up?"

"Sure."

He was next to me in seconds, telling me that the old woman who used to live in this house never let them climb this tree. He told me his name, Adam, and said that he, too, came from a family of all boys. He then proceeded to tell me about all the other kids who lived on the block. "There's little kids and there's big kids," he said. "How old are you?"

"Almost nine. You?"

"Seven. You're going to be right in the middle."

"In the middle of what?"

"The little kids are my age and younger. The big kids are all older than you. You're right in the middle. You have a bike?"

"Yeah."

"Let's go to Schneid's."

"Who's that?" I asked.

"Schneid's is the candy store." I went in and asked Mom if it was okay, and she just told me to be careful and gave me a dime. I really did not know what to expect. In all of the other houses that we had lived in, we were never close enough to stores that I was allowed to walk to by myself. I had been to stores, of course, but always with my parents, certainly never alone. Most definitely I had no memory of going to a store devoted to candy!

Adam told her it was only two blocks away, required crossing only one street, and most of the kids were allowed to go whenever they wanted to. "You can get a soda, a candy bar, a comic book, even a sandwich." We got on our bikes, rode the block up to Hillside Avenue. The sidewalk in front of the stores was much wider than those in front of the houses, but they were filled with litter and even some broken glass. The cars were passing on Hillside Avenue at a much faster clip than they did on the side streets. It would be very dangerous to try to ride in the street, and I stayed close to the stores but almost hit a lady coming out of one of them. There were no houses, only stores, and I rode slowly because I wanted to see what they were. On the corner was a beauty salon, whatever that was, and next to that was a pet store and then a barber shop, followed by a real estate and then the Belle Rose Grill and Tavern. Next to the bar was an office for the *Long Island Press*, and on the corner was a drugstore.

Across 254th Street, on the other corner, was Schneid's. It said so right on the sign, though the sign was old, cracked, and dirty. "Schneid's" was written in cursive, diagonally from the bottom left to the upper right of the sign. Above it, in smaller block print, were the words CANDY, SODA, and NEWSPAPERS. Along the bottom in the same size the sign said, CIGARETTES and CIGARS. The building was made of old, dark, dirty red brick. Behind the store was a driveway with an old green DeSoto in it. There even seemed to be an entrance back there. I would learn later that behind the store, down a short dark hallway, was the apartment that the Schneid family lived in.

The front entrance was a single glass door that faced Hillside Avenue, and to the right of the door was a plate glass window. But there was no window display; the front window was filled with cardboard boxes. On the glass, there was green print along the bottom, repeating, CANDY, SODA, CIGARS, CIGARETTES, NEWSPAPERS. In addition, there were the words ICE CREAM and MAGAZINES, and in very large letters across the middle of the window was the word LUNCHEONETTE.

We laid our bikes down on the ground next to the door. As we entered from the bright street, I was surprised at how dark it seemed inside. I was also immediately surprised at how old it seemed. I was expecting sparkle and shine, and I got dust and grime. The floor was wide boards that had a lot of wear and no covering of any kind other than some sawdust that, though gathered heavily in the corners, was also lightly spread throughout so that it got caught up in your sneakers.

On the left, as you entered, was the counter, behind which stood the soda fountain, the malted milk machines, and the sinks. There was no one sitting at the counter at the time. Behind it stood a man doing dishes. His head was completely shaved and he had a large scar above his eye that extended down his cheek. I noticed that he had a small dark tattoo on the back of his hand, but I couldn't make out what it was.

On the right, across from the front door, was a section about ten feet wide filled with different kinds of candy. I went over and looked: Baby Ruth, Chunky, Fifth Avenue, Butterfinger, Milky Way, boxes of Bazooka bubble gum, several kinds of Hershey's chocolate bars, Three Musketeers, Good & Plenty, licorice, a whole section of cough drops: Smith Bros. and Luden's. Juicy Fruit, Spearmint, and Doublemint dominated the gum section. And there were packs of baseball cards. My eyes were darting up and down the shelves, each new discovery brightening the smile on my face. There was a small, cardboard sign: ALL CANDY 5 CENTS, but then some of the other boxes had their own smaller signs: one cent for the bubble gum, ten cents for the cough drops and cards. Above the candy rack were shelves with toys and model airplane boxes, some of which were quite dirty and greasy-looking.

I noticed to the left of the candy rack there was a wall filled with magazines, comic books, and newspapers. I went over to it and started looking at the comics: *Superman, Archie, Donald Duck, Scrooge McDuck, the Phantom, Spider-Man, Baby Hughie, Little Dot, Richie Rich, Nancy and Sluggo*—they were all here. Adam was paging through one of these, and so I reached for a *Superman* and looked through it and then noticed that there were also *MAD* magazines, and I got one of them down. I no sooner got it open than I heard a gruff, angry voice shout, "Are you going to buy that?" Terrified, I put the magazine back on the shelf and turned around to verify that he was talking to me. Scarface was looking straight at me and before I could answer, he asked, "Are you going to buy *anything*? If you're not, be on your way."

Adam was laughing at me, but I remembered that my mother had given me ten cents, so I could either choose to buy one comic book or two candy bars. It did not take me long. "Yes," I answered and grabbed the *Adventures of Superman* off the shelf. I went up to the counter and gave him my dime. He took it unceremoniously, threw it on top of the drawer to his cash register where several other coins already sat, and said, "*Now*, be on your way." He could see the shock on my face. "Unless you want something else?"

"No," I said.

"Then be off with you."

I wanted to look around some more, to linger, but I dared not. The old man then started on Adam, who said, "I'm going." We headed for the door, got our bikes, and rode home.

"See ya later," I told Adam. For the next hour, while everyone else was still unpacking and moving boxes, I sat in my new bedroom and read my first comic book.

5

Over the years, Schneid's became a comfort zone, a home away from home. When we wanted spending money for Schneid's, we had to earn it. My brothers had gotten jobs delivering newspapers for the *Long Island Press*, but you had to get working papers for that, and for working papers you had to be at least twelve years old. I'd sit with them after school and help them rubber band the papers and stuff them in their bike baskets, but they did all the deliveries, and they collected all the pay. For me, there were always jobs if I went looking for them. Mr. D'Amato, a neighbor, paid me a dollar an hour to pull weeds at the Saint Greg's ball field. I'd take my bike over, work for a while, round up to the next hour, and tell him at the end of the week how much I had done.

I mowed our neighbor's lawn, the ones who lived right behind us, every Saturday morning for four dollars. The first week, it took me from morning until night. They wanted the grass cut, raked, and bagged, the sides edged, and all the sidewalks and the driveway swept clean. I had never used an edger before, and it had not been done for a while, so the grass was craggy and thick and stuck out over the sidewalk.

I put my hand on the top of the edger and pushed and pushed, each inch a struggle, each foot a major battle. By the end of the day, my hands were bleeding and blistered, but the lawn looked great. The owner came out and smiled. Gave me an extra dollar and promised it would get easier each week. After a month or so, I was able to knock it out in a few hours.

In the winter, we would go door to door, asking neighbors if we could shovel the snow off their walks and driveways. Each blizzard was a huge commercial opportunity. We'd set flat rates: five dollars for sidewalks, ten for the driveway. On a good day, we could make fifty dollars, fighting the cold off with hot chocolates.

■ ■ ■

I never went in looking for trouble, but sometimes I just naturally slid into it. I did like to joke with certain countermen more than others. Schneid's only hired men, boys really, teenagers mostly. James Gianturco was a particular foil of mine. Older than most, he was in college, wiser and more mature but willing to banter, quick with a wisecrack if I got on his case. Once, when I was around ten, I ordered a "black-and-white malted." Chocolate syrup with vanilla ice cream was the standard black-and-white, but when he served it to me I told him that was wrong: I wanted vanilla syrup and chocolate ice cream. He raised his voice. "That's not a black-and-white!"

"What is it, then?" I asked him.

He cracked a thin smile and shot back, "I don't know—I guess it's a white-and-black—but you know what a black-and-white is, and you should have ordered it right," as he was dumping the malted in the sink. He cleaned the container and proceeded to make a white-and-black. Spurred by the abuse of this power, I was not finished. When he served it this time, I said, "I want some whipped cream on top."

He had had enough. "Malteds don't come with whipped cream."

"Ice cream sodas do," I said, adding, "I want a cherry, too."

"No whipped cream, no cherry," and he grabbed the container back from where he had placed it on the counter in front of me. He saw that I had not yet put my money down. "Thirty-five cents."

"I'm not paying unless I get whipped cream."

"You're not getting whipped cream, and you're not getting a cherry. And if you don't put thirty-five cents on the counter, you're not getting the malted."

"Well, I don't want it if it doesn't have whipped cream. You can drink it. I'd like a black-and-white ice cream soda instead." I was actually smiling, thinking I was clever and cute.

He threw the container into the sink so that it bounced and splashed the malted all over the sink and the counter, some of it onto his apron and down onto the floor. He turned red and picked up the wet dishrag. "Get the hell out of here." He pointed to the door.

"Not until I get my ice cream soda." He came at me across the counter, and I leaped back from the stool just in time to avoid the swipe. He was livid, and I was laughing. He balled the rag up and threw it at me, hitting me in the shoulder and leaving a wet deposit on my shirt. "I could sue you for this," I complained.

Was I nuts? He took off his apron and threw it to the floor and started to run around the counter from the back, yelling, "You little wise ass—I'm gonna beat the crap outta you." I ran for the door and just got out before he could grab me, and I ran across Hillside Avenue in front of traffic. I was scared. What the hell was I thinking? Fortunately for me, he did not desert the store. He was the only one working at the time, and he came out and shook his fist at me and yelled, "You better not come back here...*ever!*"

I just kept running until I got about two blocks away, and then the enormity of what I had done began to sink in. *Does he know where I live? Does he know my name? Oh my God, does he know Pop?*

I stayed away for almost a month. Adam did not understand. "How serious can it be? So you pissed him off, so what?" I started to creep back up there and peek in and see who was working. If he wasn't in sight I went in.

Finally, about three months later, we had the inevitable encounter. Abe, the scar-faced owner, was working the counter. Adam and I were sitting on stools when James came in, ready to start a shift. He looked at me and stopped in his tracks for just a moment and stared at me. There was no way I could run around him. I was terrified. He walked up to me and towered over me. He was at least six feet and stocky. I knew that he could crush me with one blow. I melted as he stared into my eyes. I caved. I looked at my feet and mumbled, "I'm sorry." Then I looked back up at him and said, "I was just kidding around."

"You little shit," he said. "Stay the hell out of the store when I'm on." Although Abe paused for a moment to witness this interaction, he had no desire for details. Anybody banned from the store was probably banned for a good reason. Both he and his wife, Lynn, had thrown me out before. As James walked past me, I tried to finish my soda, but he turned and said sternly, "I said *get out! Now!*" I left my half-finished soda on the counter and left, Adam laughing at me.

Fortunately for me, he quit about six months later and moved down the block to work for Ernie's German Deli. The next time I encountered him I was actually with my mother, picking up cold cuts for lunch. He and my mother seemed to know each other. He looked at me and said to her, "Is this your son?"

"One of them," she said.

He looked at me, clearly trying to decide if he should rat me out. I looked at my feet.

Bewildered, my mother asked, "Is there a problem?"

He hesitated, smiled at her. "No," he said, "no problem." He looked at me. "Is there?"

"No," I said, "no problem."

Mom certainly didn't want to pursue it. She'd already had one embarrassing incident at a local store. Brian had begun working the cash register at the King Kullen, and he devised a scheme to get free food. Mom would do her shopping and bring the cart to his register, and he would quickly ring her up and pack the groceries into brown paper bags. But he wouldn't ring everything up, skipping about every third item. This scam had been working for a while, but one day, as my mother was leaving the store, the manager stopped her at the door and asked to see her receipt. He then spread all her groceries out on the counter and checked their prices against the numbers on the receipt. He made a small pile of the items she was stealing. She was mortified and tried to tell him that she had no idea, yelling at Brian, "What are you doing?" The manager knew better. He rang up all the items and told her she would have to pay for them or get charged with stealing. Fortunately, she had the extra cash. He then fired Brian on the spot. Ever after, she had to walk twice as far in the other direction—all the way over to the Bohack on Little Neck Parkway—for her daily groceries.

6

When Vinny moved down the block, Adam and I welcomed him, and I was happy that I was no longer the new kid. Vinny's father had grown up in Bellerose and was moving back after living for fifteen years farther out on Long Island. He bought a house on the same block he had grown up on. We had met Vinny before, when he had visited his grandparents, first-generation Italian immigrants. Despite the gaudy display of crucifixes and sacred heart pictures in their houses and Virgin Mary statues on their lawns, they did not attend mass every week. They were sure to be in church on Palm Sunday, though, collecting the free palm fronds to adorn their icons.

Vinny had an older brother and a younger sister. Older than Adam, but younger than me, all of us barely in double digits, Vinny was bigger than both of us. He was already growing hair under his arms, and the beginning of a beard was evident on his face. We looked past his swarthy complexion and greasy black hair and trusted him at once.

The three of us grew tighter and tighter. We pricked our fingers with a pin, pushed them together until our blood mixed, and became blood brothers, a bond that we promised would hold forever. We shared secrets, slept over one another's houses and were comfortable with one another's parents.

For the sake of their own peace and quiet, parents drove their kids out of the house whenever they could. The culture was shaped by group street games: stickball, hide-and-go-seek and ring-a-levio, a tough game, with open-street tackling, thrown elbows, shoulder blocks, and suffocating bear hugs.

One of our favorites was I declare war. Adam took a piece of chalk and drew a circle, five or six feet in diameter, with a much smaller concentric circle in the middle of it, just a foot in diameter. He then divided the space between the two circles into triangular pie slices of approximate size, enough to assign one to each player, maybe leaving a few blank in case someone new were to join us midgame.

As usual, I wrote "Ireland" in my triangle, and Vinny wrote "Italy" in his. We could never predict what Adam might do. He'd write "Scotland" one time and "Tahiti" the next. This time, he wrote "Vietnam," and both Vinny and I looked quizzical. "Where the heck is that?" I asked.

"It's in Asia. My father says China and France are having a war there, and it could turn into World War Three." He raised his hand, threw the ball down, and said, "I declare war on Ireland!"

Instead of straight up, he bounced it at an angle, and it careened down the block a little. "Shoot," I yelled, as I ran and caught up to it, grabbed it, ran back to the circle, and called, "Halt!" I had cooperated in letting the game start, but I was upset that he had cheated. They had each gotten a good thirty or forty feet away before I could stop them with my order to halt.

But now they were not supposed to move, and I could yell at them. "First of all, Adam, I wasn't ready. Second, you know you're supposed to bounce it straight up in the air!" Rules were supposed to be inviolate, passed down from the big kids to the little kids.

"Stop crying and try to get one of us." He laughed.

I took the three giant steps that I was entitled to, but when I threw the ball at him, he moved his hip ever so slightly. I was not sure whether it would have hit him or not, but he clearly had cheated again. I was screaming, "You can't move, damn it, you know you can't move." They both ignored me and ran back to the circle.

I spotted a car approaching and announced it, in a loud sing-song voice, "Car, car, k-a-r!" thus commanding the game to be suspended until it passed. We gave the car a very narrow lane to pass through. Adam fell to the ground as if he had been hit. The ruse didn't work, as the driver didn't even bother to stop. A garbage truck turned the corner, and we all picked up something to throw at it. I reached back and threw a rock as hard as I could. Unfortunately, my rock sailed right over the top and smashed the back windshield of a station wagon that was just beyond it.

We heard a sort of whooshing sound, like something too big being sucked in by a vacuum, followed by the screeching of tires as the driver slammed the brakes on. The window was shattered, a thousand tiny lines and cracks emanating from a small hole. The window almost looked intact, but it was distorted, like a window in a comic-book Bizarro World. As the car came to a stop, the window swayed like a curtain in a mild summer breeze and then collapsed in on itself, silently raining down inside the car, leaving an open space. The driver was looking through it, right at us. We scattered. I ran into the alley behind the stores on Hillside Avenue and went down to the bottom of the cellar entrance to the beauty parlor. I sat on the dirty ground, hunched up and shivering.

After about ten minutes, I came up the stairs, walked down the avenue for two blocks, and then came up the side street so I could look at the intersection from the other direction. I peeked out and saw a patrol car. A uniformed officer was filling out a form and talking to the driver. Then I noticed someone sitting in the backseat of the squad car: Adam!

I retreated a few steps, all but lost my breath, and began to tremble. I looked again. The cop was now leaning into the window of his car, talking to Adam. I could not let him take the fall for me. I walked nonchalantly right up to the scene.

The driver saw me first, said something to the cop, and pointed at me. I turned around, as if to see what the driver could be pointing at, feigning that he must be pointing past me. As I walked up, the cop just hung his thumb to the side and said, "Get in."

I got into the back of the car, and Adam yelled at me right away, "Why'd you come back?"

"I didn't want you to get blamed."

"They couldn't do anything. You should've stayed away."

"How'd they get you?"

He looked at his feet. "I ran home. The guy saw me, knocked on my door, and even got my mother to call the police. I denied everything, but..."

The cop got in the car and called the station house. "Yeah, I've got two kids. One of 'em broke a windshield, threw a rock through it. Chickenshits. They ran...throwing rocks at a garbage truck. Yeah, yeah, I can bring 'em in, and we'll put 'em in the back room, stand 'em up on the table. Yeah, see if either one of 'em has any hair on their balls." He was laughing as he put the mike down and turned to us. "Either one of you girls have any hair on your balls?"

We ignored him, just looked at our feet, and hoped he was kidding.

"Cause we're gonna have a little pool down at the station house. Take some bets, throw some money on the table, and make you drop your drawers, you little cowards. Running away just like little girls."

"Look," I said. "I threw the rock. You got nothing on Adam. Let him go."

"Where do you live, little girl?" he asked me.

"Over there," I signaled with my head.

"C'mon." He sent Adam home and walked me to my house. He knocked on the door. Mom was wiping her hands on her apron as she answered the door, horrified, and both of her hands went up to cover her open mouth as she saw the cop.

After a few minutes, Mom agreed to pay for the guy's windshield, which would eventually cost her sixty-eight dollars. The guy agreed not to press charges. The cop, despite his unconscionable threats, worked out the issue for us as best he could. Then he told my mother he'd like to talk to me alone. I got scared all over again. He took me to the squad car and put me in the backseat. He leaned through the window.

"Listen, kid," he said. "Everybody makes mistakes. You screwed up when you ran away. But you showed moxie by coming back and fessing up and not letting your friend take the rap. Next time, don't run away. You screw up, stick around and take the heat. Make it right."

■ ■ ■

Adam wanted to be a racecar driver when he grew up and was always pushing the envelope, seeking new thrills. Ice-skating on Pea Pond in Queens Village wasn't exciting enough for him. The pond was set off in some woods north of Hillside Avenue, west of Springfield Boulevard, behind the Dunkin Donuts. Adam's father had dropped us off, with Vinny, right after dinner and was going to pick us up at the donut shop at ten. It had been below freezing all weekend, so the pond was solid. We skated for a while but still grew cold as the temperature approached single digits.

We gathered sticks and built a small fire right at the edge of the ice. While gathering the fuel, Adam realized that all the slopes through the woods leading down to the pond were also frozen solid. You could ski down them. We worked our way higher and higher toward the highest ridge, about a forty-foot slope. I fell a couple of times and decided to go back to skating on the pond. Vinny and I were playing makeshift hockey when we heard Adam yell. It was a cloudy, quiet night, no stars or moon in sight. It was so dark that we couldn't see him right away, and by the time we found him, he was writhing in tremendous pain.

Vinny and I pulled him close to the fire, but he kept screaming, "I think my leg is broken, you guys, I think it's broken." Tears were beginning to leak out of his eyes and roll down his contorted face. Vinny stoked the fire, and I got my skates off and ran to one of the nearby houses to call for an ambulance. By the time I got back, the ambulance was arriving, and the cops were right behind them. After getting our personal information, they tried to call Adam's parents, but there was no answer. They said one of us should go with Adam to the hospital while the other one waited for Adam's father at the coffee shop, as it was almost time for him to pick us up. Adam motioned for me, and I sat in the back of the ambulance as we pulled away from the pond. They cut his pants leg off, and I grimaced as I saw the bit of bone that had broken through the skin. I could see the ambulance's red lights reflected in the windows of the houses as we sped through the neighborhood to Long Island Jewish Hospital.

Adam was strapped down on the gurney with an IV flowing into his arm. He saw the look on my face. "Is it bad?" he asked.

"Yeah," I said, "it is." I thought about lying, but I knew my expression would betray my words. Then I laughed and said, "But you're not going to die or anything; it's just a broken leg."

I had to wait outside the emergency room while they prepped him, and I was relieved when Adam's father and Vinny arrived. Adam emerged a few hours later, with a full-leg cast and a big grin on his face. "What a night!" he exclaimed. His father stopped at the new Burger-N-Shake on Lakeville Road and Union Turnpike and treated us all to a midnight feast.

7

Even before school was out, we started anticipating the Fourth of July. Someone in the neighborhood would announce a run to Florida. Anyone with a truck could go, load up with fireworks, come back home, and make a bunch of money.

There was a unique language and hierarchy associated with fireworks. The cheapest, least desirable firecrackers were referred to as Chinese ladyfingers, which were about a half inch long, solid red, with just a smidgen of gunpowder. They would sort of pop rather than bang and were reputed to be legal. They were easy to find and were a good insurance policy in case you couldn't score anything else. You could usually buy them for five or ten cents a pack.

Next step up the scale was the ubiquitous firecracker, also, of course, manufactured in China, but this nuance escaped us. Popular brands were Tiger and Panda. You could either open the pack and separate the firecrackers for single lighting, or poke a hole in the middle of one end, pry out the first fuse, and light the whole pack at once. Everyone would run as the pack hopped off the ground, spun erratically, and scattered firecrackers. Depending on the dealer, the brand, and the quantity purchased, packs would range from a dime to a quarter apiece.

Packs were arranged into mats, which were packages consisting of eighty packs. Mats wholesaled for anywhere from five to ten dollars. You would pay on the high side if you didn't know the dealer. On occasion, you would bump into a true petty criminal, one who had probably been busted before. You had to be cool. If you just walked up and asked him to sell you a mat, you were likely to hear "Get the fuck out of here, kid," as an answer. Or, if a friend of a friend brought you to him, he might take you to the back alley and lecture you: "What're you fuckin' stupid, kid? Cops are everywhere. You tryin' to get me busted? You're not a cop's kid are you?" After some reassuring and apologizing, the wannabe thug would do you a favor and sell you a mat for ten bucks, and you'd both go away happy, you thinking that you got away with something, him with double his usual price.

Ash cans were on the next level of the hierarchy, the big boomers, the really dangerous stuff. Ash cans were cylindrical silver bombs about an inch and half long and half an inch in diameter; a hard green fuse about an inch long extended from the middle of the cylinder. They created a powerful explosion and were the favorite weapon for small-time destruction. In the same category were cherry bombs, exact replicas of cherries, red and round with a green fuse, and M-80s, which looked like a large version of the red ladyfingers. Larger than ash cans and more powerful, these were the fireworks that sent people to the hospital.

I bought a gross of ash cans for ten dollars, and I sold them for a quarter each, no deals. I blew my first dollar of profits on ten punks from Schneid's. Punks looked like sticks of incense, but without a flavored smell. They burned slowly, stayed lit, and were the favored method of lighting fuses. We heard from the big kids that some punks grew naturally in the swampy areas of Alley Pond Park. We ventured into the muck and picked some, dried them out, and tried to burn them, but they never worked right.

Finally, the big day arrived. Vinny, Adam, and I gathered early. We had sense enough not to light anything before lunchtime and spent the morning walking the neighborhood from Schneid's to the park, following rumors, trying to see if anything else was for sale. One of the biggest threats on the Fourth itself was from the police, especially early in the day. They would definitely confiscate anything they saw. They didn't arrest anyone; they just took the fireworks and either resold them later or gave them to their own kids, setting them off themselves. We kept a sharp eye out for squad cars.

As the afternoon came on, we decided to get started. This was the time to be creative. We could create our own rockets. We each went home and got an empty coffee can with the top off but the bottom intact. If we put a firecracker under it, the explosion was amplified, and the can jumped a few inches off the ground. When we put an ash can under it, it blew fifteen feet into the air. We coordinated, attempting to light three coffee-can rockets so they'd take off at the same time. Then we lit them sequentially, watching the cans shoot up one after the other.

Adam dropped an ash can into the sewer on the corner. The sonorous boom could be heard at least a block away and caused sewer water to erupt out of the sewer and into the air, the stink lingering for hours. Vinny found a bullfrog in the weeds, tied an ash can to its leg, and pureed the poor thing. This was over the line for me and sickened my stomach. We had heard tales of kids tying ash cans to cats, and I guess this was his inspiration, but fortunately, the one frog was the only fatality of the day.

■ ■ ■

Adam suggested going to see a girl he had met at school earlier in the week. We biked over the few blocks and met Kathy, who was sitting on her porch with a friend. Kathy had shoulder-length blond hair, blue eyes, and lots of freckles. She was wearing a cotton print tank top and dungarees. I could not discern a bra strap and imagined the impressions of her young nipples on the front of her shirt. Her friend Pat had cropped black hair and dark eyes. She was wearing a gray sweat shirt, much too hot for a summer day. The girls were talking about a new folk singer named Bob Dylan. Attempting to impress them, I mentioned what a good singer he was.

"He's a terrible singer," Kathy said disgustedly. Pat threw her head back and laughed.

Knowing that he was gaining fame, I disagreed. I had never actually listened to him. "No, he's really a good singer."

"No, he's a good poet," Kathy insisted. "Let me prove it to you." She went into her house and played her album, moving the needle to a particular song, "A Hard Rain's A-Gonna Fall."

She turned the record off and came back out to the porch. "See, now listen to that voice and tell me he's a good singer," she said sarcastically.

The guy sounded like a dying cat. I began to laugh and shake my head. "No," I said with a heavy sigh, "you're right. He is most definitely not a good singer." So why had they been talking about him in such respectful tones when we arrived? I was truly baffled.

Fortunately, she was on the same wavelength and wanted to convince us that he was a genius. "Now," she said, "I am going to play the record again. Listen beyond his voice to the words. Focus on the words." And we did. Quietly. And she played it again. And again. And then we talked about what the words meant. I did everything I could to relate and join the dialogue, but I had absolutely no idea what she was talking about. Crooked highways? Dead oceans? Sad forests? I was lost.

"He's talking about hypocrisy. America is supposed to be this egalitarian society, but our culture is rampant with poverty and racism. We pretend to be classless, but class distinctions are everywhere. We can't be content to sit back and ignore it; we can't pretend not to see it when it's so obvious!"

"So what's with the rain?" I asked stupidly.

"Ugh! You're impossible." She was totally exasperated. "It's portentous, don't you see? This class structure is getting too rigid. It's going to collapse or implode. It's unsustainable."

Though a year or two younger than me, these girls acted a generation above me in maturity. Not content to sit on the porch and gab about folk music, I told Adam I had to get home. As I left, I saw that he was being invited inside to listen to the rest of the record.

■ ■ ■

Pop and I helped the neighbors set up for their annual backyard party. We brought out the food, paper plates, plastic utensils, and napkins. Just as the coals were ready, Mr. D'Amato threw on the hot dogs and hamburgers as people started to arrive. My mother showed up with potato salad and a big pot of beans. Other families brought salads, vegetable casseroles, and desserts. Kids were encouraged to eat first, and we showed no hesitation. One hot dog, one hamburger, some potato salad, and a Coke, and I was all set. Mustard, ketchup, and sauerkraut completed the picture.

Meanwhile, the grownups concentrated on the booze. In addition to the case of beer that Pop bought, every family brought something: vodka and orange juice, gin and tonic, scotch and water, rye and ginger ale. Every adult had a drink in one hand and a cigarette in the other.

About eight o'clock, we began to hear firecrackers in the distance. The sun was setting, and it was going to be dark soon. Most of the grown-ups had even dug in and had their first burger, though some were having more fun with their third or fourth drink. We each went to our respective parents with the same question: "Can we start?" Most of us got the same answer: "Wait a little longer till it's dark out." This was signal enough for us to head to our respective houses and collect our goods. We met back at the corner. The protocols were clear, if unwritten and unspoken; they had been established over years of experience. Kids stood on the curb and threw the fireworks into the street, as far as possible into the middle of the intersection. At peak, there would be over twenty kids and the noise was loud and constant.

The barrage stopped for two reasons. First, whenever a car was spotted, someone would yell out, and everyone would stop lighting until it passed. Drivers throughout Queens seemed to be well aware of the proliferation of fireworks and would proceed with extreme caution. Once a squad car approached, and everyone instinctively grabbed their bag of fireworks and ran like hell. A few of us ran into the D'Amato's backyard and stashed our fireworks under the food table. If the cops were interested in pursuing anyone, they didn't demonstrate it but rather rolled right along. Maybe their kids already had enough?

The other reason the onslaught stopped was when someone wanted to light something bigger than a firecracker. You stepped one foot into the street, held your pyrotechnic above your head, and yelled out what it was you wanted to do. "I've got an ash can!"—or a roman candle. Eventually, the crowd recognized you, and the bombardment stopped, and you could traverse to the middle of the street, capturing everyone's attention, and light it off. Sometimes, alas, this was the time to joke. Although it was rare that anyone would be stupid enough to throw a firecracker when a car was passing, some might throw a firecracker behind the back of another kid. If it landed too close, an argument would ensue, but the conflict rarely went beyond words. The rest of the participants wanted to get on with the show and would start heckling the victim, "C'mon light your ash can, or get the hell out of the street."

As the night evolved, we became more and more emboldened or more and more stupid, depending on how you looked at it. No longer content to just throw stuff into the street, we began to want them to explode in the air. We held on longer, taking more risks, watching the fuses, and throwing them later. We got a higher percentage to explode in midair, sometimes only feet from our hands, sometimes causing a painful backlash from the discharge. Earlier in the night, people were stopping the action to go out in the street and light full packs. Now, people were just lighting packs and throwing them into the street. In fact, the truly foolish would light a pack and hold it from the other end until the first firecracker exploded. Then they'd throw it and have the whole pack exploding in the air, scattering firecrackers in every direction as it descended.

Don D'Amato, one of the big kids, began experimenting with ash cans. He had figured out that the hard fuses actually progressed in two steps. The first burn illusively just paved the way for the second burn. He explained it to me, yet I could not bring myself to believe him. Even though you lit it and saw the lit fuse appear to enter the ash can, it didn't immediately explode. Instead, the burning fuse ignited the main fuse, which burned down to explode the powder. Thus, though many of us had enough guts to hold one until it seemed like the fuse was about to ignite, when we threw it, it would often still sail and then bounce and explode on the ground. To prove it to us, Don finally sacrificed one of his ash cans. He pulled the fuse out, laid it on the ground and lit it. Sure enough, there was a slight burn the length of the fuse and then a larger, smokier, more dramatic burn from the top down after the first one finished. Though none of us understood the chemistry of this, Don had seen enough to convince him he could hold the ash can longer. "But the first light is alive and enters the ash can," I said, trying to talk him out of it.

"Yeah, I know, but it's not strong enough to ignite, and it doesn't burn through to the powder."

He announced that he was going to have an ash can go off high in the air. He asked me to light it for him, so I used one of my wooden matches. And he held it, and he watched it, and he watched that first burn go into the ash can. Then he reached back and flung it high into the air, and it reached a crescendo and exploded on the way down. He had done it. Now he wanted more.

He now accepted it as routine that he could hold it through the first burn, and he started to hold it longer into the second burn. He figured out that if he could hold it until the second burn was about halfway down and then throw it, it would explode at the peak of its ascendancy. He mastered this and then for some unknown reason wanted to hold it longer. He got ready by clearing space around him and cocking his arm into the pitching position and then having me light it when he was ready. He watched the fuse past the halfway point of the second burn and almost into the ash can. I was backing away as he threw it, and I was just in the nick of time. It exploded less than a foot from his hand, and we all felt the concussion from the explosion, hurting our ears, feeling the wind from the flashback.

"*Shit!*" Don yelled. He shook his hand, looking at it and blowing on it, then put it under his arm and walked in circles. "Shit, shit, shit." Clearly, he was hurt, but how badly? It took a good three minutes or so of him walking in circles and cursing before he held it out under the light long enough for us to get a look at it. His hand was red and swollen, his index fingernail cracked and black, and there was one small puncture wound with a drop of blood glistening on the side. He could not move any fingers without pain.

Suddenly, he had an idea and ran into his father's yard and stuck his hand into the cooler, submerging it in the ice water among the floating beer and soda cans. None of the adults noticed, as they were deep into their drinking cycle. After a few minutes, he withdrew his hand: the swelling was not getting worse, the bleeding had stopped, and he could move his fingers. He laughed and said, "I think I found my limit!"

8

For a couple of summers, the city sprang for an extra parkie. Ross, about twenty-five, was a second-year law student from NYU. He lived in the Bronx and took his duties quite seriously. Discontented with the lack of any programs, he decided to organize a softball league. I became catcher and captain of one of the four teams. The first year, we won the league. Mostly, all we had to do was show up. Several of the other teams were composed mostly of Navajos, a group of kids from the other side of the parkway. They were the first group in Bellerose to consider themselves a gang and adopt a name. They tended to come to games only when they had nothing else to do. We won several games by forfeit, so the championship was not cause for much celebration.

The next year, Ross informed me that at fourteen, I had aged out of his league, and he convinced me to share umpire duties with him. He put on equipment and called balls and strikes from behind the plate, and I worked the bases. There was a close play at second base, with Adam tagging Pauly, one of the leaders of the Navajos, who actually slid on the asphalt. There was a no-sliding rule, and I called him out. He jumped up, yelling and screaming, arms waving, telling me he beat the tag. I tried to explain to him that he was out for sliding; it didn't matter whether he got tagged or not.

"Bullshit!" He was right up in my face, cursing and bumping me with his body. "You can't fuckin' call that. He missed the tag. I'm fuckin' safe." He walked back and stood on second base. I looked to Ross, who took off his mask and walked out toward us. Only then did I take a step closer to Pauly. Pauly pointed his finger at Ross and yelled at him, "Don't you come out here. This's between me and him," indicating me with his thumb. Pauly relished a good fight. Although a year younger than me, he was better built—stockier and stronger. He wore tight black pants and a black T-shirt, the uniform of his gang. He was actually playing softball in short Italian boots. I was trembling.

Ross kept coming, walking slowly and talking calmly. "Pauly, David made the right call. You are out. There's no sliding. We can't have people sliding on cement. There'd be too many injuries."

"Fuck you, too. That's up to me. I slid under the tag; I'm fuckin' safe. Get the fuckin' game goin'." He was in a rage, turning red, spittle flying. I turned my back and walked back toward first. I wasn't going to push it, but Ross walked right up to him. Ross was in great shape; his muscles rippled under his tight, white undershirt. He obviously worked the weights and was not going to be intimidated by this kid.

"Pauly, you're out. Go back to the dugout."

"Fuck you and the horse you rode in on."

Ross turned and thrust his finger up in the air toward the gate as if he were umpiring in the major leagues. "Now you're out of the game, *and* you're out of the park."

"Fuck you, Ross. Who the fuck do you think you're dealing with?"

Ross reached out and grabbed Pauly by the arm, making it clear that he would drag him to the gate if he had to. Pauly yanked his arm away and took a defensive stance, yelling, "Don't fuckin' touch me! Get your fuckin' hands off me." He stared Ross in the eyes for a moment, defiance seething and burning. Then he turned and took a step away from him, toward me, throwing his borrowed mitt back toward the dugout. "I don't wanna play your stupid fuckin' game anyway."

He walked over to me, stopped, lit a cigarette, and flicked the match at me, saying, "You and me. We're not done here. You're fuckin' dead. You got that?"

Aware that every pair of eyes in the park was on me, I simply said, "Fuck you!"

He leaped at me, but before he could do much damage, Ross was on top of him and others were helping pull him off. It took three of them to get him out of the park. We continued the game, and I was aware that he was waiting outside for me, watching through the fence as he paced, chain-smoking. I was terrified. I knew that he was stronger, faster, and crazier than I was. I was hoping he would leave when the game was over, but he hung right outside the gates with his friends, taunting me through the fence.

"You gonna come out and take your beating, or you gonna hide behind the parkie like a pussy?"

I went inside the park house with Ross and Vinny. Ross told me, "Wait till I close. I'll go with you." I had played many games of chess and Camelot with Ross, who respected and befriended me. I thought it was okay to let him big-brother me out of this situation.

But Vinny had another view. "You can't punk out; you'll be a joke. You have to go out and fight him. I'll make sure it's fair, one on one."

Vinny was right, and I sighed. "Thanks, Ross, but I have to do this alone."

Vinny and I walked out of the gate together, and Pauly called, "Hey, Pussy, you gonna fight me or what?"

"Fuck you," was the best I could do as I put my skinny arms up and made fists out of my tiny hands.

He took a final puff on his cigarette and flicked it into the street. He laughed and said, "This is gonna be too fuckin' easy." He bounded up to me, swinging a hard right, which I tried to block, but it was too strong and came through anyway, followed by a left undercut to my belly, followed by another strong right to my face. He had landed three brutal punches, and I staggered back and tripped over a bicycle. When I hit the ground, I moaned.

Vinny was disappointed. He leaned over me and said, "Don't fucking say 'ow'—take it like a man!" He took my hand and pulled me up.

I didn't complain again. Pauly was on top of me, pounding me, landing punches at will, with me barely able to block a few and not really landing any on him. It was, in fact, too easy, and Pauly got bored. He knocked me down again, sat on my chest, pinned my arms to the ground, and asked, "Do you give?"

"Fuck you!"

"You stupid fuckin' asshole." He rapidly smacked me four or five times in the face, my arms still pinned to my sides. Vinny walked up and said, "That's enough."

Pauly, knowing Vinny could take him, said, "Stay back, Vinny. You know he's gotta say he gives." To me he said, "Just say you fuckin' give, asshole."

I could taste the blood trickling into my mouth, the tears fighting to get out of my eyes. I was tempted to curse him again, but I knew I would be putting Vinny in a bad situation. I did not want to force him to interfere. I sighed heavily. "I give."

"About fuckin' time." Pauly got up to congratulations from his boys. "Let's get the fuck outta here."

Vinny gave me time to get myself up then said, "Let's go back into the park and get you cleaned up. You can't go home like this."

He helped me into the boys' room and told me to wash the blood off my face. He saw me fighting tears, and he lit into me again. "Don't ever fucking say 'ow,' and don't *ever* fucking cry. You understand me?"

"Yeah, I got it."

And he was on my side.

9

Summer brought out the best in Adam's father, who suffered from diabetes. Every day, he had to give himself an injection of insulin. His skin color was pale, and he had blotchy patches on his arms and face. And he was moody. You would never know if he was going to be short and irritable or happy and carefree. But when he was in good spirits, he was just like a kid. He'd get a silly grin on his face and giggle and suggest that we all do something together. He loved to pile a bunch of kids in his car, take us somewhere, and act like he was one of us.

He was a car nut and a tinkerer. He built his own go-kart, complete with twin engines. We went to go-kart races set up at Grumman, the huge Long Island aerospace manufacturer where he worked. Adam would compete, often winning the trophy. I'd get to ride the go-kart around the parking lot during warm-ups. We'd also go to the stock-car races in Freeport. He'd hang out in the pits and try to sell helmets and other safety equipment to the drivers from the trunk of his car. Adam and I hit the stands and watched the races or played in the pits, trying to meet the drivers. We watched them work on their cars, being sure not to stare at the blue light from the welder's torch, knowing it could blind us. His dad waited until the parking lot was almost empty, hoping for one more sale, and it would be after midnight before we left.

The best thing he did for us was the annual trek to Coney Island. He had a station wagon, a woody, and he'd pile in as many kids, big and little, as he could fit. He'd park a few blocks away from the amusement park, on a city street, to avoid having to pay for parking. As we walked, we'd see the lights and hear the noises, and excitement would grow. First, we'd eat at Nathan's; cherishing the foot-long hot dogs but salivating over the thick-cut French fries. Then we'd play some games, shooting water guns and pitching nickels, trying to win stuffed animals.

Finally, we hit some rides. The Steeplechase had an admission price, and then you had to buy ticket books for individual rides. We rode on the Steeplechase racehorses, similar to those you see on a carousel, but on a series of tracks at the top of a hill. The horses released and rolled down the track, gaining speed as they descended, and we had to hang on tight as they took the curves. The winner of a race got to ride again, for free. At the end of the ride, there was a slide that dropped you onto a floor covered with round, rotating metal plates that flung you in all directions, quickly ejecting you to the pit at the side.

After the Steeplechase, we'd hit the roller coasters: the Thunderbolt and the Tornado, working our way up to the Cyclone. We'd ride the Wonder Wheel, sure the cars were going to slide off into oblivion. When our money started to run out, we'd walk along the boardwalk, and Adam's father would treat us all to the Parachute Jump. Each year, this ride was the most terrifying. You'd sit on a flimsy metal swing, just like the ones in the playground. A seatbelt wrapped around you, but it was worn, cracked, and dirty and looked like it could break. The seat was attached to a bunch of wires, and when everyone was belted in, the pulleys hoisted us up slowly. If you looked down, you'd get dizzy and couldn't even recognize the people on the ground; they truly looked like bugs scurrying around. I looked out over the amusement area and the parking lots and saw the skyline of the city in the distance. Then I looked out over the ocean, watching the distant horizon retreat, deeper and darker than ever before. And then I hit the top, and for just a moment the seat dropped out from under me and I was floating freely, hanging on tight as my heart and stomach lurched, almost leaving my body with the deep breath I exhaled as I suddenly plummeted to the earth, screaming all the way.

■ ■ ■

Joe Stayer, one of the big kids, was afraid to come. He used to get a case of nerves, and be trapped in the bathroom with "the runs." His mother would come out and tell us he couldn't do it. But one year, he finally made it. As soon as we got there, he wanted to break our routine, wanted to ride the Cyclone right away, figuring if he got that out of the way, he could relax for the rest of the night. He rode in the first car, next to Kevin. He got scared and put his head down, leaning on the safety bar.

When he got off the ride, blood was dripping out of the sides of his mouth, and he looked like he was going to pass out. He had bitten right through his tongue. Adam's father left us there while he took Joe to Coney Island Hospital, where they put six stitches in his tongue. He came back hours later, swollen and unable to talk. He never went on a ride again.

Joe had just graduated from high school and would be going upstate to Ithaca in the fall, on a music scholarship. He had some gigs with his father on the weekend, doing weddings and bar mitzvahs in the city, but during the week he only had to practice his saxophone for several hours every afternoon. We were off to the beach in his sky-blue '55 Chevy, two or three mornings a week for the entire summer. Joe didn't pull the big-kid–little-kid stuff with me, even though he was four years older. He treated me with respect, and we talked about all kinds of stuff from movies and sports to his anxieties about college and my anxieties about high school. Mostly, though, Joe liked to talk about girls.

Not just talk about them—he liked to look for them, look at them, and talk to them. He would beep at girls walking on the street, and on the rare occasion when one waved back, he might stop the car and say hello. This scared half of them off, but some came to the window, often to my side, and chatted, flirted, teased, and now and then left a phone number.

On the Southern State Parkway, Joe would be watching the drivers, hoping to get a smile from a pretty face. Refusing to pay the ten-cent toll at Valley Stream, Joe would pretend to throw in a dime as he stopped and went through. The bell went off, but no one ever came out to chase us down. At Jones Beach we usually parked at West End 2. Despite the long walk, several hundred yards from parking lot to ocean, this was the beach preferred by the college students. Families were attracted to the shorter walks from the East lots. On the West End, kids ruled. Radios were blaring and bodies were glistening from the iodine and baby oil concoctions that the girls slathered on.

Joe provided a running commentary, rating the girls and giving especially good grades to the ones with the big tits. Joe was a "breast man," he liked to boast. He'd been there, and he liked to tell me of his exploits, successful and unsuccessful. He had dated the football coach's daughter at Saint Francis Prep—in secret, because her dad warned the football players that anyone who ever went near her would be kicked off the team and out of the school. He did not put the same fear into the band, however, at least not into Joe, and he described to me what it was like the first time he undid her bra: her voluptuous breasts just spilled out, and he buried his face in them. I would get hard from his re-telling of these experiences, covering my bulging boyhood with a towel.

10

In 1963 Pop bought his first car, a 1950 blue four-door Oldsmobile Super 88. It had a manual shift on the steering column and a steering wheel that looked as big as a riverboat's. He paid a hundred dollars cash. He took the family to Lake George, our first-ever vacation. The small village was a commercial paradise: miniature golf courses, a drive-in movie, souvenir stores, a Ferris wheel, diners, and a small stand that sold submarine sandwiches.

About two miles north of the village, not so far out that it was a long drive, we stopped at the Osprey. The office manager walked us around the property. She took us down to the lake, where they had a private dock with rowboats and paddle boats, and they offered daily water-skiing, all for free with the room. Across the street they had a swimming pool and a giant trampoline. In addition to the standard rooms, they had a number of cabins that included full kitchens, and we rented one of those for eighteen dollars a night. Mom and Pop took the room with the two single beds, just like at home. They broke out the scotch and settled down for a drink. My brothers borrowed the car and went off to town to do some food shopping, and I took a stroll down to the lake.

I saw her from the top of the hill as I headed down to the dock. She looked about my age. She had long blond hair and a deep tan. She was swimming to the side of the dock in water about ten feet deep, playing with a rock, dropping it, watching it sink slowly to the bottom, and then retrieving it. She had on a tight bikini and was gracefully kicking her legs ever so slightly to stay afloat. All her limbs were splayed, and she could have been floating down in the air. She looked so graceful. Her hair spread out in the water like a giant fan. I reached the dock and stopped, watching her every movement. She came up for a gulp of air and saw me staring at her. She unveiled a captivating and warm smile and said hi.

At first self-conscious and speechless, I finally mumbled hello as she climbed up the wooden ladder. She reached for a towel that was draped over the rail. "I'm Tanya. You're a little early."

"I'm sorry," I stammered, bewildered. "Um. Early for what?"

"Skiing silly. My brother Stephen should be here soon, though. We start at two o'clock." She walked past me to the motorboat that was on the other side of the dock, got in, and put on a white T-shirt. I could not stop following her with my eyes, so I walked over and sat down near the edge of the dock, by the boat.

"Do you live here?" I asked her.

"Just in the summer. During the school year, we live in Seaford, Long Island." Her last name was Fedorov, and she was the youngest child of the Russian immigrant family who owned the motel. It was her mother who had shown us around. She had bright-green eyes, but I kept looking at the wet patches spreading on her T-shirt from her bathing suit. She busied herself getting towlines and life preservers out of a giant box and setting them up on the dock.

"You ready?" I nearly jumped out of my skin. Her brother had come up behind me so quietly that I had no idea he was there. He was talking to Tanya and treated her like a younger sibling, bossing her around, nastily telling her what to do. Other guests began to arrive, and a small line began to form. Stephen started up the motor and untied the rope at the dock, and without really looking at the guests, he sort of yelled over his shoulder, "Just checking the boat out, be right back!"

He took off at full throttle, the front of the boat nosing up into the air, a three-foot wake cresting away as he left. Tanya was thrown back, slightly surprised at his hasty departure, but then sat down and put her arm out to wave. I didn't know if she was waving to me, but I waved back anyway. They went way out onto the lake out of sight for a few minutes and then came roaring back, sidling up next to the dock to get into position. The person at the head of the line got into the water and put a life belt on, but Tanya pointed at me and said, "He was here first."

I immediately put my hands up and said, "No, no, that's okay. I can wait."

I did not want to go first. I was not even sure that I wanted to try it. She asked each person if they had ever skied before. Some had, many hadn't. She gave general instructions and then laid out the rope as the boat slowly pulled away from the dock. Each skier would get about a ten-minute ride, going across the lake and back. If you fell, you would get three opportunities to get back up.

After three or four people, it was my turn. I put the belt on snugly, trying to get in the right position, sitting in the water, legs into chest, tips of skis just sticking out of the water, towline in between the two skis. Stephen pulled out slowly, and I kept bobbing to the side, ready then not ready, shaking like a fish on a hook, worried that he would take off when I was completely to the side, wondering what I would do if I ever got up. As the rope went taut, Tanya yelled, "Hit it," and Stephen pushed on the throttle. I let the force of the boat pull me, my arms pulling in on the rope, and within a moment I was up. I was water-skiing! This thought startled me, and within seconds I was down. I had crossed my skis and lost control. Now I was in very deep water, a few hundred yards out in the lake, and it was much harder to get in the ready position, but I did so.

When Tanya yelled, "Hit it" again, I did much better. I got up and stayed up. I consciously enjoyed the experience. I liked looking directly at the skis, watching the little crescent waves that they made as they sliced through the water. If I tried looking around at the enormity of the lake and the surrounding mountains, I got shaky and focused again on my immediate surroundings. The towrope and the boat were enough to handle. Then I got a little cocky, pulling on the rope and leaning to the side, skiing out over the wake. I came back across, jumped the wake again and headed for the other side, but this time when I went down, I went down hard, crashing into the water head first, losing one of my skis. They circled back and laughed once they saw I was fine.

"You get one more try," Tanya yelled, but I said, "No, please, that's enough." She had her brother pull the boat next to me, and she dropped the ladder and helped me into the boat. The touch of her hands on mine, ever so fleeting, was electric. I tingled as I sat across from her. I tried not to stare but could not help myself—her butt was thrust toward me as she leaned over the side and retrieved my skis from the water. For the first time in my life, I was in lust. I adored her, could not stop looking at her.

They took me back to the dock and gave rides to the rest of the guests. I stayed and watched, even though it took over two hours. When they had satisfied the last guest, it was Tanya's turn. They let yet another Fedorov, a young boy about ten, in the boat as state law required a lookout separate from the driver. Tanya told Stephen to hit it before the rope was completely taut, and she came up fast. He went just a short way out and circled back in. As they neared the dock, she stepped out of one of the skis, and it floated on a trajectory in toward the dock. She now had both her feet on one ski, and as they headed out into the lake, she was crisscrossing back and forth across the wakes, creating a large wave as she did so.

They were gone for fifteen minutes, and I was watching a family on the beach. A little girl about four years old had gotten out of the water, and her mother wanted her to change. The mother took the girl's bathing suit off, and she was standing there stark naked. I looked at the small crack where her legs met, the folds of skin to the side of it. I was staring. I had never seen this before. I was surprised at the way it sloped into the body, rather than hung out. The mom put her underwear on, and I looked away, embarrassed that I had been looking at a child. I was confused. My brother had told me that a cunt was like an asshole in the front, but this was nothing like that.

I heard the motor and saw the boat cut in front of the dock at full speed. Tanya let go of the tow rope and skied right up to the dock, sinking in the water just a foot or so before the ladder. They stowed the gear and tied up the boat and walked off together toward the family cabin. I waited in vain, desperately trying to will Tanya to turn around and look at me.

When I was looking at the recreational notice board the next day, I saw the announcement for the teenage dance at the dock. The rest of the family wanted to go into the village, but I stayed back, had a sandwich for supper, and went down to the dock after it got dark. There were only about a dozen kids there, mostly girls. Tanya was in charge of the record player, and she was whispering and giggling with a couple of girls her age. She took off the Beach Boys and put on "Louie, Louie." A few of the kids there were too young to be teenagers, but most were around thirteen or fourteen. Nobody was dancing. I hung around in the shadows for a while, caught her eye once or twice, but was too shy to walk right up to her while she was with her friends.

I saw her two more times. She treated me just like any other guest when I went water-skiing again, but was friendlier to me one evening. I had checked a rowboat out and was rowing around the nearby point when I saw her. She was sitting in about three feet of water, shampooing her hair. She had it all bunched up on top of her head, full of suds, scratching it. When she saw me, she called out, "Don't tell anybody. We're not supposed to wash our hair in the lake, but it feels so good." She held her nose and dipped her head backward into the lake, arching her long neck, her wet T-shirt revealing her form. I rowed over to be near her, and we talked for a little while. She asked me why I hadn't come over the other night, but I just shook my head. She said, "Well, you should have. Bye," and walked off toward her house.

We had to leave early the next morning, and I never saw her again.

11

Halloween, like the Fourth of July, had its rituals: tricks and treats. Not content to get sacks of free candy, we also liked to trash the neighborhood. We brazenly stole pumpkins right off neighbors' porches and smashed them in the street. On Halloween evening, Adam, Vinny, and I gathered at Schneid's, ready for vandalism. We went to the drugstore and bought shaving cream, making sure to buy the can with the cylindrical dispenser that allows the cream to shoot out a few feet if you really shake up the can and point it at the right angle. We went to the grocery store for eggs and flour. Then to the five-and-dime next door for big sticks of chalk.

All we needed were the nylon stockings into which we would pour the flour to make our weapons. Adam had a brilliant idea to fortify our supplies and get the stockings. We split up, and each of us took different blocks in our neighborhood. We knocked on doors and asked the people who answered for help. "I'm on a scavenger hunt for a Halloween party, and I need to collect some things. I was wondering if you could help. Do you have a nylon stocking, a raw egg, or a 1906 copper penny?"

I did this for about a half hour, hitting almost ten houses. A number of people saw through the ruse and just said "no" and closed the door. One or two were angry, and one even told me I should be ashamed of myself. But I collected another six eggs, two nylon stockings, *and* one 1906 penny from an old couple who must have been in their eighties. He bought the tale hook, line, and sinker. "I must have a 1906. How old was I in 1906?" the old gent asked his wife.

They invited me in and had me wait while he went upstairs. The furnishings in the house were ancient. The patterned carpet that was over the badly worn hardwood floor was threadbare in spots, and the path that led to the kitchen was completely worn through so that the wood was showing. Above the mantel was a portrait that must have been of the couple when they were younger. He was dressed in a double-breasted suit, and she wore a flowing dress with a high lace collar encircled by a tasteful string of pearls. Even the sepia tones could not hide the fact that she had been beautiful and he had been handsome. Observing the wrinkled bags they had become, I shivered.

There were colorful vases and black-and-white pictures in old wood frames. And there was a fat cat, a Persian. She was sitting on the lap of the old woman, across from me on a sofa that was protected by a faded slipcover. Both were staring at me. I attempted a weak smile, but they were unmoved, the woman petting her cat softly, waiting patiently.

The old man came down with a fishbowl full of pennies and spread them on the coffee table. At first, he just wanted reassurance from his wife that he was born in 1886, meaning that he was twenty in 1906. Had he been saving his pennies since then? The wife, though, while gently reassuring him that he got his year of birth right, started asking me questions. What are you going to do with these items? Where is this party? Why a 1906 penny?

I kept wondering why Adam threw this twist in, and why I listened to him. I guessed he'd thought it would be too suspicious if we just asked for eggs and stockings. The penny would add convincing legitimacy to our request. I think she was clearly on to me, but did not want to crush the spirit of her husband, who was having fun searching for the penny. By God if he didn't find one. He held it up and said, "Got it." As he came over to me, his wife had had enough and gently put the cat aside and stood up to cut him off. "Dear, are you sure you want to give it to this boy?"

"Yes, hon." He looked at me for support. "This will help you win the scavenger hunt, right?"

"Yes, sir," I said in my most deferential and appreciative voice. "I think the penny is the hardest item to get, and I have everything else." I held up my brown paper bag to demonstrate. "I just need to rush back to the party to see if I'm first." I stood up and moved toward the door to demonstrate that time was of the essence.

She was relentless, though. "Do you have to *keep* the penny, or do you intend to return it?"

"Oh, I think they're going to keep it. You know, to show the other kids that I really got it."

"You could return it to us tomorrow."

He tried to help me again. We had become allies—male bonding and all. "Oh, hon, I have lots of pennies; I don't need it."

"But maybe the 1906 is valuable, which is why they sent these kids out on this scam, um, search." She was enjoying herself, smiling at me as she pretended to misspeak.

This got his attention. He had been just about to relinquish the penny to me, but he drew his hand back and looked at the penny up close, examining it on both sides. He was worried now. "Do you think so?" He was asking his wife, not me.

"Might be."

He was only slightly deterred, but he had made a decision. "I'll loan it to you on one condition," he said. "You promise to return it to me."

"Well, I guess so." I faltered. "Maybe you just want to give me a raw egg?"

This pushed his wife over the edge. She had been unsure of herself up to that point, but now she was righteous. "You had better be on your way," she said icily and put her hand on the doorknob.

Silently, I took the few steps to the door, happy to be getting out alive. "Well, thanks, anyway," I said to the old man. He looked me in the eye. "Is there really a scavenger hunt?" he said, his own eyes welling up ever so slightly.

"Yes, sir, there is," I lied.

"Here." He held out the penny. I took it and thanked him. "Bring it back to me if you can."

"I will, sir. Thank you, sir, thank you very much. I am going to win, thanks to you." Had I laid it on thick enough? When I ran into Adam at the end of the block I was absolutely conflicted. On the surface, I was the bravura punk: "You should have seen these old coots looking for a 1906 penny. Can you believe it? I actually got a 1906 penny!" At the same time, I was filled with shame, embarrassed that the old lady knew I was a fake and sad that the old man had his doubts about me. I put the penny into my pocket and resolved to return it to him, while saying, "We got enough crap; let's start doing something with it, for Chrissakes!"

As we roamed the neighborhood, smashing pumpkins and chalking dark houses, we bumped into my brother Kevin by the playground. He was covered in egg and shaving cream. "What happened to you?"

"I got ambushed by the guys from Dirty Dan's," the rival candy store, just three blocks, but a gulf away, from Schneid's.

"Where are you going?"

"To get some more eggs. I'm gonna go back and get even."

"We have eggs and shaving cream. You want us to go with you?"

"Sure," he said, "but there are a lot of them. Let's get some help."

We walked up to the corner. The little kids worked Schneid's while Kevin hit the bar. Together, we drafted about ten more people. We cleaned out the rest of the egg case at Ernie's. We divvied up the eggs so that each person had about half a dozen, though Kevin retained almost a full dozen for himself. A crowd was gathering at Dan's, too, and we sent an emissary up, who came back egged. "They want to meet by the playground. They think the cops will come if we do it on the avenue."

"Do what?" I asked.

Kevin answered like a wounded warrior, "This is going to be a war, Davey; are you in or out?"

"I'm in, of course," I stammered. Kevin had never included me in anything. *He must be desperate,* I thought. We pumped ourselves up as we walked the four blocks to the playground, strategizing, plotting. I even heard the words "flanking maneuver."

When we got to the playground they were nowhere to be seen. Had they faked us out? Were they getting ready for another ambush? Suddenly, we saw them up the block, on the far side of the playground, their turf. "That's not neutral," someone said, a little worried.

"Who gives a shit?" said Kevin, "Let's get 'em." He started jogging up the block, and the crowd followed him. He was barking out orders on the way. "Some go up this side." He pointed to one sidewalk and then the opposite one. "Davey, little kids go up this side." He stayed in the middle of the street, and his troops did what they were told.

When we got to the corner, we all stopped. If anything, they had even more people than we did. They, too, were spread throughout the intersection. But they were not hiding, not planning an ambush. They were ready to rumble. Their leader was Billy Mackay, a six-foot-four stud who drove a brand-new souped-up GTO, with a rack on top and a bunch of surfboards. He had all the girls in the neighborhood drooling over him. He stepped forward, as if claiming the intersection as his, daring someone to challenge him. Kevin took the bait, emulating the macho courage. He, too, stepped into the street, dumping his carton of eggs at his feet. He fixated on Billy, very quickly drew back, let an egg fly, and nailed him. Billy shrugged his shoulder to the side and took the egg on the top of his arm. It splattered on his black leather jacket, and some of the insides even flew up into his precious and always well-coifed hair.

The battle was on. Eggs began to fly in all directions. Everyone was getting hit at once. The scene had a certain amount of beauty to it. Dimly lit by the streetlight on a moonless night, the white oval shapes looked like small birds darting back and forth against a cloudy sky. There were so many eggs flying that some actually collided in midair, raining on all that were underneath. The barrage lasted only a few minutes before the munitions began to run out.

One of the tactics we had agreed to on the walk over was that each of us should keep one or two eggs in reserve for potential hand-to-hand combat. Sure enough, they charged across the street, wielding their shaving cream cans and flour sacks. I had foolishly put one of my reserves in my pants pocket. There were definitely more of them than us, all of them big kids. We broke ranks and started to run. As soon as I turned to flee, one of my reserve eggs broke in my pocket and was seeping down my leg, looking as if I had lost control of my bladder. I glanced back to see that Kevin had held his ground. He was surrounded by the opposition and getting pounded. He just crouched down and took it for a minute until Billy, admiring his guts, said to his cohort, "C'mon, let's get the chickenshits who're running."

I got pelted by a few eggs, covered by shaving cream, and pummeled by flour sacks. I dropped most of my weapons. I tried to hide behind a car, but they found me there and attacked me again. I ran into a backyard and jumped the fence into the next yard. Staying in the dark shadows was good. I kept moving, hopping from yard to yard. I lost my pursuers. I hid under a big bush until I heard the noises die down.

I cautiously came out and crawled back to the battle scene, half expecting to see my brother lying there, crumpled and defeated. It was eerily empty and silent, yet clearly a battle had taken place. The street was covered with broken eggs and shaving cream. There were empty egg cartons and empty shaving cream cans scattered about. The middle of the street looked like a soup truck had spilled its cargo: the yellow of broken and spread yolks was interspersed and interlaced with the white of the shaving cream and bits of eggshells.

Realizing I was still in enemy territory, I decided to get the hell out of there, apparently just in time. I heard voices, but I retreated into the shadows of a neighboring yard. It was some of the Dan's crowd, laughing and recounting stories about their victory. They, too, were covered in dried-up goop, but they had a right to celebrate, as they did get us running and chased us away from their turf.

What would Kevin do? Certainly not cower in the shadows. I remembered that I still had one reserve egg left, miraculously unbroken in my top shirt pocket. I took it out and cradled it, looked at it and talked to it: "C'mon, baby, do your stuff!" I stepped out of the shadows onto the sidewalk and hurled the egg in their direction as I yelled, "*Dan's sucks*." Unfortunately, my shout gave them time to react, and they scrambled as the egg landed among them, striking none of them directly, but at least splashing their shoes a bit and definitely pissing them off.

Enough of this courage crap, I thought, as I bounded back into the shadows, hopping fences in reverse order and staying in yards all the way to the end of the block. Not sure where I retreated to, they stayed in the street, a few of them holding the corner and a few of them walking up the block parallel to where I had run. When they got to the next corner, they were only twenty yards away from me as I sat under someone's backyard porch and listened to them.

They were excited, angry, and disappointed that they had not gotten a good enough look at me to see who I was. They had no idea. They referred to me as a coward, but I was more comfortable with the persona of a brave sniper who had infiltrated the enemy camp. I felt good about myself and tried to relax, conscious of my pounding heart. They gave up the search and walked back up the block to join their friends. I waited a few more minutes and then darted across the street and into the shadows and traversed that whole block, this time more quickly, on the front lawns, not needing to hop fences. Running from shadow to shadow, I encountered and scared a few trick-or-treaters and angered at least one homeowner, but I made it all the way back to Schneid's in about ten minutes.

The rest of the little kids were licking their wounds. Abe had closed early, not wanting to deal with the excesses that were predictable on Halloween. The older kids were in the bar, done for the night. Even some of the kids from Dan's had joined them, comrades again, buying one another beers, regaling each other with stories.

Not content to let the night end, Adam had another idea. "I know where there is a party we could crash."

"Whose?"

"Well, she's older, a junior, I think. She lives over on Little Neck Parkway. C'mon, let's just check it out. But we need some stuff." We went into the deli and bought some chocolate syrup and honey.

When we got to the house we saw that there was indeed a party going on in the basement. Clearly, though, from what we could see through the window, these kids were all much older than us, dressed up and listening to music, bobbing for apples and dancing. Adam read the concern on my face. "We're not going to crash it," he said. "We're going to trash it."

We did some reconnaissance and discovered that there was a separate entrance to the basement, up the driveway toward the backyard. There was a concrete stairway leading down about ten feet. The stairway was protected on three sides by a low brick wall. We hid behind the back wall and sat with our backs against it. Vinny lit up a cigarette.

"What are we doing here?" I was growing exasperated.

"Just wait." Adam kept looking around. "There," he finally whispered, pointing. "She might be coming to this party." Across the street was a girl, a few years older than us, decked out in a pink party dress and all made up, her hair looking like it had been done in a beauty parlor. "Get ready," he ordered.

"Ready for what?"

"We're gonna get her!" He gave me the jar of honey, which he opened and handed to me. Vinny got the chocolate syrup. "When she gets to the bottom of the stairwell, pour this stuff on her," Adam commanded. I felt sorry for her already.

Adam slipped into the neighbor's yard and used the slight shadow along the house to get to the front and hide behind a bush. Sure enough, the girl was coming this way. She looked so happy in anticipation, so pretty. As she came up the driveway, Adam crouched at the end of the bushes, so that I could see him, but she couldn't. He waited until she started down the stairs so that we could trap her. "*Now!*" he yelled, and he jumped out and ran at her.

He squirted her with shaving cream as she screamed and ran down the stairs. While she knocked, he squirted more shaving cream on her. Vinny leaned over the wall and poured the chocolate syrup straight down into her hair. It streamed down her face and onto her pink dress. She was screaming hysterically, but the music was blaring, and no one inside could hear her. She collapsed to the ground, and Adam gave her another squirt of shaving cream on his way up the stairs. She started kicking the door. As he ran up the stairs, he directed me, "Now the honey!" I looked at the honey and threw it to the ground, next to me.

There was no way I was going to pour it on this poor girl. Vinny looked at me without saying a word.

The door opened, and her friends saw her. We had to bolt fast, and I ran out of the driveway, up Little Neck Parkway, and all the way home. I was done for the night. At the corner, Adam popped out and asked me, "Did you get her good with the honey?"

"No," I said, "I missed." Vinny was not in sight.

"Oh, that's too bad, that would have been a great final touch." He was beaming, ecstatic with his performance. "Where's the honey?"

"I left it there."

"You left it there? That cost me fifty cents!"

"Tough shit! That was terrible. There was no reason to do that to that poor girl!" I was finally honest, almost crying from pent-up emotion, but to no avail.

He just laughed. "It's Halloween, people expect to get tricked."

"You think that's why she wore a new dress and got her hair done?" I was yelling now, incredulous that he was going to justify what he had done. Realizing that I was really pissed, he dropped it. "All right, all right, already! What now?" he asked.

"I'm done," I said. "School tomorrow, remember?"

I went in and took a long shower, leaving my meager pillowcase of candy by the door. Mom asked me if I had had fun trick-or-treating.

"Yeah, it was great."

12

Queens experienced somewhat of a blue-collar cultural awakening in the early sixties. National League baseball had returned to New York City after a five-year absence. A World's Fair blossomed amid the evolving infrastructure of parkways, subways, and apartment complexes. A massive amusement park celebrating America's history, Freedomland, sprouted on the edge of the Bronx. Meanwhile, the nation elected its first Catholic president, John Fitzgerald Kennedy; the Beatles invaded our shores in a wave of hysteria, singing simple songs about love; and I got accepted to Bishop Reilly High School.

Public school was for paupers, Protestants, and pagans. The nuns, reinforced by our parents, had indoctrinated us for eight years: the best way to heaven is to stay in Catholic school. Even though I was sick of the discipline, the punishment, the humiliation, and the blame so prevalent at Saint Greg's, I never considered not going all out for Catholic high school. I certainly never even imagined that I had a choice. I knew full well that it was going to be tough, as the brothers and priests who taught high school were even stricter than the nuns, but I was absolutely dedicated to pleasing my parents, performing up to their expectations.

The application process rolled out like a very big competition, almost like vying for a scholarship to college. The archdiocese of Brooklyn administered the entrance test right across the whole city. The individual schools vied for the students with the best test scores. Like almost everyone else, I listed Archbishop Molloy first, even while knowing that only the brightest got accepted. Bishop Reilly came next, the school that had just opened in Fresh Meadows. I liked the name, and I was interested in the novelty of it, the newness of it. Unlike many of the Catholic schools that were either all girls or all boys, Reilly was going to admit both genders. The school was designed as two wings on a single core, and the students would intermingle in the common areas, which included the cafeteria, library, and administration. All of my classes, though, would be all boys, taught by brothers and male lay teachers. Still, there would be dances, and the concept sounded more enticing than an all-boys school. My parents were completely supportive. In fact, it was a school run—and therefore subsidized—by the diocese itself. Tuition was only $300 a year; half of what it would have cost them to send me to Molloy.

The nuns tried to prepare us for high school mostly by scaring us: teachers there would not be as nice as our nuns, would tolerate no shenanigans. Homework would take hours a night, and we would be expected to *type* papers.

But it was hard to take them too seriously. The BVMs—Sisters of the Blessed Virgin Mary—wore full habits: floor-length black robes, rosary beads, and white starched headgear that left only the outline of their faces exposed. The effect was often to squeeze the humanity out of them, and they each had their own peccadilloes: Sister Mary Clarice liked to take her sixth graders over her knee and spank them in front of the class, humiliating us beyond imagination; Sister Mary Elizabeth Joan was a slapper—she was the one who once slapped me in the face for stopping in the hallway and getting a drink of water without permission; Sister Mary Catherine told us stories about hell, how we would burn and scream for forgiveness, trying to get us to imagine an infinity of pain.

Sister Mary Lou Ellen had her own quirk. Her ruse was to ask Terry Otes, the tallest kid in the class, to straighten a picture of Bishop Sheen that hung in the back of the room above the coat closet. She would direct him, and all of the kids in the class would turn in their desks and watch him. Sneak a peek back at her, though, and you could catch her squeezing her pimples, wiping the blood and pus with a tissue that she kept up her sleeve.

Most of the nuns were of Irish descent, and the highlight of their year was always the St. Patrick's Day annual show. We would all have to get our moms to make green costumes, and we would rehearse skits for weeks. We always started out serious, with Saint Patrick casting the snakes out of Ireland, and ended up silly, leprechauns chasing gold and leading the whole auditorium in song: "My Wild Irish Rose," "Too-Ra-Loo-Ra-Loo-Ra," "McNamara's Band," and "Harrigan."

On the last day of eighth grade, as we suffered through the humiliating class march to the end of the ball field one last time, some of us boys celebrated our freedom by fastening our school neckties to the fence, dousing them with lighter fluid and setting them ablaze. As we watched them burn, we saw the nuns coming from the school; we ran away, not brave enough to stand our ground.

As Labor Day drew near, I grew more and more anxious. I was in the second class at Reilly. The kids I knew from the first class, the sophomores a year older than me, told me that the upperclassmen needed to assert their superiority. I had better be careful at the bus stop as they would expect the freshmen to be at their beck and call. They were planning to harass and haze us. I talked to my parents about my fears, but they dismissed them outright. "Don't be ridiculous," Pop said.

I was terrified the first day as I got off the Q43 across the street from the diner where everyone else was waiting to transfer to the next bus. I was prepared for the worst, remaining anxious even as the bus pulled up and we all got in, showing our bus passes and dropping our nickels in the box. Nothing happened. Not that day, not ever.

Meanwhile, I got into trouble early, but not often. The punishments were too degrading. I got caught chewing gum in Spanish class and had to stand for the rest of the period with the gum on my nose. I was sent to detention for talking in class and had to stand in front of the detention hall holding hands with the roughneck whom I'd been talking to in the first place. He was much more angry than I was, and when I tried to take his hand in response to the Brother's order, he just grabbed my wrist, squeezing hard, cutting off my circulation, and whispered to me as the Brother turned away, "If you ever mention this to anyone, you're dead!"

The worst part of high school was gym class—well, not gym class per se, but the mandatory showers after gym class. The locker-room showers were communal, ten or twelve boys taking a shower at the same time. And the brothers standing around watching, making sure every one of us took a shower. Not only was I totally unprepared for hanging out with a bunch of naked boys, I was caught off guard by the vicious humor. The more mature boys made fun of the freshmen. They called us humiliating names, made fun of our size, and threatened us. On occasion, with the brothers looking the other way, they would take a particularly vulnerable boy and hold him upside down, sticking his head in a toilet bowl while they flushed. Every day was an unspeakable horror. I'd try to undress slowly at my locker, waiting for the mad rush to thin, and then I'd carry my towel in such a way as to cover my genitals while I walked to the shower. I'd get in and out as fast as I could, barely rinsing off the sweat, and pray that I didn't get singled out for abuse. Carelessly, though, my eyes would wander, and I'd notice the variety in size and shape. I'd be amazed at the uninhibited, the ones who were comfortable walking around, standing around talking, unabashedly flaunting themselves.

■ ■ ■

I was friends with one girl, a sophomore who was dating Don D'Amato, and I stopped to talk to her one day in the cafeteria, right at the invisible line that separated the boys' side from the girls'. I didn't even know it wasn't allowed. Brother Syrus came up behind me and dug his hands into my neck, gripping like a vise, and drove me down to the floor, my knees buckling and my eyes tearing from the pain. He looked at me with a subtle disdain, a sick smile on his face, as he said, "Get off the floor and get back to your table."

I decided to learn how to keep my mouth shut, and fly below the radar. This treatment was not for me. The brothers had their pet whipping boys, and I resolved not to become one of them. One afternoon I was sent to deliver a package to the principal's office. On the way back to my classroom, I could hear that an announcement was being made, but there were no speakers in the halls, so I could not tell what it was. It was an odd time for an announcement, in the middle of a class. When I returned to my classroom, the announcement had just finished, and the shock was evident. Everybody's mouths hung open. Even the teacher was stunned and speechless. I sat in my seat and leaned over to my neighbor, knowing I was risking detention, but I had to know what was going on. "President Kennedy has been shot. He's in critical condition. We're all supposed to pray for him."

I felt the crushing emptiness immediately. The fear was dark and deep. My mind became an abyss that my thoughts could not cross. I felt faint, dizzy. Brother Thad snapped us out of it. "Get on your knees and pray to God that he makes it!" We had to kneel in the aisle next to our desks for the next hour, our heads bowed. I couldn't pray at first. I was too scared. What did this mean? Who would shoot the President? The first Catholic President in the nation's history. He was a young family man; we all knew that. I prayed for his kids, for little John-John and his sister, Caroline. I prayed for Jackie. I prayed that the Russians would not use this as an opportunity to bomb us. I finally remembered to pray that he might live.

There was no levity on the bus that day, none of the usual ruckus. Adults on the bus were crying, holding each other for comfort. Kids remained stunned, shocked. Along Hillside Avenue, crowds were gathering in front of the stores that had TVs in the windows. The overwhelming silence was palpable. At home, we became glued to the television. All events were canceled for the weekend, even professional sports. There weren't even any commercials. When news came that he had died, we all cried. Over the next few days, the images of the riderless horse and of Oswald being murdered by Jack Ruby were burned deep into our collective memories. The world would never be the same. We would never feel at peace again; we were sure of it.

13

And yet, life went on. One day after school, Pop picked me up in his Con Ed truck so that we could visit the World's Fair site. The entire area was under construction. The steel shell of Shea Stadium was rising on the north side of the Willets Point elevated subway station, and the virtual city that would be the fair was under construction on the south side.

Pop grew animated while recalling the 1939 World's Fair that had been constructed on this very same site, now known locally as the Flushing Meadows. He told me how it had been called the Corona Dump, a bleak and uninhabited refuse heap, composed of the ashes from Brooklyn's incinerators. Robert Moses, whose vision had transformed the twelve-hundred-acre dump in 1939, was going to do it again. This time, he wanted to leave a permanent legacy: a public place of rolling hills, lakes, tennis courts, gardens, and walkways. He would turn the vast, generously named meadow into a public park that he hoped would be named after him. Located almost at the geographic center of the city, it would rival Manhattan's Central Park.

The landscape had been leveled and was crawling with heavy machinery—cranes, dump trucks, cement mixers, and bulldozers—all moving about in syncopated harmony. It looked like some giant version of a boy's dream toy collection. From a distance, the trucks moved as if in slow motion, climbing to the tops of hills to dump supplies, digging out holes in the ground, and leveling sites for new buildings on a scale beyond imagination. There were hundreds of construction workers in hard hats, blueprints spread out everywhere, pickup trucks scattered around, and continuous, deafening noise from the jackhammers, welders, and carpenters.

Pop talked about the fact that some of the corporate sponsors of the fair were the same ones from twenty-five years earlier, with the famous updating of the General Motors Futurama exhibit being the most prominent. He described the 1939 visions that had become reality: the extensive roads and parkways making the automobile a new necessity. And he explained that when the fair ended, they tore everything down. He said they would do it again, but this time they would salvage a few exhibits, like the Unisphere, the symbol of this fair. It was to be a massive globe, 140 feet tall, made out of stainless steel and ringed by circles representing satellites. It was to symbolize the fair's theme, "Peace Through Understanding." Along with the New York State pavilion, it would remain after the rest of the fair was gone.

We had been to Freedomland, right across the East River, in the Bronx. With its staged reenactments of historical events like the Great Chicago Fire and the gunfights in the Wild West, it was spectacle on a huge scale, with seven different themed areas. You entered into Little Old New York and experienced the city of the eighteen hundreds with trolley cars and surreys with fringes on top and people walking around in period costumes.

I'd felt transported when I'd been there, as if I were really visiting another time. We thought of it as the East Coast's answer to Disneyland. Pop promised that the fair would be even better, almost six times bigger.

When the fair finally opened, my first visit was as a student. As our class gathered at Willets Point, a station that would never again be a quiet neighborhood stop, the brothers gave us instructions on how to behave. They had let us know in advance that this was to be a unique situation: we would not attempt to stay together as a school or even as a class. In fact, once we went through the gates, we were on our own. We could stay as late as we wanted, and we had to get ourselves home, just as we had gotten ourselves there. There would be no chaperones, no organized groups.

I split off immediately with a few of my school friends, and we ran off giggling, glorifying at the freedom. We headed right for Futurama, foolishly waiting on the longest line at the fair. But the wait was worth it. We marveled at the futuristic vision and imagined diving comfortably under the ice floes of Antarctica and checking into an underwater hotel. Thinking that I would be getting a lifelong friend, I signed up for a pen pal at the Parker Pen pavilion by choosing a card from a barrel, writing a letter to a high school boy in India and dropping it off, only to be let down later when I never got a reply. Our only assignment from the brothers was to see Michelangelo's *Pietà*, the wonderful sculpture of a sorrowful Mary holding the deceased body of her son at the foot of the cross. Another long line led to a moving sidewalk, and we had about a minute to glide by, the lighting bathing the small room in an eerie blue, and the crowd hushing in reverence while drifting past the holy icon. We took the nine-minute simulated helicopter ride around the Panorama, a scale model of New York City, trying to pick out our individual houses and getting a view of the layout of the boroughs that you could never get from a map.

For my second visit, I went with Adam and Vinny, and we planned a dream day. It was a Saturday in the summer, and we had discovered that you were allowed to leave the fair, after having paid your admission, get your hand stamped and return during the same day. We were there when it opened, spent the morning on the rides and exhibits, left at noon, and walked the half mile across the train platforms to Shea Stadium for a one o'clock Mets game. After the game, we walked back to the fair and stayed till it closed at ten o'clock that night, watching the fireworks and the dancing fountain display.

The three of us went again the very next week. We became experts at the layout, knowing where the best foods were, seeing some of the major exhibits for the second and third times, and riding the US Royal Tires Ferris wheel, in the shape of a giant tire, over and over again. Eventually, we got around to some of the minor exhibits, the more educational shows, like the Wonderful World of Chemistry at the DuPont exhibit. I lived for the Belgian Village, where we would splurge on waffles with a rich malt taste, freshly baked and steaming, and topped with real whipped cream and fresh strawberries.

The price of admission was just one dollar for students, not much of a barrier to us going as often as we liked. Even so, we realized one day that the fair was so huge that there must be a way we could sneak in, a fence that we could hop, or a wall that we could scale. We reconnoitered inside the fair and spent the better part of a day scouting and scheming. We realized that the easiest way to sneak in would be to walk along one of the tall retainer walls on the Grand Central Parkway. There were admission gates at several of the side streets that crossed the parkway, and if we walked down one of them and then slipped onto the parkway wall itself, we could walk on top of it and find a spot with an easy ingress. The boundary of the fair right at the side streets had a fifteen-foot fence, but once you got a hundred yards or so away from the street, the tall fence was replaced by a standard six-foot galvanized fence like the kind around many a backyard. We knew we could scale these in an instant.

About a week later, we decided to try it. We took a new route: Q43 bus to Jamaica, the E train to Queens Plaza, then transfer to the 7 from the other direction, from Manhattan toward Flushing. We got off the 111th Street station, before the fair stop and walked along Roosevelt Avenue, diverting from the subway el, as we got closer to the fairgrounds. We went down 114th Street to 44th Avenue, and as we crossed the street, we were happy that there were sizable lines at each entrance booth, occupying the time of the ticket takers, not allowing them any leisure to be watching as we slipped behind some bushes and began our walk along the wall. We had gone about fifty yards in when we encountered a barrier, an overgrown bush that was blocking the path. Vinny pressed into the bush and grabbed the fence on the near side with his right hand, turning his body toward the fence, sidestepping his way around the bush, reaching around to the other side to grab the fence with his left hand, and then pulling his body over. It looked easy enough but was definitely scary, as the cars were whizzing by on the parkway directly below. The traffic was steady at sixty or sixty-five miles per hour.

I copied what Vinny had done, grabbing the fence with my right hand, sidestepping the bush, and reaching around with my left. But I was not as tall or as broad as him, and as I reached with my left hand, extending my body as much as I could, I let go of my right hand before I had a firm grasp of the fence with my left. I lurched to grab the fence, but my foot slipped, and I fell off the wall. I experienced a moment of absolute terror. My feet had no traction at all, and I was on my way down, knowing that I would break a leg or two at best, and at worst I would be killed by oncoming traffic. I stretched up to try to grab the bush but the branches broke and only served to slow me for the shortest fraction of a second. That fraction was all Vinny needed. He leaned down and grabbed my arm as I fell, and he caught me. He was strong enough to hold me while I thrust out with my other hand and grasped the top of the wall. Hanging onto the wall, I was able to use my feet to boost myself and pull up while Vinny steadied me and guided me back. I embraced the fence and hugged it to me. I was safe. Vinny had saved my life.

Adam, similar in size and stature to me, immediately announced that he was not going to make it—was not, in fact, going to try. Vinny convinced Adam to squeeze himself between the bush and the fence, with us assisting by pulling as much of the bush away from the fence as we could. Reluctantly, Adam did this maneuver and made it to our side, scratching up his arms pretty good and tearing his shirt. He was near tears, covered with sweat, and breathing heavily. We were all trembling as we stood on top of this retainer wall, still short of our goal of sneaking into the fair. We continued sidestepping for a while, much more carefully, never letting go of the fence, and cringing a little at each and every car that sped by ten feet below us, creating short burst of drafts that clawed at our feet and tried to suck us to our doom.

I kept blubbering to Vinny, "You saved my life."

Nonchalantly, he said, "You'd have done the same for me."

"Right," I said sarcastically, knowing I did not have the strength to do what he had done. "I would have caught you." We all laughed.

We were behind the House of Good Taste in the industrial area, not one of the most popular spots in the fair, aware that people out on the main pathways connecting these three fully furnished houses could see us. A few, in fact, had stopped to watch us, wondering what we were up to. We realized that it would not be long before one of them somehow busted us. We decided to just be brash and go for it. Almost as soon as we had arrived at the area where the fence was smaller, we decided to climb it, knowing we were in full view of a few people. We had nothing to lose, though, and we were not about to try to go back around that bush to escape, and so, on the count of three, we just did it, all three of us climbing the fence at the same time.

Adam briefly got caught on the sharp edge at the top of the fence, ripping his pants to go along with his torn shirt, but we were over it in a matter of seconds and just walked briskly out from behind the building nearby. Of the few people who were watching us, most laughed or smiled or pretended to ignore us, but one, a middle-aged man, decided to get involved. "You punks, what do you think you're doing?"

"Going to the fair, just like you," Vinny said, looking him dead in the eye, unintimidated as usual.

Adam and I, meanwhile, were both scared, and we wanted to run the other way, but Vinny puffed up his chest and walked right past him. We kind of jogged to catch up to Vinny, looking over our shoulder at the stranger, seeing that he was still outraged at our behavior. He began to yell, "What you did is illegal, you know. What's more, it's immoral! Everyone else has to pay. Why do you think you don't have to?" He was looking frantically around, but much to our relief and his disgust, there was not a policeman or a security guard or any kind of fair staff in sight.

Vinny then turned around and gave him the finger, and so we had to run, blend into the crowd, not comfortable until we got all the way to the other side of the fair, to the live porpoise show in Florida, beneath the giant orange tower. For the rest of the day, Adam and I were both watching the people, afraid that we would bump into him again and that he would have us arrested. Vinny blew it off and enjoyed himself much more than we did. Toward the end of the day, when it was time to leave, Adam asked the two of us, with a straight face in his sincerest voice, "Do we have to jump the fence to get out?"

I just laughed at him and said no, but Vinny was merciless, stopping in his tracks and asking him, "Do you think they have cops at each exit who somehow know who paid to get in and who didn't?" in his most belittling and humiliating voice.

Lamely, Adam countered, "I don't know."

Vinny just shook his head and lit a cigarette.

By the time I went with my family, I was a pro. We picked the Unisphere as our meeting place when we went in different directions. We enjoyed the opportunities to merely sit there, as the breeze would often send a light spray from the fountains over the crowd, providing some relief from the heat. I enjoyed being the expert, leading them to the best exhibits and demonstrating my familiarity with the culture of the fair. I wanted to sit in one of the Bell booths and make a simulated videophone call with the whole family. These were scattered throughout the fair and looked like small glassed-in bus stops. But they were always crowded, and Pop refused to wait on the line. In fact, Pop had enough of the lines before it even got dark out, and we left early.

The fair closed for the winter and reopened again the next spring. Adam, Vinny, and I remained regulars. We never tried to sneak in again, realizing that we could save a lot of money by bringing lunch from home and avoiding the high-priced food. Many times, we just went in for a few hours after a Mets game. The crowds were much smaller the second year, and from a business perspective the fair was a bust, never recovering the investors' money. When they closed the gates for the last time, razing began almost immediately, amazing us that buildings that had looked so permanent had been constructed for only a two-year life-span. Freedomland went bankrupt at the same time and Walt Disney abandoned the dream of having a New York amusement park, listened to his advisers, and headed for the more temperate climate of Florida.

14

In late fall, darkness set in during the supper hour, and by six-o'clock it felt like the middle of the night. Three nights a week we gathered to play basketball at Teen Center, inside PS 133, just four blocks away. Getting there was foreboding. The night felt uneven, quiet, and empty. I had so many fears, but there were two in particular that always haunted me on these short but interminable walks. The first was the very vastness of space. On a clear night, as I looked at the stars, I was sure that there was life out there. I fantasized that if visitors came, they would be motivated to kidnap and experiment. I searched the heavens, sure that someday a light would appear, spot me, and drag me up into a spaceship. I imagined brain-sucking, body-probing physical and emotional tortures. It was my disappearance itself that frightened me the most: the awareness that I could be gone, torn away from my parents—and they would never know what had happened to me!

The second fear was much more parochial. I had to walk past a line of tall bushes down the block, the spot where darkness was complete. There were no streetlights on this end. If murderers or monsters were lurking for me, this is where they would hide. I never let my guard down as I approached them. Since there were bushes on both sides of the street, the only choice was to pass by running as fast as possible in the middle of the road. I would take a deep breath of the cold night air, grip my gym bag tightly, and run, eyes straight ahead, never actually looking at the bushes themselves. After I got through this spot safely, the rest of the walk was a dream: adequately lit, the school in sight. As I got to the door, my relief was complete, my mind instantly erasing all fears and anxieties.

The ref, Nick, was the only grown-up at the center, and it was his call how many basketball games would be played and how he would divide up the teams. He had to be flexible based on the number and ages of kids who showed up on a particular night. The center was open to all teens, but you never knew whether big or little kids would predominate. If there were plenty of both, Nick would hold two games. The first game would be for little kids, ages thirteen to fifteen, and the second for the sixteen-and-older group.

I concentrated on defense. I was not fast and did not have a great shot, but I played hard and played long, always willing to run up and down the court for the full game. When I got the ball, I would be more inclined to pass to an open man, only taking a shot when a lane cleared and everyone else was covered. I could hit the lay-up pretty well, but my jump shot was weak. In these games of two fifteen-minute halves, scores would range from the thirties to the fifties. An average individual score would be eight or ten points. On those nights when I was lucky enough to hit double figures, I floated home, riding on a wave of self-esteem.

Despite the fears, I often went alone, meeting acquaintances and friends that I only saw there. Friday nights were special, though, as it was the only night that either Adam or Vinny was allowed to go with me, and there was a lot more going on than basketball. The Boy Scouts met then, and we liked to make fun of them as they vied for their badges. The Navajos, growing more like a street gang each year, liked to hang out, drink beer, and smoke cigarettes.

They would call us names just for going in, referring to us as collegiate, as if this was a great insult, indicating that we were studious, serious, and straight. The banter was lighthearted enough, and they would try to get us to hang outside with them and shun all semblance of authority or obeisance to any rules.

It was here that I first saw someone touch a girl's breast. Dennis Doyle had been a sleazeball from an early age. Constantly in trouble for talking back to the teachers, he had been suspended from school a few times. He and his entourage spent their evenings committing petty crimes: shoplifting, window-breaking, tire-slashing, can-opening parked cars, tearing off aerials, and cursing out anyone who crossed their paths.

They were hanging on the steps, smoking cigarettes. I had seen this girl before at Saint Greg's; she was a grade lower than me, and I knew her to say hello to. She had bleached-blond hair cut in a short bob, and she was wearing tight blue jeans, a tight sweater, and a faded leather jacket. Even more so than boys, girls looked like completely different people when out of their school uniforms. Dennis had his arm around her while they sat on the railing that lined the walkway to the stairs. It was an iron railing, about three feet tall. He was kissing her roughly and sloppily, noisily sticking his tongue in her mouth and sucking, almost slurping, on her lips. All the while, he was pushing against her breast with his right hand, smashing it into her body and pulling it out again, almost as if he were kneading bread. When he came up for air, he offered her out to others. She put her head down and said softly, "Dennis, don't."

"Shut up, bitch," he said. "C'mon, who wants a free feel?"

Several of his cohorts shuffled over and clumsily squeezed one of her budding breasts as if it were a Pensy Pinky and they were checking its bounce. When he offered her to me directly, I declined and was embarrassed as he taunted me, calling me a chickenshit. I was too scared to touch her; I just wanted to go in and play basketball. Yet I lingered, watching. I was not afraid to touch her breast. I was more afraid for her. I was afraid of what she must be feeling, scared of her humiliation, scared of what could make someone willingly endure this treatment, scared of what made Dennis do it.

She was clearly not enjoying this. It gave her no discernable pleasure of any kind. She seemed quite aware that the whole scene was a demonstration of his power and control over her. Yet she stood there and endured it for a good six or seven minutes before she balked. Softly with her head down in hopes that only he could hear, she said, "That's enough."

This only enraged him, and he grabbed her by her hair and pulled it tightly, wrapping and intertwining it in his fingers. Tears immediately welled up in her eyes. He then used the grip to pull her whole head up toward him, causing her to yelp as her feet almost left the ground. He bit her bottom lip and crushed one of her breasts with his other hand, and then he yanked himself away, letting go of her and pushing her back down with just enough force to signal total disdain. He said, "It's enough when I say it's enough, cunt."

As he walked away, she leaned against the railing and cried. This scared me the most. No one went over to her. No one comforted her. He huddled with his boys to block the wind and lit a new cigarette. My heart went out to her, but she would never know. I crawled into the gym and played basketball.

We didn't like to shower at the school gym, so we felt pretty clammy and manly as we hit the night air and walked up to Schneid's for a toasted corn muffin and a hot chocolate. We talked about the game, made plans for the weekend, and stretched our time out as the big kids came in for cigarettes. Later, lying in bed, I couldn't shake the image of the breast girl. At the same time that I revisited the anguish in her face, I wondered what the thrill of touching her would have been like.

I had only recently begun to learn a few truths about sex. At home, it had never been discussed, save a stray comment Mom made once about the ugly and disgusting nature of the male body. I had seen a naked woman on my paper route. I was delivering the *New York Post*. Unlike the *Long Island Press*, which went to almost every household, making it easy to deliver a route, the *Post* went primarily to Jewish families, and my fifty customers brought me all over Bellerose and Glen Oaks. I collected on Saturdays, and she had answered the door dripping wet, holding a towel under her chin down to her knees. She said, "Just a minute, sorry. I was in the shower."

She left the door open as she turned and walked to her kitchen to get her purse. She made no attempt to cover her back, and I made no attempt to turn away. I watched her strut, her butt and hips seductively signaling something to me, but I had no idea what. Out of the corner of her eye, she saw me watching her, and she dropped the towel as she went through her purse counting out the change. She was middle-aged, forty or so, brown hair and brown eyes. Her breasts were large and full, if sagging a little. I saw her bush—her beaver or snatch, my brothers would have called it—glistening with drops of water. It completely covered her cunt, so that neither the crack nor the folds could be seen. She took her time. I continued to stare, and I started to sweat. What if she asked me in? What if she wanted me to fuck her? I didn't know how, but I guessed that she would teach me. She picked the towel up and held it in front of her again as she walked over and handed me eighty-five cents, indicating a thirty-five-cent tip, larger than I had ever gotten at this house before.

"Thanks," I said.

"Oh, you're welcome," she said with a big smile on her face. As she closed the door, she let the towel fall to her feet, giving me one last, close-up look. The next Saturday, and every Saturday thereafter, there was a note saying that my money was in the milk box on the porch, including my fifteen-cent tip.

■ ■ ■

We had a counselor at school, a priest with large, basketball-palming hands. He didn't always wear his cassock; often he just had his starched white collar on with street clothes. He was only thirty or so and tried to use his youth to signal that he was like us. He told us that masturbation would become a strong temptation, but we must remember that abuse of one's body was a mortal sin and must be confessed as such. He was dead serious when he told us that it could lead to sterility, blindness, and even insanity. I became afraid of my own body.

When Adam told me that he had begun masturbating, I was embarrassed to admit that not only did I not do it, I was not even sure how to do it. He laughed and said, "Yes, you do." When he saw me avert my eyes, he knew I was serious. "Davey, you just grab it and pull it up and down, like this," demonstrating on a stick. "And it happens. You'll feel it coming. Really you will. Be careful, it spurts pretty far, and you have to clean it up so your mother doesn't see it."

Over the Thanksgiving holiday, Vinny was all excited and told me and Adam that Joe Stayer had brought a porno film down from Ithaca. It was a rainy Saturday afternoon, and his parents were away for the weekend. We went to his house and knocked on the door. He let us in, but as the rest of the big kids gathered, they threw us out. My brothers insisted that all little kids leave. "Out," Joe said, laughing at us.

"C'mon, please let us stay," we pleaded.

"No! Out! Now!"

We went out, dejected and angry, but Vinny had a solution. "Let's go around back," he said.

There was a small well, or pit, dug outside the basement window, starting at ground level and going down about two feet. If we knelt or lay on the ground, we could take turns sticking our heads in the well and looking through the window. They had tacked a white bedsheet up on the far wall and set up the film projector. Joe was mounting the film, threading it through the projector into the other canister. Joe looked up and saw me, but he just shook his head and laughed. He did not come up and chase us away. He did not seem to tell my brothers.

The big kids were drinking beer and eating peanuts. They put the lights out and started the projector. The black-and-white film was grainy and flawed, filled with scratches and black streaks running across the screen. It was running too fast, the characters all moving at a higher speed than normal, but in a jerky, stilted way. A title flashed up that said, *Motel Wives*. All of the characters looked like foreigners, and the film had English subtitles written across the bottom of each scene. We could barely read them, as the rain intensified. It was pounding on us now, flowing into the well and draining out the bottom. We were getting soaked, but we didn't care.

A skinny little man, dressed in a suit, complete with a bow tie and a bowler hat, would answer a knock at his motel door, where he had been sitting on the bed reading the Bible. A pretty young woman said that she had had another fight with her husband. She was crying. Then the scene jumped, and somehow they were both naked, sitting on the bed. He climbed on top of her and entered her, thrusting his pelvis up and down while she writhed around dramatically. The subtitles said, "Ohh," and "Ahh," and "More." There were no close-ups, but I felt that I finally understood what fucking was.

By this time, all three of us had jammed our heads into the well, and we could barely move. The film was so poorly spliced and edited that it became clear there was no additional plot. The guy would suddenly be dressed again. He'd answer a new knock at the door, a new woman would appear, and they would suddenly be naked and start fucking, though always in a new position, sometimes even from the back, doggie style. With the new positions, the subtitles got dirtier, with captions that said, "Fuck me hard," or "Fuck me like my husband won't!" The skinny little man would reply, "Do you like it like this, Mommy?"

In the middle of one of these scenes, the film broke, and they all yelled at Joe, who had to turn the lights on and attempt to fix it. We were now shivering, turning blue from the cold. I had had enough. Vinny announced that he was going home to "jerk off," and Adam nodded in agreement. I went home and took a warm shower. I held my penis for a moment, but I didn't even get hard, and I dropped it right away. I lay in bed that night, praying for forgiveness, wondering if I had to confess all of this on Saturday.

15

A few times a year, we would plan a day trip into the city. We never called it Manhattan or New York, just "the city." We knew that that was where the rich lived: the artists, the actors, the businessmen, the politicians, and the sports stars—anyone, really, who was wealthy and sophisticated. We thought of them collectively as the jet set. But we also knew that a lot of poor people lived there: perverts, derelicts, drunks, panhandlers, shopping-bag ladies, drug dealers, porn peddlers, petty criminals, and schizophrenics. When we took the bus and subway in from Queens, we knew we were entering another world.

We developed street smarts, both intuitively and through direction. Our parents' instructions not to talk to strangers became extremely relevant when we went to the city, because strangers inevitably approached us, either offering to sell us something or promising to sneak us into an adults-only peep show. Mom was clear in her advice: "Ignore them. Don't make eye contact and keep moving. Never stop to talk, never look them in the eye— that's how they trap you."

But observing and, yes, interacting with the ne'er-do-wells was part of the attraction. Stumbling upon a game of three-card monte captivated us. Smart enough to know the game was rigged, we enjoyed watching as if it were street theatre. The cast consisted of two to four players. One set up a card table or sometimes just a milk crate. He set out three playing cards, all slightly bent in the middle to allow him to pick them up quickly and move them around from spot to spot, using speed and sleight of hand to keep them moving, picking them up and putting them down in different spots in rapid succession.

A crowd gathered as he ran his mouth on about how easy it was to follow the queen of hearts. We tried to pick out the shill before he emerged from the crowd. He'd amble over, watch for a few minutes, place a bet, find the queen and "win" ten or twenty bucks. We laughed as we watched these two black males, who we suspected were buddies or brothers from the same block in Harlem, pretend not to know each other. We became even more amazed when some tourist took the bait and laid their hard-earned vacation money down, sure that they too could follow the queen, stunned when they turned over the jack of clubs and said good-bye to their cash.

The third member of the troupe was always harder to spot. He might be as much as a whole block away, and he would usually be roaming around some perimeter. His job was to look for the cops and to signal the warning if one began to approach. He simply yelled out, "The Man!" The play was over, and the actors converged to collect the scenery: shill, spotter, and dealer working as a team, uncaring that the suckers now saw that they had been conned. They melted into the crowd in moments. If the cops did arrive, a tourist might complain to them, but the cops would just shake their heads. I saw folks lose up to a hundred dollars, ten bucks at a time, knowing their luck was about to change. Reluctant to realize they were duped, they became angry and expected the police to "do something about it."

"What would you like me to do, sir?" The cops were always polite in their unresponsiveness.

"Arrest them."

"They're probably back on the A train by now. Take it as a lesson. This is New York. Be careful with your money. Keep it in your pocket." On the rare occasion when the victim still wanted to file a complaint, the cop sighed and directed them to the station house.

■ ■ ■

Vinny had great-aunts who lived in a fourth-floor walkup just off the East River. The building was only about ten feet from the exit ramp of the Fifty-Ninth Street Bridge. The stairs were narrow, dark, and dirty, and we ran up them, laughing and bumping each other, stopping to look out the window right into the eyes of drivers coming in from Queens. When we finally arrived at their apartment on the fourth floor, they checked us out through the peephole and then unlocked the multiple dead bolts that kept intruders at bay.

Entering their apartment was akin to entering the Fun House at Coney Island. The long dark hallway that led to the kitchen was slanted at such a dramatic angle that you felt like you were walking sideways. We were in awe at the steepness of this floor, wondering how the building could still be standing at such an angle. Vinny called them his *zias*, Italian for aunts, and they spoke not a word of English.

All three of them, only two of whom were actually sisters, had come from Italy together and had been living together for decades in the same apartment. I never understood the source of their income, because they said that they very rarely left the apartment. These women were in their seventies and could no longer manage the stairways, except for an occasional trip to the doctor. One of them, Vinny's mother had told him, had not been out of the apartment for five years. They had everything they needed delivered to their door.

In addition to the slanted floors, the apartment was remarkable for its musty smell. Every inch of available wall space was taken up with bookshelves, sofas, tables, dressers, and various other pieces of furniture, all of which were piled high with books, clothes, cardboard boxes, and knickknacks. The walls were covered with crucifixes, sacred hearts, and an assortment of prints and paintings. Above a certain height, everything was covered with dust. Either they did not own a step stool, or none of them could any longer risk climbing it. Up to about five feet, the surfaces seemed relatively clean, but you could see the years of accumulated dust on the top.

The kitchen, on the other hand, glistened. The Formica counters, although spotted with burn marks, were sparkling. The zias were excited to see us; they had laid out a banquet more fit for dignitaries than three teenagers from Queens. Platters of antipasto including everything from olives, fruits, and cheeses to various kinds of fish. Multiple loaves of hard Italian bread. Cold cuts: prosciutto, turkey, roast beef, Swiss cheese, and provolone. Mustard, mayo, horseradish. Sweet and hot peppers of various shapes and sizes. Italian pastries, mostly cannoli. And to wash it all down, much to our giddy delight and nervous embarrassment, red wine and coffee.

After hugging and kissing each of us on the cheeks, grabbing Vinny in particular and making fun of his zits, pinching and pulling on them while laughing and nattering away in Italian, they ordered, "*Mangia*, mangia." Eat we did, for an hour or so, mostly making sandwiches out of the cold cuts and bread and ignoring much of the rest. But as you cleared your plate, if you did not put something else on it, they would begin to do it for you, repeating their refrain, "Mangia." When I tried to tell them I was full, they ignored me. When I finally began to push away, holding my stomach and moaning, "No more, no more," they got sad. We had eaten maybe 20 percent of what they had laid out for us.

They cajoled us into their living room for more coffee, but the dank and musty smell that prevailed—as if there were dead rodents in the walls—was too much, and we tried to leave. They got sadder then accepted the fact and hugged and kissed us good-bye. Vinny taught us how to say *grazie*, and that thrilled them to no end as they babbled away at us, or to us.

If we didn't eat at Vinny's zias', lunch would be at the Horn & Hardart Automat, which was always available to provide a respite from the winter weather, allowing us to escape the cold and biting winds. The warmth enveloped us as if a mist had encircled our bodies. Immediately we began peeling off the outer layers of hats, scarves, and jackets, as we would find a table that wasn't too dirty or too crowded with strangers. It was rare that we could get a table of our own.

Near the door was a cashier who would exchange twenty nickels for each dollar. We would circle the whole cafeteria before making our selections, straining our necks to look through the little glass doors and attempt to get a good and complete view of the food we were about to eat. The choices were endless:

soups, salads, sandwiches, hot entrees and vegetables, Jell-Os and desserts, all available for multiples of a nickel.

After pouring the requisite amount in, you had to be adept at opening the sliding-glass door, holding it open, and slipping out your purchase. The workers had little tolerance and less trust if you tried to tell them that you put your money in but the door snapped closed before you could get your purchase out. Some would just out and out ignore you; others would tell you to wait. They might eventually go and retrieve the item for you but would never give you a refund.

Then you had to hope that the stranger or two who sat at your table would leave you alone and would not smell too badly. The best were the businessmen, who would be content with their newspapers or work from their briefcase. The worst would be the bag ladies who spent a dime for a cup of coffee and then tried to stay all day and tell you their life stories, all the while grubbing the scraps left on other people plates. Or the ones who hit the hot dog condiment stand, trying to get away with scoops of sauerkraut, relish, and onions for their lunch. I was always embarrassed for them when they got caught at this petty theft, trying not to stare as they were thrown out. Most of them left screaming and kicking, not humiliated at all but miffed at the indignity, maybe wanting to work up the blood a little before being thrust back out into the cold.

As darkness fell, we reveled in Times Square, enthralled by the lights. We admired the huge Camel sign, smoke coming out the hole at the end of the cigarette. We hit Radio City for a stage show, with the marvelous Rockettes, and a movie, stopping to watch the ice skaters in Rockefeller Plaza, wondering who got to skate there, never dreaming that money was the only barrier to our partaking.

During Christmas season, we looked at the window displays, amazed at the early attempts at animatronics. We saw the horse-drawn buggies, trailed by the droppings that steamed in the street, and imagined that only the super-rich could afford the rate. We smelled the roasting chestnuts but never tasted them. We went by the majestic tree, sneaking past the police barricades to go up and actually touch a branch and get back out without getting caught.

On a Sunday afternoon, we bought student tickets to see the New York Rangers at the old Madison Square Garden. We got there about two hours before game time and hung outside the players' entrance, getting autographs from two of our heroes, Jacques Plante and Boom-Boom *Geoffrion*. Our seats were up in the rafters, allowing us to see more than half of the action, the skaters disappearing into the lost space underneath our balcony's overhang. We waited, holding our breath, to see when and where the puck would come back out.

Adam tossed a penny on the ice. If a player fell, we imagined that he hit Adam's penny, and we laughed. Another student threw an egg. Noticing right away, the refs stopped the action, got shovels and scrapers to shave ice over it and then scoop it all up. Ushers and guards searched the student section looking for the guilty party, but we were cool, straight-faced, and innocent-looking. "Isn't it terrible?" I'd say. "I think it came from the other side, over there," pointing across to the balcony directly across the ice from us. We littered our row with pistachio nutshells, emptying the huge box that we had bought at Schneid's for thirty-five cents. By the end of the game, our hands and lips were stained red.

In the summer, our diversions of choice were found in Central Park. This expanse of open green meadows, lakes, and ball fields brought absolute joy to our hearts. Often we would find a bicycle rental shop and rent bikes, sometimes bicycles built for two, and ride amok all over, ignoring the rules about which paths to stay on and which direction to go in. We were never shocked if we bumped into a film being shot or a mime or other street performer trying to make a living. After dropping off the bikes, we stopped at a cart and had a cream soda and a hot dog with onions. We walked into the park, sat on the grass, and watched a softball game, and then we just hung out and watched the parade of characters.

Sometimes the best theater was unplanned. We rented a rowboat on the lake near the Bethesda Fountain. We saw two queers, as we all called them then, who were having an argument while they rowed around. Both were exquisitely and tastefully dressed, one in a blue suit, one in a sportier tweed. They were having a fight over one of them cheating at the baths. But they were yelling at each other in a controlled, staged way, not threatening anything physical, one content to row and one to be rowed.

"I am so upset, I am going to take my new thirty-dollar pipe and throw it into the lake."

"You wouldn't dare!"

"Wouldn't I? You don't think I would? Well, I will!"

"Go ahead then."

"I will."

This went on for at least ten minutes before he actually delivered on his threat, hurling his pipe far from the boat and watching it splash into the lake. His friend was surprised and horrified that he'd actually done it and began to row furiously to the spot where it splashed, arriving there to order, "Go find it." This prompted the one who threw it to cry, but not to get in the water.

Before long they were both crying and then apologizing. During the whole show, we circled them in our boat, always keeping enough distance away to not intrude or appear to be enthralled, but clearly they knew we were watching and seemed to appreciate us as an audience.

The late-night E train that took us home, with its yellow corn-row-plastic stitched seats, was filled with dirt and old newspapers, but we grabbed a few seats and quietly rocked along with the movement of the train, lights flickering and dimming, sparks flashing from the wheels, clear tracks ahead and green signal lights as far as the driver could see.

We studied the map, tracking our way through the city and then into Queens, imagining the neighborhoods above us. In Jamaica, waiting at 179th street for the Q43 bus that would take us east, we were on our toes, knowing that we were vulnerable in the dark, happy when some other white adults would show up, nervous if a group of blacks came by, especially if they were sharing a cheap bottle of wine. All of our parents had told us, "Be careful in Jamaica. Be careful of the niggers."

Finally, the bus came, and we talked quietly as we bounced along Hillside Avenue at a speed fast enough to give the potholes some meaning. Finally, we got off in front of Schneid's, which was closed. Late-night showers were needed to get the grime and grit from a day in the city flowing through the sewers of Queens to the sea.

16

The summer we turned sixteen, Vinny and I got jobs at Mendelsohn's, the corner drugstore, for $1.25 an hour, plus tips, each of us working three nights a week. There were two pharmacists, Mr. Stewart and Mr. Prowse, who had bought out the store from Mendelsohn.

My primary duty was to deliver prescriptions, which I did by bicycle. Virtually every delivery meant a tip, anywhere from a dime to a quarter. On a good night, there would be enough deliveries to keep me out of the store all night. Each delivery could be milked for a few extra minutes, even a quick break at home to watch a few minutes of *Batman*, *Lost in Space*, or *Star Trek*. If I had to go all the way to Glen Oaks for a delivery, I could stop in one of the stores on Union Turnpike for a soda.

On a slow night, I'd be stuck inside the store, and the hours would feel like weeks. Take off all the items on a particular shelf, dust each one, line them up on the floor, dust the shelf, and then return the stock. Some of the merchandise was ancient, and the dust was real, but the work was boring, and I would do it carelessly, my mind drifting. And I'd watch the clock move in slow motion. Sometimes I'd try to trick myself. Dust a whole section without looking up, sure that a half hour or so must have passed, only to be shocked that it had been seven minutes.

Prowse kept all the good work for himself. Restocking the candy rack every Wednesday could take an hour, but if Prowse were on, he did it. Stewart, on the other hand, let us do more on our own. He was content to stay on the phone. It didn't take us long to figure out that he was having an affair with one of the customers. We delivered to her house a lot. She was younger than him, an attractive redhead with a sad smile. Sometimes it really would be a prescription. Her husband was very sick—terminal, we thought. Often though, we'd peek in the package and see a treat and a note. He was in love with her. After hours, we'd sneak down the block and spy on them. She'd sit with him right in her own driveway. But all we ever saw them do was talk.

In the back of the store was a small office, with a trapdoor in the floor that led into the cellar. Once a week or so, we'd go down to cut up the empty cardboard boxes and compact them for the trash. All they stored down there was Kotex, which came in huge boxes. Vinny and I would write each other notes on the boxes, sometimes in code, mostly inane stuff about cars, baseball, or music. The boxes were marked Feminine Napkins, but I had absolutely no idea what that meant. I opened a box up one time and looked at them. They looked like thick diapers, with sticky fasteners to "attach to underwear."

There was a lot of stuff in the back of the store that confused me: opium and codeine, vaginal creams and suppositories with instructions to place in vagina. I imagined that this must be another name for cunt, but I wasn't quite sure. Was the whole thing the vagina, or just the inside part? And what the hell were those napkins for? The mystery disturbed me, not casually, but deeply. I sensed my ignorance and was too ashamed to ask anyone for clarity.

■ ■ ■

By day, we were still kids, content to play handball or stickball in the park or to seek out thrills elsewhere. We'd ride our bicycles farther and farther from Bellerose, often exploring the horse stalls in Elmont, next to the Belmont racetrack. We'd seek good hills for skateboarding, which was becoming a big craze. We got adept at making them. Adam's father had power tools in his basement and taught us how to cut out the wood. We started by disassembling roller skates and attaching the wheels to the board. Then we found out you could buy wheels just for skateboards, and we grew more and more sophisticated. As our boards improved, we looked for steeper and longer hills, took more and bigger risks. One day we were in Queens Village on a steep grade with a great turn in it. Vinny hit a rock, spun out, fell, tumbled, and hit his head on the curb. He was out cold. I knocked on the nearest door, and they called the police, who arrived within minutes. Vinny was just coming to, and they asked him what had happened. He pointed at me and said that I had snuck up and hit him—that I had tried to kill him! Was he kidding or just dazed and confused? It took a good hour for all of us to work through it and for them, and him, to believe it was an accident.

As night fell, we morphed from our innocence. We were on the prowl, coming of age as a group. Looking for girls became our nocturnal passion. We walked up to Glen Oaks, a large development of garden apartments north of Bellerose. Adam introduced us to some girls he had met in school. The first time I met Glenda, her mother was not home. She had the ground-floor apartment to herself and invited us in. She was a healthy four-teen, full breasted, long black hair, huge brown eyes, prominent, if stereotypical, Jewish nose, and a wonderful, generous smile.

We hit it off right away. Although she invited me to her bed-room, it was not an invitation to go beyond some light petting and kissing. But what a kisser! She taught me the art of French kissing: purposeful, slow, and deliberate. "This is what a girl likes," she told me. "Don't just try to bury your tongue down my throat. Rub your tongue along my tongue, let me guide you; let me pull you in. Then move it around, first, your tongue on top, then mine. When you need a breath, back away ever so slight-ly and use your tongue to caress, and I mean caress, my lips. Gently, lovingly. Run your tongue along my bottom lip, then I'll run mine across yours, and then we'll do top lips. After a few minutes of this, you can go back into my mouth like before, but then this time when you back out, run your tongue to the back and nibble on my ear, then run your tongue up and down my neck, but *no hickeys*."

I followed her every command, tried every move, and en-joyed every second. Clearly, pleasing her pleased me. She re-turned the favor, using the same technique. Then she clamped her teeth down on my neck and sucked slightly and gave me my first hickey. "How come you can give me a hickey, but I can't give you one?"

"'Cause my mother would kill me and never let me have boys in the house again. Besides," she said, "hickeys aren't really en-joyable, are they? I mean, guys like to wear them as some kind of badge of conquest or something, and some girls like that too, but I mean, they're the sluts, aren't they? I'm not a slut!"

I lay on her bed all evening. We kissed, and then I stroked her long black hair, and we talked. She told me of her life, how hard it was not having a father. Apparently her father had run off when she was just a baby, and her mom had to work two jobs just to get by. They had a two-bedroom apartment, sparsely furnished: the beds, couch, and even the kitchen set looked tired.

Meanwhile, Vinny and Adam were squaring off with two other girls. It got to be eleven o'clock, and Glenda announced, "Everybody has to go. My mother will be home soon." She would not tolerate our complaints. "If you want to come back and do this again, you better not let my mother catch us."

We left and began the walk back home. It was a hot summer night, and we were feeling randy, comparing notes. I was not comfortable sharing with the others what Glenda and I had done, even though we had apparently done less than them. Everyone got the French kissing, but they each said that they also copped a feel. I had not tried. Even though I had just met her, I respected her. I desperately wanted to be sure that I knew what I was doing.

"Let's go for a swim," I suggested.

"Where?" they said simultaneously.

"I don't know. Let's go skinny dipping in someone's backyard." We decided to cut south before getting to Little Neck Parkway. We would not want to trespass too close to any of our houses and would not want to get caught by anyone we knew. On a dark side street, I spied a pool with easy access. The driveway was in the shadows, and the gate was open. We would have no trouble, but we must be quiet. There was one car in the driveway, and a few lights on in the house, but it looked like whoever was home was watching TV in the living room. We knew these cottage designs, knew that the kitchen was in the corner of the house and that if someone came into the kitchen, they might be able to see us.

Just in case, we planned our escape carefully, went to the darkest shadows behind the pool, and peeled off our clothes. We piled them for easy grabbing. We were prepared to run through the streets naked if we had to. We actually were quite anxious, but we had come this far, and no one wanted to back out.

I climbed over the wall and eased into the water gently. After the kissing lesson, the long walk, and the anxiety over this adventure, we were all sticky with sweat, and the cool water was exhilarating. The others followed me in, and we swam around silently. And then it happened: the kitchen light went on, illuminating the half of the pool that was closer to the house. We swam, too noisily, to the shadow side and bunched together. No one panicked, but we did lower ourselves into the pool so that only our heads were sticking out. We whispered, trying to decide what to do. Should we get out and run? Should we stay where we were? We giggled as we decided to wait it out, hoping that the lack of movement would keep us safe. We were right. We saw the middle-aged man leave the kitchen with a drink in his hand. But he left the light on.

"Let's get the hell out of here," Adam said, and Vinny nodded. We slid over the wall and out of the pool and were struggling to get into our wet clothes when Vinny decided to shake things up. He had his shorts on, but he put his T-shirt and sneakers down in the driveway and went back up the ladder.

"Oh shit, Vinny, what're you doing?" My heart was racing, and I could not believe it when, without a word, he took a leap off the ladder and did a huge cannonball into the pool, splashing loudly and sending a wave sloshing over the side. We all began to laugh out loud but were shocked into silence when the yellow bug light above the kitchen door came on. I had my sneakers and shorts on and had been messing with my T-shirt, too anxious to know which way was inside out. I took off like a shot out of the driveway, past the door as it opened, not looking to see who was coming out. I ran as fast as I could down the block away from the house, not knowing and not caring what was happening behind me, but I could not help hearing the shouts: "Who's there; what's going on?"

I got about a block away, turned the corner, went another short block and turned. Then I hid in the shadows behind a parked car. I waited. I listened to the sound of my heart, which was thundering so that I could feel each beat. I waited, catching my breath and wondering what was happening to my friends. I didn't hear anything, and I didn't see anything until a car came cruising slowly from that block. I cursed myself for not noticing or not remembering what kind of car had been in the driveway. I crouched farther down behind the parked car. The dark car came to the corner and stopped. The driver seemed to be looking around. I began to scout the ground, prepared to crawl underneath the parked car if I had to. The car turned the other way, and a few minutes later I saw Adam come out of the shadows from across the street, jogging toward me. As he got to the corner, I called him, and he turned toward me immediately, laughing. How could he laugh? I was going to die of fright. "What happened to Vinny?"

"I don't know. The guy came out, and I hopped the fence into the next yard and heard the guy yell, and then I just ran."

"Yeah, me too. Did you see that car go by?"

"Yeah, was that the guy from the house?"

"I don't know."

"*Boo!*" We jumped out of our skins and took a step to run again, when we both realized it was Vinny. Leaping out of the shadows, he scared both of us, but at least his antics broke the tension. I began to believe that we were going to get away with this...until I saw the same car coming down the avenue again. We all crouched down behind the parked car, laughing nervously. Vinny was still carrying his sneakers and shirt and was examining his feet for cuts and bruises. "That house next door has a nice pool. I saw it when I came through this yard. Let's go for another swim; I want to clean my feet off."

Not knowing whether he was serious or not, I simply said, "I'm going home."

■ ■ ■

The amorous adventures lasted all summer. Except for those few nights when Glenda's mother was going to be home, we headed up to Glen Oaks. Most, if not all, of the girls in this crowd were Jewish. As such, one of the first things that any of them let us know if we asked them out on a date was that we would not be able to marry them. We had no problems with that.

It was the make-out summer, with no one going all the way. One night Adam could not join us. Glenda was on the phone with her cousin, and Carol, who paired off with Adam each night, and I were sitting in Glenda's living room on the couch, in the dark. She began to rub my leg. She and Adam had been pretty much exclusive for most of the summer and whenever they were together would shamelessly make out and grope each other for hours, not caring who else was in the room. At the end of the night, Carol's face was usually red and swollen.

She started out by talking about Adam, but then proceeded to tell me that I was "just as cute as he was," and then came right out and asked me what I thought about her and Glenda trading Adam and me one night.

My imagination was running wild, and I was thinking that maybe she and Adam really were having sex while Glenda and I were still making out and doing some playful petting. In reality, Glenda kept me away from her breasts, telling me that if she let me have them, I would want more and would not stop until we went all the way, and I should remember that I was not Jewish. I would laugh and say, "I don't think I have to marry you if you let me touch your boobs," but I never got in there anyway. I was okay with this, as I loved the making out, and we were actually becoming pretty good friends. I got up the guts to ask her about Kotex, and she taught me all about periods and pregnancy. She laughed at my innocence. I loved her hair and could stroke it all night as we lay in her room and talked, her head in my lap like a child.

Now I was reliving some of those nights, imagining what Adam and Carol had been doing in the next room, remembering that more than once, Glenda had found them in her mother's room, a forbidden zone that Glenda tried to protect. Just what would we be trading? "What does Adam think about this?" I wanted to know. I was loyal enough to him that there would be no way I would do anything with Carol behind his back.

"Oh, we've joked about it," she said. Then, reflectively, coyly, she added, "I could talk him into it." As she said this, she began to twirl her finger on my upper thigh, over my jeans, making little circles and edging closer to my groin. I began to grow hard. I was finding it difficult to maintain this conversation.

Embarrassed, I tried my damnedest to will my penis to shrink. Carol got the cutest look on her face when she could see the bulge in my pants, and she began to outline the shape with her finger, tracing around my penis but ever so slightly brushing it as if by accident. I thought I was going to explode in my pants right then. She leaned over and kissed me, full on the mouth, and I lingered for just a minute, tasting her tongue. I grew ravenous for more and jumped up, brusquely shifting her aside. "Adam is my best friend, you know."

"We didn't do anything," she defended herself.

"I know, I know," I stammered. "We need to keep it that way."

Her endearing and lovely smile came right back, though, as she said, "Unless he agrees to a trade."

Bam! The overhead light came on. Glenda had finally finished her phone call, checked the time, and discovered that it was late; her mother would be home any minute. We had to go. In fact, just as she finished telling us, the screen door opened, and in walked Mom. Carol jumped off my lap and straightened her skirt, making it look like someone had been messing with her in the dark. I noticed a wet spot on my jeans and tried to keep my hands in front of it. "Well, well, well," said Mom, "what have we got here?" She gave a stern hard look at Glenda but then, surprisingly, turned to Carol and me. "So," she said, "are you Davey or Adam?" I was astounded that she knew about us.

"Davey," was about all I could manage.

She actually gave me a warm smile and shook my hand. "How nice to meet you…at last," icicles forming on the last two words as she looked suspiciously at Glenda. Then she came right out and asked me, "Are you supposed to be in my house when I am not home?"

Glenda tried to interrupt with a pleading, heavily empha-
sized, "*Motherrr!*"

But Mom put her hand up to silence her daughter, looked me
in the eye, and said, "Well?"

"No, ma'am," I said in my best Catholic school deferential
tone.

"Then why are you in here?"

All I could think of was thank God Glenda had to make a
call, and Mom was not catching the two of us in her bedroom.
"Glenda had to make a phone call, and Carol and I were just sitting here waiting for her..."

"In the dark?"

Trying to pretend that I had never been there before, I said,
"Um, I didn't know where the light switch was." Even Glenda
and Carol couldn't help cracking smiles.

"Do you think I'm stupid?" she said.

I got serious too. "No, ma'am."

"Well, then, try again." She smiled, sat down, and lit a
cigarette.

Heavy sigh. I got a defensive and slightly hurt tone. "We
weren't doing anything; we were just sitting here talking, waiting
for Glenda." Glenda was beaming at me; somehow I had rescued
the situation with just the right attitude.

Miraculously, this seemed to work, and Mom backed off and
said, "Okay, then, come into the kitchen and tell me about yourself. I understand you're not Jewish?"

Oh, shit, this friendly behavior might wind up being worse
than getting yelled at. "Irish Catholic," I said proudly and then
added, "But don't worry, I have no plans to marry your daughter." This made Glenda frown but elicited a "good" and another
smile from Mom.

We sat in the kitchen as she made herself a cup of tea, offering me one, but I declined. We got along just fine, and she told me how hard it was to raise a daughter all alone, how worried she was leaving Glenda alone at night, and how *thankful* she was that I came over to be with her. What *had* Glenda been telling her? We talked for an hour, Carol having made her exit right after Mom arrived. She actually hugged me on the way out and told me to be careful on the way home.

The next night, Glenda was depressed; she had been crying, her face was red and puffy. She had attempted to put eye makeup on, something she only did rarely, and it was running down her face. "What's the matter?" I said.

"We're moving."

"Moving?" This had come out of nowhere. "When, where, why?" At least I didn't ask how.

"End of the month...upstate."

"Why?"

"Mom's got a job offer that will allow her to only work one job, and she said that I'll be better off not being home alone so much." She went back to crying, sobbing. I held her tight and promised that we could still be friends. By the weekend, she was packing and Mom had quit work so that she was home all the time. I helped pack one night but avoided her after that. After she moved, I never heard from her or saw her again but her kissing technique lived on!

17

Drinking was nurtured, if not encouraged, in most respectable Bellerose homes. Typical Irish values prevailed, and the typical male dependence dominated. The one thing Pop would do for himself on payday, before handing the rest of the cash over to Mom, was to stop at the liquor store and buy a bottle of scotch. He'd get home and open it with a childish, silly grin on his face. He would pour some into a juice glass and drink it neat, hopefully while Mom was not watching. If she was, he would put the cap on and push the bottle toward the back of the counter. But if she missed it, he would make himself a scotch and water before heading off to the living room to read the paper.

When I was sixteen, my parents had a New Year's Eve party, which was in full swing by about ten o'clock. They hosted their parties in the basement, making good use of the built-in bar. I did not want to spend the evening with my parents and said I was going out. "Be back by midnight," Mom yelled up the stairs. I went up to Schneid's and met Vinny, and we concocted a plan: get one of the bigger kids to buy us some booze. We had heard that Orange Tango was a good complete drink, a screwdriver in a bottle.

We hung outside the bar, waiting for someone we recognized. Joe Stayer came along and agreed to buy it for us. We scraped our dollars together and waited across the street at Schneid's while he went into the liquor store. As soon as he came out the door, we crossed the street, yelling his name as excited as children on Christmas morn. His face took on a look of extreme anguish as he snarled at us out of the side of his mouth, "This is not being cool. Get away from me and walk down the block."

We froze, realizing the mistake, anxious that he not betray us. We made as if going back to Schneid's, and he made a left down the street as if walking to his car. He waited for us in the shadows under a tree. We walked over, not surprised that he was angry. "I could get arrested for this, and you approach me right in front of the store. I have half a mind to just keep this stuff, except it tastes like shit." He started to hand the bag over to us then withdrew it. "Look," he said, quite earnestly. "If you get caught, I didn't buy this for you. You asked a stranger outside the liquor store." We were reaching for the bottle.

"Okay?" he asked.

"All right, all right," we replied.

"All right, *what?*" He was serious.

"All right, we stopped a stranger in front of the liquor store, and he bought it for us, and we don't even know his name."

"Same story whether it's the cops or your parents who catch you?"

"All right."

"All right." He held out the bottle, and we almost dropped it as we both reached for it at once. "Happy New Year," he said, big smile on his face as he walked away, his own bottle in its own brown bag tucked comfortably under his arm.

We decided to go to Vinny's backyard to drink. His parents used the basement as their living room. Like many of the Italian families in Bellerose, they used their upstairs living room as a showcase for furniture. They bought expensive couches and covered them with protective slipcovers and never sat on them. We would not be noticed walking up the driveway, deep into the dark shadows. The night was crisp and clear, stars prominently displayed, temperature hovering right around twenty. We could see our breath.

Vinny unscrewed the top and took the first swig. He grimaced, as if sucking on a lemon, and handed me the bottle. I took my shot. The taste was pungent, almost sickeningly so. Strong, yet artificial, with a metallic aftertaste, barely a hint of orange. "Joe was right; this does taste like shit."

"Who cares?" Vinny said. "It'll do the trick. Try holding your nose." And he demonstrated, holding his nose, thrusting his head back and taking a long drink, two or three gulps.

I pulled it down from him, spilling a little. "Don't drink it all." Then I copied him and held my nose and took a few gulps. I couldn't drink any more if I'd wanted to, not sure that holding my nose was doing anything, because the taste was still unbearable.

We heard a noise from inside his house and a light went on in the back bedroom, projecting almost into where we were hiding. We went deeper into the yard, into the corner formed by the right angle of the galvanized fence. We had not yet been there five minutes, and the bottle was half empty. We thought we weren't feeling anything, but we must have been, because my next guzzle did not bring forth the same grimace. "I'm getting used to the taste; it's not so bad!"

Two more times back and forth and the bottle was empty. We drained out every last drop. "Let's get out of here," Vinny said. He had the presence of mind to put the empty bottle back in the brown paper bag. He even looked for the cap but couldn't find it. We walked back up toward Schneid's and dropped the bag into the trashcan at the bus stop. We had been gone not more than fifteen minutes, and we arrogantly joked that we hadn't had enough and wished that we could score another bottle. Then we realized that it was now after eleven o'clock, and the liquor store had closed. Abe, too, was locking up, and we looked at each other and wondered what the hell we were going to do. We began to walk, because it was too damn cold to just stand there.

The vodka started to kick in, and we were laughing at nothing. We were talking about what good friends we were and how great this was to be walking around drunk on New Year's Eve. Temperature was falling, but we didn't seem to care much. We went to Adam's house, and he convinced his parents that he could come out till midnight. Vinny and I were hopelessly blotto now. He fell over a tree stump. I walked up to the tree and punched it hard, fist closed, and yelled at it, "Don't trip my brother."

Vinny lay on the ground on someone's front lawn. "Your brother?" he said.

"Sure," I slurred. "You're like my brother." I helped him stand, and he threw up, getting some on his shoes. "I'm sick," he said, looking quite pale. "I'm goin' home ta bed." Adam and I walked him home and bade him Happy New Year.

"I have to go home, too," Adam said, and we walked to his house. "Are you going to be all right?" he asked, and I assured him I would.

The next thing I remember was Brian shaking me, waking me up. It was midnight, and my brothers and a few of their friends had come out to bang pots and pans together, scream, "Happy New Year!" and pound the ceremonial shiny new penny into the street. They found me laid out on the front lawn. I did not remember walking there from Adam's. "Davey, what the hell are you doing down on the lawn? It's freezing out." I just lay there, slow to respond, then got up and started to lurch, trying to walk. I looked at Joe Stayer and tried to give him a conspiratorial smile. "*My God*, he's drunk," Brian said to Kevin. They immediately went into protection mode. "Let's get him in the house before Mommy and Daddy see him." Then to me, "You'll ruin their party if they see you." They helped me in and got me to my bedroom and told me to sleep it off. I just collapsed on the bed.

A number of people came and went in the hallway to use the only bathroom in the house. When Pop came up to pee, he peeked in and saw me on top of the bed with my clothes on. It didn't take him long to recognize a drunk. He put the light on but turned it off quickly when he saw my painful reaction. "Okay, get your shoes off, and your pants, and get under the covers. You look like shanty Irish."

Clumsily, I did so and informed him, "Dad, I'm drunk."

"I can see that," he said. "What did you drink?"

"Tango."

"Ich! Where'd you get it?"

"One of the big kids."

"Who?"

"Can't tell you."

He accepted this—even respected it, I think. "Okay," he said, "sleep it off. Are you going to be sick?"

"I don't think so," I said and then belied this with a dry heave.

He brought a big bowl to my room. "Never drink junk like that. Stick to Scotch and water. It's the sugar in the soda that makes you sick. Throw up in here if you have to. And keep your door closed and your light off. Don't let your mother see you like this."

Another coconspirator. "I'm sorry, Pop."

"That's okay, pal. Sleep it off."

He put out the light and closed the door.

"*Pop!*"

"What," he said, cracking the door just a bit.

"Happy New Year."

When I awoke in the morning, my head was pulsating. I could not lift it off the pillow. I dry heaved a few times but still did not throw up. It was almost a full minute of just feeling the pain before I remembered what had caused it. Guilt overcame me. I was sure my parents were going to be furious with me. I lay there for a while but could not stand it. I wanted to get up and take some aspirin. I knew the cure, had observed my parents and brothers often enough to know the drill. God, I hoped the aspirin actually helped.

I stumbled out the door, and my father heard me right away. He did not get up from reading the paper. Rather, he called out, "How's your head?"

"Terrible. Pounding. Going to explode."

"Take some aspirin and put a cold washcloth over your eyes."

I did so and lay back down, closed my door, and prayed that the pain would abate. I had taken two aspirin. After about fifteen minutes, I crawled back to the bathroom and took two more. Back to bed, and after a while the pounding began to slow down, and I began to have the belief that I was going to live. That I was not going to die from this headache.

My father came in to check on me. I assured him that I was getting ever so slightly better, and I reiterated that I was sorry. When he went back to the living room, I overheard him talking to Mom: "The hangover is punishment enough. He'll learn from this." At least I was not going to get the once-over from Mom; Pop protected me from that. In another hour, I moved out to the living-room couch and apologized to Mom. She was unforgiving, cold, and quiet. Her eyes flared in disgust. I finally threw up, but I made it to the toilet bowl and did so cleanly. The taste of Tango came through my nose, and I heaved until I had nothing left. Washed up, back to the couch, cold washcloth all day, vaguely aware that the college football games were on the television, drifted in and out of sleep. By evening, I began to feel human. Took a shower. Tried to eat but couldn't. Went to bed at nine o'clock, vowing never to drink again.

18

Our image of gangs was derived from *West Side Story*'s Jets and Sharks. Gangs were an inner-city phenomenon, born in poverty and nurtured in the angst of abandonment. The streets were preferable to the cockroach-and-rat-infested tenements of the slums. Abusive fathers drove these kids to bond with each other. Violence was a matter of survival. The 1961 film had romanticized gang lore: gang members were good-looking, sharp-dressing magnets for the opposite sex. Misunderstood by their parents, they were really tender and loving. The tough-guy image was just a cover-up.

Out in the suburbs, gangs formed as a diversion from the boredom of having it all. The romantic notion of being in a gang was fueled by the fear of the future. Eighteen was the magic age: you could legally drink, and you could legally drive. But you also had to register for the draft. If you were lucky, you could defer the war by going to college. But for many, the specter of Vietnam lurked just off the horizon. The body counts were reported every night on the evening news.

We started calling ourselves the Bellboys as a knee-jerk re-action to the gangs that were forming around us: the Whelans from Union Turnpike, the Crips from Springfield Gardens, the Bandits from Hollis, and the Black Angels all the way from Jamaica. We were pretenders, at best, still dressing in madras shirts and penny loafers, while real gangs were dressing in tight dungarees, white undershirts, pointed black shoes with Cuban heels, and black leather jackets.

Cars reduced the travel time between neighborhoods to mere minutes. When they got bored on their own turf or were hassled to move by the cops, groups of guys from other neighborhoods would cruise the known hangouts, looking for trouble. A dis-respectful word tossed at an inappropriate time would lead to a fight, and the fight might lead to a brawl. But we weren't rough-necks. We were jocks who mostly wanted to be left alone. More often than not, we would agree to a rumble and then not show up. Or if we did, we would throw more words than punches. It was more like a game, a ruse, a dangerous pastime that could lead to a split lip or a black eye.

On occasion, the stakes were raised. One night, a carload of Whelans pulled over in front of Schneid's. It was the middle of the summer, and there was a big crowd, dozens of people mill-ing about. The guys stayed in the car, opened the windows, but kept the convertible top up. They were drunk and crossed the line right away, singling out Kathy. "Hey, Blondie, how 'bout a blow job?"

Kathy and Adam had been fast friends ever since discover-ing Dylan together. We had all known her for years. She blos-somed into a classic beauty: slim, angular face, high cheekbones, iridescent and captivating blue eyes, and a smile that melted your heart. She hadn't cut her hair in years, and it fell almost to her waist. Outgoing, generous with her laugh, she was a fun flirt. But she was also smug and self-assured. She turned, looked straight at their car, and gave them the finger. The guy in the passenger seat opened his door and gestured for her to come over, saying, "Sure, baby, you can fuck me instead!"

Vinny flicked his cigarette at them and said, "This is bullshit; let's go!" We swarmed the car like cockroaches on a half-eaten donut. Vinny shocked us all by whipping out a switchblade and cutting through the back window of the convertible top. Don started jumping up and down on the top itself, until his boot finally ripped through and he could kick the driver in the head. Those of us on the fringe waited till we could get close, and then we poured beer on them or threw cans and bottles at them through the window and the holes in the ragtop. They were helpless, trapped in the car. Even the girls got involved: Kathy grabbed a can opener and scratched the side door. The car was trashed and the punks humiliated. Someone must have called the cops. We scattered as soon as we heard the sirens. Like roaches reacting to a light that comes on in a dark kitchen in the middle of the night, we disappeared into the woodwork. When the cops found out the victims were from another neighborhood, they lost all sympathy. "Get in your car and get outta here!"

About a week later, a few of us were drinking at Vinny's house, his parents having gone out. We each had a quart bottle of Budweiser. I went to the bathroom, and when I came back I began to finish mine off. Vinny and Adam were laughing like crazy. "What the hell is so funny?"

"Well, we pissed in your bottle while you were in the bathroom." I didn't believe them, but I put the bottle down and didn't drink any more.

"It's just a little," Adam said.

"Fuck you! Are you serious?" They tried to stop laughing but could not help themselves.

"Yeah," they said.

"Fuck you guys!" I stormed out of the house and slammed the door. I just started walking, spitting, trying to gather saliva so I could spit some more. I was heading for the playground. I wanted to use the water fountain to clean out my mouth. I noticed some kids in the handball courts, drinking, but did not pay any attention to them. I climbed the fence and went to the fountain, swirled several mouthfuls of water around and spit them out. As I wiped my mouth on my sleeve, I turned around and discovered that I was surrounded.

The guys from the handball court formed a circle around me. "Well, well, what have we here? If it isn't one of the Bellboys!" I saw that it was the Whelans from the car that we had trashed. I immediately tried to run and break through two of them, but they had me down instantly. There were four of them. Three of them grabbed my arms and pushed me up against the fence. "Hold him," the one who had been the driver said. "You fucked up my car, you asshole. Now I'm gonna fuck you up," and he punched me in the stomach causing me to double over. But I did not cry out; I remembered my lesson in taking a beating.

He said, "I'll be right back." His buddies kept holding me. He jumped the fence, walked over to a car parked in the street, and broke the aerial off. He came back and told his buddies to turn me around. They pushed my face into the fence and held my arms out spread-eagled. They then took turns beating me with the aerial. Each lash was a new crescendo of pain. I could feel the searing heat well up after each blow while I was bracing myself for the next one. I refused to cry out. I grimaced and held my breath and took each shot. After they each hit me two or three times, they noticed the blood on my shirt, and one of them said, "That's enough. Let him go."

They released me, and when I went to walk my legs betrayed me, and I collapsed at their feet. One of them kicked me, but the driver said, "Leave him alone. That's enough."

They left, laughing. I lay there for a few minutes and then pulled myself up and got over the fence. I walked back to Vinny's and stumbled into the basement. Vinny and Adam saw me crumple to the floor and asked me what happened. "A few of the Whelans jumped me and beat me with an aerial. But I didn't say 'Ow,' Vinny, and I didn't cry."

"Fucking bastards," Vinny yelled, and he and Adam ran out the door. But they came back in about ten minutes, frustrated that they couldn't find them. "Don't worry," he said, "We'll get even. Let me see your back." I took off my shirt, and Vinny grimaced. "Oh, shit, man, this is fucked up." He took me to the bathroom, washed me down with a facecloth, and poured peroxide on my back.

For the first time, I cried out. "God, it hurts!"

They felt bad, guilty that their little practical joke had caused this. "I'll make it up to you," Vinny said.

"Yeah, how?"

"Do you want to get blown?"

"Fuck you!"

"No, I'm serious," Vinny said laughing. "Joyce is waiting for me up at Schneid's. You can have her tonight."

"Will she do me?"

"She will if I tell her to!"

Joyce was madly in love with Vinny, who was using her with no pretensions. He let her blow him, often. We all knew it. We also knew that Joyce blew others for money: some of the bigger

guys and even some older men from the bar. But she did Vinny
for free. Whenever he wanted her to. And he treated her like a
dog, like the slut she was, and never said a kind word to her, at
least not publicly.

"Let's do it," I said, with a heavy sigh, not knowing what
to expect, having not had sex of any kind yet. We walked up
to Schneid's, and there she was, smoking a cigarette, leaning
against the light pole. She could not have been more than fifteen. Long black hair, as dirty as hair can get, disheveled and
hanging in strands all over her face. Vinny walked up to her and
whispered into her ear. She answered loudly, "Okay, but let me
do you first."

"No," Vinny said, "I promised Davey he'd be first." He had,
of course, made no such promise, and I began to think that the
prick really did piss in my beer. After promising her that she
could do him after she did me, she finally walked over to me.
"I've never done you before, have I?" She didn't seem sure.

"No," I said. Vinny had warned me not to be nice to her, no
matter what; never to kiss her, just get her to do it. "Where can
we go?" I was anxiously ignorant.

"Behind the store," she said and led me into the shadows
behind Schneid's, outside the private apartment, for God's sake.
The store was open, but the back was dark.

"Take it out," she said, and just as I began to open my fly, we
heard someone coming. Abe was bringing the trash to the back
of the store. He saw us, and we stepped out of the shadows.

"What the hell are you doing back there?"

"Just looking for something," I lamely mumbled, and I
grabbed Joyce's elbow and said, "Come on."

The bitch stalled. "Where are we going?"

"Just come on," I said and pulled her.

"I don't want to leave Vinny." He was across the street smoking a cigarette and laughing his ass off.

"Don't worry about him, he'll wait…won't you, Vinny?" I yelled across the street.

"I'll be right here," he said.

We walked in front of Schneid's and headed toward the next block, in the opposite direction from my house. Like many times before, I begged God not to let my father show up. I was terrified that someone would see me with her. She dragged, walking slowly as if she knew I wanted to go fast.

"Do you think Vinny loves me?"

"Sure he does," I lied.

"No, I mean it," she said plaintively. "Do you really think he loves me?"

Heavy sigh. "I don't know. Let's not talk right now." God, was this ever going to happen? We went behind Dirty Dan's, and I directed her down a stairway that dropped about twenty feet to a cellar door that looked like it hadn't been opened in years. The stairs were filled with street trash and had a distinct smell of stale urine. Hoping we would not bump into any rats, I was sure the corner shadow down there was deep enough that it would not be visible from the sidewalk.

I leaned into the corner, unzipped my fly and took my penis out. I was not yet hard; I was too scared. She had begun to crouch down but laughed when she saw how soft I was. Humiliated, I said, "Don't fuckin' laugh at me."

"Oh, just give it to me," she said, still laughing. She gently took it into her hand and stroked it tenderly; she even slid her hand down into my underwear and rubbed my balls. This was working, but she slowed things down a little by asking, "Will you kiss me while I do this?"

"No," I said, "Just blow me already."

I was hard enough now, and I was ready. She got into a crouch and got her head close to my penis and then looked up at me and said, "Do you think Vinny will ever love me?"

I could not believe it. "Oh, Goddamn it, I don't know," I said. Why could I not just lie to her and promise her that Vinny had told me that he would love her forever? Wouldn't that get me a blow job quicker?

"Please," I begged, "just do it." Mercifully, she put her mouth on the head of my penis. She was wet and cold, and it woke me up and got my adrenaline going instantly. I put my head back and was ready to enjoy this fully.

After just a few seconds, she stopped and said, "Do you think Vinny knows I love him?"

Dear God, this was unreal. "Of course he does. You tell him every day, and you tell everyone you bump into. How could he not know? Now *just do it*!"

She smiled at me and took me back into her mouth and tongued the shaft up and down and then settled the head between her lips and sucked generously and my juices began to stir for real and—*then she stopped again*! "How can I get Vinny to love me?"

Unbelievably, I yelled at her, "Well, for starters, you could stop blowing every guy you run into!"

She immediately stood up and looked at me in the eyes. "Does this bother Vinny?" Was she for real?

Fearing I had lost my chance, I said, "Of course it bothers him. But don't stop now. You have to do me, or Vinny is going to be really *pissed* and maybe never talk to you again!"

She considered this for a moment and then got back down and went to work for real. I had no comparators, but I felt this girl was a pro; she was good. I closed my eyes and went to another place, a place of pure pleasure.

But it just took about a minute before I exploded into her mouth. She leaned back and spit then wiped her sleeve, saying, "I only swallow for Vinny." She looked down and said, "Oh you're a mess," and she used her sleeve to try and wipe the come off my pants. She finished rubbing it in with her hand and then wiped that on her coat. God she was filthy. I tucked myself away, zipped up, and proceeded to go up the stairs.

"Don't leave. Walk with me back to Schneid's," she said.

I didn't answer but also didn't want to abandon her in that stairway, so I waited for her to come up the stairs. My back was throbbing now. I had hidden from the pain during this encounter, but it reappeared with a vengeance. I walked up the block to Schneid's, trying to stay a few steps ahead of her as she pleaded, "Slow down! You think Vinny is still there, don't you?"

I did not talk to her. I despised her. I pitied her. I hated her. I hoped I was not going to get herpes or something worse. I felt so sorry for her.

Vinny, of course, was gone. "Where is he?" She was crying.

"I don't know," I answered, but I suspected he was back at his house, finishing off the beer. "Wait here," I told her. "I'll see if I can find him." I went to Vinny's house and was not aware that she had followed me. They were drinking the beer, had finished mine. "You drank the piss?"

Laughing, Adam said, "We didn't piss in it, you fool."

Then there was a knock at the door. It was Joyce. Vinny saw her and turned on me. "You brought her here?"

"No. She must have followed me."

He went to the door, and they yelled at each other for a while. "How dare you come here? I told you never to come to my house!"

"But I love you and you said you would wait...just let me do you..."

"No, for coming here, you can't do me tonight!" He got blown so often that he could turn it down?

But after ten minutes of back and forth, he left with her and came back alone about a half hour later, really enjoying his cigarette.

■ ■ ■

It was only a few weeks later, one of those hot, sticky nights, and the crowd in front of Schneid's was enormous—could've been close to a hundred kids. Nights like this created static in the air. Even Abe and Lynn were wired, tightly controlling who came in and out, assuring that they kept their eyes on everyone, sensing that they got ripped off whenever there was a big crowd. Wet dishrags were snapping all night. If you were not making a purchase, you were not welcome in the store.

The altercation started suddenly. Vinny recognized one of the kids from the Whelans and slugged him. There was kind of a popping sound as he hit the ground, and blood slowly dripped out of the side of his mouth. Vinny was looking at the guy he decked. He'd let his guard down and didn't see the others approaching him. Pushing and shoving surged through the crowd and—*smash*! Vinny had been slammed into the side panel next to the front door; it shattered as he went through it, and broken glass came down on top of him. He tried to duck and cover his head as the upper piece fell. I observed the whole thing as if it were in slow motion, and I stood there, helpless. I watched the shards drop and pierce his skin and his arms fly up, and I felt the sound hush the crowd as everyone turned to watch the last instant.

Vinny screamed, "Motherfucker, look what you did to me!" He walked away from the door, shaking bits of glass off him, circling the corner. Blood was dripping everywhere on the pavement, mostly from his arms. His face was also covered with blood. There was a shard sticking out of his right eyebrow, oozing into his eye and blinding him. There was also fear in his eyes; the pain was intense, and the shock was setting in. "What am I gonna do? What am I gonna do?" He repeated as he kept walking in a circle.

I went over to him. "Vinny, you've got to get to a hospital, man."

He seemed more interested in continuing the debate. He went over to the last guy who pushed him and said, "You did this to me, you fuck!"

"I was just reacting, man. You swung first. Listen, I've got a car. Let me take you to the hospital." Off they drove, injured victim and his attacker.

Abe came over and singled me out. "What happened?"

"It was an accident, Abe. He tripped and fell."

His look of warm concern turned into angry despair. "Don't you Goddamn kids ever *think* about what you're doing?"

"I guess not," was my quiet and sad response.

"I have to call the police," he said. "I'll need their report to collect my insurance." I started to pass the word, and the corner cleared in five minutes. A few of us stayed, knowing that we belonged, feeling a right.

Abe swept up the glass. The cops came and asked their questions: How bad was the boy injured? Would there be any charges filed? None of us gave up anybody's name, so they focused on their minimal task of getting Abe his police report. They completed their paper work and left. Abe had called his son, who arrived with a piece of plywood that they used to cover the hole.

I hung around and helped where I could, working with Abe to scrub the blood stains off the sidewalk. The weight of the incident sat directly on his shoulders. He finally turned to me and said, "How do I know which of you are thieves and which of you still have a few of your parents' values?" I just shook my head. I didn't know myself.

Vinny was stitched up at Long Island Jewish. His physical wounds would heal fine, but his anger and his rage would only continue to smolder.

19

At Reilly, adherence to authority ruled, symbolized in part by the mandatory jacket and tie. While my friends dressed the same way for public school as they did for hanging out, I had a dual existence. They were cutting classes and dropping out while I was finding a voice. I was developing a worldview that was different from theirs, different from my parents'.

The war was escalating, and the debate that would divide the country, divide the generations, had begun. Mr. Pellegrini, my social science teacher, stood firmly behind the domino theory, explaining and defending LBJ's decisions. "If we don't stop them now, the communists will overtake all of Asia, and then they'll set their sights on Europe, and then where will we be?"

"We'll be here, practicing democracy," I argued. "Why are we interfering in a civil war? Do we know what the people of Vietnam want? Do we care?" He not only allowed but actually welcomed the debate. He respected me for having an opinion and for being willing to share it.

After class, he counseled me, pushed me toward college, be-lying his in-class position. "If nothing else, do it for the defer-ment. Avoid the draft." I had few options. Knowing that we had no money, and being completely ignorant about financial aid or scholarships, I chose the path of least resistance and applied for Hunter College, part of the City University of New York. As a city resident and a high school graduate, I would be subject to CUNY's open admissions policy: a guaranteed slot, tuition free.

"If you're going to San Francisco, be sure to wear some flow-ers in your hair." Scott McKenzie's beautiful ballad became our theme song. It was 1967, and I lost myself in the summer of love. The romantic notion of marijuana had been popularized by the music industry. Ever since Beatlemania invaded our shores, we had a growing awareness of the ability to enhance creativity. Even the Beach Boys were rumored to have crossed over: good vibrations did not come naturally. Prior to the Beatles, it was the Beach Boys who had represented rebellion, with surfing being the ultimate rejection of our parents' values. "Beachcombers" were bums to our parents but heroes to us. When *Sgt. Pepper's Lonely Hearts Club Band* came out, we mined every lyric for hid-den meanings, imagining that the Fab Four's fame was a direct result of their experimentation with various substances.

The brothers at Reilly had sensed this invasion. "Jazz musi-cians used marijuana," they said, and it led to brain damage and early death. Their anecdotes and stories were infused with rac-ism. They showed us the film *Reefer Madness*, presenting it as a documentary. We stifled our laughter as best we could.

But the culture for substance abuse had been well shaped. Our parents continuously smoked tobacco in multiple forms. Our fathers drank whenever they could. Our mothers took diet pills to lose weight, and when these "uppers" deprived them of

sleep, they took sleeping pills, or "downers." They took tran-
quilizers for their nerves. All legal, all prescribed. They tolerated us sneaking a drink or a smoke, setting the rule that you
had to be sixteen to smoke at home. This substance abuse, these
dependencies, were so deeply imbedded in our culture, such a
part of the mainstream, that there were commercials on TV for
them, and no one acknowledged them as hazardous. Sure, there
were alcoholics, but they were societal dropouts who lived in the
street and died of cirrhosis. There were no warning labels on the
products, no major concerns.

Yet they believed that none of their abuse was of drugs.
Drugs were what the junkies did up in Harlem. Marijuana was
categorized as an equal of heroin and cocaine. If so, then drugs
rode the subway out to Queens. Jamaica became a major distribution hub. We were reminded, even as teenagers in high school,
not to talk to strangers or to accept rides in cars. Fear was presenting an image of pushers, desperate criminals, sitting in stolen cars outside our schools trying to deal drugs to us.

The reality was much less dramatic. It was early evening,
and I was on my way to the playground to see if I could get into
a softball game. Joe Stayer cruised by and asked me if I wanted
to go for a ride. He said he was going out to Long Beach to see
Bill Mackay's new beach house. I hopped in, and we each drank
a beer on the way. Shortly after arriving, the two of them disappeared into a back bedroom. Curious, I walked down the hallway and tentatively peeked in. Bill tried to cover something on
his bed with a pillow, but Joe said, "Don't worry; he's cool." Bill
looked over his shoulder tentatively but then accepted Joe's judg-
ment and uncovered his treasure. He had one of those round
trays that they use to carry bottles of beer in the bar: "My Beer
is Rheingold, the Dry Beer." In the middle of the tray was a pile

of dried weeds or herbs or something. It took me just a second to realize what it was, and when I did, I audibly took a short sharp breath. I was surprised and scared but immediately realized I did not want to betray Joe's trust, so I tried to narrow my eyes back to normal. Joe caught some of my hesitation out of the corner of his eye, and he winked at me and nodded in approval as if to say, "It's all right."

Bill took a corncob pipe out of his pocket and proceeded to stuff the weed into it, packing it down, not too tightly. He used a wooden kitchen match to light the stuff, and he took in a few puffs, inhaling quickly and ensuring that the pipe was well lit. I could see a red glow on the top of the bowl when he sucked in. He passed the pipe to Joe, who also took a few puffs and then passed the pipe to me. I was a little apprehensive, picturing the inmates in *Reefer Madness*, but I kept it to myself, and without hesitation I took the pipe, put the mouthpiece up to my lips, took a deep puff, and swallowed the smoke. I immediately felt a burning, tearing sensation in my throat and lungs, and I coughed violently. This exhalation forced the burning weed out of the bowl, sending it a foot up into the air and scattering it all over his bed. Joe cracked up, doubled over, laughing, but Bill pounced on his bed, looking for the burning bits and patting them out with his hands.

"You blew the bowl, Goddamn it. What the fuck, man? You can't cough into the Goddamn pipe!" Looking at Joe, he said, "You told me he was cool!" Joe was still laughing. Bill scraped the remains together and stuffed what he could get back into the pipe. He looked at me and said, "Can you handle this?"

"I'm sorry, man; it's my first time."

His demeanor softened instantly, and the famous grin the girls swooned over flashed at me. "Oh...why didn't you just tell me? I would've warned you." He went back to his pile and took a pinch of fresh grass to top off the bowl. He did this slowly, carefully, with the precision of a craftsman, as he politely explained, "It feels pretty harsh at first. You'll cough a lot. Take your hit and get the pipe out of your mouth and pass it. Pull the smoke deep into your lungs and hold it as long as you can." He relit the pipe and passed it to me, and I did as instructed, holding the smoke for a few seconds before coughing it out. Joe stopped his laughing and got in on the action. We smoked the whole bowl; then he refilled it, and we smoked another.

I got wrecked. My sense of reality was definitely distorted. My head felt cloudy even as my lungs and throat ached. I needed a drink and went to his kitchen, but I did not feel like a beer. I poured a glass of orange juice, a magic elixir. Soothing my throat, exquisite; it was the best tasting orange juice I had ever had. I realized then that I was high, and I giggled over the thought. Laughing came easier than usual—I was standing there laughing at my own thoughts when Joe and Bill stumbled into the kitchen.

I saw them and immediately froze, holding the refrigerator door half-open, about to place the carton back, as if I were playing the children's game of statue. Somehow, they looked at me and knew, and they froze and held their positions for a few seconds. When I unfroze, putting the carton back and closing the door, they proceeded in as if nothing had happened. But for the next hour or so, which felt like a day, we played this game, taking turns being the lead on freezing and unfreezing. Bill did it next, stopping for a minute in midsentence. "Does anyone want to wa...tch TV?" as if in a continuous stream from where he had left off.

We all picked up the game instantly, framing the rules as we played, but with no discussion, no acknowledgment of what we were doing. The person who put us into the freeze had to lead us out. Time passed slowly in this surreal pretend time warp. We went through motions, watched a ball game, got drinks and snacks, and went to the bathroom, but always subject to freezing on command.

Finally, Joe said we had to leave, and after freezing one more time at the door, we drove home with the radio blasting, talking about girls, as usual. We never discussed the game—or played it—again.

When I got home, I felt transparent. Pop was watching the same Mets game that we'd been watching in Long Beach. This connection seemed to have added relevance to me, and I sat down with him, but I talked more than usual. There was a new technology, videotape replay, that allowed the broadcaster to show a good play minutes after it had happened. They superimposed the graphic, Videotape Replay, so that the viewers would not be confused and think this was the live game. I was fascinated and jabbered on about the possibilities, but Pop was underwhelmed. Did I just imagine that he was looking at me differently?

All of a sudden, I was sure that he knew I was stoned. I had to get out of there. I went to the kitchen and made myself a peanut butter and jelly sandwich. Our dog accompanied me, salivating. I stuck half my sandwich in a bowl, filled it with milk, and gave it to him. He loved it, but got confused by the peanut butter sticking to his mouth, using his front paws to wipe at his jawline. I was laughing at him when Mom walked in and said, "What are you doing?"

I felt busted again. I was swinging from highs to lows in instants. "Nothing," I said. "Just having a sandwich."

"What's wrong with Magic?"

"Uh, I gave him some peanut butter and bread and milk."

"Oh," she said, "That was pretty stupid!" She walked away, shaking her head.

■ ■ ■

They say that pot is not physically addicting, like heroin or cocaine, but users tend to become psychologically dependent. I craved it. My free time became absorbed with acquiring and smoking it. Grass became a great equalizer. Gangs that used to war against each other began getting high together, dealing to each other.

One day, Vinny and I bought a "nickel," a five-dollar bag, from Dennis Doyle. It tasted terrible, and we had smoked most of it before we realized that it was actually parsley and oregano, with a little bit of pot thrown in. We did not get high, but we did get headaches. Vinny went ballistic. We went back to the corner but were told that Dennis had gone home. We went to his house and rang the bell. The screen door on the front porch was locked. After a minute, we rang the bell again, and finally his mother came out and tried to tell us that Dennis wasn't home. Vinny told her that she had better get him, taking a dramatic drag on his cigarette and looking her right in the eyes. She was visibly frightened, and I thought she would go in and call the police. But Dennis poked his head out and told her, "Ma, it's okay. Go in the house."

"Who are these boys?" she wanted to know. "What is going on?"

"Ma, just go in the house, please." When she did, Vinny cut to the chase. "You sold us beat shit. Give us our money back right now."

"I can't," he said. "I spent it. I didn't know it was beat. I swear." He was shaking.

"Bullshit," Vinny yelled. "You cut it yourself, you little prick. Now get our money."

Dennis leaned into the screen door and said, "Shhh, c'mon, you guys; my mother is going to hear you."

Vinny drew his arm back suddenly and punched at him, right through the screen, landing hard, right on his nose. Dennis's knees buckled and he slumped, almost fell, but then stood back up. His nose was bleeding, and he wiped it on his sleeve. His mother had been watching through the window, and she came running out to the porch. "What's going on here? I'm going to call the police!"

She went to go back in, but Dennis stopped her. "No, Ma, don't."

Vinny chimed right in. "Do you want us to tell your mother what's going on, Denny-boy, or do you want to give us our five bucks back?"

Dennis turned to his mother, "Ma, I need to borrow five dollars." She hesitated, and he started to cry. "Please, Ma, please." She got her pocketbook, came back with the five dollars, and gave it to Dennis, who put his hand through the new hole in the screen door and passed it to Vinny.

Vinny grabbed it, and as we were walking away, he said over his shoulder, "I wouldn't show my face anytime soon, Dennis. And I wouldn't think about beating anyone else if I were you." We could hear Dennis's mother as they went back into the house, near hysterics, yelling at him, asking him what this was all about.

There were, of course, other dealers who were not too far removed from the stereotypes that our parents feared. They were friends of friends who cruised by the corner, leaning out the car windows looking for customers. They sold nickel and dime bags. The transactions took place off the avenue, down the block, or outside the playground, with few words spoken. Slip the five and take the small manila envelope, folded over and scotch-taped.

Because the police began to patrol more regularly, and because it was inevitable that someone's parent would be by for a pack of cigarettes or a carton of milk, we had sense enough not to smoke on the corner. We walked through the neighborhood. If someone else scored first, you might be expected to spring for the corncob pipe. Or you might take up a collection, getting a buck each from five people and then making the deal. The pot came "dirty," cut stems complete with sticks and seeds. We stuffed the whole mess into the pipe. A nickel came with enough for four or five bowls, enough to keep a small group stoned for the whole night. And so we rode the coaster: giggling and talking through the highs, stuffing our faces through the munchies, listening to the pounding of our heartbeats, and thinking through the spinning paranoia of the crashes. The crash could be delayed by smoking some more to reinvigorate the high and staying with people, talking, laughing, and joking, avoiding the bleakness of being alone and thinking, wondering what the hell you were doing this for.

Everybody knew that the dealers scored in Jamaica, buying ounces or pounds and distributing nickels and dimes. "Let's cut out the middleman," Adam suggested one night. "Let's go to Jamaica and score for ourselves." He had heard that the parking lot at the Burger King at Hillside Avenue and 175th Street, a couple of blocks from the end of the subway line, was a major wholesale distribution point. We took the bus, nervously discussing tactics. As we got off on 179th Street and walked toward the restaurant, all my ingrained fears surfaced.

We had been taught to be careful in Jamaica. As compared to lily-white Bellerose, Jamaica was a true melting pot. Blacks,

Puerto Ricans, and Asians seemed to outnumber the whites. All of our experiences with Jamaica had been similar: it was the way station to transfer from buses to the subway, on our way to the city or Shea, and it was a place to shop, especially during the annual Jamaica Days sale. Specialty shops for men's wear, shoes, and women's wear lined Jamaica Avenue, under the elevated train, the same one we used to take to Brooklyn. But all the stores now had bars and grates, overhanging doors that came down at night to protect the windows. It was not the place for teenage white boys to hang out after dark.

The restaurant was twice the size of any of the so-called fast-food places in our neighborhood. The parking lot was huge, surrounding the store on all four sides, and was relatively full. It was also dirty: wrappers and paper cups blowing and rolling around, broken glass, and dozens of cigarette butts. Here and there were small groups of men, mostly black, hanging around cars, smoking cigarettes. All eyes were on us. We went into the store and ordered some Whoppers. All of the workers were black or Puerto Rican, as were most of the customers. All of a sudden it occurred to me that I was the minority, and I was terrified. I slumped my shoulders and shrunk my neck into my flannel shirt collar. I was willing myself to be smaller, to be inconspicuous. I could feel the blood draining out of me, and I was growing even paler.

I just wanted to go home, but Adam insisted on waiting around. We ate our burgers slowly and watched the scene, avoiding eye contact and turning away from the innuendos. All of a sudden, Adam said, "Turn around slowly and look to your right, in the parking lot, there is a deal going down." I did as he suggested and saw the tail end of a transaction take place. A white guy was just pulling his arm out of a car window. He immediately went over to a different car, got in, and drove off.

"C'mon," Adam said, and he got up and walked out.

He waited for me outside, but when I got there, I said, "Let's not do this." He laughed and said, "Don't be such a chickenshit." He walked over to the car we had been watching, leaned right into the window. He talked to the driver and then waved me over. The driver leaned to the back and opened the back door and told us to get in. Adam went to do so, but I put out my arm to stop him. My knees were shaking. He brushed me aside and got in. The driver stared at me. He had a dark, scarred face and the whites of his eyes were yellowed and dim, crossed with large red streaks.

"You gettin' in, white boy?"

I shook my head.

"Suit yeself," he said. He closed the door and pulled out, Adam looking at me as the car pulled away. I didn't know what to do. I felt like everyone else in the entire world was staring at me. I had never felt so alone, never imagined such despair. I wondered if I would ever see Adam alive again. How would I explain to his parents that I just stood there while someone drove away with him? My very brain was tingling; every fiber of my being was alert. I went back into the restaurant and ordered coffee. I watched the clock tick the seconds away. Fifteen minutes passed, then a half hour. It was well after rush hour now, and the crowds were thinning out. There were not so many people in the street or the restaurant.

An attendant asked me to lift my feet while he swept around me. Finally, the car pulled up, and Adam got out. He looked unharmed, if a bit disoriented. He looked around for me, and I bolted out the door so that he could see me. He came over and said, "You fucking abandoned me!" But he was giggling as he said it.

"I'm sorry, but I wasn't getting in that car, and I didn't think you would. What happened?"

"I got fucked up with this nigger, that's what happened! I scored a clean ounce for twenty bucks, that's what happened!"

I was totally panicked, afraid. "Holy shit, keep your voice down. What're you, crazy?"

"This is some good shit," was all he could blurt out.

We rode the bus back, got off a stop early, and went into Woolworth's to buy the manila envelopes. We went to his house, up to his room. He told his mother he wanted to play me the new Jefferson Airplane album he had bought. He put the record on loud, locked his door, and used the album cover to divide up the ounce. We split it into six nickels, agreed to sell four to get our money back, and keep one each for smoking. Our dealing days had begun.

■ ■ ■

Everything about who we were began to change. Inspired by the Beatles, we grew our hair long, wore colorful, flowery shirts and bell-bottomed pants. We spent more time alone in our rooms, listening to music, burning incense and candles to mask the smoke, and less time with the family watching television. We grew more and more secretive, lying about where we were going and who we were going to be with. We started staying out later and sleeping in. Gone were the innocent days of sitting in front of our own houses, talking, playing cards or passing around a transistor radio, claiming "Poetry in Motion" as your own song, giving you the right to hold the radio while it played.

Adam began to go to Jamaica by himself, buying pot by the pound. Sometimes Vinny and I would chip in forty dollars each and divide the pound into three. Adam began selling dirty dimes and ounces, leaving the nickel customers for Vinny and me. I was less concerned with dealing for profit, and I certainly was less interested in returning to Jamaica on a regular basis. I was happy to let Adam do the risky work, even if he took an extra chunk off the brick before we got to it.

Vinny and I were more interested in getting high for free. We learned to clean the grass. After getting our cut, Vinny and I went to his house and broke it down. We'd start by rubbing the stems between our palms, crushing the dried leaves and separating them from the stems. We removed all sticks and stems, and then carefully extracted most of the seeds. Dirty pot was fine for pipes where the sticks would burn and the seeds would pop and explode. True connoisseurs preferred joints. After cleaning the grass, we rolled it. Vinny was more adept than I, more of a perfectionist. We figured Abe must have known that something was going on when he started selling cigarette rolling papers in unprecedented numbers. He even began to stock the novelty items—chocolate papers and such—but we stayed away from them.

Vinny had started hanging out more with some of the Navajos, Pauly, and even Dennis Doyle, who had been forgiven. On a cold night, we abused our night center privileges, letting the two of them in as guests. We met Adam in the entrance area, but instead of going to the gym, we snuck down a hallway and sat at the back of a second-grade classroom.

Vinny lit a perfectly rolled joint and passed it to me. I inhaled deeply but did not pass it instantly, and Pauly leaned over to take it, saying, "Hey, man, don't bogart that joint," and we all cracked up. As it progressed around the circle, Adam produced a fancy, feathered roach clip, allowing him to extract every last bit of the resin that wicked at the end of the joint without burning his fingers.

"Where did you get that?" I asked.

"At the Shrunken Head," one of the new head shops that had sprung up in the neighborhood shopping centers to market drug paraphernalia. In addition to roach clips, papers, and pipes, they sold black lights, posters, candles, beads, incense—all the accoutrements you needed to feed your head. We drew pictures on the blackboard, but before we left, I lingered and erased the dirty ones.

The gang violence ebbed as more and more kids turned on. The crowds at Schneid's continued to swell, spilling over into the streets. I still had the dilemma that Pop might walk up at any time. All of my friends knew to yell out, "Hi, Mr. O'Connor," when they saw him coming to give me fair warning. I would try to hide, as he would weave through the crowd to get in the door. If he did see me, he would just say hi or maybe ask me what time I was coming home.

After he left, I might get razzed or ranked on a little bit, but so many kids knew him from baseball at Saint Greg's that little disrespect was intended. I brushed off the teasing but often became consumed with guilt. I knew that I was up to no good, knew that I could never tell my father the truth about what we did. But the shame would be momentary, lasting only until the next kid asked me if I wanted to go smoke.

Abe and Lynn began to have more and more trouble controlling the crowds. So many kids came in and out and didn't buy anything that they knew they were being ripped off. They had to develop ugly tactics to try to maintain some measure of control. Abe would just yell and sometimes use his large and imposing body to ease a kid out. But Lynn, short and slight, needed a weapon. Her dishrag became a regular extension of her arm. If you weren't smart enough to see it coming, her first deployment would be a wave of it, swinging it in your direction as if by accident, spraying dirty water on you. If this didn't work, and you didn't leave, or if you mouthed off to her and showed disrespect, she would lose her temper and swing the damn thing right at you, hitting you on the arm or shoulder and getting you wet and angry. In rare moments, if riled enough, she would slap you right in the face with it.

20

The summer had gone by in a smoky blur. In the fall, I would be starting Hunter College, commuting by bus and subway to East Sixty-Eighth Street near Park and Lexington, while continuing to live at home. Right after Labor Day, I had to attend a freshman colloquium. The "invitation" said that it was mandatory.

It was going to be held at Kirschner's Resort, in South Fallsburg. Pop said mostly Jews vacationed at these Sullivan County resorts, and it would probably be lush. I knew that our neighbor, Berk, had spent many a summer going to camp in the area, often bringing home garter snakes and chameleons that he had captured. I had never been away by myself and was quite anxious. I pictured Borscht Belt kitsch and expected to be miserable. I had to schlep my luggage into the city, to meet on campus and travel up with my classmates. I decided to bring a joint with me, in case I needed to escape.

I toned down my wardrobe, but despite my parents' advice, I refused to cut my hair, which was just starting to touch my shoulders. I expected to see other "heads" there but could pick none out. Indeed, most of the other guys had short hair and were quite conservatively dressed, a few even wearing ties. For a bus ride to the Catskills?

In 1870, Thomas Hunter, an Irish immigrant and social reformer, founded the school that would come to be named for him. Originally called the Female Normal and High School, it was quickly renamed by the New York legislature to the Normal College of the City of New York. Its primary mission was to educate teachers. It became known as an outstanding liberal arts school. Although Hunter had gone co-ed in 1964, it still had a majority of female students.

I was timid and shy, avoiding eye contact and keeping my head down. I brought one of Mom's paperbacks with me: Jacqueline Susann's *Valley of the Dolls.* I chose a seat in the back row, next to the window. I hunched my body into the corner, shrinking myself as small as possible and climbed inside the book to avoid the inevitable, but meaningless, social chitchat. The story was a distorted and tawdry tale of struggling actresses and models. Liquor and pills promised instant love, instant excitement, but led to ultimate hell. I was enthralled.

When we got to the hotel, I learned for the first time that I would have a roommate. The unexpected realization that I would be sharing a bedroom with a total stranger sent a dark chill down my spine. It was an unnamable fear, an anxiety that I wouldn't know how to relate, that I would appear inept, and scariest of all, that he might see me naked. Derek, my roommate, was Jewish, with short reddish-brown hair, dark features, and thick, black, plastic-rimmed glasses. He looked like Steve Allen, but he seemed to have no sense of humor at all. We had two single beds, with just one lamp on a small table between them.

The first afternoon was to be free time, and I went down to the pool and spotted who must surely have been the most beautiful girl in the school. She was wearing a two-piece bathing suit. She had a blond, shoulder-length pageboy and dark sunglasses. She already seemed to know a few other girls, and they were hanging on the side of the pool, talking, splashing around a little, and laughing. I sat in a lounge chair across from them, and she caught me staring at her. I tried a smile but weakly flubbed it, and it probably looked like a grimace. She put on a quizzical look and turned away.

When I went back to my room, Derek was lying on his bed, reading my book. He jumped, tried to quickly put it down, then realized he couldn't hide it, and picked it back up to show me that he borrowed it. "I hope you don't mind?" he said. There was no way I would be smoking pot with this kid.

I managed to meet a few guys over the weekend, even got into a poker game, run by Howie, who liked to parade around in his underwear. I lost ten dollars, got caught in the hallway after hours, and had to give my name to the monitor. Great. Good start. I never met the babe, or any other girls, shying away from all opportunities.

I never lit the joint. It was the first time I had gone three days without smoking pot since the beginning of the summer. I felt good. My lungs were clearing, getting stronger, and I swam some laps in the pool, the first physical activity I'd had in a month. It became clear that my fellow students were quite serious. There were lots of questions about grades, curves, and testing. The curriculum looked challenging. On the last night, I flushed the joint down the toilet bowl.

When classes started, I settled into a new routine. I worked after school, and by the time I got home, I barely had enough strength to do the reading and homework that was required. During the week, I refused to go out at night, and after a while my friends stopped calling for me.

Come Friday nights, though, I often binged for forty-eight hours, hanging out at Schneid's and smoking pot. The weekend before Thanksgiving, Adam asked me to do ups with him. He stole two of his mother's diet pills, which were reputed to contain meth-amphetamine. Whenever I stopped by Adam's house, his mom couldn't shut up. Adam's father was always working. He had quit his job at Grumman's and was setting up his own business selling car parts. He was hardly ever at home during the day, even on the weekends. His mother, on the other hand, welcomed any company. She was indeed heavy, not overly fat or huge, but definitely on the plump side: short, stocky, large-boned, heavy.

I wondered if she ever slept. She was up early, and she was up late. Adam, on the other hand, was a slow starter. I had plans to meet him at eleven o'clock, but he wasn't at Schneid's, so I knocked on his door. His mom let me in, brought me into the kitchen, and poured me a cup of coffee. She sat down and started talking. She went on for ten minutes before I could get a word in edgewise. Mostly she talked about television. What had been on the game shows, question by question. Or the news. Or the soap operas. She talked about those characters as if she knew them. In the afternoon, she would set up her ironing board in the living room and watch soaps while she ironed. She talked about things that I had absolutely no interest in and could not contribute to. That was okay; she was not looking for a conversation. She was looking for someone to talk to. I could envision her talking to the TV if no one else was around.

Trying not to be impolite, I asked, "Is Adam up yet?"

"Oh, no, he's still asleep." Her kitchen was spotless; it sparkled. It was totally occupied by cats—pictures, posters, ashtrays, even cookie jars—all cats. On the wall, her clock was in the shape of a cat: the face of the clock replaced the body and was accented by a head and a tail that protruded out the bottom and swung back and forth, like a metronome. As the pendulum tail swung, so did the eyes in the head, looking side to side, second by second. I watched the clock, watched the minute hand go around, counting the seconds, becoming hypnotized by the back-and-forth motion of the tail and the eyes, accompanied by the droning on and on of her voice, the words losing all meaning, running together into an endless white noise.

After another ten minutes or so of nonstop banter, I asked a little more directly, "Could you wake him up, or do you want me to do it?" She released me, and I escaped to Adam's room to drag his sorry ass out of bed. Grumpy, grouchy—these are not words that describe Adam well enough when he woke up in the morning. Stuporous and incoherent came a little closer: eyes like slits; eyes that don't register that they recognize who you are. He greeted me with, "What d'you want?"

"Ups today, remember? You fuckin' talked me into it?" I opened his window and lit a thin joint, blowing the smoke outside.

"Give me a hit," he pleaded.

"Come and get it, turkey." I expected that this would finally get him out of bed. I had smoked most of it before he managed the trip across the room, and he finished the roach and flicked the remnant out of the house.

He dicked around for another hour, taking a shower and getting dressed. I put his headphones on and tried to get into the Mothers of Invention: "Suzie? Suzie Cream Cheese." I did not share his fascination with Frank Zappa, trying to apply too much logic to the random noises and meaningless lyrics.

His mother corralled us with coffee, regaling us with her plans for Thanksgiving. It was well into the afternoon before we got to Schneid's. We each bought a soda and took the pills that he had stolen from his mother's medicine chest: Dexedrine. Brand name for dextroamphetamine. Administered in its sulfate form, it elevates the mood of the depressed and controls the appetite of the obese by stimulating the central nervous system.

For a while, we just hung out with the crowd at Schneid's. We didn't notice anything; the pills didn't seem to be working. As the light faded, the crowd dispersed as other kids went home for supper. A good three hours after popping the pills, we realized that we were talking more than usual. We took a walk through the neighborhood, and we talked nonstop, barely noticing where we were, paying no attention to where we were going. We were animated—excited, even. Listening was tough; we each wanted to dominate talking. I tried to listen, but at the same time my mind was racing, because I was thinking about what I wanted to say next, what topic interested me. Sometimes it was like having two separate conversations, but neither of us cared.

"Let me tell you about this stock-car race I went to last week," he began. "The day before the race, I met Mario Andretti in the pits, and he let me sit in the driver's seat of his car, and then he let me drive—slowly—around the track. The gears are so much closer, and the gearshift is so small. The clutch, though, is much heavier. My dad's been a sponsor of his for years, and he was really just doing him a favor by letting me drive. Then we looked at the engine, and he explained all the specs to me. Did you know that they actually have quad carbs in these cars?"

He stopped for a breath, and I said, "Yeah, yeah, let me tell you about this girl at the colloquium. She was gorgeous, drop-dead beautiful. She could have been a model. When I see her on campus, I try to catch her eye and say hello, but she is always encircled by a bunch of friends, so I don't know how to get close to her."

"That's great," he said. "In addition to the quad carb, there is, of course, a quad exhaust system..."

By the time we circled back to Schneid's, we were surprised to find it closed. It was well after eleven. Adam had an idea, one that would allow us to stay out later than usual. I called my mother and told her that I was sleeping over his house, and he called his mother and told her he was sleeping over mine. With each other, we did not discuss where the hell we were going to sleep. Sleep was not in our vocabulary; it was not something that existed in our world of possibilities.

Most of the houses had grown completely dark. Off the avenue, the side streets were quiet, disturbed only occasionally by a passing car. We kept walking, kept talking. We promised that we would listen while the other person talked. Though this took some effort, it actually allowed us to have a real conversation, a deep conversation. We talked of the universe, of order, of the definition of God, and of the stupidity and the excitement of taking drugs. We talked of relationships with family members, with other friends, and with girls. Adam always got trapped, stayed with one girl too long, even while a new girl was winning his heart. He'd wind up cheating, apologizing, and then repeating the cycle. Other than Glenda, who had been more of a buddy than a girlfriend, I had no serious relationships. All I had to add about girls were my lust stories and my fantasies.

We circled back to the corner again. It was now one o'clock in the morning. The streets were quiet, desolate. There were a few people in the bar, but we had no desire to sit in there with the alkies, our new name for the drinkers. I had just turned eighteen, and he had a phony ID, but we stayed out. Many of the alkies, especially the older ones, were antipot, antidrugs. They were also more prone to violence, and we at least had the foresight to realize that we might lip off to the wrong person. While we were standing on the corner, trying to decide what to do next, a car pulled up next to us. It was a hot muscle car, a 427 Pontiac Firebird. The window rolled down, and Richie Nolan stuck his head out. "What the fuck are you derelicts doing out so late?"

"We're just hanging out and talking."

"You want to ride around for a while?"

"Sure," we said, looking forward to the opportunity to get warm. It was about forty degrees out, and though we both had jackets on, they were light. Whenever we stopped walking, our feet got cold, and we got the shivers; my teeth chattered whenever it was not my turn to talk.

We both knew Richie pretty well, knew him from Catholic Youth Organization days when he used to play basketball for Mr. D'Amato. We also knew that he had recently become a cop. Adam and I both squeezed into the front bucket, but it was too tight, so I slipped into the back. Richie had an open six-pack next to him, three cans already gone. He finished one soon after picking us up, threw the empty out the window, and opened his fifth. Cruising down Hillside Avenue, he came to a red light at Commonwealth Boulevard. He stopped, checked both ways as if it were only a stop sign, and then proceeded through the light. This bothered me. Sure, he was a cop, but why go through a red light, why attract attention, especially when you're driving around half in the bag? He took the service road to the Cross Island down to Jamaica Avenue, made a left, and then came back up Little Neck Parkway to complete the circle and pass Schneid's. I figured he was going to let us out, and I was ready.

He'd been blasting the radio and yelling over it, telling us how all the rookies in the police academy would go out at night and get drunk. He passed right by the corner, past a patrol car that had been sitting there. The cops pulled out to follow us, and he said, "Let's have some fun." He quickly made a right turn from the left lane, accelerated for a block, made another quick right, turned off his headlights and taillights, and slowed down. The cop took the bait and zoomed up behind us pretty quickly. He put his red flashing light on. Richie went another block, laughing his ass off, his lights still out. The cop blipped his siren on for just a second, a sort of "bwoop" sound. He must have been aware that he was dealing with some sort of clown, and he had the presence of mind not to wake the whole neighborhood.

Richie finally stopped, grabbed his shield, and walked to the patrol car. He was only gone a few minutes. Adam and I were terrified, imagining ourselves getting arrested and trying to explain to our parents why we'd lied. I was wondering if they had a blood test or a urine test for ups. We turned around and saw Richie showing his shield to the cops and laughing. He came back and got in, and the green-and-black patrol car took off.

"What happened?" we asked simultaneously.

"Oh, I knew the guy, and I told him that I was just messing with him. He was a little pissed, but no big deal. Fuck him." Richie continued to do the talking, mostly about what a bunch of Irish drunks the police force was, and how the cops were probably the most corrupt people around, and how for an alky troublemaker like himself, joining the police force was the smartest thing he could do. "I can avoid getting busted, have fun harassing people, and some nights even drink on the job— for free, no less!"

He started on his sixth beer. "Now let's have some real fun," he said. He started to drive fast, quickly accelerating to ninety down Hillside Avenue, flying past Creedmoor. We came to the Rockies, a huge vacant lot strewn with boulders, and went around the side road where the back of PS 18 joined with the Rockies. There used to be a problem with teenagers driving their cars from the school parking lot into the Rockies, tearing up the place. To avoid this, the city had erected two bollards about four feet high, maybe six feet apart. Richie put his brights on and asked us if we thought he could fit through the poles. "I miss driving through here," he said with a stupid grin on his face.

I said, "No, what are you crazy? NO!"

Adam just laughed and said, "Well, maybe!"

Richie crept up to the barriers and slowly fit his car right between them, barely an inch to spare on each side. When he realized he could clear them, he began to back out. I heaved a heavy sigh of relief. He backed to the end of the parking lot and stopped. He finished his beer, staring straight ahead, his brights still on.

"Could you take us back to Schneid's now?" I asked a bit too tentatively.

"Shut the fuck up," he said, in no uncertain terms. This was an order. The nice guy, the fellow kid from the neighborhood, had disappeared in an instant. He had suddenly adopted his mean-ass, nasty-cop persona. He seemed to be focused on some anger from his past, and he became totally concentrated, determined to once again demonstrate his rebellion.

I contemplated jumping out of the car, but it only had two doors, and I would have to squeeze past the back of Adam's seat and lean over him to get it open. The door was unlocked, and I thought I could do it, but what would I do then? I did not want to be alone in the Rockies if they left me here. I just kept thinking, *He's a fucking cop; he's not going to kill us.*

I thought too long. Richie lowered his window and threw his empty out. Then he slowly raised the window and very quietly, almost spiritually, whispered, "Hang on!" He pressed his left foot on the brake pedal and floored the accelerator with his right. The car was surging. He popped the brake, and the tires screeched, burning more rubber than I had ever seen outside of a racetrack. He fishtailed and swerved a little crossing the parking lot. At first, he was holding the steering wheel with only one hand as he wound through the manual gears. I could see his eyes in the rearview mirror, and he looked scared, but he did not slow down. He grabbed the wheel with his other hand, continued to accelerate, and got a cold, steely look of intensity in his eyes.

I knew we were going to die. I was sorry that I hadn't tried to get out. I was disgusted with my own fear, realizing it was stupid of me to assume that it would be okay because he was a cop, and blaming myself that we were all going to die. I glanced down at the speedometer. As we cleared the parking lot and hit the dirt, it was just passing sixty. I held my breath, but I watched. We flew through the poles perfectly. He didn't scratch either side, but he had to hit the brakes pretty hard, hurling us toward the dashboard as he careened and swerved around a boulder. He took out a bush and dragged it under his car. We hit a lot of smaller rocks and were bumping and banging our way through the Rockies. He went straight across the main field and tore straight up the embankment of grass and across the sidewalk, down the curb, and out onto Hillside Avenue, all in about ten seconds flat.

He screamed, whooped at the top of his lungs as he straightened out the car and headed down the Avenue. "Holy shit! We did it! We motherfuckin' did it!" as if even he had been sure that we were all going to die.

Adam and I were momentarily speechless. We had survived certain death. We felt exhilarated, flying on dex, bottling up our words until we regained the ability to speak. Thank God, Richie took us back to Schneid's and dropped us off. "You boys stay out of trouble now. Don't do anything I wouldn't do." He laughed and left another patch of rubber as he took off.

We were emotionally drained, physically exhausted, but still racing on speed. It was three thirty in the morning. We were cold, shivering again. What the fuck were we going to do now? Once again, Adam had thought ahead. "I asked Vinny to leave his father's car unlocked. You know, the one he always leaves on the street in front of his house." We walked past our own houses and over to Vinny's, and sure enough, the car was unlocked. There was even an old wool blanket in the backseat. The car was a fifteen-year-old Nash Rambler, with a spacious, if dirty and worn, backseat. We got in, put the blanket over our laps and legs and began rapping again. "Can you believe what we've been through? Scary about the cops all being corrupt. I thought we were all going to die. How could they let that nut be a cop?" That kind of stuff, though often followed by: "This sucks! I wish we could go home. I am so fucking thirsty. I am so fucking cold!" All of our sentences were chopped, a meandering succession of staccato phrases. We looked out the back window and marveled at the stars.

At first light, we went up to Schneid's and helped Abe open up the place, carrying some stacks of newspapers in for him. He shared the first pot of coffee with us, and we lied to him about what we were doing up so early. We drank some more coffee, paying for the second round. He asked us if we wanted to order breakfast, but neither of us could eat. We understood how these things helped you lose weight. We hung around for an hour or so, but at seven o'clock people started coming in for their Sunday papers, and we decided to head home before one of our parents showed up.

Pop was awake. "Good morning," I said, happy that he never suspected much. Everyone else was still asleep. "Adam and I talked late into the night," certainly the truth. "I didn't get much sleep."

"Are you coming to mass?"

"We went last night," I lied.

I went down to the basement, to my new room. I had convinced Mom that a college student was too old to be sleeping in a bunk bed, and she had helped me convert the rec room. Pop had driven us to Klein's warehouse in the Bronx, where we bought some furniture that had been returned due to scratches or dents. We got a pullout sofa, a nightstand, and a dresser, all for less than a hundred bucks. I bought a portable stereo out of my own money and had acquired a few albums. My collection of 45s was much larger. Vinny and I would go to Mays, where I worked in the men's department, and I would distract the stock boy in the record department, asking him stupid questions about time card rules or weekend work schedules. Vinny would grab a bunch of records and stuff them down the front of his pants and then pull his jacket over them. We'd steal half a dozen a week.

I put on *Sgt. Pepper's Lonely Hearts Club Band* and tried to sleep. My mind kept racing even as my body experienced the full crash that we had heard about: tired eyes, sluggish blood flow, aches, emptiness, and overwhelming depression. The body is clearly not designed to go without sleep. I felt like I was in the early stages of the flu, without the respiratory symptoms. While my body ached, my mind wandered around wildly, replaying the scenes from the night over and over, reexperiencing the terror of the car ride.

At ten o'clock, after the rest of the household went to church, I abandoned all hope of sleep and went back up to Schneid's. Spent the day shuffling between Schneid's and the playground. I went home around five thirty to change, but I lied and said I ate out. I still had no desire for food of any kind. I went over to Vinny's, and we smoked a jay. Kathy, with whom Vinny had become much tighter with since defending her honor, was there with Joe, home again on Thanksgiving break. Joe and I started wrestling over a roach, fooling around. He was much taller than me, and we had our arms over our heads, and he was pushing down on me when all of a sudden I was in great pain.

"Stop," I said, "I'm hurt!" I sat down to see if it would subside, but it didn't. The pain was sharp, excruciating, starting at the top of my arm and radiating out in all directions, reaching deeper and deeper into the fibers of my body. "I feel like my muscle is torn in half or something." They ignored me. After about a minute or two I said, "Listen, something is not right. Something is seriously wrong. I need to go to the hospital." The look on my face finally stopped their laughter, and Joe ran over to get my parents. We were stoned but sobering pretty quickly.

Joe came back with Pop, and we all drove over to Long Island Jewish. In the ER, they diagnosed a dislocated shoulder pretty quickly. They shot me up with morphine. The resident got me to lie down on the gurney, and he told me that what he was going to do was going to hurt like hell, but just for a minute. He sat down on a chair, put his foot up against the gurney for leverage, and grabbed my arm, pulling it back into its socket. It did hurt like hell—an acute, sharp, mind-numbing pain as if a knife was coring my shoulder like an apple. When it slipped back into place, the relief was instantaneous, the sharp pain reduced to a dull ache.

By the time we got home it was after eleven. Joe wanted me to stop by and smoke a jay to top off the morphine, but I refused. "You may be off, but I have school tomorrow." We talked for a few minutes in front of my house. When I went in, Mom and Pop were already watching the news. Mom was relieved that I came in but gave me a lecture. "What are you doing to yourself?" she demanded.

I apologized for the stupidity, knowing that they only knew half the story. I went down and lay on my bed and cried. I knew this happened because of the ups, because I was crashing, because I really was stupid. I had been awake for over forty hours, and I wept in self-pity. I finally slept, fitfully, dreaming on and off that I was being chased. I ran through the streets, hiding behind cars, but each time I thought I was safe, there was another pursuer jumping out and getting me running again.

21

The pervasive influence of the growing drug subculture was beginning to manifest itself right in our living rooms, showing up on our televisions. A few years earlier, when the Beatles played on Ed Sullivan, Mom and Pop watched right along with us. Sure, they were baffled by the hysteria and critical of the screaming girls, especially the ones pulling out their hair. But they could relate. They talked of Frank Sinatra and Times Square on New Year's Eve. But the humor of the Smothers Brothers was beyond them. The drug nuances of the regular skit, *Share a Little Tea with Goldie*, were lost on them, and they just thought it was inane. They asked Kevin and me what we were laughing at, never suspecting that we were as stoned as Goldie. They did not understand the hoopla around CBS's censorship of the show. They thought it was related to the antiwar stance the show took.

I got Pop to watch a special on Channel 13, educational TV, a film by Yoko Ono that consisted of thirty minutes of a housefly crawling around on a woman's bare breast. It would crawl up to her nipple and flutter its wings and dig into her flesh, all the while accompanied by Yoko's background screeches, as if she were trying to give voice to the fly. I called it art, and Pop called it the end of civilization as we know it. Timothy Leary had advised us to turn on, tune in, and drop out, and my parents just thought he was a freak, not knowing that that label was one their kids would become proud to wear.

By late 1967, it had become clear that Secretary of Defense McNamara's prolonged bombing of the North Vietnamese was not getting the desired results. President Johnson had begun to accelerate the escalation. Ground troops were deployed; American boys were getting killed in record numbers. For the first time in our history, there was talk that we could lose a war. In October, there was a massive protest in the heart of Washington, right in front of the Pentagon. Celebrities like Arthur Miller and Norman Mailer were involved. The president was incensed. Pop called the protesters traitors and said they should be arrested or drafted and sent to the front lines. As her own boys turned eighteen and picked up their draft cards, Mom's worry lines deepened.

Between school and work, my days were full, and I found it easy to keep my resolve to stay straight during the week. Vinny and Adam, however, were both succumbing to new temptations. Neither of them worked anymore; they got all of the money they needed from dealing. They entertained me with stories of daytime parties. They were cutting school and going to Joyce's parents' house, along with a number of other kids, mostly from the Whelans and the Navajos. A number of girls were joining them, and Vinny liked telling me of the sexual pairings that were taking place in these afternoon orgies.

"Who are some of the other regulars?" I asked Vinny.

86

TIMOTHY F. DEMPSEY

He got quiet at first, but then told me, "Pauly, Dennis Doyle—you know, that crowd."

"Vin, aren't those guys all doing glue?"

He whispered, "Yeah."

I had seen enough changed behavior among the glueheads to know that it was really messing with their brains. Even when they talked about it, they could only describe the experience as a dream: they were aware of their surroundings, but it was a different reality, one in which all sensory perceptions were dulled, thinking was slowed down, and doing anything serious, like driving a car, became extremely hazardous.

"Vin, what the hell are you doing?"

"It's cool, man, I got it under control."

Vinny was dealing big-time, moving pounds of pot. He saved enough to buy a used car, a four-year-old Mustang convertible. So far, he had been smart enough not to drive when he was doing glue. On a sunny Saturday, I reluctantly agreed to drive him and his new buddies around. First stop was A&J's Toy Store on Northern Boulevard in Douglaston. Glue had become such a problem that the city had passed an ordinance that not only said you had to be eighteen to buy glue, but you could only buy it when you bought a plastic model. All of the candy stores in Bellerose had simply stopped selling it. But this guy in Douglaston was cashing in on the abuse. He never checked for ID but did insist that you buy a model. The kids in Douglaston quickly learned that you could score free models simply by checking the trash bins down the block from A&J's. The glueheads were buying their models, getting their glue and brown paper bags, and throwing the models out as soon as they got away from the store.

While they went in, I sat in the car, top down, listening to the radio. To the casual observer, it looked like a pleasant enough scene. Inside I was churning, my behavior gnawing at my gut. I knew glue was much worse than pot. I had no desire to do it, but I was torn by the reality that I was helping these guys with something so dangerous.

As I drove away, Vinny, Adam, and Pauly were all business. Like factory workers, they all followed a standard procedure. They folded down the top of the bag a couple of layers so that when they fit the bag over their nose and mouth, their face would be close to the glue; this would maximize the amount of fumes that they'd inhale.

They squeezed the glue into the bottom of the bag, and they started "huffing" slowly. Unlike the media, the glueheads never referred to the practice as "sniffing." They breathed deeply in and out, like they were trying to cure hyperventilation, for about two minutes. They would then take the bag down, and grab a gulp of fresh air. Their eyes had already started to shine, and they had silly grins on their faces. They made no attempt to talk, but after being out for about thirty seconds, they would immerse again.

The second time they came up, they really started looking disoriented and confused. The third time up, the grin was gone. They looked lost. They had entered a dream, some altered reality, during which they often turned nasty. Whatever was going on inside, outside their demeanor became ugly. They cursed me for driving too wildly while I was parked in Alley Pond. They cursed and accused one another of trying to steal their glue bags. They were thrusting their heads so far into the bag that glue was sticking to them. It hung in stringy droplets from Vinny's mustache.

I was appalled and leaned over to try to stop him from putting the bag back up to his face. He smacked my hand away and said, "Get your hands off this, you fuck. This is mine; you can't have it." He glared at me as if he would kill me if I touched his bag again. I had heard of fights over glue bags where kids wound up getting knifed. I got out of the car to take a walk. It took me about ten minutes to walk around the parking lot, and when I got back, they were arguing among themselves, the glue bags in their laps. The fumes had dissipated already, and they were craving more, complaining that they did not get deep enough into their dreams.

They talked about this delusional state with great awe and respect. You achieved some kind of status if you could go into a dream and emerge later to describe it. It was like a competition to see who could have the better hallucination. Apparently, when you were in a dream state, you had some level of awareness of who you were and what you were doing, but it was distant and only loosely affiliated with your consciousness. They wanted me to drive them back to A&J's to get some more. I refused until Vinny threatened, "If you don't take me, I'll drive myself, man."

I shook my head in frustration, unsure of what to do. I did not want it on my conscience if he got killed or something, so I said, "All right, you prick, but this is the last time!"

I drew the line at going into A&J's for them. "No fucking way. You buy your own glue." Pauly was in the best shape. He went in and came out with three more models and three more tubes of glue. The models and the bags went into the trash right outside the store. I envisioned the creep reselling them. Rather than use new bags, they wanted to add the glue on top of the mess they already had so that less of the new stuff would be absorbed into the paper.

They were huffing for longer periods now, and by the time I got back to Alley Pond, they were into their dreams. They looked like junkies or zombies. They leaned back, their heads kind of bobbing around on their necks. Their mouths hung open, their eyes glazed over and collapsed into slits that were not quite closed. Pauly seemed to be in a dream without letting the bag down. He had propped his head against the side window and was leaning against it with the bag smashed into his face, but his hand stayed in position to prevent it from falling.

Vinny had no movement in his eyes, no expression on his face. He was absolutely vacant, in a stupor, staring straight ahead. There is nothing quite as blank as the emptiness in the eyes of someone emerging from a glue bag. Talking to him brought no response whatsoever. I took another walk. This time when I got back, they had regained enough consciousness to put the bags back up and huff some more. The process was no longer performed with neatness and precision. Glue was everywhere: on their hands, their clothes, their shoes, dripping down the outside of the bag. I couldn't stand it. I felt lost, alone. I drove back to our neighborhood, parked down the block from Schneid's, took the keys with me, and left the three of them there. I walked into the candy store and had a malted, chatting with some of the people who were hanging out. Kathy was there, and we had a long talk. Kathy had naturally blond hair, but as she grew into a teenager, she bleached it anyway, turning it almost platinum. She let it grow long and silky, parted it down the middle, and let it hang in front of her face while she sat in the handball courts. She was one of the few girls who drifted between Schneid's and Dan's: you could almost tell where she would be heading based on how she was dressed. Leather pants for Dan's but jeans for Schneid's.

Easily one of the great beauties of the neighborhood, she could've had her pick of the guys. We all lusted after her, all wanted to get beyond the smile to stroking her gorgeous hair and progressing to her supple body. She took to wearing sheer blouses without a bra. She drove us crazy, flirting unmercifully while grubbing up a cigarette, a joint, or a beer. She got whatever she wanted. Almost. For alas, she had fallen in love with Vinny. She told me she was all too familiar with glue, had even tried huffing with him, though she did not get into a dream and was too disgusted with herself to do it again. She said the best thing was to stay away from Vinny and Pauly when they were huffing.

About an hour later, they stumbled in, weaving and slurring their speech as if they were drunk. "Davey, man, wher'd you go? We need s'more stuff."

"No fucking way, Vinny; I'm done." I got up to leave.

"Where's my keys?"

"I'll give them to you tomorrow."

He blocked my path. "Give me my fucking keys now!" His eyes were glassy black marbles with a look of pure rage. The fumes coming off him were putrid, turning my stomach. I could not believe that this was my childhood friend. I did believe that he would hurt me if I interfered.

"Fine, man, here. I'm not your fucking mother!"

"Fuck you, Davey! You think you're so fucking high and mighty with your college books and all your bullshit. You're no bettr'n us, man."

"Fuck you, too, you asshole-fucking gluehead. Get out of my way." And I brushed by him and went home.

The next morning, Sunday, the phone rang early. I heard someone pick it up, and then Mom called down the stairs. I was surprised, because she usually would not wake me for a phone call. She would tell them to call back if I was sleeping. "Davey, it's Vinny's mother. She seems pretty upset. She said she needs to talk to you."

I took a deep breath, rolled over, and picked up.

"Davey, the police just called. Vinny's in the hospital; he's unconscious." She started crying, talking almost hysterically. "They said his car is totaled. Weren't you with him last night?"

"No," I lied.

"He said he was going out with you."

"I'm sorry; he didn't."

"They said somebody named Paul was driving, and Vinny was in the backseat. Davey, the policeman said they were sniffing glue. Who is this Paul, and why would he be driving Vinny's car? Davey, tell me what's going on."

"Is Mr. Alvarez home?"

"No, he's working this weekend."

"Let me get dressed. I'll be over in fifteen minutes. Let's go to the hospital."

I borrowed Brian's car and picked up Mrs. Alvarez. She tried to lay a guilt trip on me. "Why don't you spend more time with Vinny? Why can't you help him? He respects you."

"Yeah, but he doesn't listen to me either, Mrs. Alvarez."

She apologized and cried and told me that she knew it wasn't my fault.

When we got to the hospital, Vinny was awake; his injuries were not as bad as we expected: a slight concussion and bruised ribs. His mother lost control and started screaming and hitting him. I had to restrain her and call for help. The doctor came and helped me get her to the waiting room, where she calmed down. I went back to see Vinny and he said, "Thanks a lot for dumping me last night. You see what you did?"

"Fuck you," I said, on my way out.

■ ■ ■

As the school year progressed, I continued to drift away from Vinny. Sure, our paths would cross every weekend, but as more and more people began to hang at Schneid's, new factions began to form. We were always cordial to each other, civil in our banter. But as the evening wore on, he'd slip away with the harder-drug users; I'd stick to smoking a joint or two.

I finished my first year in college with one A, a couple of Bs and a C. Summertime was upon us again and on any given night, there might be fifty to a hundred kids stopping by or hanging out at the two candy stores. Patterns imitated our old behaviors but on a much-larger scale: cliques formed, groups intermingled, and small pods took walks through the neighborhood to get high. But now the cops stopped by a few times a night, ordering everyone on their way. As they brandished their nightsticks, they tolerated a certain amount of grumbling and even some mild heckling. We got to know them by first name. They never hit anyone, very rarely had to bust someone who was out of control.

The first time I saw her, it was out of the corner of my eye. She was on the fringe of the crowd, talking to a few girls, one of whom I knew. She did not stand out in a physical way: she was average height, maybe five foot four, a little on the skinny side, nothing prominent about her body at all. But she had the cutest Irish face. Her cheeks were rounded, naturally but only slightly flushed, and her face was framed by flowing red hair that she would toss back when it fell in front of her eyes.

Above all else, I was captured by her laughter. Across the din, I could pick it out. She had a genuine and happy cackle, and she would throw her head back and roar when something struck her as particularly funny. Her whole face retained the smile for minutes after each laugh. As I stared at her, her eyes caught mine, but I turned away. When I turned back, she was still looking at me, trying to confirm that I was seeking her out. She smiled, but then was distracted back into her conversation.

I asked Adam, "Who's that?"

"That's Cheryl."

"From where?"

"Glen Oaks. She's friends with Sarah and Lynn and those people. They all go to Van Buren."

A week went by, and there was a much smaller crowd at Schneid's, but both Kathy and Adam were there, and they came over to me. "Wanna go to a party?" Kathy asked.

"Whose?"

"Sarah Levinson."

Adam added, "Cheryl will be there."

And Kathy teasingly said, "She thinks you're cute."

"What?" I said, my heart skipping even as I pretended indifference.

"She thinks you're cute. She was asking me about you. She'd like to meet you."

"Are you shitting me?"

Adam laughed and walked away, shaking his head, but Kathy feigned offense. "*No!* Would I do that?"

"No, no you wouldn't," I said. "Sorry. Can anybody go to this party?"

"Well, I'm invited, and I'm inviting you and Adam. It'll be fine."

It was one of the larger two-bedrooms in Grand Central Apartments, just north of Glen Oaks off Little Neck Parkway.

The party was intimate, maybe a dozen or so people in the living room and kitchen, the parents obviously not home. I met Sarah, and she said coyly, as if she had a secret, "I know someone who wants to meet you."

I'd looked around but hadn't seen Cheryl. "Oh?"

"She's in my bedroom."

The color must have drained from my face as I raised my eyebrow and scrunched up my cheek as if to say, "Excuse me?"

"Don't be scared," Sarah absolutely giggled. "We've been teasing her, and she doesn't want this to be a spectacle, so she asked me to bring you back to introduce you."

I took a deep breath and said fine. She actually took me by the hand, which was already quite sweaty, and led me down the hallway. The single overhead light was missing a fixture, and the bulb was just glaring. It could have been a hospital corridor. I could hear a few *woo-hoo*s from the living room. Uncomfortable at being on show, I now had a better understanding of the spectacle comment.

Cheryl was sitting on the bed, next to a pile of jackets. She was drinking a soda or something and turning crimson, blushing from embarrassment, gaining the color that I was losing. Sarah did the formal introduction: "Cheryl, Davey. Davey, Cheryl."

We clumsily shook hands. Sarah left, dramatically closing the bedroom door behind her as she took one last look at us over her shoulder, a huge smile on her face.

I sat down next to her on the bed, and we talked for an hour. She leaned back on the coats, and I leaned on my elbow on the bed. We were close, less than a foot apart, but not touching. She rewarded me with her brilliant laugh a few times, and I was feeling comfortable when there was a knock on the door, and Sarah called, "Everything okay in there?" Cheryl called back, "Don't come in; we're not dressed," and laughed uproariously.

After a moment's hesitation, Sarah could not help herself, and she burst in to see, giggled mischievously as if she were quite aware that Cheryl was kidding, but with just a hint of disappointment in her eyes. "My parents are going to be home in an hour, and I have to clean up. Everyone has to go."

I walked Cheryl home, stopping in the shadows outside her apartment. She explained to me which room was her and her sister's, which was her parents'. I put my arm around her, and she melted into my embrace. We kissed, lightly at first, and then openmouthed and deeply. She kept her eyes closed and lingered, a slight content smile on her face. I tasted the stale remnants of cigarette.

Our relationship developed fast. I became content to spend all my free time with her. We smoked pot occasionally, drank a few beers less often. Both made her even sillier than usual, stimulating her marvelous sense of humor. She counterbalanced my dark and anxious side with an unbridled optimism. She visibly brightened when she saw me, and her attitude was often contagious. I was delighted to be with her. Our sexual relationship progressed slowly. We liked kissing and could do so for hours. We avoided intercourse. This was my doing. Cheryl had adopted a conversation style that included the phrase, "when we get married." She had reached this conclusion on her own, with no encouragement from me. But whenever we got too hot, I backed off. I knew that if I got her pregnant, I'd marry her. This was fine with her; she was ready. I was not. She became too clingy, too dependent. She was radiant in her love for me, and I began to take her for granted. I wanted to control her, and I grew mean and nasty when I couldn't.

We fought incessantly about her smoking. I had become an avid antismoker, disdaining the smell of it, abhorring the taste of it, and routinely judging people who smoked as weak willed and self-destructive. I gave no acknowledgment or consideration to the claims of physical dependence and addiction. I viewed each puff as a conscious and independent choice that the smoker could refuse if she chose to. I completely ignored or refuted the comparison to pot. She would lie and tell me that she quit, that she hadn't had a cigarette in a week. Then I would kiss her, and I would taste it, and I would absolutely disrespect her, spitting on the ground, calling her a liar, calling her *stupid*, the biggest possible blow of all.

Despite my emotional abuse, she remained loyal and devoted. She promised to do better. I, too, was erratic. For her birthday, I took her to an Italian restaurant in the city that I'd heard about. I made reservations weeks in advance, and we dressed up, me in a jacket and tie. As we sat down, my ignorance betrayed me. Not only were the menus in Italian, there were no prices listed. I was frightened that I might not have enough money. As I was too embarrassed to ask questions, I ordered the only word I understood: lasagna. Unlike my mother's lasagna, which was layered with fat and wide noodles, this came in a bowl and had the consistency of soup. But it was delicious, and we had some wine and laughed and managed to pay the bill with no problem.

I loved to plan outings and bought tickets for Ringling Bros. and Barnum & Bailey Circus months in advance, securing seats in the front row, center ring. I bought ups—black beauties—for the occasion, scoring them from Pauly at two dollars each. They were tiny black capsules filled with twenty milligrams of biphetamine. We swallowed them on the subway platform in Jamaica, and they hit us about an hour later, just as we went through the turnstile into Madison Square Garden. They stimulated our minds, and we were racing through conversations. We babbled relentlessly, barely glancing at the clowns, elephants, and black panthers that were performing just a few feet in front of us. The circus served only as a backdrop, a pleasant and momentary series of diversions to our conversation. We were equals as we made each other laugh in turn.

We talked about the power of our generation, whether or not we were changing the culture or whether the mainstream was making minor adjustments to absorb this so-called counterculture. She believed that we were a massive force.

I disagreed. "The counterculture's awareness of the disease of society offers no illusion of hope. Instead of making any attempts at 'countering,' we have decided that this is too difficult because it involves personal sacrifice, not only of time and physical effort, but of money. Our reluctance to commit, to prefer to spend our money on drugs and entertainment, demonstrates that our values really aren't so different after all."

Time raced; the hours passed like minutes. When the show ended, we mechanically got up and followed the crowd out and made our way to Times Square, where we continued to talk, sitting on a city bench, watching the traffic dwindle. We got much more serious, talking about God, organized religion, heaven, and hell. She asked me what time it was, and I answered, "Time is an illusion, created by man. It does not exist. Past and present do not exist. Each moment should be given equal respect because it is unique."

"That's all well and good, you jerk," she said, laughing and tossing her hair back. "Let me look at your watch." It was two o'clock in the morning, and we headed for the subway. Virtually alone on the platform, we waited almost an hour. We felt a bit

desolate and huddled on the lone bench, our conversation focused on getting home. We had begun to crash. After the train,
we rode the bus; tiredly watching the stores pass by, our reflec-
tions in the windows a reminder of the hollowness and transpar-
ency of my thoughts. We had finally run out of things to say.
I kissed her good night and walked the couple of miles home,
going along Little Neck Parkway. Dawn was breaking as I got
home, and my father was just getting up. "How was the circus?"
he said, and I was surprised. I had lost the idea that it was the
circus I had gone out for, just a little over twelve hours earlier.

22

Adam had been surfing for a few months before he convinced me to try it. I borrowed a board and wet suit from Richie Nolan. Long Beach was a collection of aging, decrepit hotels, complete with peeling paint and broken windows through which could be seen torn and sun-bleached curtains. The area had attracted a number of transients and former mental patients. The state of New York had redefined the regulatory authority that had been keeping a lot of people hospitalized against their will. When released, many of them returned to the streets. To address this, the state had bought a number of failed hotels and converted them to subsidized halfway homes. The buildings were surrounded by trash: Styrofoam cups and fast-food wrappers continuously blown around by the ocean breezes.

This being early spring, both the air and the water were cold—a dreary day, overcast with dark, billowy clouds, about fifty-five degrees. The wind was blowing hard, cutting right through us, but bringing the surf up. The ocean was ominous, a darker and deeper green than the "pickle," my nine-foot board.

The darkness brought the horizon in, and the water and the sky met as if they were being sucked into a black hole.

Adam and I suited up and entered the water together. He had bought a brand-new board: short, only about six feet, and much lighter than mine. We both paddled out about ten yards from shore, where the waves were breaking. He taught me how to lie on the board, use my arms to prop up the front half of my body and look for the right wave, then start paddling in advance of it until it was about even with the middle of the board. I would then have to grab each side and hop up, balancing the board while I stood up and spread my feet apart to be able to lean and steer.

He started getting up and getting rides. I was getting up, but falling right off. "You're jumping up too soon," he said. I tried waiting until the waves were farther along, but then I was missing them completely. He taught me how to sit on the board and rest. I liked this part.

I kept trying, kept getting rides that were mere fractions of the rides he was enjoying. I was growing tired. This board was too big for me. I felt I was not gaining enough speed from paddling. My legs were frozen. My face was numb. I began to get a headache. This was fun?

Adam paddled over. "How're you doing?"

"Not as good as you. I'm afraid this board's too heavy for me." He offered to trade. We slid off our boards and switched. I did a little better on his board, and he did slightly better on the pickle than I had. I finally rode almost all the way to shore. When I paddled back out to him, I had a big smile on my face: I could do this. This was fun. My legs were still frozen, my face was still numb, and my headache was beginning to pound, but I didn't care.

"Okay, let's switch back," he said, "You just need some practice on this board; you'll do fine." We surfed for a while longer, but I did not do fine. He continued to get good rides, and I continued to struggle with getting up and staying up on a board that barely moved after I hopped up. Adam paddled over to me again. My head was exploding. I hoped he was going to say, "Let's go," but instead he said, "Look at how they're breaking farther out." I sat up and looked out to sea, trying to avoid the dark abyss in the distance. He was right. There must have been some kind of sandbar, and the waves that were breaking on it looked bigger than the second break on shore.

"Let's try out there," he suggested. Without waiting for an answer he began to paddle, his feet leaving a tiny white wake as he headed out to sea. I followed, out past the sandbar, and the waves were indeed breaking better. Unfortunately, I was scared. Shore now looked like it was a half mile away. With each wave that washed over me, I felt like my head was going to detonate. I could feel my temples with each heartbeat. Was I going to have a stroke or something? *God*, I thought, *at least try to ride a wave*. I sat up on the board, tried to still my aching head for a moment, and watched the steady pulse of the sea. Adam had just caught a wave that took him halfway to shore. I saw a beauty coming; it must have been six feet high. I lay prone on the board, waited till the wave was about ten feet away, craning my neck to assure I was following the same crest and started paddling like crazy, determined to get this board going fast enough to catch this wave. Just as the wave touched my feet and started to lift my board I felt an excruciating pain: a sharp, searing blast with instant radiation down my arm. I recognized it right away: My shoulder was out; I had dislocated it again.

Reaching with my right hand across the board to try to somehow grab my shoulder just as the wave broke over me, I slipped off the board into the water. The board rose and drifted away, as the wave, undisturbed, continued into shore. The board was now about four feet away, and another big wave was on the way in. I paddled with my good arm, pulling myself toward the board and was able to reach out and grab it just before the next wave hit. I held onto the fin while the wave went over me. I pulled the board closer to me and struggled to try to get on it. Another wave came, and I held the board from the side, my body leaning over it and my head resting on it. For a moment, I just felt the pain and lived in the pain, wondering which was worse, my throbbing head or my dislocated shoulder, each symbiotically feeding the other.

After just a few seconds of feeling sorry for myself the thought occurred to me that I could die out here: a wave could separate me from the board, and I would not be able to swim. I would either be drowned or driven into the rocks and smashed to death. The vision of my mother grieving over my battered and broken body helped motivate me to fight. I managed to pull my full body onto the board and even to sit up just a little and start to scream for Adam. He could not hear me. He was too far away. I tried to paddle with my right hand, but made no progress and only increased the risk that I was going to fall off the board again. I looked past the waves to where the sea flattened to a dark plane and saw lightning out on the horizon. *Great*, I thought, laughing to myself through tears that began to well up, *a thunderstorm. Maybe I'll just get hit by lightning and die that way.*

I leaned up again. Adam was paddling in my direction, having completed a ride. I waved frantically, motioning him to me. He seemed to understand. I lay back down and just held onto the board. After a few minutes I looked up, and Adam was now closer but had repositioned himself to wait for another ride. He did not understand. I tried screaming his name again, and this time he heard me. He sat up on his board and put his hand to his ear, cupping it as if indicating that he wanted to hear me.

I used every last ounce of my energy to scream as loud as I could. I lay back down on the board, wrapped my right arm around it, and made a failed attempt to move my left arm, but it truly was dislocated, and I couldn't. I put my head down on the board, closed my eyes, felt the hammering in my head, and prayed, "Dear God, please don't let me die; don't do this to Mommy."

I was so sure that my head was going to burst that I became less consciously aware of the terrible pain in my shoulder. I just held on and rocked, afraid that with each wave something was going to happen. I felt something bump me and I was afraid that I had drifted into the rocks. I picked up my head, expecting to see the worst, but instead I saw the tip of Adam's board. He had heard the distress in my voice, though he could not make out the words. He had paddled out to ask me, "Are you all right?"

"No," I could barely speak, but I added, "I threw out my shoulder; I can't paddle."

"Okay," he took charge. "Just hold on, I'll get you in." With a determined and steely look on his face, he maneuvered his board next to mine, and grabbed the front of my board. His paddling was slow, but steady. I lay my head down and closed my eyes, willing the thumping in my head to ease, calming myself with the relief that I was going to live through this.

It got a little hairy when we hit the breakers again, but he never let go. By the time we got close to shore, I was mentally and physically exhausted. I was numb all over: I had gone to

some place beyond pain and didn't care about it anymore. I just
wanted to live. If I could just keep breathing in and out, I would
eventually be okay. I silently thanked God for sparing Mom.

When we got to shallow water, Adam asked me, "Can you
get up?"

"I think so." I slid off the board and knelt in the shallow
water. Movement brought the pain in my shoulder back to life,
and I reached over with my right hand and held my left triceps,
pulling that arm close to the body, shrinking the visible depression in my shoulder. Adam helped me to the sand, retrieved the
boards, sat me down, and looked around.

There was no one else on the beach, and the storm clouds
were growing darker and closer, the thunder audible now. He
said, "I'm going to go call for help." He jogged up the beach toward a building that was just a few hundred yards away, right off
the boardwalk. I just hung my head down and tried once again
to still the pulsating throbs that kept exploding through my head
with each beat of my heart. I began to shiver. I was freezing. The
fifteen minutes or so that he was gone felt like hours, but I was
encouraged to see him coming back with two other people, one
of whom was carrying a blanket, which they quickly wrapped
around me. The look on the stranger's face when she saw me
was frightening. I must have looked pretty bad. The warmth of
the blanket provided some instant comfort, and almost immediately after they arrived I heard the siren. I imagined that it was
an ambulance coming for me, but in fact, the first arrival was a
police jeep that came right out on to the sand and drove straight
up to us.

The cop was straightforward. "The ambulance would get
stuck in the sand. I'll move you to the parking lot." I realized
then that there was another siren approaching. The cop and

Adam helped me up, and for the first time I saw that a crowd was gathering. I was the center of attention, but I looked at everyone as if through an otherworldly haze, as if they were watching me from a distance, even though they were just a feet away. The cop helped me into the back seat of his jeep, left the door open, and very slowly drove along the sand to the parking lot. By the time we reached it, the ambulance had arrived, and the EMS crew was bringing the gurney out.

"Where's Adam?" I asked when they started to close the ambulance door.

He came over, still as calm as could be. "I'm going to get the boards on the car, and then I'll call your parents and meet you at the hospital."

The cop leaned over and said, "We'll call your parents and help your friend; don't worry." They put the siren on as we left the parking lot, and I watched the crowd disperse through the back window.

Long Beach Medical Center was only a few minutes away, but upon arrival they informed me that they could not do anything until my parents got there. "But I'm over eighteen," I said.

"That's fine," the ER doc said. "Your parents should be here soon."

I found this unacceptable and began to plead. "Please, I need something for the pain." Fortunately, he could see that I did and ignored whatever the risk was and gave me a shot of Demerol. It eased the pressure in my head within minutes. They put me in one of the curtained areas and began to cut my wet suit off. Then they cut my T-shirt off and sent me to X-ray. The technician was sympathetic as she pressed my aching shoulder up against the cold film plate.

By the time I got back from X-ray, Adam and my parents were there. The sight of them brought me instant comfort but also let me drop my guard, and I cried a little. "It hurts so much," I said. I turned to Adam. "You saved my life, man."

"You'd do the same for me."

I nodded. "Still, you saved my life."

When the doc learned that this was the second dislocation of my left shoulder, he gave me the drill. "Did the first doctor tell you of the reoccurrence probability?"

"Yes," my mother and I said at the same time.

"Well, now that you've done it a second time, there is a 95 percent chance that you will do it again. But I still believe in doing everything we can to give it an opportunity to heal. Part of that is how I reduce it. What did they do the first time?" I recounted the scene at Long Island Jewish, foot up against the gurney and all.

He smiled. "That's one way. I'd like to try something a little different." He explained to us that it would be a little slower and maybe just a little more painful. "But," he added, "it is less traumatic and might allow for healing." We agreed to let him do it his way without asking for more detail. The Demerol had been effective in calming my headache and my shoulder pain. What the hell did I care?

He laid me face down on the gurney and had me hang my left arm off the side. Then he hung a silver pail, the kind they must use to mop the floors with, on my arm and slowly filled it with water. Right from the point that he hung my arm off the gurney I began to feel pain again, but as the weight of the pail increased, so did the pain. This guy was a sadist. The whole process took almost twenty minutes, as the increasing weight ever so slowly pulled my arm back into its socket.

When it looked good to him, he sent me back to X-ray for confirmation. Then he put a cast around me, immobilizing my arm against my chest. The cast went around my whole upper torso, but kept a slit for my hand to stick out of. As it hardened this cast felt like a suit of armor and looked ridiculous.

The doctor said I should not need any more pain meds and sent me home, wishing me good luck. The storm had come and gone while we were in the ER. Everything was refreshingly wet, and the sun was coming back out.

23

The news had been expected, and though completely predictable, it was devastating nonetheless: within a month after graduating from Saint Johns, Brian received his draft notice. In six weeks, he would be inducted into the army. Mom took the news harder than he did. Pop didn't understand her reaction. Proud of his service during World War II, he would now be proud to have one of his sons go and defend his country.

Brian was stoic, neither excited nor scared. It was just something he had to do. The only way to fight it at this point would be to try to go the conscientious-objector route, maybe wind up serving the two years doing community service. Mom urged this, but he was not interested. Nor would he consider "running away" to Canada and "hiding out" with the other draft dodgers. He did not want to be known as a coward.

No, he would go. Kevin and I decided to give him a big send-off, treating him to a weekend in Lake George. We invited Don, Joe, Berk, and Adam. I left Vinny out, unsure how he would act.

I had been in the cast for six weeks, sometimes hiding it beneath a large T-shirt. Often, though, the cast was all I wore on my upper body. I went back to the doc's office in Long Beach, and he cut the monstrous thing off with a small circular saw, white plaster dust flying everywhere and settling in my hair. The stench escaping from under my arm was putrid. My first shower in a month was long and hot. My arm had atrophied, but I was happy to be free of the cast.

We drank beer all the way up. We listened to the Beatles' "Hey Jude," which had just been released, over and over again on station after station. By the time we got to the Wee White House, a somewhat sleazy motel several miles out of town, we were drunk, arguing about what the line "The movement you need is on your shoulder" was supposed to mean. After checking into the sparse room, we sat in a circle, outside on the grass, and played a drinking game. We counted off, person by person. When it was your turn, if the previous number ended in a four or was a multiple of four, you were supposed to say "zip" instead of the next number. "One, two, three, zip, five, six, seven, zip." If you messed up, you had to drink a can of beer. We made the rules more and more complicated, reversing direction of the count after every zip and then adding "buzz" to replace sevens or multiple of sevens. We went through several cases of beer. We made a huge tower out of the empty cans and got rambunctious every time someone toppled it. Returning to the room, we knocked over lamps, broke glasses, and vomited in every corner. By morning, the room was completely trashed.

Debilitated by our hangovers, Adam and I decided some grass would help. We hitched into town and saw some longhairs hanging in the park. One freak trusted us and took us to his cottage on the other side of the lake. He didn't have any grass, but he had some great blond hash. He turned us on first, smoking in a hand-carved pipe that he had whittled himself. The bowl was in the shape of a dragon's head, and he called it Smaug, after the dragon from Tolkien's *The Hobbit*. We settled into a mellow high, a mild euphoria. We happily bought a dime each.

We went to a bar, and started drinking again. After a few shots of tequila, I convinced Adam to go to the Osprey with me. I fantasized about meeting Tanya there but learned that her family had sold the motel. Adam and I walked down to the lake, liberated a rowboat, and rowed out to one of the smaller islands. There was only one house on it. On the point of the property, there was a twenty-foot flagpole with an Irish flag on top. I shimmied up and ripped off the flag. Just as I got down, we heard a dog bark, jumped in the rowboat, and got away just in time.

Back home, Pop threw a small going-away party for family and friends the night before Brian had to leave. But Mom stayed in her bedroom and cried the night away. Pop and Brian got good and drunk, and were hungover for the long drive to Fort Dix in New Jersey. Kevin and I took turns driving. The scene was intimidating: armed soldiers heavily guarded the entrance, and we were allowed to accompany Brian only as far as the PX. We said our good-byes and watched him walk across the battlement to the induction center. He turned and waved good-bye one last time. On the quiet drive back home, Kevin drove while Pop lit up a victory cigar.

■ ■ ■

The third time I dislocated my shoulder was in some ways the most frightening. I was standing in the kitchen, talking to Mom, who was making an all-too-rare excursion out of her bedroom. She was mourning Brian as if had died. He had been home briefly after basic training, but then he transferred to Fort Bragg, North Carolina, for infantry drills. He had been home again, just a few weeks before shipping out to 'Nam. Mom had actually encouraged him to desert, flee to Canada, go AWOL, and don't look back. These conversations had always been out of earshot from Pop, who would have been livid had he known what she was suggesting. Brian held to his commitment.

Mom and I were talking about the latest letter from Brian, who always tried to hide the worst from us, but we could read between the lines and knew that he was scared. I stretched my arms over my head while yawning. It was a normal, everyday stretch. My arm popped out, quite easily, without any other force than gravity. It didn't even hurt as much as the first two times.

When I looked with anguish at Mom and said, "My shoulder is out," she did not believe me. Nothing had happened that could have caused it. "Mom, my shoulder is out. I have to go to the hospital." Kevin drove us to Long Island Jewish.

We went through the routine: a shot of pain-killer and an X-ray confirmation of diagnosis, then back to the ER. What method was doc number three going to try? But doc number three had seen recurring dislocating shoulders before. He had me stand next to the gurney and grab the other side of it with my right hand, and then he took my left shoulder and yanked before I was even ready. He reduced it without much pain, certainly without much effort.

He then proceeded to tell me that now it was a 99 percent chance that it would dislocate again, most probably on a chronic, ongoing basis whenever I lifted my arm above my head. He outlined three options: 1) try to go through life without ever lifting my arm above my head—highly unlikely and not reasonable; 2) learn how to reduce it myself—in fact, there was a significant percentage of chronic dislocaters who chose this alternative; or 3) have surgery to repair the damage, his recommendation. "Is it guaranteed not to dislocate again if he has the surgery?" Mom wanted to know.

"No guarantees in medicine, but most likely this fixes it."

He put my arm in a sling, saying I could take it off in a day or two; that it wasn't really going to do me any good. I lived in anxiety, learning how to dress myself, take a shower and retrieve a book from a shelf without putting my arm above my head. Yet I knew this was ridiculous. I would never be able to play softball or go swimming? This was unacceptable, and I told Mom I wanted the surgery.

She disagreed vehemently. Mom did not trust hospitals—or doctors, for that matter. She associated hospitals with places you go to die. "Learn to live with it," was her suggestion. "Learn to reduce it yourself."

We argued. I insisted and could not understand her resistance. Finally, she played her trump card: "This can keep you out of the army. You'll be 4-F. If they fix it, you might get drafted." She did not want to see a second son going into the army. She worried every waking moment about Brian, spent many an hour in her room, crying. Sympathetic to her pain, I found this argument persuasive, but not convincing. I finally told her that I thought she was being unfair by projecting her fears onto me. "This is my life, my risk. I'm the one feeling the pain. I'm the one who could be drafted and go to Vietnam." Finally, I wore her out.

The orthopedist's office was in Bayside, and I went there alone. Mom wanted to come, but I felt a little old to need my mother. The doctor took his own X-rays, did a thorough exam, reviewed the history, and absolutely agreed that surgery was the answer. We scheduled it for the following Monday. When I got home and told Mom, she went to pieces and started crying. She retreated to her bedroom and wept for the next hour. She had thought she'd be in on the decision. She had hoped that the doctor might suggest another alternative. She was terrified that I was making a mistake and would get drafted and killed. We had the same argument over and over again.

Pop came home from work and joined in, apparently taking my side. "It's his life, and it's his decision. There's nothing wrong with going in the army. Aren't you proud of Brian?"

She exploded, pulled at her hair, yelled at him, "No, no, I'm not 'proud' of him. I'm scared for him. I'm scared of losing him." She was crying inconsolably.

"Enough!" I yelled. "Enough already!" I turned to Mom. "You don't have to worry. I'm not going to Vietnam. I'm not going to get drafted. I'll go to Canada first."

"The hell you will," Pop said. "No son of mine is going to take the traitor's way out."

"You can't stop me, Pop. I'm against the war. I'm against Nixon. I think it's wrong, and I won't be part of it. I'm against killing, and I won't learn how to do it. I'll go to Canada. I swear I will, with or without your blessing."

They were both equally stunned. I took a deep breath, went to my room, and closed the door. I turned my stereo on, but even The Beatles could not pull me from myself. "Half of what I say is meaning less." I thought about Brian, thought about the war. I was afraid of the surgery, afraid of being hospitalized. I did not want to get drafted, did not want to have to move to Canada. I weighed the situation over and over again. I was nineteen. I was active. I hated the pain of dislocation; I was terrified of the concept of having it become a routine that I would then reduce myself. I promised myself I'd go through with the surgery.

I was admitted on Sunday afternoon. Flushing Hospital was old and run-down. Nondescript red brick, it blended into the neighborhood and could have passed for another apartment building. The parking lot was typical Queens: paved over and littered with trash and broken glass. Looking up at the building, I noticed that many of the windows were open, and there were no screens. Surgical-scrub-blue curtains could be seen fluttering in the light breeze.

This was a far cry from Long Island Jewish. Admission took two hours. I was shocked when they wheeled me into a ward with ten beds. I had not readied myself for this, had not thought about it much, but I had imagined either a private or semiprivate room. The long room had a double-door entrance and two long rows of five beds on each side. There were two windows on the right side of the room and two on the back wall. The left side of the room was a soiled and faded wall that may have once been white. Although there were three empty beds, it was clear that only one of them was available, as the other two had personal belongings around them. Each bed came with a small night-stand and a chair next to it. The chairs looked like remainders from a kitchen fire. The nightstands, about three feet tall, with three drawers in them, were on wheels and were badly in need of stain.

The nurse took me to the one bathroom in the corner and told me to put on the hospital gown, opened to the back. I got it on but could not for the life of me tie it. I came out and asked her to tie it and she did so and then took me by the elbow to the bed and ordered me to get into it. As she left, Mom sat on the rickety chair, and Pop borrowed the one from the bed next to us. In this bed was an unconscious man whose face was black and red, so swollen that one eye was shut. "He won't miss this." My father chuckled, trying to be lighthearted. My mother glared at him.

The dietician stopped in to inform me that I would get for dinner whatever the previous occupant had ordered. It was too late for me to order anything.

"What happened to the previous occupant?" I asked.

"He passed away last night," she said, validating my mother's worst fears.

The dietician saw the horror in my face and added, "Don't worry. The mattress was fumigated, and the linen has been changed. It's okay." I was not comforted. All I could think of was that I would be eating the dead guy's food. "You're going into surgery first thing in the morning, so no breakfast," she continued without really missing a beat. "You'll still be out of it when you wake up, so no lunch, and they'll want you on clear liqs for dinner. I'll come around tomorrow afternoon, and we'll see about Tuesday's meals; you'll have some choices."

The anesthesiologist then confirmed that I had no known allergies. He explained to me what would happen in the morning: "They'll wake you up about five and give you a pill. Then at six they'll give you a shot. By the time they bring you to me at six thirty, you'll barely be awake. I will put an IV in your arm, and you will fall asleep. Then I will put a tube down your throat for the duration of the surgery. When you wake up your throat will hurt. For a few days. Also, you will feel nauseated and might vomit. Many people do; it's normal. Any questions?"

I had none, but Mom asked, "How long is the operation?"

"Three or four hours."

She moaned.

Finally, about eight o'clock, my orthopedist came. He asked me whether or not the anesthesiologist had visited me and if I understood what he had told me. He then described the surgery, which interested me and Pop, but Mom had to take a walk and smoke a cigarette after the first few sentences.

"I am using a new technique, one that will cause less scarring. It was invented by the Russians and is just starting to be used here, but it has been used extensively over there." He took his finger and drew a line from the topmost point where my arm met my shoulder to just under my armpit. "The incision will only be about three inches. It used to be almost six inches in this type of surgery. But it will be deep, and I will peel back the top layers of skin and muscle. There is a bunch of tendons and ligaments in there that must be flexible enough to allow your arm to move, and strong enough to allow your muscles to lift, but secure enough to keep your arm in place. The first time you dislocated your arm, it took force to push it out, and this force caused those tendons and ligaments to stretch. We always hope they will retract and heal and rebuild, but they rarely do. Now that you have dislocated several times, they are so stretched out that they have no tensile strength at all; they are as weak as rubber bands. What I am going to do is cut them. I am going to cut several inches out of the middle of each one and then pull the ends together and tie them. I will fold the layers of muscle and skin back over each other. But I am going to lay a wire along the incision point and fold the layers over it. This is the part the Russians invented. It works better than stitches and leaves a smaller scar. The wire helps the muscles and layers of skin to bind and heal, and we tape the top layer with a special strong adhesive tape to hold it all together. In a few weeks, assuming it has all healed well, we just remove the wire."

This last part confused me. "Um, how do you 'remove' the wire? Do you have to cut me open again?"

"No, that's the beauty of it. You will see about a half inch of wire sticking out from both the top and the bottom of the incision. We take the tape off and then just pull the wire out. It hurts a tiny bit as it breaks the scabs, but it feels no worse than a splinter."

Mom came back, but it was eight thirty now, and the nurses were telling all visitors to leave. Mom was crying as she kissed me, and I felt sorry for her, but I was ready to do this. I put my radio on low and listened to the new progressive-rock station, WNEW-FM. Compared to AM radio, the DJs were mellow and played songs from albums, not just the same dozen songs over and over again. After ten o'clock, the Night Bird, Allison Steele, came on. Her deep and scratchy voice was ever so sensual as she told stories and read poetry in between songs. Even her introductions to commercials were interesting. She played some great music: Jefferson Airplane, the Who, and the Doors. The nurse told me that I had to keep it very low, but I could keep it on unless someone complained.

Well, the guy next to me was still unconscious, and the guy on the other side had come back from surgery and had multiple casts on. He had been in a car accident. There were only a few other presurgery admissions on the ward, and they were all down on the far side of the room. I did get up and walk down there to look out the window. The street was quiet, and the outside seemed like a world apart. I imagined myself as a prisoner, unable to escape. I thought of what it would be like to jump from this fourth floor window, whether it would kill me or just break my legs. I chatted a little with the patients at that end, listened to their upcoming surgery stories. It was midnight now, and I tried to sleep, but as the night wore on the elderly man across from me began to go bad. He had been semiconscious most of the evening, even when his wife had come in and given him a sponge bath. He had IVs in both arms, oxygen in his nostrils, and a tube down his throat. His moaning got to me to the point where I pressed my nurse's call button. It took her just a few minutes to respond. "What is it?" she said.

I pointed. "He doesn't seem to be doing well; he keeps moaning loudly."

She smiled at me, pleased, I guess, that I had rung the bell for someone else's good. She went over to his bed and asked him if the pain was getting worse. He was barely able to nod his head yes. "Do you want me to increase your pain med?" Again, he nodded. "I'll have to get a doctor's order; I'll be right back." She was gone no less than five minutes, and she returned with a hypodermic, which she proceeded to inject, not into him, but into his IV bag. She placed her hand on his forehead, took his pulse, and told him to try to rest.

She came over to me and told me that it was nice, what I had done. I asked her what was wrong with him. "Cancer," was her one word response, but the look on her face told me it was terminal. I shuddered as I remembered my mother's mantra: people go to the hospital to die.

Next to the cancer patient was the most interesting man on the ward. An elderly, gray-haired black man, he had been asleep most of the day. He was, moreover, restrained. His arms were tied to the sides of the bed. He had one-inch gauze wrapped around his wrists and then wrapped around the bed rails. He was drunk, the nurse told me, and had been drunk for days before they brought him in. He was belligerent at first, fighting the nurses, saying that he did not want to be there and then ordering people to bring him a drink. "They restrained him for his own good."

Well, he woke up about two in the morning. "I gotta pee," he yelled. "I gotta pee."

The nurse came in but had no sympathy. "You've already wet yourself," she said, as if he should just keep doing so.

"I gotta pee; please let me pee."

She gave him a urinal, putting it between his legs, propping it up at an angle and slipping his penis into it. "Go ahead and pee," she said as she turned to leave the ward.

"*Please*, please let me pee in the toilet," he begged.

She stopped and reluctantly came back. "Are you going to behave yourself?"

"A course I goin' to behave meself; I jest got to pass me water."

With a heavy sigh, she began to undo his restraints then went into the hall and called for an attendant to help her. The attendant was a rotund black man about thirty years old who must have weighed in at 240 pounds. She now felt safer undoing the restraints. The two of them backed away from the bed, and she said, "Okay, go pee."

He got out of the bed and immediately fell to the floor, dragging the nightstand over as he did so, trying to break his fall but failing miserably. Silently, the nurse went over to him and then admonished herself: "This is what I get for trying to be nice." She and the attendant each took one of his arms and lifted him up and sort of dragged him to the bathroom. The attendant went into the bathroom with him, but they both came out in a few minutes. "How'd it go?" the nurse asked.

Disgusted, the attendant said, "He sprayed everywhere except in the bowl, but I was not going to hold it for him; I'd rather clean it up." They got the guy back in bed, and the nurse went to restrain him again, but he pleaded and cried, "Please don't tie me down…it hurts; I be good, I promise."

She took pity on him. "You better not make me regret this."

"I won't. Thank you. *God bless you,*" he called out. He had a silly, drunken grin on his face as he fell back to sleep. The attendant kept the bright light on and the bathroom door open as he noisily cleaned up the mess, muttering out loud to himself, "Goddamn drunken no-good nigger. Is this a drunk tank or a hospital, motherfucker?" until the nurse came back and told him to hush. He glared at her as she left then began his muttering again, but at a lower decibel level so that it just sounded like gibberish to me.

Once again, I closed my eyes, realized it was too hot to sleep—it must have been seventy-five or eighty degrees—and lay there sweating. Even the Night Bird had signed off at two. The air was filled with some talk-show host babbling on about the body counts in 'Nam being overinflated. I finally drifted into an early stage of uneasy sleep, half dreaming but half-conscious when I was startled, along with the rest of the ward if not the whole hospital, by the antics of the elderly drunk.

He had decided he needed to pee again and had gotten up in the bed by himself. He was standing in the bed and must have thought he could walk to the bathroom, because when he looked down at the end of the bed, he saw his food-cart tray and probably assumed this was the floor. He stepped onto the cart, and it went rolling out from under him. He sailed up in the air, landed on the cart, knocked it over, and then everything came crashing down around him. He was rolling on the floor, unleashing a steady stream of cursing.

Both the nurse and the attendant came running back in, looked at the situation, and joined in his litany of curses. Then they picked him up, dragged him back to bed, and tied him down again. "I gotta pee," the drunk yelled again. The nurse grabbed the urinal and roughly picked up the guy's penis and stuck it in the urinal. "Pee in here!" After she left, I could her him tinkling in the urinal, and then he started crying and sobbed himself back to sleep.

I had gotten no more than an hour's sleep when they came to wake me at five. I was certainly groggy enough when they lifted me onto the gurney, strapped me down, and rolled me down the hallway. The overhead lights were piercing. I recognized the anesthesiologist, though all that was showing were his eyes. I felt a little stick as he started one IV, then another. My surgeon showed up and said, incongruously, "Good morning." He used some kind of a marker to draw a line on my shoulder where he was going to make the first cut. "I'll start with a number twenty scalpel but switch to a five after I get in..." I listened with rapt attention, disassociated from the reality of what was about to happen to me. Classically, the last thing I remember was the anesthesiologist putting the mask over my face and telling me to count backward from a hundred.

■ ■ ■

I was at some level of consciousness but was unsure how to think. I had no idea where I was or what had happened to me. I felt extremely tired, as if sludge were moving through my veins. I was aware of my throat and how much it hurt and how parched I was. I struggled to a higher level of awareness, slowly, deliberately. I was able to open my eyes, but the light immediately blinded me.

A nurse noticed and came right to my side and began checking my IV. "You're okay," she said kindly. "You're in the ICU. The operation is over, and it was a complete success." I had absolutely no idea what the hell she was talking about, nor did I care.

"Water," I cracked out of my painful windpipe. I saw her check the chart that was hanging by the foot of my bed. She then got a paper cup, one of those small cone-shaped ones that come from the dispenser hanging next to a water cooler, and brought it over to me. She lifted my head up with one hand, tilting it slightly, and angled the paper cup to my lips. I was able to sip, but it made my lips hurt. I started to put my head back down but then lifted it again and whispered, "One more."

Back on the ward, they transferred me to my bed. My mother and Cheryl were there. I looked at them and said, "Make the pain stop." My entire chest hurt. I felt like I was being stabbed in multiple places at once. My entire being was pain. I knew who they were, but I did not know how they could just stand there while I was in such pain. Tears came to my eyes, and I said again, "Please make the pain stop. I feel like the pain is never going to go away. It's going to hurt for the rest of my life."

I quickly grew to crave the morphine, which brought relief within minutes. The pain stayed away for around two hours. At the three-hour mark, the pain started to get uncomfortable. They made me wait until I begged for it at the four-hour mark, and then they brought me relief again. When the needle entered, the psychological fix kicked in, and the pain subsided from its peak just from the knowledge that the magical elixir was on the way. The morphine did not just ease the physical pain; it erased the emotional worries, epitomizing the word "euphoria." This went on for two days.

I got to know the other patients. The drunk finally sobered up and did not understand why his daughter was so upset. They'd just told her that he had cirrhosis of the liver. The elderly wife of the cancer patient befriended me. He was on continuous morphine now. A retired registered nurse, she liked to do a lot of the care herself. She saw that I was a ball of sweat and offered to give me a sponge bath, and much to my own surprise, I found myself saying yes. The cool water felt like salvation. I was relieved when she told me to do my own private parts. She even pulled the curtain and turned her back. She talked a lot, and I just listened. She didn't know what she was going to do without him, but the pain that he was in devastated her. He passed away in the middle of the next night. I missed her company. Above all, I wanted to go home. I had to get off the morphine first, so I started to push the limit on tolerance: six hours, then eight, then finally I could live without it.

24

The best therapy for my arm, the way to build up strength again and prevent further atrophy, was swimming. Kevin had gotten together with Joe Stayer and rented a house in Hampton Bays. They were going to use it mostly on weekends, and Kevin said I could stay with them and use it during the week as well. I would be able to swim every day.

I scored some pot, threw all my shorts, swimming suits, and a bunch of T-shirts into a duffel bag, and headed east. The beach house was modest, consisting of a kitchen, a single bedroom, and a bathroom. Right off Montauk Highway, set back in some pine scrubs, it was secluded and landlocked. This was not the Hamptons of the Manhattan jet set, though their turf in Southampton was just minutes away. Weekends were a continuous party. Kevin and Joe, along with Joan and Pamela, their respective girlfriends, claimed the two double beds. No one else was welcome in the bedroom. All others would have to crash on the kitchen floor, which could hold a half dozen or so people wall to wall in sleeping bags. Any overflow could sleep outside under the stars.

Pot flowed freely. We smoked for breakfast and stayed stoned for the rest of the day. We drove to the beach, swam, sunned for the afternoon, and returned by dark. The shower was reserved for the couples paying the rent. The rest of us used the hose in the yard. Even so, we shared the toilet and on a regular basis overwhelmed the septic tank. Every other week or so, we had to call to have it pumped out. The father-and-son team who came to service it were from some other part of the island. Large black men, they each worked with cigar stubs in their mouths, which they would relight after getting the pump going. Dressed in blue overalls with no shirts, they had become immune to the stench that permeated the yard whenever they pried off the tank's cover. Each time, the father told us the same thing: "This here tank is made for a small house, it only 'pects one or two people. You hippies are too many." Each time, he accepted the beer we offered and never delivered on his threats to tell the landlord just how many people were staying here.

In the evening, we'd make a coal bed in the outdoor barbecue pit and grill burgers and franks, or if it was raining, make a huge pot of spaghetti indoors and everyone would eat together. Joan collected a little of everyone's pot and made some Alice B. Toklas brownies. By dark we were giggling and gaggling, half the time laughing incoherently at our own jokes, relating to each other only in that we occupied the same stupor, wandered around in the same haze.

As usual, music permeated the environment. We discovered new sounds: Julie Driscoll, with Brian Augur and the Trinity, with their organ dominated version of the Doors' "Light My

Fire," the haunting and beautiful lyrics of Laura Nyro. Of course, I'd hate it when Cheryl came out and kept playing Nyro's "Wedding Bell Blues" over and over, singing along with the lyrics, replacing the name "Bill," with "Davey." "Will you marry me, Davey?" she sang, much too seriously. What captivated us the most was the just-released rock opera *Tommy* by the Who, a story about the deaf, dumb, and blind kid who found salvation in pinball. We found the story complicated. We could rarely focus long enough to listen to a whole song, let alone an album side, so that when someone figured out a part of the story, we all became enthralled. But we argued over specific aspects. If something wasn't spelled out clearly and simply, it left room for argument. "His parents kill her lover. No, I think the lover kills the first husband...Cousin Kevin is having sex with him. No, he's just torturing him. Uncle Ernie has sex with him. Nobody has sex with him, they just threaten him. He becomes a prophet. No, you idiot, he becomes a rock star!"

"See me. Feel me. Touch me. Heal me." That's all any of us wanted, really. We knew the answers lay in the lyrics, and we would try to focus and replay a song over and over again, but we would invariably lie on the floor and laugh, sometimes acting out scenes. "Fiddle about, fiddle about!"

Joan's friend Miranda provided unwitting comic relief. Miranda had spent her high school years riding in the front seat of Billy Mackay's GTO. She had been beautiful then, and she had been in love. In the two years since graduation, he had gone on to several other girls. She still carried the torch for him and felt sorry for herself, dreamed of the day that he would come back to her.

She wallowed in the depths with the dregs of the street. One of the few girls to do glue, she'd get her long blond hair tangled in sticky knots. She'd tried heroin but couldn't stand the needle. She found her salvation in "downs," little red bullets. Seconal was prescribed as a sleeping pill, a narcotic depressant that dulled the senses, clouded perceptions, and freed inhibitions. Miranda swallowed them like candy. She'd eat one or two before dinner and have a third like an after-dinner mint. As they'd kick in, she'd want more. We'd try to ration her, knowing that she would never stop, and we grew tired of dealing with the repercussions. She was a walking train wreck. She felt no pain, hid behind her numbness. She could step on a pop-top, slit her foot open, and have blood spurting out but not notice it until someone pointed it out, which would draw from her nothing more than the inevitable, "Shit, man, not again." Her body was covered with bruises. Usually around her fourth Seconal, she would lose the ability to walk and the awareness that she couldn't. She'd try to stand up, take a half step or two, and then come crashing down, flailing her arms around as she did so, bringing lamps, tables, dishes, coffeepots along with her. And people. Her 120 pounds became dead weight. If you tried to catch her, half the time you'd go down with her, shoving her off you so you could get up and then pitying her as she lay on the ground, sometimes accusing you. "Fuck, Davey! Why'd you knock me down, motherfucker?"

Forget about trying to take her to town, to a restaurant or a club. Within minutes, she'd either be on the floor, ripping off pocketbooks in the ladies' room, or making out with some local skell at the bar. We took turns babysitting her at the house. She grew asexual, not interested, not sensitized enough to appreciate touch. Time with her was a continuous battle to keep her keys from her and try to control how many reds she took. She'd lie, cheat, threaten suicide, even promise sex, though she could never deliver. Every few hours, you'd give her one just to shut her up for a while.

Come Monday morning, I'd often have the place to myself for three or four days. Things had deteriorated at home. Ever since Brian had been shipped off to Vietnam, Mom stayed in her room all day, blinds closed, door closed. She sobbed and wallowed in self-pity. I didn't know how to help her, and I couldn't stand to be there. I wrote letters to Brian, grew excited to read his. He'd tell me the upside: pot was plentiful and branded into gold and black. Potent shit. Most of the soldiers were stoned all the time. Prostitutes were cheap, and he was getting laid or blown whenever he wanted. He'd barely allude to the fear and the danger and the horror that he was living in. I'd tell him about the Mets and the music and Miranda's latest mishaps.

I'd take it easy during the week, no drinking, maybe only one or two joints a day, later in the evening. During the day, I'd go to the ribbon of beach along Dune Road, the spit peninsula that began in Southampton and stretched between the Atlantic Ocean and the Shinnecock Bay toward the inlet that separated the cape from the lighthouse on the Hampton Bays beach. I would bring a chair and a cooler and set up on the bay side. I'd watch the fishing boats come and go. I'd talk to the squatting campers. Mostly I'd read, devouring Tom Wolfe's *The Electric Kool-Aid Acid Test*. And I'd swim in the bay, in the ocean, in the canal. I'd snorkel, picking out a crab or a lobster close to shore and noiselessly follow it as it went about its business.

We had no phone in the rental. I used the pay phone at the diner up the road to call home, collect, to check in with Mom, usually on Sunday, lying as often as not, telling her of course I went to church, not letting her know that I was priding myself on having been barefoot for weeks in a row. She had no idea that on the rare occasions my friends and I did go to mass, we'd sit in the back row and rate the girls, talk of our exploits, and have farting contests. The ritual of the religion that we were raised in had become a farce to us.

■ ■ ■

I was surprised when Kevin showed up unexpectedly on a Wednesday afternoon, doubly surprised, after seeing the car turn into the driveway, that he was by himself. I grabbed a beer out of my cooler to welcome him with, and he took it, but there was no joy in his face. He opened it and drained it, staring at me as he put it down. "What's wrong?" I asked him. "Tell me."

"Brian's dead."

My knees buckled, and I sat on the gravel. I just shook my head. "I thought he was safe in Saigon. I thought being an MP was supposed to keep him away from the war."

"Nowhere's safe in 'Nam. Some gook tossed a hand grenade into a bar. He wasn't even on duty."

"How's Mommy?"

"How do you think?"

I cried softly while gathering my stuff, tried to stifle the tears, bury the pain, displace it to concern for Mom. We smoked a joint on the way home but didn't talk. We drove in complete silence, each wondering what this forever-changed world was going to be like.

■ ■ ■

The casket was closed at the wake. Mom had a lot of trouble with this; she wanted to see him, to touch him, to kiss him good-bye.

She would pry it open herself, she said. Pop finally had to tell her the truth: there were only pieces of him in there. She took the portrait of him in his military police uniform off the stand, cradled it to her bosom, and wept quietly through the entire service. She could not rise when the priest asked all to rise nor kneel when the time came. She just sat there, weeping, moaning, and sobbing while she slowly rocked back and forth, clutching the picture tighter and tighter. At the cemetery, she was inconsolable. She tried to climb into the grave, said that she wanted to be buried with him. We had to drag her off and get her a sedative.

In the days to come, Pop and Kevin went back to work, but Mom just stayed in her room. She entered a comalike sleep state, refusing to come out, not touching her food when I brought it in. The doctor said, "Be patient. She'll come out of it." I wanted to be away, wanted to go back to the Hamptons and lie on the beach, but I knew I couldn't leave her alone.

We occupied the same house, but it might as well have been different planets. I retreated to my dark room in the basement, smoked my pot, drank some beers, and took an occasional Valium, stolen from her supply in the medicine chest. She mostly hid in her bedroom, drank some coffee and ate some toast, smoked cigarettes, and wept.

After two weeks of this, I cleaned myself up, stayed straight for two days, and went over to the rectory. I knocked on the door. Father Ambrose, her favorite parish priest, received me and agreed to come to the house to see her. She was angry when we got there and refused to come out of her room. I sent him in. I could hear the gentleness in his lilting voice, but could not pick up the words. Every now and then I heard her sob. He stayed in there for two hours, and they emerged together. She came over and hugged me and held me tight, crying hard and telling me she loved me.

"I know," I said. "I love you, too."

As I drove the priest back to the rectory, he shared his secret. "I just reminded her that she has other children. That she will see Brian in the next life, and she still has to love in this one to get there. She's worried about not being able to forgive God." He sighed, and his eyes glazed. "I told her I worry about the same thing."

25

By the end of July, Mom began getting out of bed on a regular basis. She was going through the motions in a cold and dispirited way, but she was taking care of the basics. She was eating, bathing, even doing a little cooking and cleaning. She had returned to mass on Sunday, and for a few weeks, Kevin and I joined her and Pop. I was enjoying taking a dip in the pool and sleeping in my own bed. I helped Mom with the shopping and housework, and we'd sit around and drink coffee and talk. She made me promise that I really would go to Canada if I got drafted, and I had no hesitation in assuring her.

The ads were all over the radio. The Woodstock Music and Art Fair promised "Three Days of Peace and Music…An Aquarian Exposition." Independently, Kevin and I decided that we wanted to go. Reading the *Daily News* and listening to WNEW-FM kept us apprised of the political issues and changing venues.

We were among the fifty thousand or so who actually bought tickets—for us, Cheryl, and Joan. Each three-day ticket cost us eighteen dollars. We decided to go together. We were going to leave Friday around noon, thinking this would give us plenty of time, as the music was supposed to start at six in the evening. On Thursday night, the radio was filled with reports that traffic was already building. They showed the site on the eleven o'clock news, and people were streaming in. We were all up at dawn and made it out of Queens and through the Bronx, up the New York State Thruway, over the Tappan Zee Bridge, and onto the Route 17 Quickway in about two hours.

Traffic had been heavy since before Middletown. By the time we got through Monticello and onto Route 17B, it was intense. The road was only one lane in each direction, but after the first few miles of bumper-to-bumper traffic, I was one of the first to slide out to the shoulder to create a new lane. This gained us a mile or two of passing cars, but then some Volkswagen bug driven by a girl moved over too slowly a few cars ahead of us, and was rear-ended. The shoulder came to a standstill. Instantly, while a rubbernecker was looking at the accident, I zipped back into the traffic lane.

After another mile or two of creeping and crawling, things really started to get crazy. It was late morning now; the sun was out in full force, and the heat was rising. Cars began pulling left into the oncoming lane and forging ahead. Why not go all the way? I jumped in with them, and we turned the rural route into a highway by using the far shoulder as well. On the right, they ventured back onto that shoulder again, and for a good five minutes or so we had four lanes all rushing to Woodstock at a healthy twenty miles per hour.

Of course, that was too good to last, and suddenly everything came to a screeching halt. Absolutely nothing moved for a half hour. We turned the car off and got out to stretch. The road looked like a giant, narrow parking lot between the rolling hills and cornfields. Joan took the opportunity to roll a joint, and we got high.

We could see the blue light in the distance as the state trooper was breaking through the oncoming traffic, providing a thin but effective wedge to merge the four lanes back into one, getting traffic moving again, but at a snail's pace that felt like a hundred yards an hour. Lunchtime came and went. Cars began to move to the side of the road, and people started locking them up and leaving them, apparently preferring to walk.

It was getting hotter, in the mid-eighties and climbing, and I felt like a slug leaving behind a sticky trail of sweat as we crawled along. We felt we must be getting close when we began to see people walking in the opposite direction, approaching us. Invariably, they were offering tickets for sale, clearly indicating that tickets were probably superfluous. Cheryl suggested that some of us walk backward and try to sell ours, but Kevin and I were not up for that. "What if we get there and need them?"

"Then we just buy some from someone else that is selling," she said with a sweet smile. We were unconvinced, uninterested in making a profit, just hopeful of actually getting there. Brian's beloved '64 Mustang, more or less mine now, began to overheat. The fumes became overpowering. The other three deserted me and sat on the roadway, smoking joints and laughing at my predicament. When I began to get dizzy, I gave in, pulled the car off the shoulder into a field, and said, "That's it. Let's walk." There were hundreds of cars abandoned on both sides of the road on various parcels of private land. Unlike most, we had come quite prepared: a ten-person rented tent, canned food, beer, extra clothes, sleeping bags, towels, and cameras. Unfortunately, the tent and sleeping bags were all we could manage to carry.

Some of the locals had caught the spirit and were giving away drinks of lemonade, iced tea, and water. One woman was making and giving away peanut butter and jelly sandwiches. We trudged on for over an hour. The determined drivers who were trying to get all the way into the site were being overtaken by the streaming hoards. People became parasites, jumping on the hoods and tops of cars and resting while they crept forward in slow motion.

Finally, we got to what appeared to be the entrance to the festival. There were no signs, no ticket booths, no fences; but the crowd was heading that way, and so did we. Out of nowhere, a yellow school bus came up from a dirt road, and when it turned on to the shoulder, the driver swung open the door, and people began to pile in. We didn't get seats, but we did get to put our belongings down for the last mile up to the growing throng at Yasgur's farm. The bus made a left up a dirt road until the mass of people prevented it from going any farther. The driver announced, "Welcome to Woodstock!"

When we got off the bus, we only walked a few hundred yards more. There were tents and people everywhere, and we were exhausted. I had talked to Vinny and Adam about trying to meet them and, though we felt that was no longer likely, we figured the closer to the entrance, the better.

We had never erected this size or style of tent before, and of course there were no instructions. It took us well over an hour to get it up. It was late afternoon, about five o'clock, and we were hot, tired, filthy, and hungry. We heard rumors of a lake, and so we set out in shorts and T-shirts to find it. It didn't take us long, as lots of people seemed to know the way. We could see it up ahead, the sun glistening off the water, sparkling through the trees, enticing us along. We heard shouts and laughter and knew we were close. We saw people swimming and frolicking on the shore and just hanging out. But as we got closer, we could see that many of them were stark naked.

Apparently, this was more than our inhibitions could handle. I angered both my brother and the girls when I announced, somewhat cavalierly, "Don't look at them if it bothers you." I was soundly and harshly overruled, with Joan being the most definitive: "We're not swimming here!" I was conflicted, desperately wanting a cool swim, yet not strong enough to break from the group and go my own way. As the others started to walk back, I stood there for a moment, watching them, then turning back to the lake and watching the free spirits. I hung my head, turned, and followed them all the way back to the tent. Without a swim. Because they were afraid of public nudity.

The other three decided to nap, and I took a walk by myself. Not back to the lake, though I thought about it. I got on the main "road," a dirt path that circumvented the stage, and I went all the way around. What timing: I was walking under the wooden bridge that led from the performers' area to the main stage itself just as Richie Havens was walking over it! "Hey, Richie, get it started, man!" I yelled, and he saluted me by lifting his guitar and nodding at me, rewarding me with a big, private, benevolent grin. From about fifty yards to the side of the stage, I watched him open the festival: "Freedom, freedom...sometimes I feel like a motherless child." I sat down along the dusty road and thought of Brian. Brian fighting for freedom. Brian blown to bits in a seedy bar. So that we could be free to get stoned.

I got up and walked back to the top of the massive crowd. Country Joe captured the spirit of our rebelliousness with his cheerleader's chant: "Gimme an F...U...C...K. What's *that spell*?" A huge throng of people chanting a four letter word, the usage of which was still quite forbidden at home, led smoothly into his cheerful, incongruous antiwar song. As I listened to the words, though, the emotional shock came back. My knees weakened all over again, and I sat down at the top of the hill. What *are* we fightin' for indeed? *Why* does nobody give a damn? "Whoopee, we're all gonna die!" I put my head down and cried, even as his morbid refrain was chorused by thousands of smiling, dancing people. A well-intentioned hippie with gorgeous long brown hair, in a long flowing tie-dyed dress, sat next to me and put her arm around me and gave me a squeeze. "Don't worry, babe, we're going to stop this fucking war."

"Yeah, well, it's too late for my brother, man," I said, and she proceeded to cry right along with me. I shook my head and laughed through my tears, gave her a hug back, and kissed her softly on the cheek. "Thanks," I said. "I needed that."

"You want to go into the cornfields and ball?" she asked matter-of-factly.

"Uh, no," I said, "I'm here with my girlfriend; she's back in the tent."

"Yeah, well, my old man's here too, but we can still have a quick fuck, man, to consummate the moment. We had a real natural moment here. Let's just finish it."

I thought about getting deflowered by a flower child, but I wasn't ready. "No, I can't. Thanks for the offer, though," I said lamely.

"Hey, keep your head up and smile, man, and don't forget—we're going to end this fucking war."

"Bye," I said softly, as she blended into the background.

After watching John Sebastian in his tie-dyed splendor sing about the younger generation and challenge us to live up to our dreams, I had tears in my eyes again. I made my way back to the tent, where the others were sitting around talking, wondering where the hell I was. The evening was consumed at the food-tent lines and then walking the fringes of the crowd watching the people, the music emanating from the stage more as a backdrop, like a radio left on, than the main event. As darkness fell, and the night deepened, we settled back in our tent, ready for some sleep after a long, emotion-filled day. I was drifting, though, trying to listen to the late bands. In the distance, I imagined that I heard someone calling my name. I became sure of it, and I sat up. The others said I was crazy, but I said, "No, listen, there it goes again." I lifted the flap and stuck my head out. Then I could hear it clearly. Recognizing the voice, I yelled out at the top of my lungs, "Vinny!"

"Davey!"

"Vinny!"

Our voices got closer and closer until we could see each other. Vinny and Adam had found us. In the middle of half a million people. We took yet another walk around the perimeter, mostly talking about how amazing it was that we actually found each other. It was well after midnight before we hit the sleeping bags again.

It was the middle of the night now, and everybody was sleeping. I was awakened by a crack of light suddenly thrust into the tent by someone who'd lifted the flap. I discerned the spooky shadow of a longhaired, bearded man in a fringed jacket, beads, and a floppy hat. I suddenly realized that it was pouring rain, and he was soaking, dripping wet. He asked, "Do you have any room?"

Before I could open my mouth to say yes, Kevin yelled a loud, "No!"

"C'mon," the stranger pleaded, "I'm cold and wet, and I just want to sleep. This is a big-ass tent; you must have room for one more."

My brother replied, not quite angrily, "We're packed like sardines in here, wall to wall. Go try somewhere else."

The intruder capitulated and dropped the flap, and we were back in darkness. But as he walked away, he shouted back, "You fuckin' people don't belong here."

I was somewhat troubled. *A ten-person tent*, I kept thinking, *and there are six of us in here*. "Why didn't you let him in?" I gently and quietly asked Kevin.

"If we open the door, they'll be coming in all night," he replied with authority.

I drifted back to sleep, thinking of the Christlike mien of the visitor. No room at the Inn? Is this the spirit of Woodstock?

I was up at the first signs of dawn, the best time of day for me—a time to be alone, a time to reflect. I quietly slipped out of the tent and took a walk, nodding good morning to the other early risers. The rain had taken its toll: wet clothes and sleeping bags were everywhere. Many of the flattened and drenched sleeping bags still had bodies in them: the lost souls who weren't fortunate enough to meet their friends, I thought, not imagining that there were thousands of people brave enough and willing to come to an event like this alone. I wondered if our intruder got inside a tent. Here and there I saw some people sleeping in the open, up against the sides of tents or under impromptu lean-tos. Lots of beards and long hair, of course, and I was thankful that I'd never seen his face, though I could picture the form of his hat and jacket clearly, and I was sure I would recognize his fringe and beads.

When I reached the row of portable toilets, the stench was overwhelming. There were no lines yet, and when I opened a door to go in one, I could see why. The pool of urine and stool was almost to the top of the pit. Sitting on the seat would've meant contact with the waste. I backed out, gagging, and headed off into the cornfield, which had quickly become one giant urinal. Not everyone was out there just to pee, though. People were beginning to rip off the corn for breakfast.

Breakfast. By the time I got back to the tent, others were up, and we scraped together the last bits of food that we had been able to carry in, mostly some bread and fruit, complaining again about having to leave all of the provisions in my trunk. The sun got high quickly, it seemed, and the temperature began to climb. By ten o'clock, it felt like midday. Vinny took me aside. "Let's take a walk, man."

We wandered a bit, out to the pines, away from the crowd. "I've got something that I want to share with you," he said, "but I only have enough for two." He had brought some psilocybin, a natural derivative of the Mexicana mushroom, the stuff that achieved fame in the Carlos Castaneda books. He had scored it from a Bellerose girl who made it as a model and now lived in the city. In addition to *The Electric Kool-Aid Acid Test*, I had also read Aldous Huxley's *The Doors of Perception* earlier in the summer. I was intrigued by the concept of mind expansion, but I was afraid to try anything too psychedelic. Vinny pressured me. "This shit is pure and organic; it's not like taking chemicals at all."

"I don't know, Vin. I mean, fuck man, how can I trust you? You've been different lately, man, all this glue and shit."

He looked into the distance, took a huge and deep drag on his cigarette. "Davey, I fucked up, but I'm done with huffing. I would never lie to you. This shit is good, man, it's not like glue."

The psilocybin came in oversized "horse" capsules, about three times the size of a normal pill. The capsules were clear, and the drug looked like dirt, very natural indeed. He had four, and we each took two. For a while, we just wandered around, and then went back to the tent, but the others were gone. The tent started to get hot, seemed to pulsate, and the pattern of the sun on the sides of the tent began to swirl. I felt like I couldn't breathe. "Let's get out of here," I said, with anxiety in my voice. I was trembling. The sun was blistering, and we began the now-familiar walk around the perimeter. When we passed by the medical tent near the performers' area, there was a table set up where people could get free salt tablets and a glass of cold water. I wasn't sure I needed the tablets, but it was worth it to get the drink.

We ambled over to the arts-and-crafts area at the back of the hill. The scene was surreal, punctuated by a life-size crucifix displaying a skeleton Christ. The image bore into me, and I felt so vulnerable and mortal that I had to back away from the entire area, imagining that the hollow eye sockets were following me. The music had begun again, and we were captured by the smooth rhythms of Santana, a group we had never heard of. The crowd was captivated—swaying and relaxing.

As the mushroom peaked, we both ratcheted into the hyperperceptive stage, feeling every sense magnified and intensified. We went looking for food. There were some operating food stalls, but the process was insane. You had to wait on two long lines: one to buy tickets and then another to trade your tickets for food. Minimum time to get a gray hot dog that looked like it had been sitting in your mother's refrigerator for too long was about two hours.

We overheard people talking about the free food kitchens, and we set out to find them. Away from the main area, down a tangential valley into a cluster of shade trees, we sensed we were close: the flowing tie-dyed dresses, dirty locks, and painted faces were clustered into groups. The wait for the gruel, also gray, a pasty pudding of mashed beans and god knows what else would have only been fifteen minutes or so, but the smell and look of it brought back morning memories of the port-o-sans, and I had to withdraw.

Amazingly, we stumbled right into Pauly and Dennis, who seemed to be unconscious, sleeping in the mud in front of their tent. We sort of kicked them awake. They had an impressive and established living arrangement. They had arrived at the site a week early and had even helped build the food kitchen. They were well provided, and began grilling hamburgers on a portable hibachi. Despite our salivating pleas, they said they didn't have enough to share. Peaceful, yes, but everyone out for themselves.

Our quest for food had consumed a few hours, but we were not single-mindedly focused. Movement, color, and sound distracted us. We traveled slowly, gracefully bumping into people and things, giggling and laughing the whole while. People seemed to be making faces at us, and we often returned the gesture. There was an unspoken language of facial distortion that had little meaning beyond the confirmation that others, too, shared the inward ranting of chemical miasma.

We noticed a little crowd gathering off to the side of the hill, near the entrance road. As we got closer, we saw a truckload of watermelons. A couple of farmers, dressed in dungaree overalls, were cutting them up with large knives and selling the round slices for a dollar apiece, about four times the usual price. Capitalism was thriving in several pockets of the people's fair! We bought four slices, sat on a log nearby, and buried our faces in them, sloppily slurping and spitting out the seeds. The melon was cold and stickily sweet. We closed our eyes as we savored the tender flesh.

We sat there, watching others dig the melons almost as much as we had. By the time we thought of getting some more, they had sold out. The farmer dumped his huge vat of ice and tried to edge his truck out of the crowd, yelling out the window that he would try to come back with a new load on Sunday. It had to be in the low nineties by then, with a high humidity. We went over and quickly salvaged some of the larger chunks of ice, rubbing it on our bodies for coolness and funkily sucking on it for refreshment, while again walking the perimeter, creating the scene.

When the ice finally trickled away, it was like we lost an old friend. We went back to the truck site to see if there was any more and were disheartened, though not surprised, to see only a few puddles in the mud. We stood there, looking at the ground for a minute, our feet filthy, our pants wicking the mud almost up to our knees, and realized together that our peak was over. The mushroom high was trailing; we were coming down. The psilocybin had been a mild trip; it never really took control of us, only heightened our sensations and let us melt into our surroundings. Thus, there was no "crash" as such, and we were glad when we got back to the tent to find that the others, too, were ready to move on.

The music beckoned. We'd been at the festival for a day and a half, and for the most part we had taken the music for granted, stopping now and then to listen, but not giving it full attention. It was time to settle into it. "Let's go," we all agreed, and the adventure was on. From the top of the hillside, the stage seemed a half mile away, and the entire distance, leading to the bottom of this beautiful valley where the stage sat, was filled to capacity with bodies. Standing at the top and looking over the view, you would think that every square inch was occupied, not a blade of grass was evident. And yet at any given time, there was a trickle of people who were moving, walking, and indiscriminately traversing the unseen highway of the ground, virtually flowing like a river.

Determined, we set off to get closer to the stage. Progress was slow, as you had to remain careful and focused, attempting not to step directly on people. Step by step, inch by inch, place one foot in between two people or in between one person's legs if she left the tiniest gap. Stand there spread-eagled while you looked for the next step, often brushing someone with your foot if not outright stepping on them, triggering an occasional grunt, scream, yell, or curse. "Watch where you're fucking going, man!"

"Sorry," knowing that five more of your party were trailing you.

Those who had spread blankets had long since given up the expectation that they could protect their turf. Nothing was sacred. The bodies got tighter and tighter. We stopped to reconnoiter, spread out into a longer and thinner line. Almost thirty minutes in, we were about halfway to the stage. We could see that the performers were human beings now, not dots in the distance. Taking the stage: Mountain, featuring guitarist Lesley West. The sound was outstanding; we were aligned with center stage, and the full stereo effect was pleasant. Looking back, we could not see the crescent; the bodies just seemed to flow up and over the top of the hill, like a wave of hot starch when the spaghetti pot boils over. If possible, it seemed to be more crowded up there than when we had left.

We noticed a patch of grass, not quite a foot wide and about four feet long, in front of a group that had stretched out a blanket, an old olive-green army blanket filled with holes. They were lying down, not fully prone, as they did not have enough room for that, but sort of scrunched up into half fetal positions. A few guys and a few girls, they were huddled together and almost looked as if they were trying to sleep. The people in front of them were sitting up, leaning back on their hands, and I realized that the space was theirs, that they occupied it when they lay back on the ground. I didn't care, figured that this was the best we would get, and led the six of us to squeeze into a spot that would comfortably hold one, maybe two at most. As we sat, both sets of people, in front and behind us, groaned as one. A few turned and grumbled and gave angry looks, while a few drew tighter into themselves, shrinking their own cocoons, accepting the inevitability as if the whole crowd were one giant organism, adapting itself as it grew, each cell taking up less space than it had previously needed to allow for growth from new cells.

It was dusk, and as Mountain finished, the ritual of the stage change began, accompanied by the endless stream of announcements. "Please get off the towers. Janine Wilson, your insulin is at the tent. Please come get it, your brother is worried. Don't take the brown acid; it's poison!"

Canned Heat was on next, and they had the crowd "goin' up-country," moving around as best we could, grooving to music in the incongruous atmosphere that felt like a packed subway car. We learned to relax our muscles and expand our space ever so slightly, encroaching as others morphed to adapt to our movement. The heat was tapering off, and we thoroughly enjoyed the set. A naked hippie, with hair past his shoulders and a long scruffy beard, was dancing on the crowd, pausing now and then for a few seconds to gyrate his private parts in front of some girl, only to bounce away again before offense could be registered, falling often, rebounding as if he were on a trampoline as people rushed to push him off them. For the first time, I pondered the fact that aberrant behavior was acceptable in this culture. No one was going to get arrested for doing drugs or walking around naked. There were many comments that he must've been tripping his brains out, but who knows, maybe he was just a straight exhibitionist celebrating a society that would accept him.

It was fully dark, and the stars were out when Credence Clearwater Revival came on, and I realized I *had* to take a piss. Vinny had done so earlier, when it was still light, and it took him about forty-five minutes to make it out to the cornfield and back. "How did you find your way back?" I asked him.

He noted that there were landmarks here and there: T-shirts, bras, and other "flags" on makeshift poles ten to twenty feet high. "Just pick a few on your way out and get a feel for our position in relation to them."

I set off, checking out the landmarks as I left. After relieving myself on the edge of the cornfield, I was careful to reenter the throng from the same point I had left. The approach was more amorphous, more cells breaking and joining on a continuous basis, the surface of the cell always pulsing and changing shape. As I took the first few steps gingerly, before the mass tightened in on itself, I was feeling good until I stopped and looked where I was going. For the life of me, I could not find a single one of the flags that I had chosen to guide me. I was simply too far away, had not extended my landmarks all the way up the hill.

Definitely anxious that I would never get back, I briefly contemplated giving up and going to the tent, but I courageously set out in what I knew was the right general direction, a heroic adventurer on his own exploration. The going was even tougher than before, as more people were stretched out, some definitely sleeping, and I stepped on many a body. I got close; I could feel it, though I could not see it. I stood and gazed around, my eyes locked above the crowd. There, there was one of my landmarks, a purple bandanna; there was another one, the oversized bra; and finally, there was the third, a dirty white T-shirt. Terrific; I had all three. I should be "home" soon but still could not see anybody. I just stood there, frozen, lost in a sea of humanity, helpless, and needlessly annoying folks around me, who shouted, "Either sit down or move on, asshole!"

I took a tentative step, then another. Suddenly, magically, once again I heard someone calling my name. I looked in the direction I thought the voice was coming from, and there, not thirty feet away, were my girlfriend, my brother, and the others. They were laughing at my expense, as they had been watching me suffer for a while before choosing to rescue me. I was so happy to be found that I didn't care and rushed into their waiting arms.

The music was erratically deteriorating. The Dead were just too stoned. They seemed to be tuning up instead of jamming. We kept waiting for them to actually play, but their set, never inspiring, was endless. Janis Joplin was clearly drunk, living up to her image. It was a treat just to see her, though her performance was scratchy and uneven. I stretched out; somehow, after midnight, we had gained some more space. The creature was shrinking slightly instead of growing. I just went inside myself for a while, trying to slow my mind down a little. Sly and the Family Stone wove a magic spell, electrifying the crowd, bringing us back to life and propelling us all the way to our feet, getting us up, stretching and dancing and singing along, welcoming the opportunity to stand up and jump around and shout definitely accomplishing his wish to take us "higher!"

Sly drained us. The night was almost over, and we slowly dragged ourselves up the hillside, lots of places to step now, and back to the tent, listening to the Who with our backs to the stage, feeling the eerie glow of predawn intensified by lack of sleep and overstimulation of the senses. Though tired, we appreciated our anthem. "See me. Feel me. Touch me. Heal me." Roger Daltry's lilting, haunting plea floated through the valley, surrealistically accompanying us, carrying us along. When we got back to the tent, it was light out, and we began to have a conversation about whether or not to leave. Vinny just wanted a shower. The girls wanted some decent food. I worried about my car, concerned that it would blow up if it had to go out in traffic conditions anything like what we had endured on the way in.

We were spent. We had been there forty-four hours, of which I slept for fewer than six. Considering the lack of sleep the night before we left, I had slept about ten hours in the last seventy-two. Lack of food, shortage of water, and mushroom mania added to the stress. I was physically and emotionally exhausted. The prospect of another day in the heat and the mud, to be followed by another night sitting cramped on a damp hillside, was not appealing. As I had the car, the final decision was mine, and I said, "Let's do it." We packed up to the morning-maniac music of the Jefferson Airplane urging us to "tear down the walls!"

As we hit the road, we realized we were part of a movement. A lot of people were leaving. Cars were moving slowly on the main road, but they were moving. We managed to hop on the back of a big old Cadillac, taking advantage of this commonly accepted mode of mass transit. We got back to my car, and it started right up. Kevin drove, and I tried to sleep, not caring that once he got to the Thruway, he buried the Mustang's speedometer at a hundred and ten.

We got home around noon. Mom and Pop were just getting back from church. The *Daily News* headline screamed in a half-page banner, 400,000 Hippies Mired in the Mud! I took a long hot shower and went to my room, lit a candle and some incense, and played side 2 of the Beatles' *White Album*. I needed to mellow out and to reflect. I could not separate this weekend from the context of Vietnam. The war was wrong, and I felt my brother died in vain. This knowledge, this belief, led me and others to begin to challenge all authority, not just the government's. But our rebellion steered us astray: the antidote to authority is chaos, and drugs were the fuel of this chaotic uprising.

Drugs, along with the music, served to reshape our ideals. As Sly sang, "I am Everyday People!" our values reflected who we were becoming on an everyday basis. From hairstyles to bell-bottoms to feminism to the absolute importance of individual rights, I realized that the world was changing, and the refrain from Tommy, "We're Not Gonna Take It!" would be a theme for years to come. This weekend had dramatically changed who I was, but I was too damn tired to fully understand how or why.

26

With Labor Day just a few weeks away, I switched my major to Philosophy, realizing that I was just pursuing English Literature out of some kind of inertia. Reading was an escape, a journey to other worlds, worlds where I had no accountability or responsibility. I enjoyed Salinger and Steinbeck, Hardy and Dickens, but I felt they were just allowing me to observe the human condition. They were doing little to explain, in a way that I could understand, why life was so hard. I registered for Logic and Phenomenology. I read Hegel, tried to pursue his idea of self-consciousness, his notions of freedom and reason. He explored the notion of free will as one of the defining characteristics of human awareness. He was clear that self could only be defined as a relation to otherness. I read Heidegger and his long exploration of the universal problem of being, focusing on his differentiation between the authentic and inauthentic notion of existence.

I'd ride home on the train, ponderously studying these works, paragraph-by-paragraph, highlighting important questions and

penciling notes and questions in the margins, ludicrously trying
to apply these concepts to my life. I was consciously pursuing
the question why: Why was Brain dead? Why is there war? Why
do we live? Why do we die?

I was not finding answers, but I was changing the places I
was going to look for them. I felt God slipping away from me,
realized that He could not be present in the cardboard tasting
communion wafer. I committed a sacrilege, took a wafer out of
my mouth, and placed it in my pocket, proving that it would not
burn my fingers, not burn a hole in my pockets as the nuns had
taught us. I flushed it down the toilet.

I was cognizant that religion had been the driver behind
most of the world's wars, that more killing was done in the name
of God than any other single cause. I liked to joke that if God
does exist, she has a strange sense of humor. Refusing to cat-
egorize myself, I walked the tightrope between agnosticism and
atheism.

A "queer," the word we used then, taught the course I took
in Existentialism. He was an openly gay man who dressed in
frilly shirts and tucked his jeans into his boots. He attracted
a number of groupies, in and out of their personal closets. For
the first time in my life, I felt that I was able to start letting go
of prejudice. I respected them for their intelligence and cogent
arguments. We read Andre Gide and Jean Genet, along with
Sartre and Kafka. We read Henry Miller and Soren Kierkegaard,
who might have created the notion that it is the individual who is
ultimately responsible for his own actions, and the inherent conclusion that there might not be a divine plan. We explored the
depths of fear, the pain of existence and the safety of denial. In
our dialogues, we desperately struggled for the promise of hope,
for validation to go on. I learned a new mantra: "It's the journey,

252 TIMOTHY F. DEMPSEY

not the destination, that is important." And I started to judge differently, still hypercritical of others, but less so because of the fact that they were gay or black or female or Italian or Jewish or weird in any way, and more because of who they were, what they had to say, how they said it.

I introduced discipline in some areas, let myself go in others. I became anal in my desire to make every decision a conscious choice. I stopped shaving, stopped getting haircuts. I wore the same pair of jeans wherever I went, washing them once a week or so, getting Mom to patch them if they ripped. Mom tried to prevent me from wearing bell-bottoms, decreeing that I was "not allowed." I decided that I would wear what I wanted to since I bought clothes with my own money. Vinny and I went to Kings Men's Wear in Jamaica and I bought by first pair of bell-bottoms. They were soft cotton, white, almost silky in their texture. I bought a flowing sleeved flowered shirt and a brown Nehru jacket. I blew a month's pay on a single outfit. I topped it off with a pair of brown suede Beatle boots.

I replaced my Catholicism with a new religion: rock 'n' roll! The Fillmore East was the palace of our gods. It was the temple at which we worshipped, an imperial palace in the Forbidden City. Located on Second Avenue in the East Village, it was the New York version of the original temple, the Fillmore Auditorium in San Francisco. Both were offered by the high priest and servant to the rock gods, impresario Bill Graham.

The first time I went was to an early show, eight o'clock, arriving in the city around seven. As we were walking toward the theatre, I asked Kevin to slow down. "Let's do a jay."

He laughed and said, "We're going to smoke inside." Indeed, people were smoking on the stairs, in the bathrooms, even in the lobby. It was as if grass were legal. I felt as if I had arrived at my place.

The lobby and food area was a parade of freaks. Not even at the circus had I seen so many people dressed so bizarrely: pink hair, vests with twirling lights, bellbottoms with elephant flares embroidered with custom inserts, leather of all colors and shapes. We smoked a joint and then went to our seats, high in the balcony, to enjoy the rhythmic, pulsating gospel of Sly and the Family Stone, whose raucous brand of rock was crossing the color line with ease. Like the Chicago Transit Authority before them, they were making innovative use of horns and saxophones to accompany the ubiquitous guitars and drums. Like the big bands of our parents' generation, they played music that was easy for white people to move their feet to. Despite the fact that we could barely see the stage, we were ecstatic at the power and clarity of the sound system.

There were some rules: no smoking or food in the seats, and strict adherence to the fire laws that dictated the aisles must remain clear. The security staff, bearded and longhaired hippies dressed in uniforms of bright-orange T-shirts that just said "Security," and jeans, armed only with flashlights, tolerated no rushing of the stage or dancing in the aisles. They would warn you for smoking in your seat and then toss you out if you did it again. It was a surreal culture. They knew exactly what was important to "the man," and it was safety, not sobriety.

Sly only did one encore. The lights came on at about ten thirty, and the staff became quite organized in getting the audience out. As we left, we saw the line snaking down Sixth Street for the midnight show. As we drove back to Queens, we agreed to two resolutions that would govern our future visits: we would buy the best seats in the front orchestra, and we would only come to the late show.

We needed to plan in advance, as the good seats sold out fast, so we took turns going to the box office to buy the tickets. Although there were some other outlets, this was before the days of computerized ticketing, and the best seats were always obtained at the box office. Each week, the Sunday *New York Times* Arts and Leisure section published the new shows and the day that tickets would go on sale. We always tried to be there the first day the box office opened. On occasion, for the superstars like Jefferson Airplane or the Who, we went in the night before and spent the whole night on line, securing center seats within the first ten rows. The line was a party unto itself, with joints flowing freely and Graham often supplying free coffee, especially on the colder nights.

There were few acts at the Fillmore that we did not want to see, and so we just got into going every Saturday night. We saw Jethro Tull, King Crimson, and the Allman Brothers. Grand Funk Railroad. Ten Years After. New Riders of the Purple Sage. Joe Cocker with Mad Dogs and Englishmen, featuring Leon Russell and Rita Coolidge singing "Superstar." Crosby, Stills, Nash & Young. We saw the Grateful Dead every time they came to town.

I had my own ritual that prepped me for what was akin to a spiritual event. I worked till six o'clock at Mays on Union Turnpike in Glen Oaks. My boss was happy if I showed up on time, kept the stock room clean, kept the shelves stocked and relatively neat, and did my shift on the floor. It was not that hard, but on a busy Saturday it meant at least a hundred trips up and down the flight of stairs to the stockroom. Despite the occasional break to go flirt with the telephone operator, who would sometimes let me run the board while she took *her* break, I was pretty much focused on work the whole day. Then home to some supper and a shower and to steal a half hour to an hour of rest.

I would light a few candles and play an album or two. If I had one by the group we were going to see, I would spin that, but often as not I was content to play side 2 of the *White Album*, while lying on my bed, eyes closed. By the time "Julia" was playing, I had arrived at a meditative state: my mind at ease, the music floating in the background as I let my thoughts wander at will, visualizing and fantasizing chaotically, unorganized but patterned, approaching some awareness of self. I never quite achieved sleep, but I always felt rested and ready for the night.

Kevin and I adopted the unwritten dress code, wearing ragged, patched jeans and flannel shirts, our hair now growing past our collars. We arrived at the Fillmore around eleven, usually as the early show was departing. I looked with disdain at the neophytes who attended the early shows, considering them innocents, clean-cut guys with their debutante dates from New Jersey. An important part of the ritual, like the bishop cleansing the path with holy water, was getting stoned on line. Joints would appear and disappear at random. You had to be prepared to say good-bye to your jay if someone asked for a hit, recognizing that the person next to him or her wanted one too, and it would often drift away. This was balanced by the fact that someone else's would float to you, at another time or on another day. Often, Bill Graham himself made an appearance and thanked us for our patience and comportment. He saw to our needs if the weather demanded it, bringing jugs of lemonade on hot summer nights, or pots of steaming hot chocolate when it was snowing. He always told us that the wait would be worth it, the show would be awesome; then he'd hawk for an upcoming act.

He was always dressed in a black T-shirt and jeans, his hair somewhat unkempt. Although it was brushed to the side, it fell in front of his face, though he would continually swipe it back into place, as if it were an annoyance that he could not eliminate. He had the face of a pugilist with a nose that looked like it had been broken more than once. He politely answered questions but took little guff if someone started whining. Maybe someone complained because it was eleven thirty, and the tickets said doors would open at eleven.

He gave it right back to them. "Do you think I'm going to start the show before you get in?" or "Don't you think the folks in the early show are entitled to an encore if the artist wants to give it to them?" If the complainer kept it up, Graham finally asked in exasperation, "Do you want your money back?" If they said yes, he politely escorted them out of the queue to the box office and refunded their money on the spot. Then he put his arm around them, sometimes giving their neck a playful squeeze, and he whispered in their ear, "Don't ever let me see your fucking face around here again." And he smiled and turned back to the crowd and continued his well-wishing as if nothing had happened. Any security staff around were on high alert in case the customer took offense or got ornery.

We took our sacramental drug of choice while on the line. We tried to match the drug to the music or artist. We took downs for B. B. King, John Mayal, or other blues artists. We took speed to try to match energy with Rod Stewart. We took mescaline for the Youngbloods and Hot Tuna. We always had pot as our appetizer to the entrée of choice, using it to instantly kick-start the high.

A lot of the ambience and staging that Graham provided had, in fact, been piloted or perfected in the acid tests, the infamous

San Francisco LSD-driven parties organized by Ken Kesey and immortalized by Tom Wolfe. For most acts, the feature most stimulating was the Joshua Light Show: pulsating, gyrating colors projected onto a back screen somehow grooved exactly to the music as they morphed with a will of their own. Though simply projections of colored oils being manipulated in water, the effect was dazzling, mesmerizing. It demonstrated the unique ability for the audience to share a cosmic experience together. One could get lost in the pulses, following the blending of the colors, truly using the hypnotic effect to meld with the music.

The effect was contagious and would often affect the band. Groups loved to play the Fillmore, many citing it as the best venue for rock in the world. The audience got off on the energy of the music, and the band got off on the energy of the audience. Manic guitar riffs siphoned off cares, even thoughts. Stiff, uptight bodies swayed imperceptibly, while freer spirits gyrated feverishly, convulsing, anticipating, and instantaneously reacting to each note. I let go of consciousness, let go of self, and became seamless with sound, drowning as the purity consumed me.

■ ■ ■

Inevitably, we wanted to go higher. I had been holding out, afraid to trip, equating acid with the taboo drugs like glue and heroin. On a clear, crisp night in late December, Kevin and Joan led the way and enticed Cheryl and me to come along for the ride. It certainly looked harmless enough: a small blue pill the shape and size of an aspirin. Kevin had scored it from Bill Mackay, who would once again give me my wings.

Bill had become a poster child for the hippie generation. His apartment in Long Beach had become a local legend, a tropical oasis festooned with beads and candles. It was filled with plants, only some of which were cannabis, nurtured and fed with various types of fluorescent lights. He had covered his ceiling with bulbs, for the plants and for the head. When he wanted to get high, he would turn off the sunlamps and turn on the black lights. Behind the plants and all over the walls were Day-Glo posters, artfully arranged. He had a section of plant posters so that one corner of the room almost looked like a diorama with significant depth. On the walls in that corner, he had painted illustrations of Gandalf, Elrond, and other *Lord of the Rings* characters.

Mostly he had hobbits, his adopted mascots. He talked to them as if they were friends of his, as if they really existed. In addition to the posters of hobbits, he had various kinds of three-dimensional representations. He had tiny, two- or three-inch statues of dwarfs and leprechauns strategically placed in the dirt of his flower pots, often as if they were hiding and peeking out from behind a leaf. His favorites, though, the ones he named and talked to, were the lawn statues: colorful green-clothed, white-bearded older men with twinkles in their eyes and pipes in their mouths, some pot in their bowls. He shushed us and told us to listen closely and be respectful so that we could hear them talk back.

Bill himself had become rail thin, bony, and extremely hirsute. He sported a thick head of curly, dense black hair in an Afro style. But he had lost the ability to drag a comb through it. He grew a thick mustache to accompany it, and he kept it unkempt as well. It curled down over his upper lip and sought entrance to his mouth, where he would sometimes suck on it. He must have shaved the rest of his face occasionally, but he seemed to have a permanent five-day beard.

He spoke in quiet, reverential tones, as if everything that came out of his mouth was sacred, as if he were the voice of god. He not only believed in fantasy, he lived in fantasy. He played the guitar and composed light and airy songs with lyrics of fairies and dwarves. And he set to music some of the songs from the Tolkien trilogy and sang with great longing for life beyond the Misty Mountains.

Smoking a joint in his living room was our traveling to Mecca. You knew you were somewhere holy, and you partook in the sacraments with ritual respect, going through the motions of entering his universe, happy to be there. Even when completely stoned out and collapsing into giggles, he maintained an aura of a guru, an essence of spirituality that put his disciples at ease. In reality, he was a marketing genius. We were happy to pay a premium for his dope. We were honored and trekked out of our way to score from him, to experience the purchase as a rite while we let him round up.

We knew that acid was LSD, of course, but that term was mostly associated with the media hype—Timothy Leary and all that. LSD was the establishment designation, like referring to grass as marijuana, a word only our parents' generation used. Acid came with brand names, each of which promised a unique experience.

Kevin had bought Kaleidoscope, at three dollars a hit. Billy had assured him that it was a good trip but warned that virgins might want to take half a tab. As we drove into the city, I started feeling anxious even before getting the car parked: I knew that acid was hard-core, and I was afraid of the folklore around "bad trips" and permanent genetic damage. Acid alters the state of mind that you are in, rather than creating a new one. Thus, the same formula can have mild effects on one person and disastrous effects on another. I knew I'd be in trouble, due to my doubts and insecurities. I held it in my fingers for a while, staring at it, imagining what it could do. Yet, as I swallowed it, I sucked on the ends of my fingertips.

The first thing that I noticed was that colors were intensified; I could almost feel them. Everything had a certain glow to it. Looking up at one of the tall buildings and noticing how it seemed to pierce the sky right into the stars, I noticed that the rows of windows became animated. They started to move as if in a cartoon. Like a series of blinking Christmas lights, they streamed in patterns, flowing up and down and around the building. They stopped and waited for each other, like cars in a busy cloverleaf intersection.

I told everyone to look at what the building windows were doing, and they expected to see something in common. When they didn't, Joan asked me to describe what I was seeing, and when I did so, she grabbed me by the shoulders, took command of my eyes with hers, and with a big beautiful smile said, "Davey, you're hallucinating!" and laughed at me.

This knowledge absolutely terrified me, inadvertently causing the hallucinations to intensify. As I was standing on the corner, watching traffic, the front grille of a taxi pulling to a stop at the red light turned into a mouth and grinned at me, and the headlight turned into an eye and winked at me. Flabbergasted, I glanced up just as the light turned green, and when I looked back down, I had entered a complete cartoon: all of the cars were animated characters, rearing back like horses before starting, changing lanes by jumping from one lane to the next, climbing over one another, exhibiting personalities, and talking.

I don't know how long I stood there, watching. It felt like a lifetime, and a small part of my brain was wondering if I would ever return to the real world. Actually, it was just a minute or two. Somehow, I discerned a connection to reality.

"Davey, Davey." Joan was calling from another world. I could hear her, and I remembered that she was other than me, but I could not see her. This scared me, and I looked around, searching for her, but all the people had become blurs, and I could not distinguish faces. I thought I was alone, stranded in the twilight zone. I began to convince myself that I belonged in the cartoon world, that I would never need to return to the real world. Then fear gripped me at the possibility that I might not be able to return.

I closed my eyes, but the show continued unabated. Suddenly, though, I dredged up a saving mantra: Bill Mackay had said it was a good trip! I was tripping. I had taken a blue pill, and it was doing something to my brain, and this was tripping. I was able to imagine that someday it would wear off, the trip would be over, and I would return to be me again.

Time was irrelevant, but all this took place in mere seconds, and, fortunately, Joan came into my world to retrieve me. She suddenly appeared in front of me, locking my eyes again and grabbing my hands. With that human contact, the world opened up a little bit, and the people, at least, began to look like people again. I held onto Joan tightly, told her that I had been lost in another world, begged her not to let me fall behind again. If I were to wander off in another direction, anything was possible.

Joan could not contain her laughter and showed me that Kevin and Cheryl were right there, too. Cheryl was also hallucinating, creating her own world. She, too, was in precarious shape, but I could not go where she was. We could not communicate because we frightened each other. We were both in other worlds, but not the same world.

Cheryl indicated that I should have a cigarette, that it would help calm me down. I understood her intentions. She was smoking one, and it seemed to be part of her, a stabilizing part. I took one and examined it closely, turning it over and over in my fingers, curious as to what good it could do. It began to glow, took on the aura of a magic wand, and began to pulsate.

I turned to Joan. "What do I do with it?" I asked with great sincerity. Laughing, she said, "You put it in your mouth and light it!" as she handed me a book of matches. I fumbled around, unable to distinguish the individual matches from the book itself. I dropped it twice and retrieved it with great drama. It was about twenty degrees out by this time, and somehow I had gotten my gloves on, though I had no memory of doing so. Between the gloves and the wind, I could not have lit the cigarette if I'd been straight. I stared at the matches dumbfounded.

Cheryl turned away. "I can't handle this." Joan, my savior, pulled me into a doorway for shelter. She lit a match and held it up and lit the cigarette and handed it to me. I took a puff but didn't feel anything. I held out my hand in front of my face to look at the cigarette, but it was gone. In its place, my finger had become a torch; the end of my finger was spouting fire, as if I were a human match. I stood there, staring at it, unable to comprehend how come it didn't hurt if I were on fire. I got further confused, believing I was a match and needed a cigarette to light.

Meanwhile, the real cigarette burned my real finger, and the pain shot through me like a bullet. My whole body was on fire like a surge of electricity, a surge of existence, was pulsing through my blood. I dropped the real cigarette and looked at my hand and was relieved that it looked like a hand. When had I taken the glove off? I was ever so briefly back in reality until Joan yelled at me, "Jesus Christ, after all that trouble, you don't want it? Make up your fucking mind and get your act together. You're starting to freak *me* out!"

Kevin materialized. Where had he been? He said, "Let's go into a store to get warm." I wasn't sure what a store was, and I wasn't sure what warm was, but I knew I could not survive being separated from this group again, so I followed them as they entered a revolving door. This door served to connect worlds. When I entered it, I was somewhat connected to reality, somewhat lucid. I was comfortable in there, knew who I was and why I was there. It was a comfort zone, and I wanted to stay. According to earth time, my total transport had only been a second as the door revolved, but I had achieved inner peace.

When I exited the door, I had been transported to yet another world, a world of light. This was about a week before Christmas, and the store was a temporary one, selling only Christmas lights, ornaments, wreaths, and such. Somehow, in a deep recess of my mind, I understood that, but it was a very distant knowledge, like an old memory that you can't distinguish whether it is a real memory or the memory of a dream and when you try to focus on it, it slips away.

This was as close as I could get to the awareness that I was in a "store," and the lights and stuff were for sale, and people could use money and buy them. As I tried to focus on this awareness, it did indeed slip away. The lights and decorations became color patterns only, no shape or form, just blending colors like on an artist's palette. When two colors blended, the original colors were gone, and I realized that the blending colors were trying to suck me in. They were like a vortex, and they were pulling on me. I began to stretch, to elongate, and I knew that if I did not resist, I would become a blended color, and I would be gone.

I moved around the store, which was a small corner store, maybe twenty feet wide and fifty feet deep. The décor consisted of a series of tables in the center with merchandise stacked up there as well as on tables aligning the walls, so that from the revolving door, you could make one circle around the store and come back to the door from the other side, where the cash register was located. I began to move around the store, resisting the color vortex, not consciously aware that I was walking, just moving in my mind, not wanting to become a color, not wanting to be gone.

Suddenly, there was this revolving door in front of me, and I knew that if I could get through it, I would not have to become a color; I could continue to *be*. It was scary and foreboding, but I knew it was the right choice. I entered the door and once again, though knowing I was so alone, I was in my comfort zone, and I was absolutely at peace. I resolved to stay longer, and I lingered as long as I could, at least a lifetime or two. When I exited the door I had conflicting feelings: despair at having left my comfort zone combined with exuberance that I had avoided becoming a color, that I continued to exist.

I took a single step forward and was thrust back into the cartoon world, and I immediately retreated, thankful that the revolving door was still there; it had not disappeared while I entered the other world. I realized that the rest of them were still in the world called warm. I was alone in this outside world, a border world between color and cartoon. This world was much bigger and much scarier than the color world. I did not want to be a cartoon character any more than I wanted to be a color. A blissfully protective cocoon formed to encircle me. I could only distinguish form and shape within this cocoon, which had a circumference of about eight feet. Beyond that distance, I could discern a translucent wall, and beyond that wall was the chaos that I chose not to see any longer.

Yet when I moved, the translucent bubble moved with me, creating new adaptive boundaries protecting me yet distancing me, because I knew that knowledge of what lay beyond the cocoon would be lost to me. I tested this awareness. I moved about ten feet from the revolving door and instantly knew that if I went much farther, the very knowledge of the revolving door would slip away. I would never find it again, and it—and the people lost on the other side of it—would be gone forever. I rushed back to get the revolving door inside my cocoon, instantly bringing great comfort and relief. I repeated this experiment three or four times before convincing myself that I absolutely could not allow the door to get out of my sphere. I experienced a great emptiness; a huge hollow space had corrupted my thinking, pushing out connections, redirecting the synaptic responses before they could make sense. I missed the others; I needed to see them; I needed to know they were real to self-actualize.

I had been out here too long, though in real time it could not have been more than five minutes. I began to wonder if they had become colors, and I would forever be on my own. I felt guilt at abandoning them in the color world. I *had* to go back into the store to find out. I anticipated the euphoria of comfort world but knew it would be temporary and fleeting. I was barely able to enjoy it. With trepidation, I exited the revolving door and immediately encountered the color vortex. I was able to leverage my cocoon, to resist the pull. Within the cocoon the colors were impotent; they took on the visage of everyday items like Christmas lights and ornaments. I took my cocoon with me and slowly traversed color world, walking around the store.

Although I sensed that beyond my protective bubble colors were merging and blending and raging in a sort of nightmare storm, I believed that I could walk through the storm because my pellucid walls would help keep me from becoming a color. As I walked around this planet, I realized that I would live the rest of my life alone in this cocoon if I didn't get someone else in it with me. As if by wizardry, Joan pierced the shell and entered from the perimeter. I recognized her as one of me, and I grabbed her and held her in my arms, whispering, "You're safe now, stay with me."

She was laughing, playing with a string of lights, and babbling something that was indecipherable. I told her that I thought we needed to get out of the store, but I wasn't sure if the cocoon could be divided, if one of us could wait in the other world while one of us returned to rescue the others. I told her that we would have to get everybody out, or we would all become colors.

She said, with just a bit of impatience, "Goddamn it, Davey, you're fucking tripping! We're peaking now! Will you just relax and enjoy it and stop freaking the fuck out?"

Once again, this served to raise me to an awareness of reality. Mentally, I repeated my mantra: Bill Mackay said this is a good trip. Bill Mackay said this is a good trip. And I hit upon a plan. The best thing for me would be to go out of the store, as the colors were too intense for me to handle. Then I'd live with the revolving door within my range and wait until the rest of them were done tripping through the store. I executed this plan with great determination and diligence. I stood outside in my translucent cocoon, keeping the revolving door just at the edge of my sight line, and I was content to live in this world for a while. I felt secure and comfortable here and actually enjoyed the hallucination for a while, for the first time with awareness that the hallucination was different from me. I consciously turned people into cartoon characters when they entered my cocoon, releasing them, sometimes in a new form, when they exited it.

Certainly, it was the peak of enjoyment. I had fun doing this, and I did it for quite a long time; it must have been ten or fifteen minutes. The others were taking shelter from the cold and enjoying the lights, and I was enjoying the world that I had created and could control. When they emerged from the revolving door, all was right with all of the worlds. I had resisted the colors, controlled the cartoon characters, and not gotten lost. On with the trip. I attempted to keep the others in my bubble but did not panic if they drifted out. I did look over my shoulder and gazed back at the door, saying good-bye to the peaceful world I had created, wondering how to stay there.

Suddenly, Kevin said in an urgent voice, "Davey, look out, you have to act normal; they are coming to *get us*!" He pointed to a phalanx of policemen who were marching out of a subway station, in unison, ready to disperse into the city for the night shift. There must have been twenty cops, all bundled and buttoned up in their winter wools, and I envisioned them surrounding me and hauling me off because I couldn't handle my trip. I froze in fear and actually began to crouch down to try to hide myself. Joan and Cheryl were hysterical as Kevin grabbed me and said, "Get up, you asshole, or you really will draw their attention to us. I'm still dirty."

My brief euphoria at having retained my sanity was crushed. They had freaked me out, and I began to get paranoid all over again. Cheryl, too, was looking scared rather than silly. We stood off to the side and began to conspire. "What if we never come back?" But we reassured each other. We got a semblance of what time was, I repeated my mantra, and we figured out that we had been tripping for over four hours. We remembered that it was a drug and that it probably had an ending since it had a beginning. We asked Kevin and Joan for help, and thank God, they chose to try.

"Yes," Joan began, "You took a pill, and you're on a trip, and the peak is just about over, and the whole thing will last no more than eight hours, and you're five hours into it. Now," she admonished, "could you let us fucking enjoy the rest of it?"

We would come back. There would be an end to this. It registered, and I stopped the intense hallucinating almost immediately, as if I could have willed it to stop all along. I enjoyed the rest of the time in the city, marveling at Rockefeller Center, complete with late-night ice skaters, the tree with all the lights. They were no longer a threat. I smiled at them with arrogance, knowing that I had defeated them. I did not travel to another world. We had pie in an automat, and I was able to drink a cup of coffee, though I was not able to handle money and buy it for myself. We wandered around the Plaza Hotel, stumbled upon a woman, all alone, playing piano in an otherwise empty ballroom, but we lingered too long and got thrown out.

Most important, I started to *feel* again, though this awareness came with the feeling of the cold. It must have been down to single digits, and I was shivering. I again focused on the fact that there was such a thing as time. I asked what it was, and Kevin said, "It's two thirty. Let's go home." And then I remembered that there was such a thing as home, and it was not in revolving-door world, and I felt comfort...and guilt! What if Mommy knew what we were doing? What if we got busted or something? After Brian, how could we be so insensitive? How much more could she take?

We found the car and got the giggles as we shared stories of what we had been experiencing. Kevin and Joan both explained that this turned out to be very strong acid, the most hallucinogenic they had ever taken, admitting that they had already tripped several other times, though with different brands. Their prior trips had been mild, more like the mushroom high at Woodstock than this otherworldly event.

Kevin assured us that he was fine to drive. Traffic stopped as soon as we got out of the city. The Long Island Expressway didn't move for the better part of an hour. Then we started inching. We saw the flashing lights about fifteen minutes later. There were four or five cars involved in an accident, and the police and ambulances occupied the two left lanes, leaving only the rightmost lane open. I was in the back left seat at the window, and just as we were crawling past the accident scene, they were loading a dead body, wrapped in black plastic and strapped to a gurney, into an EMS truck. The entity was less than ten feet from me. Joan said, "Wow, what a bummer." I pictured Brian, in his plastic bag, in parts.

Kevin observed unabashedly, "Well, at least now traffic will start moving again." I had a fleeting moment of grief, sad that the colors had gotten another victim. We all talked about the morbid moment of pleasure that New Yorkers get when they have been stuck in a traffic jam, and they discover that it's been caused by an accident, and thus the traffic will clear up when you get by the accident scene. Inwardly, I was sure that this person had died because I had tripped, their death some kind of message to me, their very life offered up for me.

We took Cheryl home first, and I walked her up to her door. She assured me that she was all right, and we kissed good night. Next, we dropped Joan off. Down to the two brothers. Getting out of the car, I announced that I was afraid to go in. I was still tripping, and I was afraid of the house, afraid that Brian might be there. I was afraid of what it might do to Mom and Pop if they saw me "like this," as if my whole demeanor had changed, along with my persona.

Kevin was patient. "First of all, Davey, it's almost five o'clock in the morning, and they're asleep. Second, Brian's gone. He's not here. He's dead; he's not coming back. Finally, you don't look any different. Just be cool, go in and down to your room, and go to sleep." I knew that sleep would not be possible, and even though it was Sunday, I had to work in a few hours. As it was the week before Christmas, they had scheduled all of us to come in and clean up and restock after a busy Saturday. The concept that it had only been eleven hours since I left work was astounding, impossible. We stood there talking, laughing, and joking about my fears for about ten minutes when it started to snow. Kevin lost his patience. "Look, we're going to wake Mommy if we keep this up, and then you'll have to talk to them about what the fuck we were doing out here at five thirty. *It's time to go in. This trip is over!*" As if declaring it could make it so.

With no further hesitation he walked up to the door and went in. I followed, embraced my normal rituals, hungry for the ordinary. I lit a candle, put the Beatles on, and lay down on my bed fully dressed. I almost cried during "Julia," John's ode to his departed mother. The words had new meaning, but I was unclear how to reach it.

My alarm went off at seven. I had set it before going out, half a lifetime and half a world ago. I knew Pop would be up around eight, and I decided to get out rather than risk bumping into him. I finally changed out of my wet socks and put a clean shirt on; wearing the same dungarees I had worn when I went to work twenty-four hours earlier. Just a little afraid to drive, I crept over the two-inch base of new snow, fearing to hit the brakes and skid.

I told Pete, my boss, about my trip. I knew that Pete had experience in this, that he was an acidhead of the first order. He was perfect. "Stay up in the stock room; stay off the floor." I tried to restack fallen boxes of underwear, but I didn't accomplish a lot. Pete came up after a while and told me how to weather the crash, not to worry. "The trip is over; you'll be fine." I got out of work at noon and went by Cheryl's, but her mother said she was still sleeping. I dropped by Schneid's and hung out but avoided smoking dope. I went home in the early evening, ate supper with the family, watched Ed Sullivan, and went to bed at ten o'clock after being up for over forty hours. Mercifully, I slept. The trip was over. I would never be the same.

27

The health department closed Dirty Dan's. After an extensive renovation, the store reopened under new ownership as Dick's Pizza Parlor. Dick had just gotten off the boat, could barely speak English, but he made great pizza. His place became an alternate hangout to Schneid's, especially when we realized that Dick would never throw us out. You could buy a slice and a Coke and stay all night. At the front of the store, right inside the door, he had a small counter for ordering and serving, behind which were his work areas and ovens.

His tables and a jukebox were at the back of the store. This area was mostly out of his sight, and he rarely ventured there, leaving his customers to fend for themselves. We took advantage of the situation. Dick's became a safe harbor, a place to clean your pot, roll your joints, and take your drugs. We grew careless. People started to deal right out of Dick's. Users would come in, go to the back, and score a small aluminum pouch of speed. Then they'd go up to the counter, buy a drink, dump the stuff right in, and drink it down.

Occasionally, a patrol officer would stroll in, and there would be a mad rush to stash your stuff and look innocent. It was always good to have a slice and a drink at your table. The cops might ask Dick if he knew what was going on, but the poor guy was clueless.

The big bust came late on a Saturday night. Dick's was packed. Adam had just gotten off the bus from Jamaica. The two detectives followed him in and locked the door behind them. They flashed a search warrant and told everybody to sit down and not move. "Keep your hands on the tables." Adam took all of the drugs out of his pockets and threw them on the floor. A few others followed suit. By the time the detectives searched individuals table by table, everybody was clean. I had been clean the whole night, had just been hanging out. "Do you have any drugs?" one of the narcs asked me.

"No."

"What about the drugs on the floor—are they yours?"

"No."

"Whose are they?"

"Don't know. Whoever dropped them."

"Did you see who dropped them?"

"No."

"You're under arrest!"

"For what?"

"Loitering for the purpose of purchasing narcotics."

"I'm sitting here having a slice of pizza, minding my own business!"

"Either tell us who threw the drugs on the floor, or you're going into the system."

Adam's action enabled them to bust everyone who had been in the restaurant, including Dick. No one ratted Adam out. We were dragged all the way to Brooklyn for a nighttime arraignment. In the paddy wagon, we carried on like it was a party. The detectives kibitzed with us the whole way, confirming their suspicions that we were all pretty savvy when it came to drugs. We were booked and fingerprinted. We posed for our mug shots. Despite the folklore, we never got our phone calls—they made them for us, telling our parents to schlep into Brooklyn to post bail. We were thrown into a large holding tank, a cage, about ten by twenty feet. There was a long bench along each of the sides. A few other criminals were already there, and we huddled in a corner away from them. The only other thing in the room was a bare toilet bowl in the center of the cell. It had no seat, was brown and dirty, streaked and stained. I couldn't tell if it was from shit or dried blood, but I knew there was no way I would go anywhere near it.

One of the prisoners, talking to us in Spanish that no one could understand, made a big show of facing us, taking his penis out, and fondling it in front of the bowl. He finally took a piss, but kept playing with himself, talking to us and pursing his lips as if he were throwing kisses to us. We tried not to look, not to give him the satisfaction, but our eyes kept darting over there.

Clang! One of the cops hit the bars with his nightstick and yelled at him, in English, "Hey, Julio. Put your prick away before I come in there and cut it off." He slowly, coyly obeyed.

One by one, we were released to our parents, who had to put up a hundred dollars in bail for each of us. When Vinny's father got there, I heard him tell the cop, "Just give me ten minutes alone with him." He brought a baseball bat with him, and the look in his eyes was petrifying. The cops calmed him down and took away his bat before they released Vinny.

Mom and Pop were some of the last ones to arrive. They had stopped to pick up Craig Clancy, a detective friend of my father's. Although he was much younger than Pop, they shared a fondness for beer, and Craig had befriended our family, often popping in unexpectedly and usually half in the bag. Craig liked to tell the stories of the skells that he'd eighty-sixed that week, and the danger that he was placing himself in to make our city streets safe. In the days before aluminum, he liked to crush his steel cans with his bare hands to demonstrate how tough he was. Since Brian died, he had been coming over every week.

Craig got on my case whenever he saw me, telling me to cut my hair, which was now shoulder length. He was convinced that long hair provided a special weapon to any sleazy perp who might want to take me down. I usually humored Craig, though I did not like him much.

He huddled with the booking officer but then came over and told my parents he was sorry, it was too late to keep me out of the system. "Don't worry, though," he told them as he winked at me. "It's not a clean bust. They brought in everybody because one or two kids had drugs. It'll probably get dismissed before ever going to trial." He lent them the hundred bucks and got me out. I stayed in defensive denial for the long ride home, swearing I was an innocent victim of circumstance.

It was almost dawn when we got home. I was embarrassed and ashamed and just wanted to get some sleep. Pop offered beers all around, though, and we had to sit up talking for a while. Around six, I announced that I was going to bed. As I got up, Craig, with a beer-soaked, shit-eating grin on his face and my mother and father within arm's reach in our living room, reached out, grabbed me by the hair, and dragged my head down toward the ground. He lifted his knee up and smashed my head into it and then, still directing my movements by dragging my head, pulled me back up. He kicked me in the chest while pushing me back, causing me to hit the floor—hard—on my back. I was stunned, dizzy, seeing the proverbial stars. The whole attack, which he'd launched without warning, only lasted two or three seconds.

As I tried to clear my vision and look up, I could see him towering above me. My mother was screaming, asking him what he thought he was doing. Pop was just standing there, his mouth slightly ajar. Craig reached down to help me up, laughing, shaking the fistful of my hair that was entwined in his fingers, freeing some of the loose hairs to float silently down.

I refused to take his hand, pushing it away as I got myself up off the floor, tears welling in my eyes. I did not want to cry, so I just unleashed a diatribe. "You fucking animal, what the fuck is your problem?"

"Watch your language," Mom yelled as Craig said, "I told you to get a haircut. I didn't even hit you hard; I barely touched you. A perp could kill you just by grabbing your hair and bashing you around. You're helpless. I just wanted to make sure you were getting my point."

I looked at Mom, tears welling up in my eyes. "Watch my language? This asshole almost kills me, and you want me to watch my language?"

Pop reached across and slapped me with an open hand. "Don't ever speak to your mother that way!" I was stunned into silence. The slap didn't hurt, but it wounded me deeply. Pop turned to Craig and said calmly, "Get out!"

Craig was surprised. "I was just doing it for his own good."

"For his own good? This is my *son*, Craig, not one of your goddamn skells or perps for Chrissake. *Get out of my house!*" Pop walked over to the door and held it open, and Craig slowly turned and began to slink out. Mom looked at Pop with absolute admiration—he had done the right thing and had done it without being prompted. Too hurt to appreciate the moment, I stalked to my room.

The pizza place never opened its doors again, and Dick, the real victim, was deported to Italy. The rest of us had to get lawyers and endure a brief trial. The cops lied like crazy, said that all the kids threw drugs on the floor, but no, they couldn't tie any specific drugs to any individual kid. The judge wasn't buying it, and we were found not guilty. But we did not get out of there without a lecture from the bench. He pointed his gavel at our parents. "Take this as a warning and straighten your kids out."

28

Around the middle of April, Kevin told me that he and Joan were going upstate for the day to look at summer rentals. He wanted a change from the Hamptons. Did I want to take a ride with them? Absolutely. He had heard about Monroe from someone at work. It was less than two hours from Queens, had beautiful lakes, and was much cheaper than the Hamptons. We got off the Thruway, found the town, and walked into the first real estate office that we came across. He said that there would be two couples, no kids.

We looked at five properties and fell in love with the biggest, most expensive house we saw. Kevin put a deposit down, and I let him know that I wanted in. "I don't know, Davey. Mommy will expect me to be responsible for you."

Joan picked up my defense. "That's not fair, Kevin. You're not his parent, and you don't have to be the controlling big brother. Just be a friend for a change."

"Well, we do need more people to pay rent," he agreed. "I suppose you want to include Cheryl?"

"I don't know. Let me think about it. We have time."

Cheryl had become increasingly enamored of her belief that we would get married, maybe even before I finished college. Our make-out sessions had grown more and more steamy, and she was ready to consummate. I, on the other hand, continued to resist. I don't know what scared me more: my anxiety about whether I really knew how to do it, or my fear that I would get her pregnant and have to marry her. I buried my insecurities by surfacing her faults. I grew ever more critical of her smoking and school cutting. I was beginning to think of her as a distraction. "Maybe we should take a break."

"Why?" she cried. "Do you have someone else?"

"No...I don't."

"Then why? I would have thought that after all this time, the least you could do would be to tell me the fucking truth."

Truth? I didn't even know what it was.

■ ■ ■

On May 4, the National Guard opened fire on the campus of Kent State, a small university in Ohio. They killed four students who were demonstrating against the war. The anguish made world headlines. The next day, campuses across America erupted; students began strikes and boycotts. A national protest was planned, culminating with a march on Washington.

I had to go. They were shooting us down for our beliefs. We were supposed to be fighting in Asia to make the world safe for democracy, but democracy turned out not to be so safe for us. I was enraged. The decision to skip classes and go to Washington was easy. My folks were upset, concerned more for my personal safety than anything else. For the first time, Pop admitted that

Nixon might be wrong. You cannot go shooting students. But he did not want me getting shot either. They were even worried about the boycott: What would that mean to my chances of graduating college? Was I dropping out? We talked through a lot of it. I listened, and they listened, but I remained steadfast in my resolve.

Vinny and I decided to go together in his "new" car, a ten-year-old, original Morris Mini-Minor, built in England; the steering wheel was on the right. We split late on Friday. Vinny drove all the way, and we talked all night. "You've been hanging out with Pauly a lot lately. You're not doing glue again, are you?"

"I told you I was done with that."

"Well, then, what the fuck? Pauly looks like a junkie, man. I hope you're not doing dope."

"What if I was?"

"Jesus, Vinny."

"I just snort it now and then. Stop worrying about me."

"You're not dirty now, are you?"

"Not with dope."

Outside Baltimore we picked up a couple of young girls, hitchhikers. We stuffed them into the tiny backseat of this toy car. For a change, no one's mind was on sex; we were all intent on stopping the war. As soon as we hit DC, the girls took off on their own. Young people were streaming into the National Mall from all directions. We were coming together to let Nixon know that he had gone too far. We were not going to stand for it anymore. If he was going to shoot students he was going to have to shoot a lot of us. Ominously, we also saw National Guardsmen gathering on street corners in groups of five to ten, forming small back-to-back circles, helmets on, rifles up. Occasionally, a protester would stride up to one of these circles and curse or belittle them, some even spitting at their feet, calling them murderers. The circles tensed and tightened, and you could see their fingers twitching on their guns, but their eyes remained locked straight ahead, not glancing at—certainly not making eye contact with—the student agitators.

The mall area was completely packed with people, museum step to museum step. There was a stage set up at the far end of the reflecting pool, opposite the Lincoln Memorial. It felt like a big party. Grass flowed freely, and we got high. We wandered through the crowds, soaking in the atmosphere. The weather was perfect, around seventy degrees, with high cumulous clouds interspersed in a bright-blue sky. Rumor was that Jane Fonda was going to talk, so we made our way closer to the stage.

We listened to the speeches. Some black politician scared the shit out of us. "They've been killing black boys in the South for years. Now they've shot four white middle-class kids. Welcome to the club. We're all niggers now!" We learned to thrust our closed fists of defiance to the sky and felt absolutely self-righteous.

Jane never showed, but as day drifted into night, speeches gave way to folk music, replete with an endless flow of grass and an occasional hit of beer or wine. The organizers asked us all to stay the night, occupy the Capitol and march to Arlington National Cemetery the next day. We would honor all of the war dead, not just the lambs from Kent State. The clouds dispersed, and the stars shone brightly. The party atmosphere subsided a bit as we remembered the gravity of the situation that had brought us. We fell asleep sometime after two, cuddling with thousands of strangers on the grassy areas surrounding the reflecting pool.

We awoke at sunrise to a disturbance. A naked hippie was walking down, step-by-step, slowly but surely, from the Lincoln Memorial toward the reflecting pool. Guardsmen were gathering along the way, keeping others from approaching this fool. They were calling out to him, asking him to clothe himself, reminding him that he could not go around Washington naked. "This isn't Woodstock; this is our capital." Vinny and I were chuckling, both at the spectacle and at the irony: killing students was okay, but walking around naked was not. Smoking pot and drinking in public was okay, but waving your penis for peace was out of bounds.

It had been a lovely May night, but it was about fifty-five degrees. The water must have been cold, but he kept walking right through the pool. The DC police gathered at the other end, ready to intercept and arrest him. From the side of the pool, not twenty feet from us, a woman ran into the water, as if on cue, with an American flag. She wrapped it around this guy and yelled, "He's not naked anymore; you can't arrest him." Then, incongruously, the two of them put their arms around each other and began to sing, "Oh beautiful for spacious skies, for amber waves of grain..." The crowd picked it up and by the time the first verse ended, there must have been thousands of us singing "America the Beautiful."

Loud cheers and thunderous applause, but the guardsmen and police remained tense. What now? The young woman whispered something in naked guy's ear; he smiled and they bolted off to the side, arm in arm. They were swallowed up by the crowd, making it impossible for the cops to get near them without creating their own disturbance, upsetting the well-being of thousands.

All this before the sun was high. We were tired and hungry but agreed that we needed to stay and participate in the march at eleven o'clock. Some organizers used megaphones to direct the crowd. Instructions were frightening: "Maintain your composure! Do not run! Do not fight! If the guards start using their batons, lie on the ground; if they start shooting, lie on the ground. Do not turn and run; do not get shot in the back." Vinny and I just looked at each other, humor gone in an instant, adrenaline pumping. "This is real, man," was all I could say. Vinny took a deep puff on his cigarette and flicked the butt into the pool.

We joined the march. Only a few of the protesters had been scared off by the warnings. Most of us believed that Kent State was an aberration; they were not going to start shooting us in front of the Capitol. But we were absolutely terrified nonetheless, especially those of us who were first-time marchers, first-time protesters, out of our white suburban enclaves for the first time, filled with anger at our so-called leaders.

We convened at the base of the Arlington Memorial Bridge— there were thousands of us, and we were awaiting the order to march over the bridge. We could see a huge phalanx on the other side. The National Guard was organizing to meet us. They were fully regaled in dark-green camouflage uniforms, heavy steel helmets over their entire heads with Plexiglas face plates, and bulletproof body shields like something out of the Middle Ages that they were carrying in one hand, and the ominous batons for bashing in heads in the other. They lined up shield to shield, forming a horizontal wall. I was glad I was not near the front. I would have time to lie on the ground if they started using their weapons. If they had guns, they were not in sight, so the worst that I was expecting was a crack on the skull.

As the organizers with the megaphones began to move us out, they carefully assured us that the media were present, that television would capture the events. Was it supposed to make me feel better that Mom could see me get busted on national TV?

Slowly, we began to cross the bridge, the silence of the marchers deafening. No one was talking, no one was laughing; we were all dead serious—we were, in fact, risking our futures to make the statement that the government's behavior at Kent State was unacceptable.

Miraculously, like the parting of the Red Sea, as we reached the other side of the bridge, the guardsmen parted, reformed their lines vertically, along the sides of the road, spreading themselves out and ensuring that the crowd could not fragment but would be contained. The thought occurred to me that they could surround us. But there were no incidents, no violence, and no physical encounters. Instead, we all marched into the cemetery and lined up along one of the entrances...and waited. For what, we weren't sure. The megaphones started again, directing us to keep marching. We went past JFK's grave and the Tomb of the Unknown Soldier and gathered at the Memorial Amphitheater.

After about twenty minutes or so of milling about at the amphitheater, the organizers called the march a success and asked the protesters to disperse in a peaceful manner. The event was over. The anticlimactic feeling was infectious. We all shuffled around, realized how tired, thirsty, and hungry we were, and began wondering how to get back on the road, home to our families, hoping that we had somehow influenced something. We certainly felt righteous and proud.

It took us almost two hours to reach the highway, which remained congested almost all the way back to New York. We were crossing the George Washington Bridge as the sun was setting, and we were still glowing with the aftereffects of the march. The radio said that there had been over a million of us and that Washington had been brought to a standstill.

Of course, it was a weekend, and the governing process was not significantly affected, but we were smug. All the way home, cars from the march had left their lights on. As Vinny dropped me off, I gave one more raised-fist salute and then crawled into the house about nine o'clock. Mom and Pop were angry and concerned. I had not even bothered calling them. But they were interested in my account of the march, glad that the National Guard didn't act, hopeful that the country could move on.

I slept for the next ten hours, but I did not get up to go to school. As far as I knew, the boycott was still on. I had already missed a week of classes, and there were just two weeks left in the semester. I was too tired to go in, but I did call the school to see what was going on. A secretary in administration told me that about 50 percent of students were still boycotting, but about 70 percent of classes were being held. Teachers would not get paid if they did not resume classes.

I went to work as usual and read my books, guessing that they would hold finals as scheduled and that I would be taking them. By the end of the week, the dean announced that individual teachers would make the decisions about what happened to the student protesters who boycotted classes. All students were encouraged to return to school for the last week of classes, saying that for those who did there should be no repercussions, as long as the student met the teachers' requirements.

I decided to continue my boycott. According to the papers, only about 25 percent of us skipped that last week. I traveled into the city toward the end of the week to meet with each of my teachers and learn his or her views. I did not want to write the semester off. Two of the teachers told me that as long as I took the final and did the papers there would be no problems. One of the teachers asked me to write an extra report on why I had boycotted and what I had learned. The last of my four teachers whom I went to see, Mr. Levy, the hippie English teacher, simply said, "You marched on Washington? You get an A!"

29

Vinny and I were the first ones to move up to Monroe. I finished my schoolwork, and we both quit our jobs. We packed our stereos, a television, our summer clothes, and not much more. The house was set on five acres, accessible by a long dirt driveway, about a quarter of a mile off a back state road. There was no garage, no paved area, so we just parked our cars in a small clearing. The front porch was small but featured four round white columns that made it look like a Southern plantation, complete with a few rickety rocking chairs.

Before leaving, we had argued about the bedroom arrangements for several nights in a row. We wound up with eight paying tenants. At the top of the stairs, going from left to right, the first bedroom was to be shared by me and Don, the middle bedroom by Kevin and Berk, and the third by Joan and Miranda. The downstairs bedroom was Vinny and Adam's. Although there were four bedrooms, there was only one bathroom. Entering it from the kitchen, there was an area that included a sink and a toilet and an adjoining door that led into a larger section that had a second sink and a toilet but also included a shower. On the other side of this section was yet another door that led into the downstairs bedroom.

We had brought some grass and smoked a joint right after unloading the cars. It was a beautiful sunny day. We took a walk to the back of our property. Immediately behind the house was a large field that had been grown over with weeds. We crossed to the other side of it and discovered some ruins. It looked like a small stone house had burned to the ground. We imagined that it happened in the Revolutionary War. We walked beyond it and found some old property lines that had been marked by an extended three-foot stone wall that had mostly fallen into disrepair. We followed it back as it meandered toward our house. We were imagining a hundred years earlier, when men were farmers and life was simple.

We found a great sunny patch in the middle of the woods to the side of the house and decided to plant the seeds from our pot, expecting that by the end of the summer we would have a homegrown crop. We sat at the edge of the field and smoked another joint, resolving that this was going to be the best summer of our lives. It would be the first time that either of us had lived on our own.

As the sun set and we went back to the house, we realized that neither of us had brought anything to eat and we drove the mile or so into Monroe, a small town of about four blocks with two traffic lights. We found a pizza parlor, ordered a pie and a couple of beers and grabbed a booth. The waitress, who couldn't have been any older than us, brought a tray with two bottles of beer and two frosted mugs. The pizza was decent and we were about halfway through when we noticed the waitress talking to a few longhairs and gesturing over to our booth. Two guys, a little younger than us, maybe seventeen or so, came over to our table and asked us where we were from.

We said we were from the city and that we were renting a house for the summer. They smiled and asked if they could sit down. We welcomed them and chatted for a while, and it wasn't long before one of them asked if we had anything to smoke. We both lied instantly. "No."

They looked disappointed and told us that the previous summer some hippies had rented places and always brought great shit up from the city. They let us know that if we were so inclined, they would help us sell it. "Up here, you can get a better price than in the city."

Again, simply, "No." Incongruously, then they asked us if we wanted them to score for us!

We shook our heads, laughing.

"Where's your house?"

"A couple of miles out of town," I lied. "Far back in the woods."

They laughed, sensing that we were suspicious. "Listen, we're not narcs. There are two kinds of kids in this town: the freaks and the alkies. You can always find the alkies in the bar. You can find the freaks on the village green. Stop by and hang out with us sometime. Nice to meet you." They shook our hands "brother" style and headed out the door.

We drove to the grocery store on the far side of town and bought an assortment of chicken potpies, potato chips, and beer. As we were returning, we slowed down as we passed the village green, and we saw the locals we had met, along with a few other kids, hanging out on the monkey bars in the playground. They were watching the cars go by and saw us. They waved and nudged their friends and pointed directly at us. We would certainly not be able to hide in this town.

We threw down a few more beers, smoked another joint, ate all the potato chips and tried to get Vinny's ten-inch black-and-white TV set to work, extending the rabbit ears with a coat hanger. We got two channels, both fuzzy, both drifting, and almost had to choose between audio and video because we sure had trouble getting both at the same time. Though neither one of us had thought of sheets, we did remember pillows, and we hit our individual sacks.

Upon entering this house, you came directly into a huge living room that consisted of the whole front half of the house and had a twenty-five-foot arched ceiling. Off to the left side was an open stairway that went to the bedrooms, which were off a balcony that looked over the living room. Under the balcony level were the kitchen, the bathroom and the fourth bedroom. On the right side of the living room was a massive stone fireplace. This thing was about four feet wide and three feet deep, and it had andirons the size of my leg. It was built of solid stones that had been carved by a mason to about three cubic feet each. The stones retained their original grain, color, and stratification. The stone chimney was exposed all the way to the ceiling and through the roof, and it looked almost as attractive from the outside as from the inside. Clearly the defining feature of the house, it was well used. Black residue was thick. Vinny and I spent the next morning gathering and splitting wood for our first fire. We got everything ready but decided to wait for the next night, when others would be coming up, for the fire. We wanted to make everyone feel welcome.

We also desperately wanted to go see the Beatles' movie *Let It Be,* which had just been released. Drove to town, bought the local paper, found the ads, and discovered that it was playing in Middletown, about a fifteen-minute drive. We were mesmerized, enthralled, stoned of course. The movie sailed by. On the drive back, we commiserated and wondered whether the breakup of the Beatles would be permanent.

The next day, a Friday, I wanted to see if it was possible to walk through the woods to town. When we drove out of our driveway, we went left for a half mile and then right for a mile into town. By my reckoning, town was a lot closer as the crow flew. If I just traversed through the woods more directly, it should be an easy walk. Vinny was not up for this adventure. I just plunged into the woods. About ten minutes into it, I realized that I was probably in somebody's backyard and hoped that I was not going to get shot. But I did stumble upon a creek, remembered that a creek flowed through the village green and sure enough, I followed it and came out in the park right before the town.

A couple of the local freaks were hanging out, and I waved back as they shouted hello. I went to the deli and got a sandwich and brought it into the park and sat at the farthest picnic table from where they were. They did not hesitate before coming over to join me, though.

"Hi, I'm Nick." Nick looked like he had been one of the guys hanging out the other night when we had passed through town. "Donovan told us that you guys were up from the city for the summer?"

"Who's Donovan?" I said as I shook his hand. "I'm Davey."

"Well, Donovan's not his real name. We just call him that, after the singer, you know, 'They call me Mellow Yellow, quite rightly;' 'cause he plays guitar and sings and reminds us of Donovan."

"Okay," I said, still unsure. "So who is he?"

Nick looked about eighteen and had shoulder-length hair parted down the middle in the popular John Lennon style of the day, but jet black and Italian greasy. He had an ear-to-ear grin and a stoned twinkle in his eye. "Donovan met you in the pizza place the other night, didn't he? You're one of those guys from the city?"

"Uh, right," I stumbled, "I am."

The grin again and a little shake of the head as he asked, "You want to smoke some weed?"

Deep breath, followed by a what-the-fuck sigh. "Sure."

"C'mon," he said. "We can't smoke here; Super Trooper might be lurking around." We began to walk: me, Nick, and this other guy who hadn't said a word, following the creek on the opposite side of the park from where I had entered.

"Super Trooper?" I asked.

"Yeah, there's this state trooper who really likes to hassle the freaks. He's like one of the most decorated cops on the force, and he loves to get in the papers. And by the way"—interrupted by the shit-eating grin again—"he hates it when city hippies come up here. He thinks you guys bring all the drugs with you, 'cause the local kids must be innocent. So be on the lookout for him. He made a big bust up here last year of some city guys."

A few hundred yards out of town, the creek flowed downhill, and there was a small, maybe ten-foot, waterfall. Above it were some large rocks that had been pretty well decorated with graffiti. Nick and his friend climbed up there and hung their legs off the side. Nick reached into his crotch area and withdrew a plastic baggie with a good half ounce of pot. He rolled a joint expertly and handed it to me. "Guests first," he said as he lit a match and got me going. I inhaled deeply, then coughed most of it out. I bogarted it and inhaled again, less deeply, so I could hold it this time. Nick grinned perpetually, almost laughing when I coughed, and said, "This is good shit, I got this from Brooklyn, from my cousin."

It was indeed good shit. I got wrecked on the one joint, finally introduced myself to the friend, Chris, and talked the day away, learning all the local folklore and discovering that Nick and I were kindred spirits with many of the same tastes in rock 'n' roll. Nick had graduated high school a year earlier and was trying to decide whether he was going to go to college or not. Now, for the most part, he was just selling grass and getting stoned. We lay in the sun, refreshing ourselves with water from the falls until we began to burn out. I told him that I had to be getting back, and I told him more precisely where we were living. His eyes seemed to gleam an extra twinkle.

I made my way back through town by following the creek, but was a little unsure when I was supposed to divert from the creek and veer toward our house. I did so too early and wound up coming through someone's backyard, which caused a dog to get quite excited. I backed away from him, all the way to the creek, went a bit farther and then tried again, this time coming out much closer to home and absolutely on the right trail.

As I approached the house I heard Vinny spewing a stream of curses, and as I got closer I could see him standing in the small gully next to the chopping block, kicking at something. Then he reached down, picked something up, lifted it over his head, and smashed it down on the rocks. It was the television. As I walked up, I just looked at him, shaking my head. "What the fuck?"

"I tried everything," he yelled. "I've been trying all day, and I can't fucking take it anymore. Fuck television." He lit a cigarette and went back into the house.

The picture tube was smashed, and little bits of glass and tubes were everywhere. The outside cabinet was in chunky plastic pieces. He had gone berserk from too much fuzzy reception. I was sure that he would regret this action, but I wasn't about to tell him so. In any case, nothing was going to put this TV back together.

Vinny spent the rest of the day in his room, and I retreated to mine and lay on my bed, not really trying to nap but just resting, trying to calm my mind from the strong pot. I drank a Coke to relieve my throat. I hooked up my portable stereo and listened to the *Volunteers* album by the Jefferson Airplane with their exhortation that I first heard at Woodstock. "Up against the wall, motherfucker." I was trying to imagine what the walls were, and all I could come up with were the generation gap issues that I summarized in my mind as resistance to authority. The walls were the status quo. The walls were government and the policies that could allow Vietnam. The walls were the war. Tear down the walls, indeed.

I listened to the same side over and over until the sun began to set. Someone was knocking on the front door—the first weekend arrivals were here. Vinny and I bolted for the door at the same time, and he won, as I had to come down the stairs. We were excited for some more company, happy to see Don and Cara, an airline stewardess whom he had been dating. She was older than Don, short, and top-heavy. She wore lots of dark makeup and teased her hair into an outmoded beehive of frizz. Supposedly, she lived up to the stereotype of the young, single stewardess: she was promiscuous and experienced. I had not expected Don to bring her. We showed them around and Cara, upon seeing the room that was to be mine and Don's, immediately said, "I guess we can pull the two beds together," indicating to Don that she intended to seize my bed. I let her know right then and there: "Uh, Cara, one of those beds is mine. You're going to have to share a single bed with Don."

"With you in the room?"

"Uh, yeah. It's *my* room."

"Don, we have to talk." And they asked me to leave *my* bedroom.

"Fine," I said.

The house began to fill up. Kevin, Joan, Berk, and Miranda all arrived at the same time, followed shortly thereafter by Adam. In a house with eight single beds, we only had nine people. The situation should have been workable, but Cara had approached it with hostility, and it became a big deal. It was almost two hours before she and Don emerged from the bedroom, and when they did Don took me to the side and asked me if I could find somewhere else to sleep. "No way. I've been here for almost a week. I'm dead tired tonight. I am a paying member of the household, by the way. If you guys want some privacy, you can have some, and I'll come to bed later, but I've got to hit my bed to sleep." Don was not one to turn down a reasonable argument, but Cara was livid. Fortunately for me, she took her wrath out on Don and left me out of it.

We built a big fire, moved my speakers out to the balcony overlooking the living room and sat in a semicircle around the fireplace, smoking joints and drinking beer. We went through the *White Album* and *Tommy* and were blasting the Doors' *Soft Parade*.

We realized someone was banging on the front door. It was close to midnight. My anxieties jumped to the forefront of my brain. I thought it must be Nick and the locals, and I knew the rest of the guys would be pissed. Luckily, Kevin peeked through the blinds before answering the door. He turned back and said, "It's cops. Stash the grass fast."

I saw one joint sitting on the large bowl-shaped black ash-tray, which also had several roaches in it. Kevin closed the blinds and went to the door slowly and yelled out, "Just a minute," as I grabbed them and went to the bathroom to flush them. Don ran up the stairs, turned the stereo off, and closed the door to the bedroom. I pictured him eating his grass and hoped he had time.

Kevin was perfect, as if he had been trained. He opened the door only a crack and calmly said, "Good evening, officers, can I help you?"

It was two New York State troopers, and I was imagining that one of them was Super Trooper. "Can we come in for a minute?" one of them asked.

Kevin unhesitatingly said, "No, it's late, and we were just getting ready for bed. Some of us are not dressed. What is it that you want?" The rest of us were sitting quietly in the living room, almost afraid to move and in absolute awe at the deft way that Kevin was dealing with the circumstances.

"Well, there has been a complaint from a neighbor that the music is too loud, and we are just here to check you out!"

"Sorry, Officer, we won't let that happen again. Please let the neighbor know that we apologize."

"Where are you from?" the cop asked.

"We've rented this house for the summer."

"I can see that," the cop said in an angry voice. "I asked you where you were *from*!"

"Bellerose."

"Where's that?"

"Long Island."

"Are you up here to deal drugs?" This was getting ugly fast.

"Excuse me?" was the best Kevin could do.

"'Cause if you are, you've come to the wrong town. We will not tolerate a bunch of hippies from New York City selling dope to our kids. *Do you understand me?*"

"We're not here to sell drugs," Kevin said matter-of-factly. "We're just here to enjoy the woods and the lakes, like everybody else."

"Yeah, well, I just thought I'd let you know that I busted a group of hippies from the city last summer, and they're in jail now, so…I'll be back." So it *was* Super Trooper. The second cop had barely said a word.

As they went to go down the steps, Kevin lost his cool for the first time, and, cocky from his success, called out in a pleasant voice, "Call ahead next time, and we'll bake you a cake." He saw Super Trooper stop in his tracks and glare back at him as he closed the door. We carefully looked out the blinds until we saw the cruiser leave before we collapsed into cacophony. Overexcited, over-adrenalized, we were all talking at once: "Holy shit! Can they do that? Who do you think complained? The music wasn't that loud. Kevin, you were great! Kevin, you were an asshole. 'We'll bake a cake?' What the fuck was that?"

Kevin stood up and barked out an order. "Everybody get any drugs that you have and get them out of the house now. They might be back in five minutes with a search warrant for all we know, so let's do this fast."

Don finally opened his door and asked if it was safe. He had been sitting with his dope in his hands, only ready to eat it if he heard them on the stairs. Everybody yelled at him and then realized we all had something stashed somewhere, and Kevin was right. We went into high gear, searching our pockets, our drawers, and our luggage for any stray joint, pill, rolling paper,

or hash pipe. Even matches were suspect. First we pooled everything together and put it into a large plastic bag and then agreed
that a few would go out and bury it.

I grabbed a flashlight and started out the back door, but
Kevin said, "No, they might be right up the road, watching. No
flashlights. Just two people go—go very quietly, far from the
house, and bury it deep." Don and Vinny took off, and the rest
of us cleaned the house, emptying ashtrays into the toilet, going through the garbage bags in the kitchen, even checking the
ashes around the fireplace for any fragments of roaches. By the
time Vinny and Don came back, that place was clean.

We sat around and talked through our situation. I told everyone about the locals I had met in town. I ran on about Nick and
what he told me about Super Trooper. "Did you tell them where
we were staying?" Kevin asked.

"Yeah, I think I did." I was tentative, scared.

"You *think*? Did you tell him or not?"

"Yeah, I did."

"You fucking asshole! They tipped off the cops. I should
never have let you in on this; I knew you would do something
like this."

"Fuck you, Kevin. You heard the cops, some neighbor
complained about the music. It *was* very loud, and it must carry
through the woods. These guys turned *me* on, and they had good
pot. I did not turn *them* on. They are not narcs, trust me."

Don intervened as peacemaker even after I'd refused to help
him with Cara. "Let's all calm down. A neighbor probably did
complain; we have to be more careful. And we're lucky. We got
a warning. We have to put some rules together, and we have to
follow them religiously. Everybody who comes here has to follow them, no exceptions. No smoking dope in the house, *ever!*

Everything must get buried outside and you should only go to your stash at night if you can. Does everybody agree?"

We all nodded. We opened a few beers, sat back in our seats, and for the first time began to laugh over the incident. "Can you believe this guy? Super Trooper! He thinks he is some kind of hero saving the locals from the city hippies, and the locals have better pot than we do!"

Don and Cara went up to bed first and, as promised, I waited a while. In fact, I waited until everyone else had gone to bed. I poked around with the fire for a while and tried to sleep on the couch. But it was lumpy and dirty, and I began to think, *Why should I? Cara's a bitch. She didn't ask, she demanded.* I went up to my room, quietly opened the door, and saw that they were both sound asleep, Cara half on top of Don, both naked. They'd had their private time. I got into bed and drifted off to sleep.

30

The next day we put our plan into action. Each of us spent some time going deep into the woods, digging a hole, and hiding his stash. I buried a Chock full o'Nuts coffee can, marking the location with a large flat rock that I salvaged from the ruins. There was some paranoia that we would hit one another's stashes, leading a few of the others to be highly secretive and dramatic, but I was unconcerned.

By midday we were happily enjoying life in the country. We had erected a volleyball court on the side of the house and were playing three on two when we again had some unexpected visitors: a number of the Navajos had come up from the city, apparently invited by Vinny. Almost immediately, Kevin called me aside and began giving me a lecture. "You can't just invite anybody up."

"Um, I didn't invite them. Vinny did."

"Yeah, but you have to be responsible for the little kids. Why didn't you just ask Cheryl?"

"None of your business, and, no, I will not be responsible for Vinny and Adam. But listen, I'm just as surprised and worried as you are. I'll talk to them. Just back off."

Then Vinny called me over. "Davey, didn't you say that you looked at some other houses when you were scoping this place out?"

"Yeah. Why?"

"We want to rent one," said Pauly.

"I don't know if there are any left, but I can take you in to see the real estate lady that we used."

Pauly drove, and I rode shotgun, with Dennis Doyle and Vinny in the back seat. I waved to some of the townies hanging in the park. Our agent was on the phone, but she motioned us to wait. I reminded her who I was and which house she helped us with and asked her if there were any more rentals left for the summer. She mentioned one that Kevin and I had seen, about a mile from ours. I had liked it a lot. It was a little smaller, much boxier and unfashionable, but it was situated at the end of a road, up a hill from a lake, and it featured a long narrow stairway that traversed down the hillside, in between houses that fronted on the main road, straight down to a private dock on the lake. She said I remembered it well and suggested we ride out to see it.

They loved it and didn't want to see any others. It was a little more than half the price of ours, $800. Pauly and Dennis huddled together on the side, started counting out money and came back with the total in cash. The agent smiled and said, "Boys, you have made my weekend. This is how I like to do business."

As we were driving back through town, Nick spotted me from the park and waved us down. I let him know that we had rented another house. Nick asked me if he and his friends were welcome to come up and party, and I said, "Not yet, let us get settled in first; we'll be here all summer."

"No problem." He smiled. "There's a bar between the two houses that you're renting, on the near corner of the lake, Harriman's. Why don't you stop in there later and have a beer? It's a little bit of a redneck roadhouse, but they don't give the freaks too much shit as long as we don't give them too much. They have a great jukebox and dance floor and some cool pinball machines. There's not much else to do around here on a Saturday night."

We all went back to the new house and helped them unpack their stuff. We discovered that you could use the deck railing on the back porch to get up on the roof of the house, which had only a slight slope and offered a priceless view of the lake and the surrounding hills. We hung out up there and smoked a joint, talking about who else was going to be in on this house and when they would be able to move up. Pauly told me that Kathy and Cheryl would be sharing one of the bedrooms. I told them about Super Trooper and warned them to be cooler than we were.

As it grew dark, we walked down the stairs and along the lake over to Harriman's. None of the townies that I knew were there, but the rednecks were. There were two or three cliques, all looking the same: twenty-five- to thirty-five-year-old guys in black T-shirts, cigarette packs rolled up in their sleeves, tattoos on their arms, scruffy hair, dirty jeans, and shitkicker boots. There were a few women, none of whom looked much better than the guys. Most talk stopped when we came in, and most eyes were on us. We headed toward a corner of the bar, near one of the pinball machines, and pulled up a few stools. The bartender, who had been talking to one of the groups at the bar, shook his head a little bit, said something that caused the others to laugh, and then walked down to us. "Well, girls, can I get you something?" he asked.

Oh, fuck, we all thought, but only Dennis, with his hair flowing almost down to his waist, said something out loud. "*What* did you say?"

Trying to prevent a showdown, I stepped in front of Dennis, looked the bartender right in the eye, and said, "Look, we don't want any trouble. We'd just like to buy some beers. Some guys down in town told me this was a friendly bar."

"*Who* in town?"

"Nick Scapellini."

"You know Nick?"

"Yeah, he's a friend of mine."

"Where are you from?"

"Queens…in the city."

"Nick has friends from the city?"

"He does now."

I never broke eye contact, never looked down the bar to see how the local rednecks were gathering, hoping to get a chance to kick the shit out of us. Finally, the bartender smiled and grabbed a stack of coasters and set one in front of each of us. "I was just playin' with you," he said. "No harm done. What'll you have?"

Vinny elbowed his way past me, giving the guy his best evil eye despite my attempts to cut him off. "What do you have on tap?" Vinny asked coldly.

"No draft on Saturday…bottles only. Bud, Schlitz, or Genesee, take your pick, a buck each." Most of the yokels at the bar had Buds. "Four Genesees," I said, choosing the only upstate-brewed beer I had ever heard of. I put a five dollar bill on the bar and said, "My treat, and please keep the change." He laughed and shook his head again as he took the five off the bar before he went, opened the four bottles, and set them in front of us.

We took turns buying rounds and throwing quarters into the pinball machine as the bar filled up. At one point, we were close to getting killed again. Dennis was flipping the ball, and he missed one and yelled, "Fuck!"

From way down at the other end of the bar, over the noise, one of the sinister-looking rednecks yelled out, "Hey, watch your language, sweetie, there are real women here." Dennis looked right at the muscle-bound broad standing next to this redneck and mumbled, too low for him to hear, "I don't see any!"

We couldn't help laughing but surrounded Dennis and whispered, "Shut the fuck up, asshole," as the guy started moving toward us.

Just then, Nick and some of his friends walked in and immediately defused the situation. He said hi to almost everybody he passed but made his way toward us. He got to us just before the cowboy. "You know these assholes, Nick?"

"Yeah," Nick said, flashing his grin. "These assholes are friends of mine; go mess with somebody else."

"Well, tell the wise-ass sissy here to watch her language." We grabbed Dennis and turned him around before he could say anything. I turned to the guy and said, "Sorry. We'll be cool. Can I buy you a beer?"

"I'll buy my own damn beer," he said as he walked away.

Several more rounds, and I was good and drunk by the time the place closed at two. I walked out to a cloudless night and marveled at the brilliance of the sky and the twinkling of the moonlight reflecting on the lake. We all went back to the Navajos' place, Nick too, and sat around for a while smoking a joint and laughing at the evening. People fell asleep all around me, but I was too wired and decided to go back to my house and my own bed. I stumbled down the stairs and almost fell. I was making my way along the lake when a white step van came by. It slowed down as it passed me, the passenger's side door slid open, and a face peered out. He was in his early twenties, had shoulder-length dirty blond hair, a couple of prominent zits that had been popped, a dirty, ragged T-shirt and a dopey smile that displayed two broken teeth. "Want a ride?" he said.

"Uh, no thanks, I need the walk."

"Suit yourself," he said, "but I'm on my way into town, and I'll be going right past your place."

I looked at him with suspicion and began to sober real fast. "You don't know me," was the best I could do.

"No, but I know you're a friend of Nick's, and you're renting that big red house about a mile up the road."

"Are you a friend of Nick's?"

"Of course, how else would I know who you are? I gotta go make a pickup...you want a ride or not?"

"Why the fuck not?" I said, knowing it was a risk.

He pulled the side door all the way open, and I got in by going behind him. He was driving standing up. The passenger seat was filled with fast food wrappers and the back cargo area was filled with shelves of white bread, donuts, and cakes. I sat down, pushing the wrappers to the floor, and he took off, working the stick shift that was between us. Much to my surprise, he didn't say anything. He knew exactly where to go even though I was unsure, having never come from this direction at night before. I stopped him from pulling up the driveway, though, figuring anyone in the house would think it was a raid. "I'll walk up from here," I said. "Thanks."

"That's cool," he said. "Doesn't look like fun trying to turn the truck around in there, anyway." He was stretching his neck, getting a good look at the house. He stuck out his hand. "I'm Skipper," he said.

I shook his hand, laughing and nodding like an idiot. "Nice to meet you, Skipper, and thanks again." I got out and walked up the driveway, fumbled with my keys, took a leak, and discovered that the door to my bedroom was locked. I knocked on it. No answer. I knocked again, a little more loudly. Cara yelled, "We're sleeping."

"Open the door," I said impatiently. "I want to go to *my* bed!"

Don got up, opened the door, and mumbled an apology. I kicked off my shoes and plopped on the bed and fell into a deep sleep almost instantly.

When I awoke, the sun was high; it looked to be about noon. I was alone in the room, but the door was open. Others were stirring, and I went down. Kevin jumped on me immediately. "Where the fuck were you last night? We were worried sick."

"Sorry, Mommy, I went out with my friends." I poured myself a cup of coffee, but he wasn't done. In fact, he was just getting started.

"You could have let us know," he said. "You left here at three o'clock in the afternoon to go to the real estate agent, and you don't come home until the next morning? What the fuck are we supposed to think? You only care about yourself."

"You know, Kevin, fuck you. I'm sorry, I should have let you know, but you're not fucking Mommy, so stop treating me like you are."

"What happened with you and Cara?"

This was a surprise. "What?"

"Cara's really pissed. She says she can't have any privacy. You woke her up in the middle of the night, and you were drunk."

I looked around. "Where is she?"

"She and Don left."

"Early start?" It was Sunday, but I had expected them to stay later.

"No, she took her stuff and told Don she was not coming back."

"I don't give a shit if she doesn't come back, Kevin. Fuck her. I paid for my bed. Did she?"

"C'mon, you know she's Don's girlfriend—she's going to be here."

"I don't care. I intend to sleep in the goddamn bed that I'm paying for. I don't believe this fucking conversation!"

"Did you take any beer that didn't belong to you?"

"*What?*" I was incredulous. How many turns was this conversation going to take? I just stared at him, dumbfounded.

"She said that somebody drank all of Don's beers; was it you?"

"*I wasn't even fucking here, remember?* What're we doing—counting beers now?"

"It's the same thing with food. People are eating other people's food."

I took a deep breath. Others seemed to be just watching us, enjoying the show. "Kevin, get a grip. We have a whole summer ahead of us. We can share food. It'll all work out in the end."

"No, we're going to put labels on everything, and if you want to take anything you have to get permission from the owner."

"I don't fucking believe this." I looked around and gravitated to the living room. Berk, Joan, and Adam were sitting there, looking at their feet dejectedly. "Adam, are you in on this? Have you guys actually talked about this?"

They all turned toward me. "We've been talking about nothing else all fucking morning," Joan said with disgust.

"And this is the best you could do? Come up with more rules? This is worse than living at home! This is fucking ridiculous! Adam?"

He said quietly, "I agree with your brother, man. We can share food, but we should talk about it first. We should do the label thing and not just take other people's food."

I walked into the kitchen and opened the refrigerator door. Sure enough, there were masking-tape labels on almost everything in there: milk that said "Adam," butter that said "Kevin and Joan," eggs that said "Don and Cara."

"Fine," I blurted. "Do whatever the fuck you want. You people are fucked up." Just before I walked out of the kitchen, I turned back to face Kevin. "But leave my food alone. Do *not* label my food. Anything I buy, anybody can take whenever they want. And don't worry. I won't touch anyone else's food."

"That's not going to be fair to you," Kevin said as I walked out.

"Fuck you," I yelled back without turning around. I stormed over to Adam. "I am fucking disappointed in you, man; I can't believe you're in on this."

"I can't afford to feed everybody, man; maybe you can, but I can't." I got in my car and drove right through town, through Middletown, and almost to Monticello, then realized I had not taken my wallet. I did not have enough gas to keep going, so I turned around and headed back. But I went right past our house and drove over to the other house. I went to their refrigerator, which was filled with beer, none of which was labeled. I took one out and guzzled it down.

■ ■ ■

When Mom had enabled me to take title of Brian's car, she stipulated that I had to take over the insurance. The bill came due, around $300 for the next year. As I had less than a hundred dollars to my name, I realized I would have to work. Monday afternoon, after everyone else had gone back to New York, Vinny and I went into town, bought a local newspaper, and looked at the want ads. We went to check out an ad for landscaping and gardening work at a place called Sterling Forest in Tuxedo Park, which was about a ten-minute drive down the Thruway. After a very brief interview, we both got hired and were asked to start the next day.

We showed up bright and early on Tuesday, happy to have the work. The park contained numerous gardens and trails adjacent to a ski resort. They were trying to attract some off-season revenue, but had not yet mastered a design. The paved, winding trails were dirty, and the forest was encroaching on them. There were no benches or water fountains. We could not imagine who would pay three bucks to walk around here for an hour or two. We drove up to the small trailer that was serving as the manager's office. We were assigned to weeding duty, and the manager drove us out on a golf cart to a section of the park that was completely overrun. Flowers were growing, and it looked like it could be attractive, but the beauty was being choked out. There were more weeds than flowers. The flower buds looked lonely and lost, trying to poke their heads out among the taller, lanky green stems.

We went at the weeds with a vengeance, working hard at first, carefully reaching in between the flowers, grabbing the thicker-stemmed weeds at the base and tugging them out by the root. We'd finish a small section and admire our work. Exposing the black dirt and cleansing the area so that the brilliance of the flowers could be enjoyed was deeply satisfying, almost invigorating. But our pace began to slow a bit as the day wore on. The sun climbed high, and as the day grew hot, we were sweating like pigs. Mosquitoes and black flies bothered us. It seemed the dirtier and sweatier we got, the hungrier and greedier they got. They were swarming around us, biting all exposed skin, getting in our hair, and landing on our faces. We worked through the morning without a break. Around noon, the manager came out on his cart and advised us to take an hour lunch break and brought us back to our car. We drove around until we found a small sandwich shop. We ate and bought extra soda for the afternoon.

When we got back, our boss brought us to another site, also completely overgrown, but a little harder to weed. The flowers were smaller, closer to the ground, pansies, as opposed to the longer-stemmed lilies and daisies in the morning. They were almost completely hidden by the weeds. We set to work, same deal: tiring, backbreaking, filthy work, sweating and fighting off bugs. About three in the afternoon, the manager came driving up in his golf cart and pulled over to us while we happened to be standing up talking to each other, mostly about how much harder this was than we'd expected. We were stretching out our aching backs. I gave him an unassuming, slight wave and a head nod as he drove up. Vinny was finishing a cigarette.

As he got out of his cart and walked up to us, he said in a nasty tone of voice, "I'm not paying you two to stand around and talk."

We were getting minimum wage. Vinny turned to him and said, "You're barely paying us at all!" as he flicked his butt toward the garden.

I said, "Look at this pile of weeds. Do you think they pulled themselves? We're working our asses off out here. It's hot, dirty, and buggy. We take a five-minute break when you happen to pull up, and you give us shit?"

He walked over and looked at the pile of weeds. We had built a mound of dead, drying weeds that was almost three feet high. He backed off but was not quite apologetic. "Okay, it does look like you've gotten a lot of work done."

"Damn straight," Vinny said.

"Well, get back to it." He got into his golf cart and left. But the damage was done. Vinny and I sat down and tried to imagine what a whole summer of pulling weeds and putting up with this guy would be like, and we were not motivated. We put in a lackluster couple of hours and then went back to the office and quit.

Now the manager was apologetic. "I'm sorry about those remarks earlier. I get a lot of slackers out here. You guys are good workers, and you didn't deserve that. Why don't you give it another day?"

We asked for a raise, and he said, "I just can't do that."

"Then we're outta here!" Vinny said as he left the trailer and lit a cigarette on the steps.

I stayed behind. "What about our pay?"

"I don't have to pay you, you know, quitting on the first day. Your friend seems like a hothead. Are you sure you won't reconsider?"

"Sorry, no."

Heavy sigh. "Fine, come back in on Friday, and I will have your checks ready."

Back at the house, we came up with a new plan. Instead of working the whole summer to pay car expenses, we'd sell our cars and live off that money. We talked each other into it in no time flat. We drove down to the city Wednesday morning, and I was able to convince Mom to help me out, despite her concerns about hitchhiking. We put an ad in the paper. Meanwhile, Vinny just had to make a few phone calls because a few friends had already displayed interest in his car. He sold it on Thursday, and by the afternoon we were sticking our thumbs out on the Cross Island Parkway. The first ride got us to the Cross Bronx Expressway, and the next ride took us all the way to the Monroe Thruway exit. Our third ride took us right into town, and we walked up to our house. Not only was this hitching easy, it was fun. We enjoyed meeting the drivers, listening to their stories and telling ours.

As we settled in, Vinny told me, "I picked up some Purple Owsley while we were home." Acid. Darkness settled over my consciousness like a cover over a birdcage. I could imagine light, but I couldn't see it.

"Why didn't you tell me?"

"I didn't want you to worry about us getting busted while we were hitching."

"When are you going to do it?"

"No time like the present," he said.

"What do you know about it?"

"Owsley hung out with Kesey and the Merry Pranksters and worked on his formula all the time. It's supposed to be one of the purest, mellowest trips, not unlike mescaline or mushrooms. It's what the Dead took in the fucking acid tests, man."

With some anxiety, I gave in to the mildest peer pressure. We each took half a tab and had a mild, controllable, pleasant trip. Owsley was not at all hallucinogenic. It truly heightened awareness and stimulated the pleasure centers. Stress dissipated to nothingness. Curiosity thrived. Perceptions increased dramatically. The world appeared to be a good place, mellow and intricately beautiful. This was the type of acid on which you could function normally but were likely to proceed in slow motion, to marvel at the brilliance of a spider web or the veins in a leaf for minutes on end, experiencing everyday wonders through the eyes of a child as if for the first time, and yet understanding exactly what they were and who you were.

We decided to walk to the other house. As soon as we saw the lake, we both had the same idea: we had to go in. It was fully dark now, and we went to a secluded edge, took our clothes off, and went skinny-dipping. The water was ice cold and caused our muscles to contract tightly, and yet we lingered, relishing the feeling, marveling again at the intensity of understanding. Then we went back to shore. We struggled to get into our wet clothes, laughing at the difficult nature of this process, making mistakes over and over again and yet being smart enough to see car lights in the distance and retreating into the shadows until the vehicle passed. We were probably only in the water five minutes, but it took another fifteen or so to get dressed. Each moment was important to experience fully.

We finally emerged from the shadows fully dressed. Looking around at the trees and the nighttime sky, we forgot at first what we were doing. Then Vinny remembered, "We were on our way to the other house." Laughing at the revelation, we continued on. When we came to Harriman's, we tentatively went in and ordered two beers, but neither one of us liked the taste, and we became aware that we were staring at the other patrons, beginning to draw attention to ourselves, and we quickly grew paranoid and left. We walked right past the stairs up to the house and followed the roadway, taking the route we would take had we been driving. It was much longer by foot, a more roundabout way up the hill, but it allowed us to observe all of the neighbors' houses from a new perspective. We paused in front of a few and watched the occupants go about their routines, overlaying our sensibilities on top of the scene and imagining that so much more was going on than could ever be possible. We expected everyone to be relating at the heightened awareness that we were, when they were probably just getting ready for bed.

When we got to the other house, we discovered that it was empty. We had forgotten that they, too, had all gone back to the city and would not be moving up until the weekend. None of the doors or windows was unlocked, and although we briefly considered breaking in, we realized that would be stupid. We turned around and left, again taking the long way, ignoring the shortcut of the stairs even as we crossed the path not three feet from the top step.

We decided to walk the long way around the other side of the lake, bypassing the opportunity to walk by Harriman's again. We had absolutely convinced ourselves that only bad things could happen at Harriman's. When we reached the spot where we had been skinny-dipping, we stopped for a rest and a reminiscent laugh, remembering the swim as if it had occurred last summer, rather than an hour earlier.

When we finally got back to our house, Vinny crashed almost immediately and went to bed. He would be content to lie in the dark and smoke cigarettes. I went up to my bedroom. I again listened to the Airplane's *Volunteers* and became inspired, encouraged to join and take part in the revolution. If they didn't stop the war soon, we were going to have to put more energy into the resistance. I had noticed that Joan had left some magic markers in her room, and I went and got them. I began to draw graffiti and slogans on my bedroom wall. I put on the *White Album* and listened to "Revolution Number Nine" and drew nines on my walls. I copied revolutionary slogans from the Airplane and wrote them out on the wall. I drew peace signs and smiley faces. I had ink all over my fingers. I kept at this almost all night, only slowing down as the dawn approached, finally writing, "Morning maniacs," and putting the marker down.

The room looked like a subway car that had been parked in the yards at Long Island City. I was pleased with the results. I had expressed myself. I had made a statement of some sort that seemed tremendously important and—I thought—was remarkably artistic. I closed my eyes and envisioned, in the true nature of the words, a better place. I began to think that I needed to drop out of school and hitch to California and hang out with the Airplane, to join them in their revolution. I imagined that they would welcome me with open arms, and I fantasized that I would write treatises for them, drop acid with them, and take my turn sleeping with Grace Slick like everybody else. In the nature of acid-induced eyelid movies, I slipped somewhere from conscious dreaming to a sleep state, awaking only an hour or so later, but straighter, crashing mildly. I was startled at the mess I had made on the walls and embarrassed at the lack of originality I had displayed. *Kevin's going to have a fit*, was all I could think.

31

I began to spend most of my time at the other house. I was more comfortable there, more able to be myself. Concurrently, I became less comfortable with my brother. I had come home one afternoon and gone to the refrigerator to discover my name on a jar of jelly and I went berserk. "Who the fuck put my name on this jelly?"

"Why, isn't it yours?" Kevin answered my question with a question, and I fell for it.

"Yeah, I bought it, but I said I did not want to play your little name game, and I was offering my food up to whoever wanted it. You had no fucking right to put my name on food."

I angrily ripped off the label, as he said, "I didn't."

"I did it," said Adam. "I didn't think it was fair that you were the only one who was making his food available. I didn't want you to get ripped off."

"I don't fucking believe you; this is too fucking ridiculous." I was out of there again, walking over to the other house, where there were no labels, no burying of drugs in the backyard, no strict assignment of bedrooms, no rules of any kind that I could see. Yet, the dishes got done, the garbage got brought out, the food got cooked, and an awful lot of people seemed to be getting laid.

When I got there, the house was overcrowded, as more people had moved up for the summer. I went to the back deck and just about broke an ankle stopping in my tracks. Cheryl was there, in all her resplendent beauty. She had on a peasant blouse, white with purple and pink piping on the sleeves and neckline. It was not quite sheer, but you could still see the indentations caused by her nipples, and her pert breasts were wiggling around as she laughed. She was not wearing a bra, socks, or shoes. She had on cutoff jeans as shorts, barely long enough to cover her crotch. She was stunning in her dazzling innocence. Her smile was authentic, her laugh relaxed. She was driving me out of my mind with desire.

"I missed you," I whispered as I gave her a hug. We spent most of the evening listening to a new album that she had brought up: James Taylor's *Sweet Baby James*. I had never heard of him, but fell instantly in love with his melodic and soothing vocals and poignant lyrics. We talked about "Fire and Rain," exploring the folklore that he had written these songs while in a mental institution, that he was a junkie.

Kathy had brought a few tabs of Orange Sunshine. It didn't look anything like the blue Kaleidoscope or the Purple Owsley. This brand of acid was shaped like a barrel, bright orange, but was much smaller than the others, about a third the size. We dropped them into a gallon of Gallo wine and let them sit for an hour until they were thoroughly dissolved. Then we spent the afternoon on the roof of the house, drinking the wine. The trip came on slowly, as the acid was well dispersed. No one guzzled the wine, and it lasted the whole afternoon. But by the time the bottle was empty, about a dozen of us were tripping nicely.

Cheryl asked me to go down to the lake with her, and we went down the steps to the private dock. The day was hot, and the sun was strong, and the sky was blue, not a cloud to be seen. Cheryl had been in her bathing suit all day, and I was in a T-shirt and a pair of shorts. I took my shirt off and lay down on the end of the dock, soaking up the sun and sticking my feet in the cool water. Cheryl lay next to me and we played a little footsie in the water as we talked.

As the day got hotter, I began to talk about the possibility of swimming to the small island in the middle of the lake, probably about a hundred yards or so. I assured Cheryl that I could swim it with no problem. She said that she thought she could, but if she got into trouble, could I save her?

"Well, I've never been a lifeguard, but as long as you don't panic and thrash around, I'm sure I could keep you afloat."

We agreed to go for it. We slipped into the water, and I immediately began my freestyle crawl. I got about twenty yards out before I remembered to slow down and see how she was doing. Her style was sloppy; she was turning her whole body back and forth, splashing too much, and never putting her face in the water. I treaded water until she caught up, and then I tried to teach her a better style. She was comfortable, listening and learning, and we were doing fine.

We were almost there when I first saw it. I had to do a double take. Was it the acid or was there something big swimming in the water nearby? The water moved again, about fifteen feet away from us on the other side of Cheryl, but the disturbance was slight enough that I was still unsure. Maybe there was a log floating, and the ripples from our swimming were hitting it and causing the effect? Maybe I was hallucinating? I admonished myself not to panic, to control this trip. Then it broke the surface. It was an animal, a brown furry animal the size of a small dog. But it was no dog. It was swimming expertly with just its head above water, and then it went under and was gone again. I began to worry but did not want to alert Cheryl. "Let's swim faster," I told her. "Let's get over there." I began to swim harder and faster, but this was the exact wrong thing to do.

Cheryl stopped and called out, "What's the matter? Why are you leaving me? I can't swim as fast as you!" Just as she finished calling out, the water broke again. The animal was less than six feet from me, but it was between me and Cheryl, and she could see it clearly. She screamed. Her scream scared me *and it*—and it went under. She began to turn around and swim the other way, but she was flailing, struggling.

I swam over to her as fast as I could and got in her way. "It's too far back; you're too tired. Let's go to the island."

"I can't make it."

"It's much closer than the dock. You have to make it."

"What about that thing?"

"Don't worry about it. Your scream probably scared it to the other side of the lake. It's probably a beaver or an otter or something. Relax, let's go." She trusted me, calmed down, turned around, and started toward the island again. We got closer, down the homestretch. It popped up again, this time swimming in the same direction as us, parallel to us, much faster than us, and came right up to us with its head sticking out as if to see what the hell we were doing in its lake.

It was a water rat. I could see the snout, the ears, even the long denuded tail. It was the biggest water rat I had ever seen. It was in its home habitat, and we were vulnerable, easy pickings. I imagined it coming over to us and biting us, and I was terrified. Cheryl saw the look on my face, stopped again, and began to cry. "What is it? Is it dangerous?"

I was honest with her. "It looks like a water rat. I don't think it's dangerous, just curious. Keep moving; we're almost there." We made progress, but the rat hung around and watched us the whole time. We reached the shore, though the bottom was mucky and pulled on our feet as we tried to walk the last ten feet or so. We were stepping on sticks and rocks and God knows what else. We literally crawled up the shore and collapsed as soon as we were on dry land. We both just lay there, catching our breath. And then we began laughing. Cheryl jumped up, grabbed a small heavy stick, and threw it at the water rat, coming to within a foot or so of hitting it. It went under and swam away. We wondered how the hell we were going to get back.

There was an old rowboat attached to the dock next to ours that we had never seen anybody use, and we decided that someone else would come down to the dock eventually; we would call to them and ask them to come get us. We lay back down and dried in the sun. We talked about how scary the rat was, whether or not we were ever really in danger, and what would make a rat bite a human. How helpless humans were in the water compared to animals that live there! We laughed at the absurdity and at our own fears. She seemed more relaxed and carefree than she had in months.

An hour passed, and the sun was getting low. No one had been down to visit the dock. We considered just screaming for help but knew that might attract the homeowners closest to us who might or might not just call the police. I did not want to have to be rescued by the police. "Do you want to swim back?" I asked Cheryl.

"No." She looked terrified. "I am never swimming in this lake again. I would rather sleep here tonight or get rescued or whatever. I am not giving that rat another chance to get me."

She was pretty clear. "Okay," I said, playing the hero. "I'll swim back and get the rowboat and come back for you."

She thought this was a great plan and volunteered to help by keeping an eye out for the rat. She promised to hit it this time if it showed its ugly face again. She picked up a big rock. I laughed. "Please don't hit me with the rock by mistake. Maybe we shouldn't antagonize it. Just let me know if you see it, and I'll deal with it." I entered the lake tentatively and started swimming slowly, nervously. I was constantly looking around for the rat, instead of methodically swimming to the dock.

As I approached the halfway point, I realized I was tired and said to myself, "This is ridiculous. Just go for it." I stopped looking for the rat, put my head in the water, and concentrated on my stroke and my breathing. I made it to the dock in minutes, pulled myself out of the water, and turned back to look at Cheryl, who was jumping up and down and waving and clapping and yelling, "You did it!" across the water.

I smiled to myself. *I did do it, didn't I?* I rowed across the lake and rescued the damsel in distress. She got into the boat and almost tipped it, grabbing me to give me a big hug and a big, wet, loving kiss. I convinced her to sit next to me and take an oar to help. We rowed quietly, both of us exhausted. The feel of her leg rubbing against mine in the boat excited me, but I hid myself as best I could. We got back to the dock, tied up the boat, and made our way up the stairs arm in arm.

When we got in, the party was in full force, music blaring, beer flowing, and smoke hovering. If they had missed us, no one ever let on. Cheryl said, "I'm going to take a shower. Thanks again for rescuing me." Another hug, another kiss. I thought of telling her that I would love to join her in the shower, but the words never came out, and I just stood there thinking them as she went into the bathroom.

32

Mom sent word up with Kevin that she had sold the car for six hundred dollars, but that she needed half the money, and I could have the other half. Vinny said that he would come down with me, and Dennis asked us to do him a favor while we were in the city. We hitched down in the morning and had lunch with our respective parents. It was hard on Mom, selling Brian's car, letting another piece of him go. I listened and consoled her, but by two o'clock I was ready to leave. Vinny and I took a bus to Dennis's apartment in Elmhurst. It was one of those ancient, dirty, red brick buildings, twelve stories high. His apartment was on the fourth floor. The elevator was slow and creaky, noisily making its way up. The hallway was dark, dirty, and musty, almost a stale urine smell.

He had given us the key, and we had no trouble following his instructions. His studio apartment was sparse: a sofa bed left open and unmade occupied most of the room. Scattered about were newspapers, magazines, and a few books. The walls were bare except for two posters: a Jimi Hendrix Experience collage and a pensive gorilla sitting in Rodin's *Thinker* position. The tiny kitchen had dirty dishes left in the sink, and several cockroaches scurried away. I opened the refrigerator door and was nauseated when another cockroach crawled out of an open can of beer.

There was a package in the freezer, wrapped in aluminum foil. We found it underneath some packaged vegetables. Dennis had put masking tape on it and labeled it Flounder. I was wearing an old army jacket of Brian's, and I carried the package in an inside pocket. We took a subway up to the edge of the Bronx. Vinny told me to hide the package before we started hitching. I put it down my pants. My jeans held it against my abdomen.

We got one ride to the north Major Deegan, just before the Thruway and were outside the Thruway entrance when the cops pulled over. I was carrying enough cocaine to put me in jail for the rest of my life, and I was terrified. Vinny whispered as the cop pulled up, "Be cool."

"You boys have some ID?"

"Yes, sir." Pop had taught me to always be polite and deferential when dealing with the Man.

He looked at our drivers' licenses. "Where you boys going?"

"We have a summer house, up in Monroe."

"You boys carrying any drugs?"

"No, sir," we both said completely straight-faced.

"In that case, you wouldn't mind emptying out your pockets?"

"No, sir." We took our wallets and our change and keys and placed them on the hood of his car. He picked up Vinny's cigarettes and peered into the pack, took a few out and looked at them, smelled them, assuring himself that they were tobacco. He asked us to turn our pockets inside out. He grabbed my jacket and pulled it aside. He pointed to the inside pocket where the coke had been not thirty minutes earlier and said, "*All* your pockets."

God, I hoped none had spilled. I pulled that pocket out; it was clean.

He seemed satisfied but decided to hassle us some more. "You boys wait here." He went to his car, left the door open so that we could hear him on the radio, called in our names and driver's license numbers, and waited until he got clearance that we were not outlaws. As he came back he said, "You both have yellow sheets?"

"Excuse me?" I said.

"You've both been arrested before?"

Vinny didn't say a word, but my mouth just gushed forth. "Yes, but that was for loitering, and we were found not guilty, and actually, our lawyer is still trying to get the records expunged."

"Yeah, well, good luck to him. I'm going to ask you again. You boys carrying?"

"No, sir," Vinny said. "You can search me, I'm clean."

"Well, thanks for the offer," said a smiling cop. I couldn't believe Vinny had said that. He patted Vinny down head to foot. Then he turned to me. "I suppose you're clean too?"

"Yes, sir."

He patted me down, but not as thoroughly as Vinny and did not notice the extra bulge in my pants where the cocaine was resting comfortably. He gave us our stuff back and said, "You know hitchhiking on the Thruway is illegal?" Rather than lie to him, we both just remained silent. He seemed to like that and said, "Walk up to the entrance. It's much safer where the cars have already stopped."

"Yes, sir; thank you, sir." And he was on his way.

Two rides later we were in the homestretch. The coke was now in Vinny's pants. At the Thruway rest area he had volunteered, "You carried it half the way; we should share the risk. I'll take it the rest of the way." We had gotten off the Thruway and were walking through the small downtown area of Central Valley when another patrol car pulled up next to us. Vinny and I had been hitching for weeks and had not met a cop. Now we were being stopped for the second time in one trip while we were carrying more drugs than either of us had ever seen before, *and it wasn't even ours!*

This was a local officer, driving a brown sheriff's car, and he was taking a new tack—"Where were you in the army?"

"Uh, I wasn't in the army, sir. This was my brother's coat."

He reached out and twirled the gold button on the front of my jacket, the one with the insignia of the American eagle, the symbol of freedom. "Did you know it's illegal for someone who has not been in the army to impersonate a soldier?"

Was this guy fucking kidding me or what? I laughed, which seemed to piss him off big-time, and so I straightened up quick. "Sorry, sir, no, sir, I'm really not trying to impersonate a soldier. I'm just wearing my brother's jacket."

"Are you wearing it to demonstrate your support of the war?"

He may have been fucking with me, but I was beginning to get scared. I decided to play the sympathy card. "No, sir, I'm wearing it to honor my brother. He was killed in action in Saigon."

"Are you in support of the war?"

"No, sir, I'm not. I'm opposed to the war and would be opposed to any war. But I support my brother and the other guys who wear the uniform—they didn't start the war."

He just glared at me, took our IDs, and went to make the now too-familiar phone call. As he came back he said, "You're the two guys who were picked up in the Bronx a few hours ago." I couldn't believe it. Did they remember our names from the radio or was there some sort of a tracking program going on? We were not fugitives, just two kids trying to get to their summer house so they could sample some of this cocaine they were muling. Vinny was losing patience even while I prayed he would keep his mouth shut.

"We weren't 'picked up,'" he said. "We were just talked to on the side of the road."

The cop ignored him. "Take the buttons off the jacket," he told me. "You can wear the jacket but not the buttons."

"Yes, sir. Thank you, sir."

"And walk to the end of town before you start hitching again."

"Yes, sir."

"And don't ever walk through my town again, or I *will* bust you!"

"Yes, sir—I mean no, sir. Thank you, sir."

"Get the hell out of here before I change my mind."

■ ■ ■

When we reached the Navajo house, it was about eight o'clock. Dennis and a few others came out to meet us as we walked up the steep steps. He was all excited to get his stuff, and we were all excited to tell our story, making sure Dennis understood just how close we came to getting busted doing this little favor for him. He finally said, "Yeah, well, you had an adventure, and you didn't get busted, so no harm done." He turned to walk away, putting the package in his pocket. Both Vinny and I were shocked. "What about our cut?"

"I'm sure you already took your cut," he said, laughing and throwing his long hair over his shoulder. "It's good shit, isn't it?"

"We didn't take any," we yelled at the same time.

This time Dennis turned around to face us. "Yeah, right, you went to my apartment and got an ounce of coke and hitched with it for six hours and never sampled it?"

"That's right," we said.

"Bullshit," he said and began to walk away again.

Vinny sprang off his feet like a colt and grabbed Dennis by the back of his long hair. He pulled him forward, slapping him, not too hard. Hanging on to his hair, he then dragged him toward the house, pushed him against it, holding his head against the wall and making a fist with his other hand. I flashed back to Craig Clancy in my living room. So this is what he was talking about! "We told you we didn't take any, you little prick. We put our lives at risk and carried this shit all the way up here, and you're going to give us a decent cut right now, or I'm going to beat the shit out of you and take the whole thing! Got it?"

Dennis was scared, his usual smirk buried beneath his quivering lip. Vinny would pulverize him easily, and he knew it. Then, tactically, he began a nervous laugh. "I really had you going there, didn't I? I was just kidding, just fucking with you. C'mon inside, and I'll cut your share."

We went into the house and cleared the kitchen table. Dennis grabbed a butter knife and some aluminum foil and opened his package. Most of the guys gathered in a circle around the table to watch the ritual. He took the knife and broke off about 10 percent of the powder, and started to wrap it up. Vinny reached out and grabbed his wrist. "More." Without speaking, without even looking at Vinny, Dennis cut off another piece about the same size. Again Vinny said, "More." Now Dennis was going to start protecting himself. "C'mon, Vinny, that's a hundred dollars' worth right there; that should be enough."

"That would have been enough if you hadn't tried to rip us off and disrespected us," Vinny said, as he grabbed the butter knife. "Now we'll take a little more," and he cut off a piece slightly larger than what Dennis had given to us already. We now had almost half the rock. Vinny held the butter knife straight up under Dennis's chin, looked him in the eye, and said, "You got a problem?"

"No," Dennis said. "Just fucking take it."

I searched the house and found Cheryl. She and Kathy were sitting in one of the bedrooms, listening to Joni Mitchell. "Hey, you guys want to come with me and Vinny and do some coke?" Their eyes lit up. We took the stairs down to the road and stopped at the dock. It was a still, overcast night. Vinny carefully used his driver's license to cut a few lines on the flat surface of the oar from the rowboat. He rolled up a crisp dollar bill. We each did a line. Then we each did another, switching nostrils. It was the first time I had ever done coke, and I didn't even think about it, didn't spend the energy to make a conscious decision, just rolled right along. The rush was instantaneous. My head felt clearer, my mind raced, and my bowels wanted to move. Another line, and I was going to shit my pants. "Let's head home," I said, but as we passed Harriman's, Vinny wanted to stop in for a beer. I agreed, somewhat reluctantly, because the girls wanted to. Even though neither one of them had yet turned eighteen, the bartender never asked them for proof, and they enjoyed hanging out in the bar.

I went to the men's room, which was predictably disgusting. I had no choice. I was not going to be able to make it back to the house. Fortunately, there was a barrel-bolt lock. The bathroom was the size of a closet and almost as dark. The bare overhead bulb, hanging on a thin chain from the ceiling, couldn't have been more than forty watts. I used the roll of paper towels to wipe the urine off the toilet seat and then put about three layers of toilet paper all around the seat and across the front and back. I lowered my jeans, but not far enough for them to touch the floor. Rather, I used my legs to spread them apart at the knees and keep them there while I crouched onto the seat. I unloaded the world without straining. Someone started banging at the door, and I yelled, "Just a minute."

This farmer did not want to wait. "What the fuck are you doing in there? I got to take a piss," and he banged on the door some more for emphasis.

"Yeah, well, I'm taking a shit!"

Silence for a moment and then, "You poor motherfucker. Well, hurry it the fuck up."

I finished wiping, washed everything I could reach, twice, and then washed my hands and face a third and fourth time. I looked in the cracked and rusted mirror and smiled. I felt great, still had a bunch more coke, and had Cheryl out with me for the night. As I came out, one of the rednecks pointed at me and told his friends something, and they all laughed. *Fuck them*, I thought.

Vinny, Kathy, and Cheryl were in the back room, on the dance floor, by the jukebox, playing the Moody Blues' "A Question of Balance," the futile quest that we all have searching for answers. Ironic, I thought, after what I had been through, but they just grabbed my hands and formed a small circle and starting singing the chorus to the song, "It's not the way that you say it when you do those things to me; it's more the way you really mean it when you tell me what will be," as we all hoped for miracles in our lives.

They had bought a beer for me, but before I could finish it one of the rednecks came back complaining about "all this English shit," and filled the jukebox up with quarters and punched in about an hours' worth of country music. We finished our beers and continued our journey.

We walked to our house, and Vinny and Kathy joined the crowd around the fire. I sat on the porch with Cheryl, and I reached over and rubbed her arm. "Would you like to go up to my bedroom and relax and listen to some music?"

She smiled and nodded.

I got Vinny to the side and asked him to give me half of the coke that was left, quietly, so that no one else knew we were breaking the rules. I wasn't worried, inasmuch as I knew I could eat the whole thing if the cops showed up, and I wouldn't let it out of my sight.

Cheryl and I went up to my room and snorted a line almost immediately. I locked the door, put the stereo on, played Ten Years After, with the lead guitarist Alvin Lee on their hard-rocking song "Little School Girl," and its popular chorus, "I want to ball you."

Cheryl lay back on the bed and invited me next to her by patting the pillow. Not a word was spoken as she leaned over and kissed me, and we stretched the excitement of our heightened sensuality. I slipped my hand under her tie-dyed T-shirt, beginning a passionate, tender tour of her body. We used the coke to our advantage. I surprised her by asking, "Where are we going with this?"

With dead seriousness, she looked at me and whispered, "Wherever you want."

I asked her, holding her hands, "Are you sure?"

"Oh, yeah," she said. "I've been waiting a long time for you to get here."

"Okay," I said, "I'll be gentle," as if I had experience at this.

Without saying a word, I gave a full thrust down, feeling the resistance but pushing hard anyway, and she gasped and said, "Ow," with a grimace.

"I'm sorry, did I hurt you? Are you okay?"

"I'm fine," she said. "It just hurt a little. Finish!"

Finishing did not take me long but did little good for her. As I pulled out she winced again, and I asked her if there was anything I could do. "Just hold me," she said. She fell fast asleep. My mind was racing. I had kept Cheryl at bay for so long, carefully weighing the risk each time we had an opportunity. I looked back on the day as if it had been a dream, as if I had lost the potential to make choices, as if I were just going along for the ride. But I knew I still had responsibility. Conscious or not, choices had been made. Now I'd done coke, pretty hard-core. I'd hitchhiked dirty, just plain stupid. I'd committed statutory rape. Finally, I'd lost my own virginity. All in one day. After a while, I slept soundly, Cheryl cradled in my arms.

When I awoke, I just lay there a while, watching her sleep. Her head was just below my neck, nuzzled into my chest. Her mouth was puffy, open slightly, just a drop of spittle in the corner of her lips. Her hair was frizzed out across her face. I brushed it away and patted it down, and she stirred slightly. I looked at my clock radio to see that it was ten thirty. I felt smug and happy. I wondered if this relationship would last until the end of the summer. Would it last for years? Was this the girl I would marry, after all? *Whoa, get these thoughts out of your head.*

But the door was open for the previous day's realizations and implications to crest. I had come so close to wrecking my life. Although we took it so casually and as a matter of course, Vinny and I also realized what the law was and how hard they were cracking down on drugs. I was fully aware that the amount of cocaine we were carrying had definitely been in the felony zone. *They might have put us away for decades. This was not loitering, for Chrissakes! And Dennis? Fucking Dennis! He's a dirtbag, and I'm muling coke for him?* I was glad that I had been with Vinny and not alone. I might have let Dennis get away with it. Sure, I would have gotten something out of him, but not as much as Vinny had.

My body was drained. I was not feeling a hangover headache or a sick stomach. It was not like a crash from speed or the heavy head from downs. The reaction that I was experiencing from having too much cocaine could only be described as a craving. I was thirsty and craving a drink. I was hungry and craving some food. But mostly I was craving some more coke. The energy I felt I was lacking could only be replaced by a line. My nose itched, literally, and I wiped it with the back of my hand and realized that my nose was sore, that the skin was already breaking down at the surface from snorting this drug. The awareness hit me that this shit really was addictive. I would have to be careful. Tomorrow I would have to be careful; today I wanted another line. I wondered if Vinny had any left.

I tried to slide out of the bed and set Cheryl's head on my pillow without waking her up, but I was not successful. She woke and looked at me, standing there, stark naked, flaccid, and sweaty. "Good morning," I said with a smile. "Get some more sleep if you can."

She smiled back and said weakly, "Okay," sank into my pillow, and immediately fell back to sleep.

I pulled on my jeans and searched my bag for a clean T-shirt, couldn't find one, and went down topless. I went to the refrigerator but couldn't find anything that I owned. I took a container of Tropicana orange juice with Kevin's name on it and took a long drink, right out of the carton, spilling some of it on my bare chest. No one seemed to be around, and I couldn't even remember what day it was. I went to the bathroom and brushed my teeth, and that felt so good that I ran the shower and took a long one. When I was finished, I went out through the door to Vinny's bedroom, as he was just waking up. He reached over to the table next to his bed, took his cigarette pack and tapped it against the table, slid one out, and lit it. He took a big drag, and as he exhaled it, he smiled at me and said, "Some fucking day, huh?"

"Where's Kathy?" I asked him.

"She went back. Nothing happened between us. 'Parently, she's exclusive to Adam. I borrowed your brother's car and drove her. What about you?"

I put the biggest ear-to-ear shit-eating grin on my face. "All right!" he said as he got out of bed and stood up to give me a high five. "How was she?"

"She was a virgin," I said, puffing out my chest like a fucking rooster, not revealing that I had been one, too. I felt guilty and ashamed that I had said it even as I was saying it. I knew I had betrayed her by spilling this, even though it was an important part of the guys' code to compare notes. Before Vinny could even react, I added, "I shouldn't have told you; that should have been private—"

He cut me off. "Hey, it's cool. I won't say anything...to her or to anyone else." Then he slapped me on the back and put his arm around me. "So you broke the fucking cherry? First time?"

I nodded.

"Awesome, isn't it?" he asked.

Mostly, it was painful and uncomfortable, quick and dirty. "Yeah, man, it was exciting. Uh, Vinny, do you have any more coke?"

He took a deep draw on his cigarette, finishing it and stubbing it out in the ashtray before looking up at me with eyebrows raised as if he were looking up to the top of a building. "You finish all yours?"

"Yeah, me and Cheryl did it up. I don't know, maybe I wasted it. I rubbed some of it on her."

This brought a big smile back to his face. "No shit? You dog, you." He reached into his pocket and drew out his stash. "I guess you deserve a little celebration for popping your first cherry." He cut two lines, and we each did one. He lit another cigarette, looked at his stash, and said, "What the fuck, not enough here to save." He cut the rest into three lines, did one, told me to do the middle one, and then he did the last. "I gotta take a shit," he said, and lifting up his arm and smelling under it deeply. "Not to mention a fucking shower."

"Where is everyone else?"

"They went out to breakfast."

The coke made me feel industrious. I had not contributed much to this house in the last couple of weeks, and I also realized that Vinny and I had broken the no-drug rules, and Kevin might or might not have been aware of that. I decided to clean up the house. It had not had a good cleaning since before we moved in, and it was pretty grimy. I started by gathering the aluminum that Vinny and I had carried our coke in, and then I went after all the ashtrays. I cleaned the ashes out of the fireplace and took them outside and dumped them. I filled two garbage bags just by picking up all the beer bottles, potato chip bags, and cigarette packs that were lying around. I swept the floor, and then I tackled the kitchen.

By the time Kevin returned and Vinny got out of the shower, the place looked good. "What, did you hire a maid?" Kevin said sarcastically.

"A simple thank-you will do."

Surprisingly, he stopped and looked at me. "Thanks. It looks good. That was a good idea." Our amity was short-lived. "Rumor is that you and Vinny copped half of Dennis's coke. You didn't bring any into the house did you?"

"Of course not, Kevin; that would be against the rules."

Vinny couldn't help laughing and turned to go back into this room. "Well, now I understand why you cleaned the house," Kevin said.

"Davey!" Cheryl called from the bedroom. Kevin looked up there and scowled. "She stayed all night?" he asked.

"Obviously," I said and went up the stairs without giving him a chance to continue and without wanting to see whatever nasty look he was offering me. Cheryl had gotten dressed already, but she met me at the door and gave me a hug. I went to kiss her, but she pulled away and said, "Aargh, my mouth feels like a toilet bowl. I need to take a shower, and you need to deal with the blood." I followed her eyes to the sheets on my bed and saw the two big circles of blood and the surrounding droplet marks. So, this is why they call it popping the cherry? I couldn't help feeling like a stud, but I was smart enough to ask, sensitively, "Are you okay?"

"I'm fine," she said. "I'm happy we did it. But I want a shower."

"Go ahead," I told her. "Vinny just finished."

"No, not here; back at my place. I want to be able to put on some clean clothes afterward."

I rolled the sheets into a ball and stuck them under my arm. I opened the door and yelled to Kevin, asking him if I could borrow his car. She punched me in the arm even as he said yes. "Deal with the sheets later," she whispered. "Don't carry them out in front of everybody with me here." I jammed them under my bed and only then noticed that the blood had seeped through to the mattress. I took the blanket off Don's bed and spread it out over mine.

33

Two weeks later, Cheryl and I were arguing. She seemed depressed, even morose. She said that she needed to go back home for a week or so, and I selfishly wanted her to stay. "*Why* do you have to go?"

Exasperated, she finally blurted out, "I missed my period! I want to get tested."

My heart must have stopped beating, and I could feel the blood draining from my brain. I could not control the images. She was pregnant; I was going to have to marry her. My life was over. "How late are you?" I finally remembered to ask.

"Just a couple of days."

"Doesn't that happen a lot?" as if I really knew anything about the menstrual cycle.

"Not to me; I'm very regular."

"Are you sure it's mine?" I couldn't believe I said it. The words were formed deep in my brain, by some other force, and they just came out.

She punched me in the stomach...hard. "Fuck you." She started crying and turned to leave. I grabbed at her and tried to turn her back toward me, but she shook me off and cursed me out again. "You prick, you fuck! You *know* I haven't been with anyone else!"

I knew I deserved this, and I was sorry for what I had said. I was also sorry for what I had done. I was thinking of myself, struggling to think of her. Reeling, getting dizzy. What the hell was I supposed to say? "I'm sorry," I said. "It's such a shock. You're so young." Then I got defensive. "You told me you started taking the pill."

"I did, but I had just started on it. It might not have had enough time, and besides it's not 100 percent, anyway."

"It's not?"

"No."

She was still crying, and I realized I had to start caring for her. I hugged her, pulling her in close to me. "I'm sorry for what I said. I know it hurt, and it was stupid of me. Maybe it will come. Maybe it's just late because of the pill."

She sniffled and squeezed me back. "I guess that's possible. I don't care. I'm going to go get a test. I'll be back in a week or so."

"How are you getting home?"

"Adam's going to drive me."

"Okay, good luck." What else was I supposed to say?

■ ■ ■

The next few days dragged, but then Nick came by on Thursday and asked me if he could bring a few friends over to the house and party. *Why not*, I thought. It was just Vinny and me this week.

Nick came over with three of his friends, and we took a walk in the woods and smoked a jay. I let him know that we were going to abide by the rules, and he assured me that he would help me enforce them.

He brought me a picture of Super Trooper from last summer's newspaper article, and we tacked it over the dartboard that we had set up in the corner of the living room and threw darts at it. Another carload of townies showed up and then a third, driven by Skipper. Nick saw the concern on my face and to a certain degree shared it, but he told me that he would handle it. "What're you doing here, Skipper?"

"What'd you mean? Davey and I are friends. I gave him a ride home one night, right, Davey?" He was smiling a vicious grin. I just looked at him without saying anything, and Nick went into a serious mode that I had never seen before. He looked at Skipper and said, loudly so that everyone else could hear, "If you're a fucking narc, Skipper, I will personally cut your balls off if you rat on my friends."

Skipper pulled back and looked shocked but then smiled. "Nick, I'm not a narc. You don't believe that shit about last summer, do you?"

"So it's a coincidence that you were over there almost every night except for the one when the cops came and busted them?"

"Yeah, Nick, I guess I got lucky is all."

"Yeah, right. Remember what I told you, Skipper."

Nick turned to me and whispered, "Do not let this asshole know about the outside dope rules, just stay clean while he's here. I'll spread the word." Nick circulated among the crowd, and everyone seemed to nod in agreement. No one trusted this guy. We got a fire going and took up a collection, and Skipper offered to go get some beer. Nick insisted on going with him, and they brought back a couple of cases. It was going to be an all-alcohol night.

This was the first time that I had really met some of the town girls. Mary was the cutest and the friendliest, but she let me know early on that she had a boyfriend in college. She gave me insight on all the guys. Donovan was the favorite, due mostly to his boyish, blond good looks, but also to his "sensitive" side. He recited poetry and drove the girls crazy. Nick was a lot of fun, but needed to grow up and stop living with his parents. Skipper probably was a rat, though they thought he maybe got caught and let those guys take the fall rather than take the heat himself. She did not think that he would turn us in, though she advised me to be careful. She laughed and said, "You don't seem to have any dope here anyway!"

I met Natalie. Older than most of this crowd, she worked as a waitress in the coffee shop in town. Many of these kids never even thought about going to college. She told me that she used to date Skipper until last summer, and that she believed the rumors and, in fact, broke up with him over it. She was unattached at the moment and told me that she had not had sex in months and was, in fact, quite horny. She was coming on to me. I said to her, "Surely there are a lot of single guys in Monroe."

She looked around the room. "These guys are boring."

I told her that I had been going with Cheryl, and she said she knew, but "I heard Cheryl was in the city; you're not married to her or anything, are you?"

No, but would I be next month? This might be the last chance I had to up my count. Cheryl was not due back until Saturday. Natalie leaned toward the plain side and had short nondescript brown hair. She was taller than me and would not usually have been my type at all. I quaffed another beer, and she started to

342 TIMOTHY F. DEMPSEY

look better. The party wound down. It was either make another beer run or move it to Harriman's, and I got Nick to lead the latter choice.

Natalie had been sitting on the floor next to me, looking up at me while we talked. She stood up and stretched, looked at the fire, and then watched as the last group was getting ready to leave. "Well, are you going to ask me to stay, or should I be going?"

I looked up into her eyes and without hesitation or conscious thought, I said, "Stay." She turned to Nick and said, "Have fun at Harriman's." They left, and she immediately reached down and took my hand. She pulled me toward the stairs and said, "Do you like downs?"

"What? Do you have some?"

"Tuinals."

"Never tried them."

"They're like Seconals, only a little stronger. I have a prescription for them. They help me sleep." She took out a prescription bottle and took out one of the blue and white capsules, swallowed it with a swig of beer, and offered me one. I took it and did the same. I opened the door to my bedroom, and she pulled me in and closed the door. Then she attacked me. This was definitely a new experience, and I was a bit taken aback. She undressed me and then undressed herself. We were lying on the bed making out and groping when I heard a knock on the front door. I thought the other townies had returned, and I was disgusted. I stopped and listened as Vinny answered the door, let someone in, and then had a conversation.

I imagined that it was Cheryl and became alarmed that she was going to run up the stairs, open the door, and catch me. She'd accuse me of being unfaithful and then tell me she was pregnant. I held my breath and strained to hear the voices, but I could not make them out. Vinny got rid of whoever it was. I heard the door close and then a car door slam and a car drive away. Natalie was on top of me again, but the Tuinal kicked in, and I fell asleep in the middle of the act. I woke up a few hours later, scrunched next to her, but she was sound asleep and snoring. I rolled off the side of my bed, moved over to Don's, and went back to sleep. My mind was too clouded from the Tuinal and beer to focus, but I had a haunting feeling, deep in the recesses of my clouded state, that I had done something terrible to Cheryl. We slept until noon. Vinny woke me up, knocking at my door. "You gotta get up man; I gotta talk to you."

I opened my door and said, "What?"

He looked at Natalie, who was stirring awake, and said, "Out here."

In the hallway, he informed me that it was indeed Cheryl who had been here in the middle of the night. "I told her that you were asleep, and she started up the stairs." Vinny looked at the floor. "I stopped her, man. I told her you were with someone. She wanted to know who, and I told her, but the name 'Natalie' had no meaning to her. So I told her you'd just met her." He paused. "She was pretty pissed, man."

"What did she say?"

"'Fucking asshole,' 'motherfucker,' stuff like that."

"And then what?"

"Then she left."

I woke up Natalie and said, "I'm sorry, you have to go."

She looked at me, laughed, and said, "You fell asleep while you were balling me, stud."

"I'm sorry," I said, "but you gave me the Tuinal."

She laughed again. "Hey, no problem. I'm sorry your girl-friend came back early, stud; I hope you work things out. I hear she's a sweet kid." She got dressed and came down to join Vinny and me for a cup of coffee. We had no car, and I had no idea where she lived, but I offered to walk her home. "Don't worry, stud, I have to work, anyway. I can walk. It will help me clear my head." She leaned down and gave me a big wet kiss, "Bye, stud."

"Thanks," I said, as if she were a hooker or something. One-night stands didn't appeal to me. I fell asleep in the middle of the act, and all I could feel was guilt. I took a shower, got dressed, and told Vinny I was going over to the other house to see if Cheryl was there.

"Davey, it's not that big a deal. She's been away for a few days, and you fucked some townie. She'll get over it."

"She thinks she's pregnant!"

"*Who,* Natalie?"

"Cheryl."

He took a deep drag on his cigarette, looked me in the eye, and said, "Different story. You better get the fuck over there."

I walked out the driveway and made my way toward their house. As I reached the lake and made the turn past Harriman's, I imagined that I heard the most beautiful tune coming out of the mountains. As I got closer to their house, I realized that it was real. Somebody was playing the flute, and they were pretty good at it. Just as I neared the stairway up to their house, I re-alized that the flute music was coming from their dock, and I turned and went down there. As I approached I saw that Cheryl was sitting there, along with Kathy and some guy I had never seen before, who was, of course, playing the flute.

As I approached, Kathy smiled at me, and Cheryl scowled at me. The stranger put his flute down and stood up and faced me. Kathy said, "Davey, this is Jonathan. Jonathan, Davey."

We shook hands. They could all see the puzzlement on my face, and Jonathan explained. "I was hitching home, and they gave me a ride. I decided to spend the night."

Cheryl walked past us and up the stairs toward the house. She was crying. I looked at the other two. Kathy locked my eyes and ordered me, "Go after her."

I took a deep breath, turned to Jonathan. "Nice to meet you...nice music, man." Before he could thank me, I was off and running after Cheryl. I caught up to her in the middle of the stairs and reached out and grabbed her arm. "Wait a minute."

"Fuck you," she said.

"I'm sorry," I said. "I really am."

"Oh," she yelled at me, "you're sorry? *For what?*"

I was grateful to Vinny for letting me know exactly what had gone down, so there was no reason for me to try to cover up or bullshit my way out of it. The best strategy was to cop to it and ask for forgiveness. "I'm sorry for what I did last night. I got drunk, and she gave me a down, and before I knew it I was in bed with her. I fell asleep in the middle of it I was so drunk. It didn't mean anything."

"Do you love her?"

I laughed, knowing she was serious, but I was unable to control myself. "Cheryl, I don't even like her."

"So you fuck people you don't even like? That makes me feel so much better."

I took a deep breath. "That's not what I mean. It was a one-night stand. I never did it before. I'm sorry. I really don't know what else I'm supposed to say. I didn't think you'd be back." Again, I knew that was a mistake even before I finished the words.

"Oh, and if I didn't find out about it, that would make it okay?" She started running up the stairs, and I followed her, catching her easily. We were three-quarters of the way up now, and people on the deck were watching us. I didn't care whether they could hear us or not.

"That's not what I meant."

"Well, what did you mean?"

"I don't know. I'm just sorry. I love *you.*" What a spot to say these three words for the first time. But I did; I did love her. At least I thought I did. In any case, it didn't seem to help much.

"You love me?" she said sarcastically. "Yet you don't even ask me what the results of the test were!" She tried to turn to run the rest of the way up the stairs, but there would be no privacy up there; the Friday crowd was beginning their partying.

"Cheryl, please. Sit down." I sat down on the steps and pulled her to me. She did not fight; she did not run or pull away. She sat down next to me. "What were the results?"

"I got my period, you asshole. That's why I'm back early. I didn't even have to take the test. I was so excited and happy; I couldn't wait to get back and tell you. I thought you would be worried. Instead you're out fucking someone else."

"Cheryl, I'm sorry. And boy, am I happy that you're not pregnant." I pulled her close to me. "I'm happy for you, and I'm happy for us. But I was going to be here for you. I was going to support you, no matter what. I do love you." I took her face and cupped it in my hands and kissed her tears, one at a time.

34

Fourth of July was on a Saturday, and we decided to have a party. We had an early evening barbecue: ribs, chicken, and corn on the cob. Berk had brought some Orange Sunshine as a present for the house, and he gave each of us a tab for dessert. I had finally become confident enough that Sunshine was safe. It was a different trip. I had confidence that my mental state was strong, that I could control the acid without fear or anxiety.

For the first time, I took a whole tab. We each took one. We spent the evening floating around the house, in and out. We kept the stereo off. The chopping block was busy, but hardly any wood got split. People just took turns swinging the ax into the stump.

I took a walk into the back field and despite the fact that it was now completely overgrown with four-foot-high weeds, I made my way to the ruins. I sat in the center of them and imagined what had happened here. This had been a two-room house, and I sat in the front room and could tell that there was a fireplace on the side wall. I imagined a family scratching existence out of the ground, gardening, raising chickens, and hunting. Suddenly, they were attacked by a bunch of redcoats, or maybe Indians, and raped and murdered. The house was burned to the ground. I shook my head. *This is too dark, cut it out. The damn thing probably burned from a lightning strike decades after it was abandoned.*

I strolled through the field and looked at the weeds up close, noticing that some of them had flowers and buds. I stopped and watched a beetle eat a leaf. It paused only a moment when it realized my presence, waved its antennas at me, and then went back to dinner. It showed no fear, had no imagination, did not know that I could torture and squash it at will. I felt strangely connected. I climbed over the boundary wall and went looking for the pot plants. If they ever germinated, I couldn't find them.

When I returned to the house, just at dusk, I had the most peaceful feeling. Everyone here was tripping; everyone was mellow and happy. Don had the silly, almost girlish grin that he shared with just a touch of guilt when he was unabashedly enjoying himself. Berk had the wise, intellectual smile that he punctuated occasionally when someone made him laugh. He collapsed into a cackle that emanated deep in his chest and infected the whole room. Kevin and Joan were bickering over nothing, but giggling. No one cared, no one paid any attention. If anything, they became aware of their own behavior every now and then and laughed at themselves. Vinny was grooving on the fire. He was in charge. He had it blazing, the largest fire we'd seen yet, and he kept feeding it, poking it, shifting it. He was more than in charge of the fire. He was the fire.

Don looked at me and said, "You have a bug in your hair." I looked at him puzzled, thinking he was kidding, but he came over and reached into my hair and sure enough he pulled out a small black fly of some sort. It was still alive, and he took it to the porch, having carefully opened the door, and set it free, watching it fly away. He came back in feeling like a hero, like a liberator. "Let me see if you have any more prisoners," he said, chuckling, but looking through my hair nonetheless. The energy in the house was utterly blissful. Each moment was unparalleled intensity. And the intensity was pure joy. There was not a harsh word, not a harsh thought. Kevin and Joan devolved into Abbot and Costello. Who we were was a family. For this trip, we loved each other and accepted each other, quirks and all. Ridiculously, I sang "Our House," from the new Crosby, Stills, Nash & Young album, *Déjà vu*. *Our* house was a very fine house indeed.

When Don was done grooming me, I realized that I was dirty and sweaty and itchy from my walk through the weeds. Even though he did not find any more bugs, I imagined that my hair and skin were crawling. I looked at my arms and saw the sweat and the small grains of dirt that had dried, encased on my follicles. I imagined that I was filthy, disgusting, swarming with germs. "I'm going to take a shower," I announced as I ran up to my room and grabbed my robe. I had not changed my clothes for two days and everything about them grossed me out.

I locked all the doors in the bathroom suite. I ran the water, stripped off my clothes and entered the shower. It was too cold, and I jumped back out, turned the hot faucet some more, and reentered in a minute, able to adjust the water to perfection. I put my head under it and let it run down my back. I found a bar of soap on the floor and lathered my whole body. I watched as the dirt dissolved and ran down my legs, coloring the water brown as it circled and then flowed down the drain.

I knew that all the dirt I could discern was coming off my body, making me clean, making me pure. I stepped out and found shampoo on the sink and washed my hair. It was like a ritual, a religious ceremony. I imagined all the germs flowing away. I rinsed and washed my hair again. I used the shampoo to wash the hair on my genitals and then under my arms. I could not get clean enough. Each moment in the shower was pure ecstasy. Why had I never taken a shower while tripping before? Nothing could feel better: not sex, not food. I let the water rush over me, through me, around me as I lathered and rinsed until the water began to run cool. The hot water was gone: it would become ice cold soon. I did not want to lose the joyous sensation. One last long rinse, and I was done.

Just as I was turning the shower off, there was a loud, hurried knock at the door. "Just a minute," I said, actually marveling at the timing of whoever had to piss.

Kevin said, "Davey, the cops are here, and they want you to come out." I instantly froze, all the fears of my bad trip beckoning me, triggered by Kevin goofing on me about the cops marching through their shift. The moment was interminable. I was afraid deep to my soul. My pulse quickened. My mind turned to dark thoughts. I imagined that there really were cops out there; that I was going to get busted and hauled off to prison in my red terry-cloth robe. I imagined that I was going to freak out, that I would not be able to handle the situation, that I would go crazy insane and have a bad trip that I never would come back from. I'd be in a straitjacket in a rubber room, crying for my mommy. I melted down into this fear, and it became who I was. I wallowed in it and trembled to my bones. I slipped off the edge of reality and caught just a glimpse of the abyss before I realized that he was goofing on me. He had gotten me. He had pulled it off.

I shook the water out of my hair like a dog coming out of a lake. I laughed at myself, laughed at his cleverness, laughed at the fact that he could get me that way. I leapt into exhilaration again, puffing up like a proud bird because I'd avoided the darkness and rejoined the light. I could handle this trip. I would control it. But I could not get my robe on. I was laughing so much, at myself, at Kevin's cunning, at my inability to get my robe on. I was back to pure joy. Rather than being angry, I was thrilled at his ability to scare me, to know me so well as to guess that I would fall for his trick. I pulled the sleeve on my robe inside out then outside in a half a dozen times before I finally was able to get it straight, to actually put my robe on and tie it in the front so that it would not fall off. Contributing to my laughter was the thought I had of coming out naked, of walking into the living room dripping wet and asking Kevin what he wanted. Although I knew that this would blow his mind completely, I was not uninhibited enough to pull it off. After finally getting my robe right, I opened the kitchen side door, and there was Kevin, leaning against the kitchen counter, looking intense. "You got me," I said, "I believed you."

He looked straight into my eyes and tried to keep the game going. "Davey, I was serious. The cops *are* here."

I laughed again, savoring the moment, and said, "Right, Kevin, I am sooo scared." I turned into the living room and smashed headlong into an invisible wall. I could not move. Every fiber in my being froze. Terror consumed me, became me. I was face-to-face with a New York State trooper who was standing at the front door, his hand on his pistol as if he would draw it and shoot me if I made a false move. It was as if he was guarding the door. He was not the only one there. There were cops everywhere. There was one in the kitchen, by the back door. There was one in Vinny's room, pulling the sheets off his bed and looking underneath. There were two more in the living room, using their

352 TIMOTHY F. DEMPSEY

fingers to comb through the ashes in the bowl-shaped ashtray. The one at the door pointed at me and said, "*You! Don't move!* Take your hands out of your pockets and put them at your side."

I obeyed and stood there with my hands outstretched. The cop in the kitchen came over to me and checked the robe's pockets. "What were you doing in there?"

Was he serious? "Taking a shower," I said, calmly.

"Did you flush anything?"

"Uh, no, I was taking a shower, not a shit."

He actually raised his hand as if to hit me, and I crouched down preparing to receive the blow. Instead, he restrained himself and said, "Don't be a goddamn wise ass! Which is your room?"

"Upstairs, first on the left."

"Get dressed."

I walked through the living room as if in slow motion. Even the memory of joy was gone, sucked into another galaxy. Don was standing there, his jawline lowered, his smile history. Berk was sitting on the couch, but with his owl-wide eyes he told me: *this is real. Be cool.* No hint of humor. Vinny was in his bedroom watching the cop go through his stuff. The girls were all on the couch, trembling. Where was Adam?

I made it to the stairs and slowly walked up to my room as the front door cracked open, and I realized Adam was out on the front porch—with a cop, and the cop was hassling him. I stopped and turned and tried to look, but the guard by the door just pushed the door closed again. When I got to my bedroom, I was surprised to see that there was another cop in there, and there was at least one in each of the other bedrooms. The place was crawling. The cop in my bedroom was holding my firecrackers and showed them to me as I entered. "These yours?" he said.

I just pulled my lower lip as if in surprise that those horrible things had turned up in my room and shook my head no. "This is your bedroom?"

"Yes," I said.

"I can bust you for these, you know?"

"They're not mine."

"Whose are they then?"

"Don't know."

"Right. Get dressed."

He just stood there and watched me. Modesty was not going to help me now. Only seconds before, I'd been contemplating walking around nude. Well, here you go. I opened my robe and dropped it on my bed, picked up a pair of jeans and the cop reached out and grabbed them away from me. "I can't get dressed if you take my clothes."

"Shut up," he said. He went through my pants pockets several times before handing them back to me. I pulled them on. I then got a T-shirt out of my drawer but thought it was inside out and repeated the bathroom scene of pulling the sleeves, first one way then another, for a minute or so before I finally attempted to get it on. I got it wrong the first time, took it off and tried again, finally got it right, and actually smiled at my success.

"What the hell are you *on*?" the cop asked me as he escorted me back down the stairs.

Still tripping my brains out and trying to cement the knowledge that these pigs were real and not hallucinatory, I was able to say, "I'm not *on* anything."

"Right," he said. "I suppose you're just a damn retard!"

As we reached the bottom of the stairs, I slipped behind the guard and opened the door. On the porch, another cop was doing something to Adam. He quickly took his hand off Adam's back, looked at me, and said, "Get back in the house." The inside guard, pissed that he had let me slip by, grabbed me and shoved me so that I fell over the ashtray, and we all came clattering down to the floor. I lay there and looked at him, wondering if I was going to get a beating or what. He glared back at me. The cop from the porch opened the door and gave Adam a slight shove to get him back in the house. He walked across the living room and said to his troops, "Anything?"

The cop in my room held up my firecrackers and pitifully said, "Just these." They all looked crestfallen. The cop coming out of the girls' room said, "And this!" He held up a shiny new hash pipe that looked like it had never been used. Several of us could not help ourselves and looked at Miranda as a betrayer. The head cop picked up on this and went over to her and said, "Is that yours?"

She said, "Yes. It's clean. It's a goof present for my father. I bought it for Father's Day, but I haven't been home."

The head cop walked over to our dartboard as if seeing for the first time that his likeness was our target. We were in the presence of Super Trooper. And what must have been every squad from precincts for three counties. I came to the realization that there were floodlights on each of our windows, and as I looked out, I saw a cop stationed at each one. Had to be over twenty cops altogether. They were expecting Al Capone, and so far all they could find was a pack of firecrackers and an unused hash pipe!

They were going to be pissed. They were going to plant something. I could feel it—they were not going to be embarrassed. Super Trooper stood under his likeness and said, "You guys think you're cute, don't you?"

Nobody said a word. "Nobody makes a fool of me," and he tore his picture off the dartboard and threw it into the fireplace. Then he shocked us all by saying, "Whatever you are doing up here, you got away with it for tonight, but don't worry, we *will* be back." He signaled his minions, and they all streamed out and populated the many police cars that surrounded the house. They collected the lights into a van, and miraculously, they were gone. They took my firecrackers. They took Miranda's hash pipe.

Adam proceeded to tell us that Super Trooper had done some mild torture on the porch, crunching his boot into Adam's ankle, asking him what we were doing here: Are you selling drugs or just taking drugs? Over and over, Adam told him, "We have nothing to do with drugs; we're just enjoying the summer. If anything, we drink too much, which is why we wanted a place so we would not have to drive drunk." They certainly had discovered enough empty beer bottles. They did not confiscate them.

35

I convinced myself that the cops would not allow the summer to end without a bust. The specter of spending time in a jail cell in some godforsaken upstate town horrified me. I pictured myself being kissed and gang raped by smelly, broken-toothed, tattooed, trailer-trash redneck degenerates. I'd die first, I vowed. I decided to stay away from Monroe for a while.

I developed the art of hitchhiking, learning to lock on the driver's eyes and attempt to pull him or her to the side of the road with a needful glance, wide puppy-dog eyes, a slight tilt of the head, willing them to follow my body language and pull their machine over. If I was able to seize their eyes and get them to actually see me, feel me, I'd end with uncurling my fingers from the fist with stuck-out thumb into an open-palmed plea, plaintively laying my hand out flat, exposing my vulnerabilities, asking them to feel my pain, share the pain of existence with me for just one moment, experience my desperation, and please, just give me a fucking ride, and I'll be fine.

No level of subterfuge was too low. I'd strategically place Cheryl, absolutely alluring in her tank top, skimpy cutoffs, and youthful exuberance, on the edge of the road, and I'd sit back on the shoulder, just six feet away but right out of the driver's periphery. Guys would slam on their brakes to stop for her, and I'd instantly jump up and run for the car door, opening it for her, making it impossible for them to just take off when they saw me. She'd get in first, while I grabbed our backpacks. Most of the time, this ruse worked, though I'd be greeted with glares. Occasionally, I'd be rewarded with the knowing laugh of someone who was aware they'd just been taken advantage of, but who had enough of a sense of humor to go along with it, someone who was respectful enough of the planning that went into the con to appreciate it. A few times, though, we were greeted by pure and unadulterated anger. I'd always rationalize that this guy was a real creep, must have thought he'd get in her pants for sure, and as he would yell, "No fucking way," or "Get the hell out of my car, both of you," I'd put up my hands and back out, ensuring that Cheryl got out, too. Sometimes they would desperately look at her and plead, "I thought you were alone." She'd smile politely and simply say, "Nope." I'd quickly get our packs, no dispute, just a curt, "Sorry, man," and flinch with my arm up protectively as his tires spat gravel at us when he floored his accelerator.

■ ■ ■

I was back home on a Saturday morning at the beginning of August. While Mom was making breakfast, I went to the front porch to retrieve the *Daily News*. The headline on the front page read, 30,000 Gather at Cancelled Festival Site. I had heard of the

Powder Ridge festival but had lost track of the date. It was on again, off again, the now-familiar plight of most of the Woodstock follow-ups. Promoters wanted to repeat the spectacle, and many of the artists wanted to play in a festival atmosphere. Usually, though, the neighbors and local citizens organized to stop them. Despite the fact that it was peaceful, many people had an image of Woodstock as a bunch of crazed, stoned, naked hippies roaming the countryside. Not too far from the truth. Just as I was finishing the article, the phone rang. It was Adam, and he asked, "Did you see the paper?"

"I'm just looking at it now."

"Let's go," he said. "I've got my mom's car."

"Can I take Cheryl?"

"Sure."

I called Vinny, and he said that he was driving up with Dennis Doyle. Not only had they made amends, but they were scoring and dealing together. We agreed to follow each other. I broke the news to Mom and suffered through her predictable look of anguish. The hurt flashed in her eyes, causing her cheeks to rise for the briefest moment before she took control and tried to cover it up. I had come home just the night before, announcing that I would remain for the weekend. It was as if each time I came home, she hoped it would be for good, that my wandering days were over, that I would never again place myself in harm's way. But she'd lost her will to fight over it, capitulating quickly into a quiet, defeatist despair.

We were on our way within the hour. Traffic was light, and we were at the ski area by noon. A number of cars were leaving already, but it seemed like more were arriving. Because of the early departures, we were able to pull almost up to the gates. It didn't look like it could be thirty thousand, but it was a big tent city filled with hippies. The promoters had lost their license at the last second, stopped by a court injunction, and although they announced the cancelation, they were not organized enough to shut the site down. The food booths that were usually there for the skiers were open, selling hot dogs and sodas.

Among the five of us we had three small tents: Cheryl and I set up mine; Vinny and Adam set up Adam's, and Doyle set up his own. After settling in, we split up and went for walks to case the site. Cheryl and I took off together. It was like an open-market bazaar. Drug dealers were everywhere, hawking their wares. Standing at strategic crossroads, their goods displayed on small tables, they began a price war. "Acid two dollars a tab," someone would yell, and twenty feet away someone else would call out in competition, "Acid a dollar fifty a tab." We scored, and each of us dropped a tab of Orange Sunshine.

We continued to stroll. There were small pockets of people sitting around, smoking joints, passing pipes, drinking wine and beer. There was no authority, no staff, and no security. But it did look like they were setting up a small stage at the bottom of the largest hill, tucked into a small valley. We stopped and watched and sure enough, they had some speakers coming in and some mikes. It looked like someone would be performing, but nobody seemed to know who.

As we wandered back, we saw Doyle sitting in front of his tent. He was holding a match under a teaspoon, heating up some white powder. He had some decent-looking works, a sterile needle still in the package. He added a drop of water, and the powder melted. He deftly loaded up, used his belt as a tourniquet, got a good vein in his forearm, above his left wrist, and shot up. In broad daylight, with a bunch of strangers walking around and watching. "Was that dope, Dennis?" I asked him.

"Nah, just speed," he said.

Later he would score some coke and shoot it. After that he would score some acid and shoot it. Each time, he would politely offer to share, and each time, we would decline, though Vinny was clearly wavering. I guessed that he would be right there with Dennis if the rest of us weren't watching. It became a running joke that the other campers around us would chime in on whenever Dennis appeared, whether it be coming back from a walk or just crawling out of his tent after a nod. "Dennis, we have some wine if you want to shoot it up."

Another stranger would opine, "You can't shoot up wine."

"Dennis can; he shot up peanut butter before."

There was a long line for the water truck, and I decided to stock up, fearing they might run out. After waiting in line for the better part of an hour, I first soaked my head under the spigot and splashed water down my back, ignoring the few behind me who complained that the water should be saved for drinking. I filled up all our available jugs and canteens. Unfortunately, the water had a gritty, tinny taste.

As evening fell, Cheryl and I went back to the stage area, where they had mounted a sheet as a screen and were setting up a projection machine. First they showed an Abbot and Costello routine in black-and-white. This absolutely loosened up the crowd: "Who's on first? I don't know...third base!" I laughed as hard as if I were hearing this familiar refrain for the first time. Simultaneously, I was imagining what it must have been like for my mom, who had seen them perform this skit live at the Kings Theatre in Brooklyn. The trip was mellow. The feelings were all good, the pathways were clear.

The valley filled up. Although a much smaller scale than Woodstock, the protocols of Powder Ridge were similar: find a spot, stretch out, stake it, and try to hold it, like the board game Risk come to life. It was fully dark out as they changed films and rolled the Disney cartoon version of *Alice in Wonderland*. This became an audience participation event, with people calling out to encourage Alice as she contemplated taking the pills, one to make you taller and one to make you smaller. "Take the acid, Alice." "No, no, take the speed." "Look out for the white rabbit!" There was a light breeze rolling down the mountain. The camaraderie was clean and easy. It was less intense than Woodstock. We befriended our immediate neighbors. They shared a jug of lemonade with us, assuring us it was not spiked. A marijuana and tobacco cloud hung low over the crowd. The stream of joints was endless, and more and more of us just started passing them, unable to draw another toke. With all the acid flowing in this crowd, we felt like Alice was definitely tripping right along with us.

Two Mr. Softee trucks on either side of the stage annoyed me. I thought they were too noisy and should be moved. I didn't mind these guys making some money hawking their ice cream, but why did they have to interfere with the show? I walked over and spoke my mind to the vendor, and he shook his head in disgust. I was guessing I was not the first complainer. But then he used his thumb to indicate the back of his truck and said, "I'm driving the generator, asshole. If I leave, you have no show." I walked to the back of his truck and only then noticed all of the large cables that were emanating from his truck were linked directly to the equipment behind the stage. Humbled and feeling quite stupid, I took the time to apologize and thank him. He seemed to appreciate it. I bought a couple of cones and gave him a nice tip.

When the film finished, we all thought that might be it for the night, but there was a stirring at the stage. A young woman with a guitar was talking to the roadies, and then they set out a barstool on the stage. She was short, in a floor-length peasant dress, with long black hair. When she turned to step up to the stage, I could see that it was Melanie. I jumped up and was one of the first to start a standing ovation to welcome her.

She thanked the crowd, got us to settle down, and then did a two-hour set, telling stories in between songs, apologizing for all of the other artists who did not show up. She was the quintessential performer for that moment on that speck of the planet. She oscillated between her haunting and self-reflective ballads: "Beautiful People," "Look What They've Done to My Song, Ma," and "Tuning My Guitar"; and her silly nonsense songs: "Animal Crackers" and "I've Got a Brand New Pair of Roller Skates." She closed with her soon to be classic, "Candles in the Rain."

"Some came to sing. Some came to pray. Some came to keep the dark away." The audience stood as one, holding up lighters, matches, and even a few candles. This would become a trite and predictable ritual of our generation, but in this instance it was spontaneous, original, and absolutely authentic. It was one of the best musical sets I had ever seen. She had the crowd singing along with her, and we called her back for three encores until she pleaded with us, "I have no strength left, and I've done all my songs. I love you. Thank you and good night." As the crowd dispersed, we kicked around the hillside for a while, surveying the remnants of a rockfest: abandoned sleeping bags, collapsed and forgotten tents, trash everywhere. It looked like the new foundation of a garbage dump. The bazaar atmosphere had devolved to ridiculous levels. "Acid, twenty-five cents a hit."

36

Back home after Powder Ridge, I slept most of the next day. Vinny called me in the evening and asked if there was any way I could borrow my father's car to do him a favor. I told Pop we were going to Jones Beach, and he threw me the keys. When I drove over to Vinny's house, I was disappointed to find Pauly sitting on the porch with him. When they got in the car, Vinny asked me to take them to Elmont.

"Vinny, I'm not taking you to cop dope."

Pauly answered, "Davey, man, I wouldn't do that to you. You know that. C'mon Davey, man, I just need to pick something up." Vinny just looked at me, and I shook my head, mourning the relationship we used to have.

Of course it was dope. I knew it, yet I took them anyway. The slums of Elmont, on the west side of Belmont racetrack, were strings of hundred-year-old mill houses in disrepair: peeling paint, holes in the roof, shutters askew. As kids on bicycles, we had always pedaled hard through these neighborhoods, cognizant of the looks we would get from the "colored" men hanging out on the stoops, drinking gin. But we had never been hassled, never bothered.

But now I was scared. Times had changed. The "brothers" on the stoops were harder up now. Smack habits are much more expensive than gin habits. Pauly directed me to the right house, asked me to keep the car running. Fortunately, Vinny stayed with me. He was casual, smoking a cigarette, his arm hanging out the open window. I suggested we close the window and lock the doors, and Vinny laughed at me, told me to calm down. Everything would be cool. There were two old black men sitting on the rickety porch that had once been painted a beautiful sky blue, barely visible now through the years of neglect. Dirty and grimy, what little blue was left was peeling. Here is this skinny white boy walking right up to them, bearing the name of some pusher who referred him. One of them looked back at us as he opened the screen door, with the bottom half of the screen torn and hanging down, and yelled, "You boys coming in?"

We both shook our heads without saying a word. Vinny dragged harder on his cigarette and flicked it into the street. "Don't think so," he mumbled to me.

Pauly must have been in there five minutes when I started to get nervous. "What do you think is happening?"

"Maybe he is trying the stuff."

"You don't think he's getting ripped off, do you?"

"If he is, he deserves it," Vinny said in a cold, even voice. "This is some fucked up place he took us. 'Davey, man, I would never do that to you,'" he mimicked.

"You're the one who got me into this, Vinny! I'm in my father's car, damn it. Why'd you set me up?"

"I owed him."

I didn't want to know for what.

It had been almost ten minutes now. The palms of my hands were sweating. "Do you think we should leave?"

"No fucking way, man. You can't leave him here. Five more minutes, then I'm going in."

That last five minutes was an eternity, but just as Vinny was opening the car door, the screen door opened, and out came Pauly, followed by the same two black guys plus a third, all in the same uniform of white "wife-beater" T-shirts. Pauly staggered toward the car. Vinny helped him in the backseat. "Davey, man," Pauly spoke in a low, guttural voice, "Get the fuck out of here, man." The three black guys were coming toward the car, smiling, and the lead one holding up his palm as if to say, "Wait a minute now."

I burned rubber. They watched us run, laughing and slapping each other on the backs. We had amused these dealers with our petty white-boy fears. Pauly was definitely nodding, eyes glassy, rolling around in his head. I unleashed my anger. "Pauly, you told me you weren't scoring junk."

He opened his eyes to slits, but his demeanor got serious. "Davey, man…grow…the…fuck…up. What the fuck did you think we were picking up, a fucking newspaper, man? This is fucking Elmont, man; of course I was picking up some shit." Then he relented, smiled, and said, "And good shit it is, my friend, good shit it is." He nodded off in the backseat of my old man's car.

It turned into a hot, steamy night, the kind where everyone in New York felt compelled to say, "It's not the heat; it's the humidity." Vinny said there was a party at Dennis Doyle's, and I dropped off him and Pauly. I was disgusted with both of them, and I took Pop's car home and walked up to Schneid's. There was nothing to do, and I was growing bored when Adam came by, and we walked around the block and smoked a joint. It was almost pro forma. It was expected; it was what we did. The days of giggling and stopping to carry out some antic were gone. We smoked a joint out of habit, pure and simple. It was almost like we smoked a joint to get straight, to not be depressed about how hopeless everything seemed. But it affected us like an appetizer, stimulating our hunger—we wanted something more.

We walked over to Doyle's and found the party raging. His mother would be away the whole weekend. The stereo was blasting, and there were lots of kids sitting around, drinking and smoking cigarettes, talking and making out. All in all there were about twenty-five kids in various rooms. Sex noises were emanating from his mother's bedroom, but no one seemed to know who was in there.

I walked into the kitchen and encountered Dennis, Pauly, and Vinny sitting around the classic fifties dinette set, a round table with a bright-yellow laminated top and six aluminum chairs with matching yellow backs and seat cushions. Adam and I joined them. Their tone was serious, focused. There was polite but nervous laughter. They were messing with some drugs and drug paraphernalia, which were spread out on the table. They were getting ready to shoot up. Curious, I sat down to watch the process up close.

Doyle took a small glassine envelope and spilled some speed into a teaspoon. He heated it up with a cigarette lighter, one of the old-fashioned kinds, rectangular with a snap-open top and smelling strongly of fresh lighter fluid. As he heated the spoon, the meth melted, and he picked up a homemade contraption. The needle was not attached to a syringe, but rather to a dropper, like the kind you use to put drops in your ears. The needle was stuck in the end and held fast with electrical tape.

Crude, clumsy works. He deftly put the needle into the spoon and squeezed the end of the dropper to draw the speed up. He turned it upside down, snapped it with his finger to ensure all the air bubbles were out. He tied a belt around his wrist and made a hard fist, causing the veins in the back of his hand to protrude. He skillfully slid the needle into one of the veins and squeezed the dropper, injecting the speed into his vein. He then left it in place as he squeezed the ball again, drawing some blood back into the needle. "It's important to aspirate," he said calmly, "to know you've got it right." Was this a clinic on shooting up? He took a bottle of rubbing alcohol and poured it over the whole contraption then poured a little into a shot glass and aspirated some into the dropper several times, cleaning it out. "Next," he said.

I watched, still with more curiosity than horror, as they went around the circle, shooting speed, aspirating the blood, cleaning the instrument. Doyle was in charge, his expertise taken for granted. I asked questions throughout. Why do you do this, why do you do that? Mostly, I wanted to know, "What does it feel like?"

Even Adam did it. My heart was racing as I realized that everyone in the room had shot up except me. They didn't look any different, weren't acting any different. Their conversations continued, though their laughter had a new edge, a small twinkle in their smiles. Their eyes, though, were exploding, their pupils routing out all color. I shocked myself as much as I did them as I asked, almost inaudibly, "Can I try?"

Doyle looked deep into my eyes. "Are you sure?"

I took a deep breath and exhaled as I answered, the words clearly belying the body language. "Yeah, I mean, it's only speed, right? I mean, I wouldn't want to do dope."

"Sure," Dennis said, "it's only speed." I sat spellbound as he meticulously followed the procedure. He cleaned the needle with alcohol, then heated the end of it with the flame. He heated the speed in the spoon, blew on it to cool it a bit. He filled the needle while Pauly checked my arm, looking for a good vein. He told me my hands looked great, so there was no reason to shoot into my arm. "Make a fist and hold it tight," Dennis ordered, and I blindly obeyed.

Dennis grabbed my wrist and squeezed, tightening up the circulation. It hurt a little, but I remained silent. I was fascinated at my own behavior; caught in a spiral I could no longer control. I observed as if I were a third party. One of the veins emanating down from my forefinger into the back of my hand rose prominently. Pauly flicked it with a finger, causing it to tingle. He wiped it with a clean cotton ball soaked in the rubbing alcohol. Doyle took a big drag on his cigarette and got into position. Very carefully, very gently, he injected the needle into my vein. He slowly pushed the speed, aspirated some of my blood back into the dropper and then reinjected this mixture back into my body. He put a cotton ball on the site as he gently withdrew the needle. He was a pro. I felt no pain. I was mesmerized, watching as if I were no longer present in my body, but rather floating above it.

The drug hit instantly, and my heart began racing. I am not sure if it was anxiety or speed, but my mind drifted immediately into worry. I was not concerned about the drug; I was worried about the possibility of air bubbles. "Sometimes one sneaks in, and it can kill you," Doyle had said. "It takes a few seconds, though." But everything seemed fine, and I realized I was experiencing the rush of instant methamphetamine on my heart. I was beginning to sweat a little, and my heart continued to race at speeds I almost felt as a continuous stream, as if there were no moments to count in between each beat, as if my heart was putting out hundreds of beats a second like the staccato of a machine gun. I heard it as well as felt it, but the rush passed after a minute, and I began to distinguish each beat, though still at a rapid pace. I had no conscious high, no feeling of euphoria, no sense that I was stoned, and no justification for putting my body at such risk.

I turned to Dennis. "Thanks, man."

He shook his head, dragged on his cigarette again. "Don't fucking thank me, man. You got your wings now, but I ain't proud of givin' 'em to you." He was serious. Despite the fact that he was injecting stuff all the time now, he was genuinely sad at welcoming me into this exclusive but growing club.

He cleaned up the table and announced that the speed was gone. It had been a dime bag. Often, he would have taken the whole thing himself. It provided enough for two to get good and high, but since we had split it six ways no one was particularly wrecked. I, for one, was fine with this. I had a good buzz, yet was glad that I was not fucked up. I was processing the answer Dennis gave me to my thanks: I had my wings. I put a fucking needle into my arm and shot up with speed. I feared this realization, frightened of who I was becoming, yet rationalized it immediately. *It's not dope; you won't get addicted; you're not going to be a junkie.* I'd just done it to try it; I was not going to become a junkie. I wondered if this was what they all thought the first time they shot up.

Pauly put a big smile on his face and asked, "Anybody want to shoot some acid?"

Thinking he must be kidding, I asked, "You're not really going to shoot acid, are you?"

"Why not?"

Doyle commented, "I've done it. It's great…a real trip. Let's go!"

Pauly started grinding two tabs of sunshine into a fine powder. He got a tablespoon and mixed the powder with a few drops of water and went through the heating routine. He did himself first, then Doyle. This stuff was affecting them immediately, and they were laughing and carrying on. Vinny and Adam followed suit, and once again it was my turn. There was just a little left in the spoon. They were no longer as meticulous with the alcohol and the cleaning.

I beat my fear into submission, desperately wanting to belong. Vinny looked at me. "Well?"

"Sure, let me do it." Less than a half hour after putting a needle into my arm for the first time and lamenting that I was on my way to being a junkie, I was doing it again. Only this time, my reaction was more than a rush, more than a runaway heartbeat and a mild anxiety attack. I was tripping before the needle was out of my arm, allowing me to look at the needle in a whole different way: it seemed permanently implanted into my hand, as if it were a part of me.

Doyle was a little rough as he pulled it out, used no alcohol or cotton ball. He was tripping, and he was no longer the pro. He just sort of yanked it out, like pulling a meat thermometer out of a turkey. He tore the site ragged. I realized that I was bleeding. The blood oozed rather than dripped, and I stared at it with fascination. Doyle yelled at me "Don't get blood on the table, man."

I instinctively pulled my hand up to my mouth and sucked the blood. It tasted salty and sticky and somehow sweet, and my hand lingered there longer than was necessary. Everybody in the room was glowing; smiles were exaggerated, voices were full of giddiness, but no one was making any sense. It was all gibberish.

They all seemed to light cigarettes at once. Pauly pulled something, some kind of a package, out of his pocket and set it on the table. "Kid stuff is over," he said. "Let's get it on." I was paralyzed as I looked at the cellophane bag of fine white powder. This was heroin, this was what I'd helped him score—had that been the same day? All of a sudden I felt the kitchen was way overcrowded. I could barely move; I could barely breathe. I was hanging on to a small thread of self, remembering who I was, fighting the urge to belong, readying myself to flee the scene. I was done. I could not, would not, shoot up smack. I would not, in fact, ever shoot up again.

I escaped into the living room, where I bumped into Emily Adelman and Carrie Cox, some friends of Joe Stayer whom I had last seen the night I dislocated my shoulder. They struck me as an unlikely couple. Emily was stunning in her beauty, with silky jet-black hair falling almost to her waist. She had model features, sharp lines, high cheekbones, an exquisitely pointed-up-ever-so-slightly nose and a winning, beautiful smile that she saved for rare occasions. All that and smart to boot, she was talking about the futility of escalation in Vietnam. I sat down in between them, forcing myself into their conversation. Carrie was short, plain, not particularly attractive, the type of girl about whom the guys always joked, "Put a bag over her head, she'll be fine." She did, in fact, have a great personality. *Must be hard for her*, I thought, *to be best friends with Emily who has guys drooling over her all the time*. Me too. I adored being near her, talking to her, being in her presence.

I had lost the concept of time. The living room was a safe cocoon, with familiar pictures on the walls and soft, comfortable furniture. I tried to keep the doorway to the kitchen out of my range, ignored the random noises that periodically escaped from that room, that room of evil.

Emily turned on me suddenly. "What about you? What are you going to do about the draft?"

"I don't know. Go to Canada?"

"Good for you. That is the absolute right thing to do. Either that or go to jail. Do not cooperate; do not partake in this immoral, unnecessary genocide. Do you know about the *Manual for Draft Age Immigrants*?"

"Uh, no. What's that?"

"It's a guide about how to go to Canada and get in without getting hassled. You can usually get a copy of it at the counseling center of your school."

"I'll look for it...thanks." With that, she turned to Carrie and said, "Let's go," and just like that they were out of there. I peeked into the kitchen and was stunned to find it empty. The revelers had dispersed, and I hadn't even noticed. I wandered all over the house. Vinny was watching television. Pauly was lying on the floor in Doyle's room, headphones on, eyes closed, an Al Kooper album on his chest. It was hard to tell if he was awake or asleep.

I kicked at Vinny. "I'm leaving. I want to get home before my parents wake up." He agreed and as we readied to go, we grew into a group, Adam and Pauly joining us at the door.

Doyle tried to stop us. "Why don't you stay and sleep here?" None of us wanted to. As we were walking along Hillside Avenue, the night air and the false dawn raised our spirits a bit, reinvigorating us, releasing us from our drug-induced stupors. We were passing a house that had done some massive cleaning, and in front there was a pile of stuff with the trash: an old sofa and chair, a lamp, and a mirror. We stopped and sat down on the old furniture. We started "playing," carrying on and pretending that we were in a surreal restaurant, and this was the décor. A car went by, and Adam instinctively held the mirror sideways as if it were a tray and he were a waiter serving us. The car slowed down and stared at us, and we thought this was a hoot. We decided to prepare even better for the next one. Vinny rummaged through the boxes and found a bottle and a rag, and we set the scene to look more realistic. The rest of us took positions as if we were sophisticates having a posh dinner and engaging in captivating conversation.

When the next car passed, a few minutes later, we were ready: we all froze like statues, some with a pretend glass halfway to their lips, others midgesture. We looked like a three dimensional tableau. We were performance artists. We were just playing, having fun, but the folks in the cars were not entertained. As they got a good look at us, they drove away with a slight look of terror in their eyes. Game over.

37

I needed a break. The drinking, drugs, and sleepless nights were taking a toll. My body ached as I dragged it around, sluggishly seeking the next high. I wanted to hike and swim, try to cleanse my body and my mind. I hungered for nature. Cheryl and I opted for Lake George for the Labor Day weekend. Kevin was going to Monroe and agreed to drive us to the Thruway.

"Did you hear what happened to Billy Mackay?" Kevin asked. I shook my head no, expecting to hear some exploit about his thriving drug dealership. "Things got a little dry, and he took a job temping for some electrician. He was working at the bottom of an elevator shaft when the elevator car above him came crashing down, flattening him like Wily E. Coyote. By the time they raised the car and peeled him off the floor, he was near death, but still breathing. His bones were disjointed, not just broken. They seemed to be floating within his squishy skin, rather than providing a structural frame for his skin to stretch out on. But, somehow, his organs remained viable."

I was spellbound. "Where is he now?"

"Davey, he's been using your room in Monroe for the last week, but before you freak out, let me tell you the rest of the story. He had us absolutely entranced last weekend. He said he had entered a fantasy world, but he was determined to emerge from it. He dreamed of rodents, who have the ability to disconnect and flatten their bones when they need to slide under a door or slip through a crack in the wall. He'd been hospitalized for weeks.

"At first, he was beyond pain and lived through his dreams, unable to distinguish between sleep and wake states, preferring the generous oblivion of consciousness avoidance. As the swelling in his head went down, he started to experience intense pain. They dosed him with significant amounts of pain killers. He became dependent on morphine. He drifted through dark states of delirium. He imagined that the doctors were elves, administering potions to his soul. The pain was goblins gnawing at him, trying to consume him, but he regenerated, and they couldn't kill him.

"Eventually, he began to achieve a state of bliss. The elves were winning; the gobbling goblins became less frequent. Speech and recognition returned. Then his father pushed him back down.

"His parents had never visited his apartment, trusting and respecting his wishes that a bachelor's pad remain a private place. Several days after the accident, while he was still out of it, they had the landlord let them in, unsure if he had any pets but aware that he had lots of plants that needed watering. They found everything: pot, hash, acid, ups, downs, rolling papers, and pipes. They sat in his living room, among the stolen dwarfs and eerie posters, and they cried. He said they turned on each other, blaming each other for who he had become. They blamed the accident on him, figuring he was stoned and somehow caused that cable to slip.

"Then they went to work, demolishing the apartment. They wiped out everything, flushed the drugs down the toilet, tore the posters off the walls, and even took apart the light fixtures. They destroyed all his plants, hauling huge black plastic bags down to the Dumpster. They threw away the trolls and the dwarfs, placing the statues by the curb.

"Then they used his accident as an excuse to break his lease. They wanted him to come home to them when he recovered. They got lawyers and began suing everyone they could think of: the master electrician and the company he worked for, the elevator manufacturer, the building owner.

"His dad reamed him out, called him names, judged him, and dismissed him. Billy met fire with fire, called his father names, belittled his mother, and vowed never to move back home.

"When they released him last week, he called Miranda. He's been staying with her in Monroe. He walks with a cane, a staff carved with a dragon's head on top and the texture and shape of a snake for the body. His voice has not returned to its former grace. He speaks deeply now with a hard edge to his voice, emanating from a place of darkness. He smiles rarely, put away his guitar. He and Miranda are wallowing in despair, feeding off each other's lost dreams, taking downs, rarely coming out of your bedroom."

"What about the troopers?"

"Never came back." Kevin finished this extraordinary tale and dropped us off at the Monroe Thruway entrance. Hitching was uneventful, and we were in the state campground at Hearthstone Point before dark. We set up the tent, built a campfire and huddled under the stars.

In the morning, we hitched a ride to the Lake George stables, just a few miles north of the campground. Cheryl got a small, docile Pinto, named Louise. I said that I was experienced, despite the fact that I had only ridden a horse once before. I got a handsome chestnut-and-sorrel dappled Palomino, with a silky white tail. His name was Stan, and he seemed to have some fire in his belly, but I thought he respected me. He could have walked the trail without guidance. Louise seemed content to follow him. We paid the higher hourly rate, allowing us to walk the trail without a guide.

Not content with an easy ride, I wanted to demonstrate my imagined prowess and go off-trail for a little exploration. I went down a small ridge and let Stan eat some flowers, which he stubbornly decided he would like to do for the rest of the day. I pulled in the bit hard enough to convince him that we were going to move on, and we went back to the trail. Louise, on the other hand, had just stopped on the trail at the point we had left it and waited for us. Cheryl was laughing and having fun. She was enjoying the view. From here you could see a good part of the lake, which lay just a mile or two below us, set in its own valley, with majestic mountains rising from both sides. To the south, we could just make out the village. Bright layered cumulus clouds floated gracefully above, so close that it seemed like we could climb a little higher and be among them.

We were out about half an hour when the trail started winding back down the mountain. I basked in my perceived horsemanship. There was a turnoff that went through a canopy of trees into a shaded area that almost looked like a tunnel through the forest. Stan resisted at first, but then traversed it, and we went up about a hundred yards. A fallen tree was blocking the path. It was a majestic old northern red oak, with a girth that must have been four feet, and it was forty or fifty feet long, resting about three and a half feet off the ground. There was no way around it, and I decided to back off and turn around. But the path we were on was very narrow, and this time Louise had followed us, so I was trying to convince Cheryl that she had to get Louise to back up or turn around. Louise was much more comfortable waiting for Stan to do something. I opted to back out and squeeze past Cheryl and Louise and retake the lead. I thought I had successfully communicated this to Stan, because he took two steps back and then shuddered a little bit. I was sure he was about to turn around, but instead he reared back and flexed his hind muscles, took two fast, muscular steps forward, and leaped into the air. He had decided to jump, and by the time I realized what he was up to, we were airborne. He was holding his forelegs up high; they were clearing the tree, and he had to pull his hind legs over.

The whole maneuver probably lasted about three seconds, but I experienced it in slow motion, observing myself even as it happened. I held onto the reins with both hands, letting go of the saddle horn, which I had been holding as I tried to get Stan to turn. Instinctively, I even lowered my body down into a crouch and looked like I knew what I was doing, as I had seen jockeys do on television. I believed everything was going to be fine, and I was actually enjoying the moment, savoring the fact that I was on a horse that was jumping high over an obstacle. I was pure adrenaline, feeling heroic. I was HopaLong Cassidy! Just then my instincts failed me. As Stan's hind legs cleared and he began his descent, reextending his front legs until they touched the ground, inertia kept me going in an upward trajectory. I just kept sailing, right off his back, flying above his head, still going up for another fraction of a second. Just as I could hear his back legs hit the ground, gravity pulled me in for a rapid descent, and I fell crashing down through a thick sticker bush of some kind. I sort of bounced and tumbled into some rocks. Trying to protect my head by wrapping my arms around it and pulling my face in toward my chest, I rolled as effortlessly as tumbleweed on an open plain. As I came to a rest, I tried to roll farther away, convinced that Stan was still coming and he was going to trample me to death.

Fortunately, though, Stan had stopped and was just looking at me as if to say, "Hey, idiot, I thought you wanted me to jump. Why did you get off?" I looked past him and saw Cheryl and Louise, safely looking at us with concern on their faces. Cheryl said, "Are you all right?"

"Mostly embarrassed is all." At least that is what I thought until I tried to stand up. My legs buckled a little at the knees, and my back and my ass hurt like hell. I looked at my behind as I got up and saw that the landing had torn right through my jeans, which now had a big hole in them, and my bare butt was showing. It had a large raspberry on it, which would turn black and blue that night and be sore for weeks.

Stan started to walk away, and Cheryl encouraged me, "Get your horse; get your horse." I ran after Stan and grabbed the reins then realized he was heading down the hill to get back to the trail. I held the reins and pretended to lead him, trying to regain some shred of dignity. When we got back to the trail, Louise was waiting for us, and I mounted Stan and resolved not to take any more excursions. We ambled back to the stables, enjoying the scenic views of the lake and the distant mountains that had graced many a postcard.

The stable hand asked us how the ride was, and we just said it was fine. I had no desire to share my foibles with him. I had to consciously turn away from him so that he would not see my butt hanging out, and Cheryl had quite a time trying to contain her laughter. When he heard that we were going to hitch back to the campground, he told us he was going into town and offered to give us a ride in the back of his truck. "Let's go all the way into the village," I suggested to Cheryl, and she agreed. Looking at my long hair and unkempt beard, the driver asked me if we had any grass. "No, but do you know where we can get some?" So much for purity and cleaning out my system. My bruised ego needed a boost. Besides, pot was natural.

He told us that he had some friends who worked in the sub shop, and he took us there and introduced us. His friend said that he was tapped out of grass, but that he did have some acid that he had just copped. When I asked him about brand, he just said it was locally made but was in the same family as Sunshine and Owsley. We bought one dot, a wet drop on a green blotter, and split it. I did not want to trip in town, worried about what we would do if it was too hard to handle, so we hitched back to the campground.

It was late afternoon, and the sun was high. It was getting quite hot in the tent, so I timidly suggested that we get naked. Cheryl hesitantly slid out of her clothes just as the acid really kicked in. It had been well marketed. Not quite hallucinogenic, it was stronger than Sunshine. We lay on the floor of the tent and looked at the patterns in the watermarks throughout the canvas, marveling at the changes in shadow and texture as the breeze moved the leaves and branches, and when the wind was a little stronger, the tent itself. When the tent undulated, the patterns shifted only their nuance, but we interpreted this as if it were a revolutionary new art form, a free form reminiscent of the Joshua Light Show.

Cheryl sat up and said she was a little dizzy, maybe from the heat, and I rubbed her back from my prone position. She was sweaty, and my hand was sweaty, and the feeling that I was getting from these mixed body fluids was turning me on. I started to trip more intensely, even as my erection grew, unembarrassed and uninhibited, not inches from her face. I closed my eyes and rubbed her back more sensually and tried to will her to lean over and take me into her mouth. Her thoughts couldn't have been further away, as she said, "I think I'm going to faint."

I sat up and said, "Put your head between your legs." As she leaned over I rubbed her neck and her back, and she seemed to recover, so I allowed my hands to slide around her side and began to caress her breasts. I imagined that I could feel every blood vessel expanding. She, though, gave me absolutely no hint that she would return my advances, and so I suggested softly, "Let's make love."

"I don't think so."

It was not a nasty or definitive declaration, so I persisted. "C'mon, it'll make you feel better."

She thought about this for a second and agreed to try. Even though I felt she was just humoring me, I didn't care. I would take it. I said, "Let's do a new position; let's try sitting up." I sat Indian style, and I eased her onto me, getting her to wrap her legs around my back. I closed my eyes and held her tight and just as I was about to try a thrust up, she leaped off me as if she had a bucket of cold water thrown on her. She was standing above me, looking down, and she seemed to be shaking all over as she yelled, so loudly that I feared anyone around us must be listening, "I can't do this. I'm sorry, but I cannot fucking do this! Do not make me do this!"

"All right," I said, "Stop your yelling. I'm not going to 'make' you do anything you don't want to do."

Fortunately, this relieved her instantly, and she sat back down and repeated, "I *am* sorry." She lay down and looked as if she was going to pass out.

I took a deep breath and turned away, ashamed of how I had pushed her. I realized it *was* hot; we were suffocating. "Let's get out of the tent," I said. Fortunately, we were aware enough to get dressed. We walked down to the lake and went for a swim in our clothes. The water was cool, almost cold to our hot bodies, but it was characteristically clean and invigorating. Cheryl stayed near shore, looking for rats. I went out and floated where it was around ten feet deep. I dove down and examined the rocks on the bottom. There were a number of small perch sharing my curiosity, and I imagined that I was communicating with them, that they were reading my thoughts.

Back on the rocks, Cheryl asked me, "What's happening when we get back home next week?"

"What'd you mean? I'm going back to school in a week."

"I know. But you only have a year left. Shouldn't we start to plan for the wedding?"

Now it was my turn to freak. "Look. I am *not* having this conversation. Not while we are tripping. Not now, for Chrissake! This is our last weekend of the summer."

"Yeah, well, I need a commitment. What happens if we keep doing this, and I do wind up pregnant? You gonna be cheating on me again, or what?"

Once again, I was beginning to feel trapped in this relation-ship. But the best I could muster was, "No, I won't do that."

■ ■ ■

On Tuesday morning, there was a light rain falling, and as much as we knew it was not fun to pack up in the rain, we decided to head to Monroe. Kevin and the others were supposed to move out on Labor Day, but the lease was good until the tenth, a few more days. We thought that having a couple of nights alone in the big red house would be a fun way to end the summer. We were also both dying for a hot shower and some clean sheets on a real bed. We had had enough nature.

The hitch was dicey, as I had to continue to be sure my butt was not on display to a potential ride. Fortunately, we had no incidents or mishaps and made it to Monroe while it was still light out. We walked through town, but the park was empty. We dropped the gear off at the house, also empty, and walked over to the other house so Cheryl could get her stuff. Vinny was hanging out with Pauly's little sister, Maria, and her boyfriend, Mike, who were there for the first time. Vinny was obviously strung out. His eyes were black and swollen, almost shut.

"What happened to you?" I jumped on him.

"I got into a fight with some fucking farmer in Harriman's."

"Vinny, you look like the other guy usually looks after a fight with you. What the fuck happened?"

"Don't ever try to take on a whole bar, man."

"Jesus, what started it?"

"Doesn't matter. Stupid shit. Look, there's worse stuff going on."

Time to sit down. "What?"

"Kathy's pregnant." Cheryl gasped. "Has been for two months, 'parently. She and Adam were not very careful. They got married on Saturday. A shotgun affair, only a few family members. Her father's going to help them out. They're getting an apartment in Glen Oaks."

We lost the incentive to tell our Lake George stories. I had a beer while Cheryl got her stuff, both of us moving in quicksand, trying to catch up to this new reality. I tried to engage. "Vinny, man, you coming back to the other house for one last night?"

"Nah, I'm done there. Besides, I'm so fucked up I'm paralyzed. The only move I'm making is to this fucking pillow." He put his head down on the ratty, dirty couch pillow and closed his eyes. In a minute, he was snoring. I saw a crumbled piece of paper, balled up on the floor where his feet had been. I picked it up, tried to straighten it while looking at it, losing my breath.

Cheryl came out of the bedroom and read the concern on my face. "What is it?"

"His notice. He's been drafted. He has to report in six weeks."

■ ■ ■

Maria was seventeen years old and as cute as her age. She had been going with Mike since the beginning of the summer. Older than she, he was in law school. She sat next to me and asked quietly, "Can we come with you?"

I raised my eyebrow. She added, "There's no privacy here. My brother's on my case constantly."

I could definitely relate. "Sure, why not?" Mike had a car, so the gesture was rewarded with a ride.

The place had been cleaned out. Stuff that I had stored in the closet under the stairs, mostly shoes, but also my prized record albums, was gone. It flashed through my mind that the Beatles' *Revolver* album, the European version that Brian had sent me from his leave in Italy, could never be replaced. I was furious, fearing that Kevin had tossed them. Just in case, I searched the garbage but found nothing useful.

We had a small fire and a couple of beers. Then we went to bed. Mike and Maria used the bedroom off the other end of the balcony. Cheryl fell asleep early, and shortly after midnight I went down to the kitchen and got a glass of water. I was naked. When I came back up the stairs, Maria was standing on the balcony. She had been watching me. She, too, was naked. Petite and svelte, she could not have cleared a hundred pounds. She had long, dark, and curly hair hanging over her shoulders tickling her pert breasts. She was leaning against the rail but turned toward me when I came up, giving me a full frontal view. She smiled and tossed her hair back over her shoulder.

"Thanks for letting us come over. It's the first time Mike and I have been able to be together in an actual bed."

"No problem. Is he asleep?"

"Yeah, he is. What about Cheryl?" I nodded yes, and we smiled at each other.

"You look great," I told her. She leaned to the side and looked down at my penis, which was beginning to stir.

She laughed and said, "So do you." I touched her hand, and she didn't pull away. I put my arm around her back and leaned over to kiss her, and she welcomed me with open mouth. Now fully erect, I realized the absurdity of the situation. Not ten feet away in different directions, were our respective lovers, sleeping after making love to us. I took her hand and led her down to Vinny's room, where we locked ourselves in without saying a word. We explored each other with a ravishing curiosity. When we had finished, I stuttered, "We better get back to Cheryl and Mike."

"Yeah, we'd better...before we get caught." Another lingering kiss, and our affair was over.

I went to sleep with mixed emotions. I felt like hot shit for having made love to the prettiest girl that came to Monroe the whole summer. On the other hand, I knew I had cheated on Cheryl yet again, just days after promising not to, and with her in earshot!

I had a troubled sleep and awoke to voices. Someone was in the house. I was sure that I had locked the door last night, and we believed that Kevin had turned in all of the other keys. I pulled on my jeans and T-shirt, just as someone was calling out, "Hello." Looking down from the balcony, I saw our real estate agent, and then as she looked up at me and said, "Good morning," a local sheriff walked into view. *Ohmigod*, I thought. *I'm going to get arrested for statutory rape, two charges.*

I just hoped the girls would stay asleep for a while and not come out. Maybe I could get rid of the intruders. I went down and shook hands with each and asked them politely, "Can I help you?"

The agent smiled. "I came out this morning to see how the place looked. Your brother told me that everyone had moved out, and I was coming to see if there was any damage or cleaning to be done before I mailed his security check back. The owner wants to put this house on the market, and I wanted to start to get it ready for sale."

"I thought our contract gave us till Saturday."

"It did," she said. "But as I told you, your brother said you were all done."

"Obviously, he never told me," I said, feeling like an idiot. The cop, who had not said a word up until then, asked me if there were others here.

"Yeah," I said, "three of my friends."

Just then, the other bedroom door opened and Mike came out. For a moment, the sheriff's hand actually went to rest on the top of his gun, until he could assure himself that there was no threat. "Is there a problem?" Mike said, as he came down the stairs.

"No," I said, "just a misunderstanding."

Mike had heard the stories of our near busts over the summer, and he started to play law student. He looked straight at the cop and said, "Do you have a warrant, Officer?"

This pissed the cop off big-time, and he yelled, "What? Who are you?"

I positioned myself between the two of them, mediating again. "Ignore him, Officer. He's a law student, and he's just kidding." I turned and glared at Mike, and he backed off.

The cop had to defend his position. "I was asked to come in here by the owner's real estate agent. I don't need a goddamn warrant!"

However, this is not what the real estate agent intended when she had gone and called the police after seeing a car parked at what she thought should be an empty house. She did not want to get me in trouble; she was just protecting herself. "This *is* a misunderstanding, Ray. Technically, they have a right to be here because of the original date on the contract." Turning toward me, she added, "But your brother verbally canceled that by telling me I could come in. I didn't mean to disturb you."

Just then, the bedroom door opened, and Maria stepped out, in her T-shirt and panties. Seeing the intruders, she stepped right back in. "Who's that?" Ray said.

"A friend of mine."

"How old is she?"

"Eighteen," I lied.

He looked at me and said, "I hope she can prove that."

The real estate agent jumped in. "Ray, you don't want to go there. Let's leave these kids alone." She turned back to me. "When were you planning to leave?"

"I was planning to leave tomorrow morning, but we can be out this afternoon if you want."

"That would be fine," she said. "I'll take your key now. Just lock the door as you leave."

38

The next weekend, Vinny heard there was a big party going on in New Paltz as the SUNY students inaugurated their orientation week. We hitched up to hang out on campus. We settled in the student union, playing pool, listening to music, and smoking pot. We scored some acid, a large red button-shaped tab with no brand name. I started tripping from the skin-contact high, breaking it in half to split with Vinny.

I grew disoriented right away, somehow losing track of Vinny and realizing I was on my own. A group of students were sitting around a table, emptying the tobacco out of cigars and stuffing the shells with pot. They began passing these around the union to all takers, and each hit was like smoking a whole bowl. I smoked huge amounts, only to start having trouble breathing. I suddenly felt like all these strangers were surrounding me, pressing in, and crowding me. But they were just caricatures of people, their faces fading in and out of focus, continuously changing shape. The union was a fog. The smoke was harsh, and I had to escape it.

It was cold outside, and the wind hit me like a rush of adrenaline. I knew that I was hallucinating, even while imagining that I was lost, that I would forever have to live outside. I went back to the door I had left from, but it had locked. I walked around the building, but it took me a while to find an open door. Just as I reentered the union, James Taylor came on, loud and clear as if he were in the room, singing, "Fire and Rain," his anthem about those who get to return from insanity. I froze, unable to move. I was a statue again, but I wasn't playing this time. I drifted away from my physical presence and became all thought. It became crystal clear that Taylor was singing directly to me, about me, trying to tell me that it was acid that drove him to the depths of insanity and warning me that acid was driving me there, too.

Fear began to win the on-again–off-again war that raged in the conscious forefront of my mind. My visible world collapsed again into a bubble, similar to the one that I had survived in the city just a year ago. It began to feel that I had experienced my whole life in this one short year. This bubble was smaller and tighter, though. It was going to smother me. I had to stop listening to this song. I had to get out of the union, away from the cigarettes, the pot, the music, and the acid. I had to rejoin my body, to take advantage of my temporal being. Only I didn't realize that I couldn't escape the acid; it was going to come with me, trail me, be me. Suddenly, I became aware that my continuing to be was deterministic: if I was still in the union when the song ended, I would never come back from this trip; I would stay insane.

Right behind me, from where I had just come a minute before, someone went out and I felt the rush of cold air from the opening door. The rush thawed me, released me from my trapped physical state. I turned and dove for the door, grabbing it before it could close, thinking if it closed, I would be trapped forever. But I got it in time, and I got out before the song ended. I had a ray of hope, a chance to survive.

I wandered around the perimeter of the building, afraid to let it out of my sight. I came back to the front entrance and sat on the steps along with a number of other partiers. I had little context for where I was, but I had a vague memory of having passed through here before. This was not home, but I felt it was some sort of a sanctuary. As I sat on the steps, I heard an angel speak to me. "Are you all right? You look a little lost." Was she a hallucination or a real angel? She came closer and put her hand on my shoulder, radiating warmth into my very soul. I looked deep into her eyes and saw my own reflection. She seemed to be part of me, not other than me. I embraced her, holding her eyes, and began to cry. "I'm having a bad trip! I need help!" Everyone on the steps overheard this comment. People gathered around, forming a circle around us, replacing my smothering bubble with a human one. She enfolded me, squeezing and holding me together. She had on a navy-blue pea coat with the collar turned up, and I envisioned this as the manifestation of her halo and wings. She was here to save me.

As she held me close, she soothingly stroked my hair and whispered, "Shhhh. You'll be all right. You're safe here." Strangers reached out and touched me, picking up the refrain. "You'll be all right, man, you're safe here." A disembodied voice called from the edge of my forming embryo, "You need some Thorazine, man. Go see the doc."

Well, as it turned out, if you had a bad trip and needed some help, the New Paltz campus was not a bad place to be. One of the students there offered advice. He had been saved from a bad trip by taking some Thorazine. He had some left over, in his dorm, on the other side of the campus. He would go get it for me. Unfortunately, I felt I had no time. Others began to tell me to go to the campus infirmary. Dr. Abruzzi was on staff. He had been the trip doctor at Woodstock. He was maybe the most knowledgeable trip doctor in the world, and he would help me.

Barely understanding their meaning, I relied on my angel. Adoringly, I pleaded with my eyes, "What should I do?" She had never let me go, would continue to keep me safe. I instinctively trusted her vibes as she nodded yes. On the way over, she kept me talking, asking me what was going on. I repeated over and over the only thing I could remember: "I'm having a bad trip. I had one once before, but I came back. This one's worse. I'm afraid I'm not going to make it back." It was the only thought I had room for. The poles of my existence, my entire being, were contained in this narrow duality. "It's a trip; I'm on acid." This thought, second to second, kept me on the brink of precarious sanity, kept me connected. To what? To my angel, my savior. Save me from what? From the trip. "It's a trip; I'm on acid." But all the while lurking in the background was another thought, trying to drive out my mantra: "This time you're not coming back." It was trying to suck my consciousness into a black hole, a hole of nothingness, an absence of being. Each time, just before the darkness snuffed out the last flickering memory of light, I'd remember, "It's a trip; I'm on acid."

My angel soothed me, constantly reassuring me that Abruzzi would bring me down. She guided me to the infirmary, helped me get inside the doors, and once again I was sliding toward the abyss. I had expected that Abruzzi would be waiting on the other side of the doors; he would take me in a bear hug and magically free me from my demons.

Instead, I bumped into predictable bureaucracy. The emergency room was the only way in on a Saturday night, but we got lost in the hallways trying to find it. The halls were empty passages in my mind, all leading in circles. I collapsed to the floor and shivered. My angel sat down next to me and cradled me. A nurse came by, asked me what I was doing. "I need Abruzzi," was all I could mutter, but it was enough for her.

She took me by the hand, led me to the ER, and left me with the admitting nurse. She asked my angel if she was family, and my angel shook her head no. "Then you'll have to wait outside." My angel hugged me, promising me she'd wait just outside the door, and then she slipped away into the ether. I felt abandoned and afraid, all alone once again.

The admitting nurse handed me a clipboard with a form on it and asked me if I was a student. Somehow, that seemed to fit and I nodded. "Your ID card, please." ID card? I could not grasp what this meant. I shrunk to the floor, sobbing, losing all hope, drifting down another empty hallway, forgetting why I was here.

Another patient with a cut on his hand, blood forming a tiny rivulet down his arm, yelled at her, "Can't you see he's freaking out? He's tripping, man. Find Abruzzi for him!" Another savior, another angel?

She relented, gave me the clipboard again, and said, "All right, all right! But it's eleven o'clock on a Saturday night; it might take a while to find him. Fill this out, and I'll try to get him here." She offered me a glass of orange juice and said it would help.

She stood there looking at me as I got up off the floor. She was waiting, but I did not know why. I had taken the clipboard. Finally, I realized she was waving a pen in my face, and I reached out and grabbed it. I looked at the form as she picked up the phone. I wandered to the side, sat back down on the floor, leaned against the wall, and tried to focus on the form. At first, it was calligraphic cartoon characters swimming all over the page. I disciplined myself to focus, and I was able to stop the motion and read some words. On the top left-hand side was a blank box, with a small word typed in it: "NAME."

"Name? Name?" I kept saying it over and over to myself. "Name? I know this. I can do this." But I couldn't, and I really began to freak. Who was I? What was I doing here? I looked up and saw the nurse staring at me, and I saw the horror in her eyes. She was beginning to freak out at the realization of just how fucked up I was.

I looked back at the form, back at the NAME box and had an epiphany: my name was Davey! I remembered my name, I knew who I was, and I wrote in big block letters across the entire form, so that the "D-A-V-E-Y" went from corner to corner. I handed the clipboard back to her with a big grin of pride on my face: "Davey," I said. "That's my name!"

"Last name?" she said.

"No, first name," I answered proudly. "*My* name." Why was she ruining the moment? I had been happy and ecstatic. I was Davey. Somehow remembering my name triggered that I was going to be okay, I was going to make it. But this nurse just freaked when she saw my joy—the joy of an innocent and proud three-year-old—at being able to scrawl my name across a complex form. She got back on the phone, and I continued to hope, knowing that she was going to find Abruzzi. But my new savior shuffled over to my side and whispered, "She's calling the cops, man. You better get the fuck out of here."

Was this my brother's routine all over again? Was my new angel really a devil? I knew that this would be the most important decision in my life, and I had to make it instantly. Though excited at the chance of having Abruzzi save me, I sensed that I was in real danger. This was not hallucinatory paranoia. I pictured myself being hauled off in handcuffs. I knew if this happened, it would be all over. I would slip off the edge. I would be held accountable, punished for eternity for not knowing who I was.

I fled. While she was screaming, "Stop, come back," I ran out the infirmary door, imagining that security was closing ranks right behind me. I did not turn back, fearing I would turn to salt or something. I could not distinguish reality from hallucination, but I knew I needed to run. Miraculously, my guardian angel appeared next to me. "Hey, I told you I'd wait. Are you okay?"

"I'm Davey." This continued to bring me comfort and solace. I said it for myself, to remind myself of the only thing I seemed to know. We wandered back to the student union, and then I heard someone else say it: "Davey, Davey!" It was Vinny. He had been looking for me, had heard that some city kid was freaking out and hoped it wasn't me. He said the guy with the Thorazine had returned. I relayed the horror of what I could remember from the infirmary.

The Good Samaritan stepped forward and said, "Here, man, you better take two of these." He handed me two dark-blue pills. I looked at them with fear; afraid he might be tricking me, giving me more acid. As if he could sense what I was thinking, he said, "It's cool, man. It's Thorazine. Abruzzi himself prescribed these. These'll bring you down, man. Take 'em." I looked to my angel, and she nodded. Vinny added, "Do it already, man. You've got nothin' to lose."

I put them in my mouth but could not swallow. My mouth was dry, and they just lodged in my throat. Someone stepped forward and offered me a carton of orange juice, apparently the tripper's elixir. I got them down, then looked up, and said, "I don't feel anything yet."

"It'll take a while, man. We'll stay with you."

The scientific name is chlorpromazine and it is generally used to treat psychotic disorders. Experiments had shown that they provide general inhibition, offsetting the psychedelic actions of LSD. Abruzzi was running his own experiments, and the students endorsed them. The anecdotal evidence was strong.

I needed to walk and did so continuously in a large circle around the perimeter of the union, babbling incessantly in a semi-coherent stream of consciousness. "We've got to stop the war, man; it's going to kill us all. We've got to stop the draft; it is so un-fucking-fair. They're after all of us. Four dead in Ohio was just the beginning. We've got to stop Nixon; he's fucking crazy, man. Why did Brian die? Does anybody have a fucking clue why my brother had to fucking die?"

People took turns walking with me, listening to me, assuring me I was going to be all right. My guardian angel. The Good Samaritan. Vinny. I never slipped back into fear. I just needed to bide my time on my way out of the darkness. I kept trying to refocus on wellness and sanity. "I'm going to be all right; I'm going to be fine; I'm going to come back." I said so over and over and over again until I started to deeply believe it. Finally, toward dawn, I started to get tired. I had wiped out my entire support group.

Vinny said, "Let's go home." My angel just hugged me, kissed me on the top of the head, and whispered, "I'll always be with you. Live in peace." The Samaritan said, "These usually knock me out by now. You'll sleep soon. Get home safely." He gave me another one to take when I got home. Hitching home took the better part of the day but was peaceful, pedestrian. Vinny slept every time we got in a car. I'd talk to the driver or just stare out the window, watching the absurdity of the houses in motion, as I seemed to be standing still. Despite the heavy dose, I stayed awake. As we arrived back in the city, I made vows to Vinny, "I'm never tripping again; I'm done!"

"Yeah, well, we'll see, man."

As I entered my home, it fascinated me that I looked normal to my parents. Mom wanted to know how the weekend was. Did I want any supper? Pop was watching a ball game. They had no idea what I had been through, no knowledge that I had been to hell and back, that I had been transformed, that I had peered into the abyss and had seen the blackness of my own soul, that I had met angels and experienced the light. And that the only reason I was here is because I knew that I was their Davey.

39

Word spread fast: hepatitis was spreading faster. I had heard of the disease before. It was mostly associated with dirty needles but could also be contracted from poor hygiene, dirty water, and unsanitary conditions. Within days, I heard that Doyle, Pauly, and Adam already had it. Adam called me and gave me the name of his doctor, who had told him that all of his friends should get gamma globulin shots, which can help prevent the onset of the disease. Vinny and I each got a shot. It was administered deep into upper arm muscle and the injected fluid moved as slowly as its name would suggest. It was a thick, syrupy consistency and must have pushed aside blood vessels as it entered. It felt as if I had a bruise from being punched.

I assumed that I was not going to get sick, that I had gotten the shot in time. I had tickets to see the Grateful Dead at the Fillmore on Friday night. I was going with Vinny. It was to be our last big fling before he followed Brian's path to basic training at Fort Dix. We had agreed to meet at Schneid's at eight o'clock. I was stunned to find him sitting against the wall, sticking a safety pin in his arm, tearing it up, making it bleed from several open sores. "What the fuck are you doing now?" I asked.

He took a long drag on his cigarette, looked up at me and said, "I'm making tracks. Despite what you think, I'm not a junkie. But I wish I was. I hear junkies are being kicked out of basic. If I look like a junkie, and snort some smack on the way in, maybe I can get out of it."

"But they know you're not a junkie, man, from your physical. You're 1-A, remember?"

"Yeah, well, I told you maybe this can work. If they think I've been shooting up ever since I got my notice, maybe they'll realize that I'm not who they want after all." He went back to his task.

My stomach hurt, and I felt dizzy, but I realized that it was more than the image of what he was doing to scar himself, and I understood, suddenly, that I was feeling sick. I was tired and achy and thought I must be coming down with the flu. It hit me like a ton of bricks. I had been a little lethargic during the day but had gone to school. I lay down after supper and uncharacteristically napped for ten or fifteen minutes. When I had left the house, I had no idea I could be feeling this bad by the time I reached the candy store.

I gave Vinny my ticket. "I'm sorry, man, give it away, sell it, I don't care. I'm just too fucking sick." I watched him get on the bus, and I felt depressed. I knew that I had made the right decision, but I was feeling sorry for myself. On the way home, I dropped into the liquor store and bought a bottle of wine to drown my troubles in. Disgusted that I was not feeling well enough to go to the concert, I could at least get a wine buzz and listen to some music.

I hid the bottle from my mother, keeping it under my coat, as I came in and told her I was feeling sick. I put on *American*

Beauty, went to bed, and drank several glasses of wine while listening to the Dead. I drifted in and out of sleep as the album played over and over. The lyrics infiltrated the conscious haze of delirium. I could not discern sleep from wakefulness, thoughts from dreams, other from self. "If I knew the way, I would take you home." But I jumped up around eleven o'clock and ran to the laundry room sink and threw up. It was a violent surging and left my throat sore and scratchy. I washed my face and gathered some water by cupping my hand. I rinsed my mouth out and then drank some. I stumbled back to bed, but before I could fall back to sleep, I was back in the laundry room, vomiting some more.

I spent the entire night this way, vomiting continually, crawling back to bed, trying to sleep, getting up to heave some more. I was drained, exhausted, feverish, and after a while, delirious. I had nothing more in my stomach, but the convulsions kept coming. Toward morning, I was retching into a towel, which was not that messy, as only a little bile was coming up. I dragged myself over to the laundry room, too tired to go upstairs, and peed into the sink. It took a while for the stream to start, and when it did, I could see that it was dark and had a pungent odor to it. It was not until that moment that I realized I had hepatitis.

I lay back down and waited until eight o'clock. When I went upstairs, Pop took one look at me, and I could see the concern in his eyes. He came over without saying a word and placed his hand on my forehead. "You're burning up, take some aspirin." I got some aspirin out of the medicine cabinet and took three, but threw them right back up. I still had the number of Adam's doctor on a note pad by the phone, so I called. I got the receptionist, who told me his office hours were full. But she listened to me and when she heard my story about how sick I was, she talked

to the doctor and then directed me to check into Whitestone
Hospital. Pop drove me right over.

During admission, when I peed in a cup, I was horrified
to see that my urine was darker, was distinctly brown now, like
weak coffee. When I came out of the curtained area and handed
the cup to a nurse, both she and Pop audibly gasped at the color.
She put me in a two-bed room, but I was the only one in it.
She immediately hung a sign on the door that said Isolation:
Quarantine in large red letters. The smaller print directed that
hospital staff needed to gown, mask, and glove before entering
my room.

She asked Pop to leave, instructed him to go get gamma
globulin shots for the whole family. She told him they would
have to stay away, at least for the next twenty-four hours. As I
tried to comfort him and tell him everything would be fine, I
had to run to the bathroom to vomit. The nurse eased him out
while I was still in there. She got me into bed and started an IV.
The pain of the needle caused my weak body to pale further, and
I almost passed out. Then I had to vomit, but I could not find
the strength to get up. I leaned over and vomited on the floor.
The nurse was not happy with me and let me know it, but it was
only then that she put a pan on my bed and told me to vomit in
it. About ten minutes later, a rotund black woman came by with
a mop and proceeded to clean up the bile I had tossed. She, too,
was not happy and grumbled about little white men who can't
even make it to the toilet. I was too sick to care but did manage
to hit the pan the rest of the time. I vomited at least once an hour
for the remainder of the day.

The doctor came by and explained that there really was not
a lot of treatment for hepatitis; the disease would have to run its
course. They would give me intravenous fluids so that I would

not dehydrate, and he gave me a vitamin B shot. He said I could not try to eat until I could hold something down.

I was too sick to care, too tired to ask any questions. I started to nod a little in between vomiting sessions and was startled when a phone next to me rang. I had not noticed it and wondered whether I was supposed to answer it. I reached over, knocked the receiver onto the floor, and then was able to pull it up by the cord and squeak out a weak hello. It was my mom. She told me that she ordered the phone, and she also ordered for the TV to be connected. I thanked her and told her that I was still vomiting but that I was able to get a little sleep.

About six o'clock, a dietician came in to tell me that I was not allowed to have dinner. "Let's be optimistic, though," she said. "Maybe tomorrow you'll be able to eat." She looked at my chart and frowned. "You'll only be able to have clear liqs though."

The aide came by, and this time she was in a good mood. "I see y'all are not dirtying up my floor!" She traded out my bile-lined pan for a clean one. "Is there anythin' I can do for you, darlin'?" she asked.

"I have to pee," I told her.

"You better go in here," she said. "We have to measure how much goes in and how much comes out." She gave me a urinal, which was an aluminum pitcher that reminded me of a vase with a handle on it. She stood there for a minute and then realized I was not going to try to pee with her watching. She smiled and said, "I be back in a few minutes to pick that up." When she left, I lifted the blanket, hung my shriveled penis into it, and peed a thick stream of very dark brown syrupy stuff that now had the color of Coca-Cola. I continued to be amazed that something this vile-looking could come out of me, and I worried about what it indicated about what was going on inside my body.

Sometime during the night, I stopped vomiting. I was awakened every two hours for vital signs, and my mind was hazy and confused, but I had this awareness that I had stopped. This awareness rolled around and surfaced in a light that said to me, "You are going to live; you are not going to die." This was a critical revelation, because it was not until then that I allowed myself to comprehend the depths of the despair that I had sunk to earlier in the day. I thought I was dying, but I somehow managed to hide that fact from myself behind a dark curtain of despair, a place where conscious thinking could find no clarity, a place where demons ran free, and being ceased to thrive.

In the morning, the dietician brought me a tray with an assortment of the hospital's finest clear liquids: water, broth, Jell-O, and tea. I tried the water first to see if there was any reaction. It tasted like honey and went down smoothly—and, most important, it stayed down. Then I sipped at the broth and experienced a reawakening of flavor. It was delicious, and I savored each drop. The tea was bitter, and I put it down after one sip. The Jell-O was not quite clear, I told myself, as I chewed and slurped a few of the light-green cubes. Too sweet. I couldn't finish half of it.

My stomach went into a churning routine that was audible. As I heard it processing, I could feel the liquid progressing through my innards. My stomach felt queasy and contracted a few times, and the memory of vomiting almost caused me to start heaving again, but I kept it down.

The phone startled me again, and it was Mom again. I put on a positive voice and told her that I had slept well, hadn't vomited in eight hours, and even had breakfast. I could feel her relief through the phone. She told me that a few of my friends had called, and I assured her that it was okay to give them the phone

404 TIMOTHY F. DEMPSEY

number. She told me that she, Kevin, and Pop had already been to the doctor's office, and all of them had gotten the gamma globulin shots. She also called my work and told them that the doctor said they should get the shots as well. I felt guilty at all the trouble I was causing from the ripple effect of this insidious disease.

I dozed on and off during the day and tried watching a little TV, but I didn't find anything interesting. I treasured the moments when a nurse came in to take vitals, or other staff came in to clean the room or give me a sponge bath. I had never imagined that isolation could be so severe. I had never felt so alone. I learned to stop jumping when the phone rang and enjoyed talking to those who called, but always tired within a few minutes.

When I was awakened for my midnight vitals, the nurse told me I was about to get a roommate. I was surprised and asked, "Am I coming out of isolation?"

"He has hepatitis, too, so he can share the room."

When they brought Dan in about an hour later, it was clear that he had more than hepatitis: he was skinny and pale, pockmarked and dirty. I could see the tracks on his arms. Vinny still had a lot of work to do before he could look this bad. Dan was an authentic junkie, and he had, in fact, overdosed earlier in the evening. Only when they worked on him in the emergency room did they realize that he also had hepatitis. He slept through the night and well into the morning, sleeping off the heroin. When he finally woke up, he did not prove to be much of a conversationalist.

Meanwhile, the doctors had decided we were both beyond the infectious period, which actually is most prevalent before symptoms show, which is why the disease spreads so effectively. We were both allowed visitors, and I was allowed solid foods.

I ate boiled chicken and mashed potatoes and enjoyed it as if it were the finest cuisine in New York. Dan slept through most of his mother's visit, and so she sat and talked to me. She was a delightful woman, older than my mom, completely gray, and pleasantly plump. She spoke to me of the sadness and heartache that her son had brought to the family with his habit. They could not understand it. He had always seemed to be a happy kid, though an only child. He never wanted for anything. Why was he doing this to them? To himself? She wept. I listened, unable to respond.

Cheryl came to visit and brought me the J. R. R. Tolkien trilogy, *The Lord of the Rings*. Adam and Kathy came to visit. Kathy was showing now, and I teased her about her looks. "Yeah, well, look in the mirror, asshole," she said without smiling. She updated me on the toll of the scourge. Most who were getting it were getting milder cases than either me or Doyle, the only two to be hospitalized. I did not tell people what the doctor had told me. I was just too embarrassed. The job of the liver is to break down substances in the blood for elimination from the body. Hepatitis attacks the liver and chews away at it, scarring it just like cirrhosis. Alcohol puts a strain on the liver as it passes through. The combination of the two could be deadly. The alcohol feeds the virus and exacerbates the damage. I had almost killed myself by drinking the bottle of wine. This fact stunned and humiliated me, and I thought I could keep it to myself. I only found out later that the doctor had told my parents in private. He wanted to know how serious my drinking problem was and whether or not I did drugs. He suggested that they get me some help. They assured him that I did not have a drug problem, that I was a good kid, a college student. They regurgitated the story that I had fed them: the hepatitis was from the dirty water at the Powder Ridge festival.

On the fourth day, I complained about pain in my arm coming from the IV site. The nurse told me it was normal and advised me not to worry about it. She had taped over my IV to keep it tight and the pressure was probably causing a little pain. The little pain got worse, but she ignored me. The arm looked swollen, and I rubbed it gently. I awoke that night in severe pain. I couldn't take it any longer and rang for the night nurse. Instead of blowing me off as her colleague had done earlier, she took off the tape to get a better look. The pain was sharp and severe, and each pull sent lightning bolts of intensity up my arm and through my spine straight to my brain. Each tug caused the needle to stab anew, and the cumulative pain became so intense that I cried. I cried like a baby, streaming tears and begging her to stop. She was empathetic but determined. She finally got all the tape off, and the arm ballooned visibly. Emanating from the needle site, there was a localized knob, the size of a baseball: hard, red, and throbbing.

She realized that my pain was real: I was not a whiner, not a complainer. "Your site has infiltrated," she said, as if I had a clue as to what this meant. "And it looks like it's been infiltrated for a while." This is what upset her. She knew that the day staff had blown it. "I'll put the new one in the other arm," she said, but I begged for a break. I had not been allowed out of bed since arrival, and I asked for permission to go the bathroom. She smiled understandingly. "Sure." My legs were weak and wobbly, and I almost collapsed. She grabbed me and draped my arm around her shoulders and helped me to the bathroom. "Can you stand?"

I assured her that I could and thanked her. I went up to the sink and straddled it with my hands. I ran the faucet and splashed a bunch of cold water into my face, relishing the coolness and the purity. I looked into the mirror and was instantly horrified:

who was this person looking out at me? The whites of my eyes had turned a deep yellow, the color that urine is supposed to be. My eyes were sunken, my skin sallow and yellow. My bones were sticking out. My hair was sticking up. I looked like I could walk with the zombies in *Night of the Living Dead*.

I moved my bowels without too much straining. I got up and glanced down and was blasted with yet another shock wave. My shit was white! I mean snow white, not a trace of color in it. I thought my eyes must be deceiving me, and I bent over to look closer, confirming that, indeed, my shit was white. No one had mentioned this. I opened the door, called the nurse, and embarrassed, asked her to look at it. She said, "That's normal for someone with hepatitis. Don't worry about it." She helped me into bed and put in a new IV, this time into my right arm. She did not wrap it tight with tape, just used enough to stabilize it. "If it infiltrates again, you make some noise this time. Do not put up with so much pain. Make them look at it."

I lay in bed and tried to get the images of brown urine, yellow eyes, and white shit out of my brain, but they lurked there, haunting me, becoming me. *How much can this body of mine take?*

I watched the Late, Late Show, *Ocean's Eleven*, starring Frank Sinatra and the Rat Pack: Dean Martin, Sammy Davis Jr., Joey Bishop, and the one who didn't seem to fit, Peter Lawford. There was a commercial every ten minutes, and after every commercial another light went out on the apartment building that was pictured as the icon for these late night movies. Before the movie ended, there was only one light remaining on the apartment building, and I knew that was me. I was the lonely person who couldn't sleep. When the movie finally ended, the light on the apartment building went out, and the image was replaced with one of an American flag blowing in the breeze. A scratchy, tinny version of "The Star-Spangled Banner" played, and an announcer simply said, "Good night." I turned the test pattern off and wallowed in a new level of despair. I took comfort in the light from the hallway and the night sounds from the staff, but I cried softly for what I had become.

I looked forward to Dan's mom's visits. I could tell her more than I could my own mom, and I tried to help her understand that even a good boy can do bad things, that it did not mean that they had done anything wrong as parents, that maybe he was just weak and gave into temptation. She helped me understand the pain I would cause to my family if I continued to degenerate. She presented me with a whole new context. She begged me to learn from Dan's mistakes and to spare *my* family.

And she cooked for me. She brought Rock Cornish hens that she had roasted with a vinegar-and-garlic glaze that melted in my mouth. She always brought the finest imported Italian provolone, which was dry to the point of being crumbly and had more flavor than any other cheese I had ever had. She would always bring enough for the two of us, but her son hardly ever ate. I tried to talk to him when she was not there, to make him aware of the pain that he was causing. He pretended to listen, but he showed no emotion, no remorse, and no regrets.

What was worse, he continued to use. When his friends visited, they smuggled contraband in. First, it was a beer, then some downs. Eventually, they brought in junk and some works. He went into the bathroom and shot up, stumbled to the bed, and nodded out. When his mother came, she suspected. At first, I attempted to lie and cover up, but she knew. She asked which friend had visited. I described him, and she began to cry. "How could he? How could he? In the hospital? In the damn hospital, for god's sake!" My heart ached for her, and I patted her back as she sobbed.

Then she pulled herself out of it and fed me. I had little advice for her—maybe try a rehab clinic? She told me that he refused her help. I feebly assured her that it was not her fault: how could someone as loving and as caring and as giving as she have caused this?

■ ■ ■

On my follow-up visit, I told the doctor the truth. Everyone who stuck a needle in his arm that night at Doyle's got hepatitis. Of course, we were all at Powder Ridge as well, so this possibility had provided a good cover. But the inner circle knew that there were people in Powder Ridge, like Kathy and Cheryl, who did all the same things we did and didn't get sick.

The doctor talked about two kinds of hepatitis: acute and chronic. It appeared that I had acute, from the nature of the symptoms. It was the more common type and often did come from poor sanitation. Chronic came from the blood and became systemic. It could eventually kill and did, in fact, spread through dirty needles. "It's possibly coincidental, because I don't think you got it from the needle. In any case," he went on to explain, "all hepatitis eats the liver, which does not regenerate. Get it two or three times in your life, and the accumulation will be fatal. Your liver needs time to recuperate." He was very dramatic, even showing me pictures of diseased livers. A healthy liver looked just like the cow's liver that Mom used to like to cook with on-ions and bacon: full and smooth, red and slippery. The diseased liver was shrunken and dry, cracked and full of black spots and crevices. It looked like something that had died and rotted out over time. He looked me hard in the eyes, saying, "It's not as notorious or as dramatic as cirrhosis, but it is a disease of the chronic substance abuser. You have to stay clean." He definitely got my attention.

Step by step, day by day, I returned to routines, first going back to school. I avoided Schneid's, avoided my friends. When they called or came around, I ceded responsibility to the doctor. I was following his orders. I had no choice. I developed a habit for vitamin C, eating the large wafers like candy. I returned to work.

I relished my quiet weekends with Cheryl. We'd go to a movie, take a walk on the beach, or just drink coffee in the diner and talk. We went over to visit Kathy and Adam. We saw new definitions of misery in this stark one-bedroom apartment. The flea market furniture was tattered and worn as if it had been retrieved from somebody's trash. The walls were faded and bare, except for intermittent screw holes and an occasional rectangular clean spot, where the previous tenant had hung a picture. The bare ceiling light bulbs were stark in their harshness. There were telltale little black mouse turds in the corners of the kitchen counter.

Kathy, seven months pregnant, was trying to keep up a good front. But all the while she was cooking, she was drinking red wine and smoking cigarettes. Meanwhile, Adam belittled her, called her fat, called her a shitty cook. He was repeatedly disrespectful to her, embarrassing all of us. He called her a whore and a tramp, questioned whether the baby was really his. I got him on the side, out of earshot. "Adam, what the fuck, man? Get off her case."

"Oh, I'm just kidding, Davey, man. She knows that." We came back into the living room, and Adam stopped behind

Kathy, who was talking to Cheryl. He took his cigarette and flicked ashes into her hair, from about a foot above so that it was not obvious, and she didn't feel it. His cigarette ash scattered into her hair. I watched the ashes blend into her dark roots as Adam winked at me, thinking I would be impressed with his childish stunt. He was proud of this prank. I walked away in disgust, sad for the both of them, my heart aching for their unborn child.

Adam slipped off to the bedroom. When he came back, he just nodded off on the second-hand couch. I went into the kitchen and gave Kathy a hug. She had a ready smile for me. We talked as old friends, reminisced a bit, looked to the future a bit. I asked her, "How long has this been going on?"

"God only knows, Davey. I think he hid it from all of us for a long time."

"Why do you stay with him?" I had obviously hurt her. Tears welled up immediately.

She laughed. "You know, nobody else even has the guts to ask me. I love you, man."

"I love you, too, babe, but you're avoiding my question."

She sighed. "Oh, God, I love him. I don't know why. I keep hoping that one of these days he'll get clean, and we'll both grow up, and then we'll grow old together. I don't know," she said, laughing, gesturing to the point of spilling her wine. She took a deep drag on her cigarette and grew completely serious as a tear escaped and rolled down her cheek. She pulled her lips into her mouth and shrunk her eyebrows down, scrunching them into the bridge of her nose, tightening her whole face. "What the fuck am I supposed to do, man? I can't crawl back to my parents. Should I live on the street, or what?"

40

One night, Cheryl and I stopped by Schneid's to pick up some ice cream. The candy store had become an outpost in a war zone. Pot was kid's stuff. Deals were going down every night for coke, heroin, ups, and downs. People were hopped up all the time, tense and short-tempered, paranoid and scared. Cops walked a regular beat; they were there every night.

I nodded hello to Vinny, but he seemed to look right through me. Vinny had slipped away from me, away from all of us. He had never reported for duty. He knew that they would come looking for him, and he figured he would just party until they showed up. He rode the harder drugs into an unprecedented area of rage.

Cheryl and I wove our way through the crowd quickly. While I was paying, Abe said, "You don't come around much anymore."

"Sorry, Abe, nothing personal."

"No," he said thoughtfully. "It's good to see someone break out. You should stay out." Just then an altercation broke out, once again right outside his front door. "Goddamn crap," he said as he reached for the phone. "It never ends."

Vinny was fighting some dealer, a much-older guy from another town. Vinny was screaming while he punched at his face, "No one shorts me on a fucking deal." The brawl turned vicious. They rolled around on the sidewalk for a while, and the guy bit Vinny's ear, drawing blood. This invigorated Vinny, propelling him to push the stranger down and slam his head against the curb. Vinny jumped up, grabbed his ear, and felt the blood. He went berserk. "Get the fuck up, you motherfucker! You bit me, you fucking animal." He went over and kicked the guy in the face, causing him to yell out in pain, just as the cops made their way through the crowd.

One of the cops tapped Vinny on the shoulder and told him to calm down. Vinny whirled in a flash, not even seeing it was a cop, and instinctively kicked up at the arm. The cop was quick, though, and backed away just in time, ducking back and drawing his nightstick out all in one motion. His partner, too, got his nightstick ready, but he also got on his radio and called for backup. Vinny, aware that they were cops now, let all the anger that resided deep in the sinew and synapses of his being spring out at once.

"Fuck you, pigs," he said, and he took one broad step toward the one who had touched him and leaped into the air three or four feet straight up. He curled his legs in and sent them out as fast as a switchblade springs out of a knife. The kick landed true on the cop's chest and sent him reeling back and down. He hit the ground hard. His head smashed onto the sidewalk, and he lay still.

His partner went into action, swinging his nightstick at Vinny, but he missed. Vinny did the same spring action and kicked him in the side of his legs, sending him crashing down. He lay on the ground and groaned, and Vinny went over and kicked him in the stomach. Vinny was in a frenzy, foaming at the mouth. He was going to kill some pigs; he was going to kill the Man. Like a flash, Pauly tackled him from the side. Vinny didn't expect it and went tumbling down. Three more of us piled on immediately, and the four of us had trouble holding him. We heard the sirens in the distance.

I yelled at him, "Vinny, these are cops, man! Let's get the fuck out of here." He was in such a fury that he couldn't speak, but he seemed to nod in agreement, and so we let him up and began to run, into the shadows, down the block, away from the corner.

The rest of the crowd had already scattered when the first backup patrol car arrived. The cops saw one of their own on his hands and knees, looking over his partner. They made no attempt to chase anyone; they just wanted to check on their fallen brethren. We all got away easily—except Vinny, who inexplicably rushed *toward* the cops and reared his leg back, as if to kick the cop who was kneeling over his partner. One of the backup patrolmen swung his nightstick down hard on the back of Vinny's head. The cop's follow-through was true and strong. Vinny crumbled at his feet.

Cheryl and I hid in a backyard and watched as patrol car after patrol car arrived, and minutes later the ambulances and EMS. We were happy to see the first cop sit up and then stand and get into the ambulance of his own accord. The second cop went away in the second ambulance, and the EMS van collected Vinny and carted him off. We were speechless, sitting in the dirt, our backs up against the porch foundation, hiding in the shadows behind the bushes. The ice cream had begun to melt and drip through the bag. The residents put the porch light on and came out for a while to see what the commotion was about.

We sat still, barely breathing, scared as helpless children. As the scene played out, I was transported to other times, to ring-a-levio and Halloween, to good times and bad. How long would I be running in the streets, hiding in the shadows? Cheryl was softly crying, and I put my arm around her and held her close. "Shhh, shhh, it'll be all right."

On the porch, a man put his arm around his wife. "It's a damn shame," he said. "It used to be such a nice neighborhood. It's the damn drugs. Maybe we should move farther out on the island?"

■ ■ ■

Neither cop had serious injuries; both recovered and were back on the job in a week. Vinny spent that week in the hospital with a brain concussion. Each day I went by his house and tried to console his mother and stay current with what was going on. He was under arrest, an armed guard outside his hospital room. At the end of the week, he was hauled off to arraignment, and a sympathetic judge gave him a choice. "You can report for duty. But I want you to bypass the draft and volunteer to serve for four years. As long as you finish your enlistment with an honorable discharge, we'll drop the assault charges. Or, you can go to trial for two counts of attempted murder of a police officer, evading the Selective Service, disturbing the peace, and possession of narcotics with intent to distribute. I guarantee that you will serve much more than four years hard time. What's it going to be?"

Tough-guy Vinny said, "I ain't afraid of hard time!"

416 TIMOTHY F. DEMPSEY

"Well," said the judge, "I'm afraid for society to let you back on the streets after becoming a hardened criminal in prison. Especially when you are this dangerous as a kid. Take my offer. Join the army." Vinny's court-appointed attorney huddled with him and convinced him to take the deal.

They cleaned Vinny up in basic training at Fort Dix, and they toughened him up in infantry training. But they made the mistake of giving him a leave before he was to be shipped off to 'Nam. As soon as he was back on the streets, he began to use.

I corralled him one afternoon at Schneid's when he first came home. "Vinny, let me buy you a malted, for old time's sake." I tried to talk to him. "Vinny, what the fuck're you doing, man? You're killing yourself."

"So what?"

"So what? What about your parents, man? What about your friends? If you can't handle it in the street, go back to the base, man. Spend your leave getting drunk at the PX, but stay off the hard shit. It's killing you."

He shook his head and laughed at me. "So what the fuck, man? So I can go to 'Nam and get my balls shot off or my guts ripped out? Come home in a wheelchair? Come home in pieces like your brother? No fucking way, man, I'm going AWOL. I'm not going back." Incongruously, he drank his malted, wiped his lip on his sleeve.

He lit a cigarette. "This ain't a news flash, man. You know the fucking army's not for me."

"Fine, man, fine. I get it. But you still don't have to kill yourself. Stay off the dope. Go to Canada. Or you're going to be spending the rest of your life in Attica."

"Canada's too cold, man; I'm heading to Mexico."

■ ■ ■

He never left the neighborhood again. He deteriorated quickly, fell all the way back to glue while simultaneously shooting heroin. He became just another junkie, willing to hit a neighbor's house to get enough to score some dope for the day, stupid enough to nod out leaning against the brick wall at Schneid's. I was hoping the army would show up to reclaim him.

Crowds dispersed when he arrived on the corner, as he no longer could be trusted not to snap. One night, he got into a pushing argument at the bar. He was obviously wasted and obviously the one who started the argument, so the bartender told him to leave. Vinny had been drinking with Joyce, whom he had begun pimping out to support his habit. She asked him not to go after the bartender. "Let's just get out of here," she pleaded.

He left with her but could not control his anger. She would later tell me that she did all she could to protect him, took him her to her apartment, let him do whatever he wanted, no matter how much he was hurting her. And then she lost him. "I'm going out to cop some dope," he told her. "I'll be back in a little while." He took a butcher knife from her kitchen drawer.

Back at the bar, the guy he had picked the argument with had finished his beer, grabbed his blue windbreaker, and left. A bus pulled up, and a young man with similar features and hair color got off. Tragically, he too was wearing a dark nylon jacket. He was a policeman's son, on his way home from college, and he'd stopped in for one beer. When he finished his beer and left the bar, Vinny pounced from the shadow and repeatedly stabbed him in the gut, leaving him to die just feet from the bar's door, collapsed in a pool of his own blood.

I don't suspect that Vinny ever realized, not for an instant, that he had killed an innocent man. He drove back to Joyce's, but barely had time to cook his works before the cops were there. He resisted, went at them with the same knife, and was killed by a single bullet that severed his aorta. He bled to death in the tenement hallway, his head curled in Joyce's lap.

Vinny's would not be the only funeral we attended. Early on a frigid morning, they found Adam dead in the back seat of a stolen car. The needle that he had OD'd with was still stuck in his arm. He had gotten the dope in, but barely had the time to aspirate a little of his blood out. The needle was empty, and just a few drops of his blood had been drawn back up into it before his body stopped all of its motion forever. By the time they found him, he was blue, frozen solid. His picture made the cover of the *Long Island Press*. His eyes were open, locked on the needle. Had he known that he would never pull that needle out as his consciousness slipped away?

The turnout for his funeral mass at Saint Greg's was low, just a few of us friends and a few family members. His folks sat in the pews on one side and Kathy's on the other. Like at a wedding. Except they didn't talk to each other, didn't seem to acknowledge each other. They did not come together to share this grief. Kevin and I sat on either side of Kathy, propping her up. Despite her weakened condition, she had insisted on coming, saying it was the least she could do for him. He, who had done so little for her. She was pale and thin; her eyes sunken to blackness, wan, and empty.

She was sustaining herself on cigarettes alone. She had gone into labor after the cops told her what had happened. She couldn't understand it. He didn't even have a jacket on. He'd said he was going down to the corner for cigarettes and would be right back. She knew better than to call the police, though, and she fell asleep on the couch, figuring he'd be home by morning.

The baby was not quite four pounds, but after forty-eight hours was beginning to thrive. They said she would live. Kathy didn't cry during the mass, didn't sob. She stared beyond the coffin, beyond the altar, beyond the church, beyond Bellerose. She was trying to look into the future, she told me, but all she could see was the past.

■ ■ ■

Even as summer once again brought its promise of hope, I had to experience one more ending. Cheryl and I went to the last show at the Fillmore East. We avoided the usual rituals and went clean: no acid, no grass, no alcohol. For one night, we got high on pure rock and roll. As the Allman Brothers jammed, drawing us out of our seats and towards the stage like a tractor beam, I felt the weight of nostalgia. I remembered the Airplane, the Dead, Jimi and the Who. Roger Daltry in his fringed suede jacket and long curly hair. Sly in his wild afro, beads flying everywhere. Ian Anderson wailing on the flute, turning that instrument into an orchestra, his Fagin frock flying all over the stage. Joe Cocker spazzing out. The pain emanating from B.B. King's guitar. The mellow sounds of the Incredible String Band and the Youngbloods: "Everybody get together, try and love one another right now."

The Allmans finished their last encore and the house went dark, ever so briefly, before the lights came back to illuminate Bill Graham as he said good night, good bye and thank you. The faithful began to file out, but Cheryl and I walked down to the first row. I sat and closed my eyes. I traveled back to the Crosby,

Stills, Nash and Young concert from the summer before. Little did we know then, that it was the beginning of the end for the Fillmore. Graham had to charge almost double the usual price for that show. While we did not mind paying it, he was offended that he had to charge it. When he announced that he would be closing the temples, he cited this concert as one of the influences on him. This was his equivalent of the moneychangers defiling what was always meant to be a holy place.

He was clear that he did not blame the performers, but he did state that he used to be able to negotiate directly with the artists, put on a concert based on a verbal agreement and a handshake, and now he was mostly dealing with corporations, cutting deals with CFOs, lawyers and agents. The thrill was gone; he had stopped having fun. He had earned a great living, and he did not deny it. But the spiritual nature of the events had motivated him; he was creating great music for the masses. When it became just another business, he was done.

A Fillmore concert was the only place I could experience total relaxation, total freedom from thought. I could ease into the riffs, flow with the rhythm, sing along with the lyrics, separate from all worries and anxieties and be a part of something outside my self. The individual connections with the artists elevated me to new spiritual plateaus. At the end of a show, I would be drenched with sweat, physically and emotionally exhausted, totally spent.

With CSN&Y, we had known we were in the presence of the highest order of Gods, the Eros and Dionysus of rock. I had been grooving on Orange Sunshine, the purest path to a good trip. My mind was soaring as I imagined a familiarity with the musicians, but I was unable to stay in my seat, so I wandered. I worked the orchestra and found a seat in the fifth row and stayed throughout the opening set, which was acoustic, with just Crosby, Stills and Nash, opening with "Suite for Judy Blue Eyes" and ending a few songs later with Marrakech express. I was sure that David Crosby was looking straight at me when he was making those weird faces, scrunching up his mustache and manipulating his eyebrows, his smile as broad as the smiley face button, as he skipped around the stage like a schoolgirl. I just knew he was tripping as madly as I was.

By the time the owner of that seat returned, they brought out Neil Young and finished their acoustic set with "Wooden Ships." Then they began their solo acts, and I wandered some more, going to the bathroom to throw cold water on my face, trying to re-energize as the night wore on. I went to the water fountain and got a drink and discovered that the guy behind me was Neil Young. I tried to strike up a conversation, but after politely and graciously saying hello, sensing I was tripping I was sure, he then said, "Hey man, my brother is up there on stage and I want to listen to how it sounds out here," in other words, I knew, shut the fuck up. I listened along with him as Stephen sat at the piano and did "For What It's Worth" from their Buffalo Springfield days. When he was done, I turned, but Neil was gone, reappearing not minutes later on stage to do "Cowgirl in the Sand." Graham Nash did "Bus Stop" from the Hollies and when all the solo acts were done, they all got together, added Johnny Barbata on drums and Calvin Samuels on bass for an exhilarating electric set. For their first encore, they announced a new song, enraged as they were from Kent State, called "Ohio," with its refrain "four dead in O-HIO!" We were all singing along, with our fists held high in the air, while the stage bathed in deep red lighting. It was a powerful moment that had brought tears to our eyes and strengthened our resolve to fight back.

They had then closed with "Find the Cost of Freedom, buried in the ground, Mother Earth will swallow you, lay your body down."

I could almost hear this prophecy again, as I held my head and felt the red blood of Brian, Vinny and Adam bathe over me. I opened my eyes to see that Cheryl and I were almost alone in the empty auditorium. I could see the worry on her face, as she said simply, "Let's go." The cost was too high. I didn't want to pay anymore. The temple closed, and the Gods lost some stature.

41

Somehow, I kept up with my studies, graduated on time. I skipped the ceremony, though. No cap and gown for me. The tragedies had sobered me. I was no longer a kid, never again wanted to hide in the shadows. My best friends were dead. I had lost my brother. I had stumbled, stoned and drunk, into the adult world, my psyche chipped, my self-image devalued, my vulnerabilities exposed. I was tired of depending. Drugs, drink, the bar, Schneid's, even Cheryl. If I stripped off my dependencies, what would be left? Who would I be? Would I be? I felt that I knew very little about myself. I felt that I must have been doing drugs and drinking to avoid learning about myself, perhaps to hide from myself.

I wanted to escape the oppression of the neighborhood, to forget the tragedies, to move on with my life. I certainly wanted to find myself. The fantasy of a cross-country trip loomed in my mind. Searchers from Kerouac to the Merry Pranksters had established a model that promoted hitting the road as a means to self-discovery, as a means to find oneself, to discover one's identity. The media said there was a generation gap. What a surprise. Yet, one of the distinctions between the generations was the boomers' having the luxury to take the time to "find ourselves," as if we had been missing or lost.

I bought a '63 Volkswagen bug, a book of maps, a campground directory, and a new tent. I told Cheryl that I needed some time; I needed to do this by myself. I was just days away from leaving when I got the notice. I had to report to Fort Hamilton in Brooklyn for my physical.

I had pushed the draft back, deep behind my daily fears, as if I was unable to face this looming likelihood. I had less than a week to get ready. I saw the campus shrink, an antiwar activist who was counseling graduates on how to beat the process. I didn't sleep for days, worrying with anticipation. The physical itself was a blur; I moved through it as if in a haze.

I thought I had a chance to beat it. After the routine of inspections, the poking and prodding invasions of various body parts, I was told to return the next day to see the specialists. I had two doctors' notes; surely one would get me out. But the army orthopedist barely looked at the letter from my surgeon. "Put your arms above your head," he ordered. I raised my left arm slowly, overdramatizing my fear to do so. He threw his pen down, sighed in disgust, walked over to me, grabbed my hand and pulled it higher into the air while watching the movement in the socket. "You're fine," he said. "Looks like your surgeon did a superb job." He cleared me.

The army psychiatrist didn't even look at the letter I had obtained from the shrink. He tossed it aside with contempt. "Anybody can get a letter from those pinko college counselors. What's yours say?"

I nodded up and down and rubbed my hands together, as I had been coached. "I'm afraid of girls, and I'm afraid of the dark, and um, I, uh, do drugs."

"You pantywaists drive me crazy! You know what? The army will help you with all that shit. Who knows—maybe we'll even make a man out of you, starting with a goddamn haircut. You're 1-A."

■ ■ ■

I spent the next week working on the bug: washing, vacuuming, duct-taping, changing the oil, and tuning it up. Berk helped me on a daily basis. The joke was the small trunk in the front of the car. It held my cooler, some extra shoes, tools, a flashlight, and a portable cassette player and some tapes. I used the backseat to hold the tent, backpack frame, sleeping bag, and pillows.

Cheryl asked me to take her to a friend's house in Vermont. She knew that it was near Earth People's Park, a commune started by a few of the West Coast deadheads who had been inspired by the concept of the People's Park in Berkeley. After soliciting donations at Woodstock, they'd found some cheap land near the Canadian border. Anyone who wanted to pitch a tent and live there for free was welcome. We imagined that it would be an easy place for me to cross over. Despite the advice from the manual, I was not yet clear that I wanted to apply for landed immigration status. I lied to my parents: "Cheryl and I are going camping in New England. I'll be back for a few days before I have report to Fort Dix."

Our first stop was the town of Woodstock, an artists' community famous for sheltering Bob Dylan while he inspired the

Band in their masterpiece, *Music from Big Pink*. It was dark by the time we arrived, and we had trouble finding the state park. We thought we were there, based on the map, but we could not find any signs or ranger stations. We did not find any camping area. We went into the town and stopped in a coffee shop where we were told that the state park was not a big draw, did not, in fact, have a ranger station, but that it was legal to put up a tent, although there were no facilities. It was beginning to rain.

We had noticed a small motel on the entrance to town and decided to spend our first night camping—in a bed. Nervous, but tired and exhausted, I took the risk and registered us as "Mr. and Mrs.," though the desk clerk looked askance as neither of us had a ring on. He gave us a room, though. It was nondescript, smelled of must and raw wood, and featured exposed wood beams on the walls and in the ceiling. It had a "color" nineteen-inch TV on which I got two channels of shadows and one real station. The radio worked better. We took separate long hot showers and joined each other under the sheets.

Cheryl's friends from drama class lived in St. Johnsbury. We arrived about four o'clock in the afternoon. They were renting a small farm on the outskirts of town. There was a sign hanging from their mailbox, Kastle in the Skye, and we knew we had arrived.

Three people were living there: Cheryl's friend, her brother, and her boyfriend. The house was a small A-frame with five rooms on the first floor: kitchen, living room, bathrooms, and two bedrooms along the back. The best feature was a small loft accessible only by ladder, crossing the A near the top, a window-to-window platform that served as the guest bedroom.

After dumping our stuff in the house, Cheryl helped her friend pick vegetables from the garden, and they prepared an organic, meatless dinner. I could not get enough to fill me up and wound up stuffing myself later with bread slathered with thick homemade peanut butter and topped off with local honey. Cheryl and I imagined that this was the best possible life one could find: living off the land, living in a smog-free, noise-free countryside. We fantasized that we would live like this one day.

The girls slipped into the bedroom to work on a quilt, and the guys settled in the kitchen, drinking cold beers. "What'd you know about Earth People's Park?" I asked.

The brother told me that the park I was envisioning was a myth. "There's a few hardy souls left, but utopia was never realized. Some real estate developer ripped off the idealistic hippies and sold them a plot of barren, rocky land that was too hardscrabble for much of anything. The dreamers had not counted on the severity of the winters, and their numbers dwindled rapidly. Those left had not been able to keep up with the property tax payments and were now basically squatting, holding an occasional fundraiser and fighting off the lawyers. The developer is quite prepared to wait them out, having already made much more of a profit than he had ever expected and is in no particular rush to repossess."

"Yeah, I don't think I need to see it," I said. "I think I'll just drive across Canada, maybe all the way to Vancouver."

"What are you looking for, man?"

"Honestly, I don't even know. I just know that I don't want to go to Vietnam."

"Yeah, but if you run away to Canada, are you really helping the cause? I mean, you're taking care of yourself, but you're not going to help stop the war."

"So what's your status?"

"Three forty-seven in the lottery, dude. They'll never get to me. But if they did, I'd go to jail, not Canada. Jail is a much stronger statement."

"Yeah, well, that's easy to say."

After sunrise on our third day at Kastle in the Skye, I said good-bye to Cheryl and crossed into Montreal near Rock Island. I finally spent a night in the tent, at the Mont Orford Provincial Park. There was a community bonfire that night, and I learned that most kids crossing the trans-Can stayed in youth hostels rather than campgrounds. I also encountered my first anti-Americanism. A stranger lectured me. "You Yankees come up here, buy land, and immediately fence it off, staking out your ownership rights. You're trying to drain our culture away from us. There's a goddamn Yankee ghetto in Toronto with long-haired deserters and draft dodgers."

I didn't know how to respond, so I tried a little levity. "Yeah, well, I'm not a Yankee, anyway, I'm a Mets fan." He didn't seem to get it.

I headed west and pulled into a hostel in Ottawa but was rejected. I had not been prepared for the grilling. Hostels were for Canadians, not Americans: I could stay in a campground or go to a hotel, but I was most definitely not welcome in the hostel. I found a campground at the Fitzroy Provincial Park.

On my third day in Canada, the car began to sputter, buck, and belch. I couldn't get any power and the car began to go slower and slower. I was able to creep to a service station at the next exit, about five kilometers. There was a mechanic on duty, and he took a look at the engine and tried to drive the car. He could barely get it to move. He told me that I had a potentially big problem, but that maybe it was just the distributor cap, not the distributor itself. I waited for hours while he had a distributor cap delivered from the dealership in Sudbury. He put it on, and there was no change. In his opinion, the engine needed a major overhaul. He could do it, but it would take him the better part of a week to get all the parts, and it would cost upward of $300. I explained that I had only paid $300 for the car and was not prepared to put that kind of money into it. I especially did not want to live at this gas station for at least a week.

He offered me fifty bucks for the car, and I took it, never knowing whether I had been scammed or ripped off, or whether his opinion was legitimate and accurate. I spent a few hours weeding through my stuff, utilizing his Dumpster, offering him some and winnowing down to what I could carry.

I met some other hitchhikers on the road and shared my concern about how I was treated at the hostel. They taught me the code: I needed to admit that I was an American, because they often asked for identification. When asked if I had any money, I needed to say, "Less than ten dollars." When asked where I would sleep if I could not stay in the hostel, I must answer, "In a ditch." All hostels would then be obliged to accept me.

The code worked, and I proceeded across Canada, staying in a different hostel each night. Hosteling was an adventure, full of surprises. Each hostel was unique, with the only constant being the questions asked and the formula answers I gave. Sault Ste. Marie was a bunch of large tents, and I was encouraged to put up my tent to the side and only use the dining and bathroom facilities. The hostel in Thunder Bay was a hockey rink, filled with cots and divided into two by a long red line painted on the wooden floor the length of the building. Women on one side, men on the other. Regina was a condemned hotel in which I was given a private room. I was told that, as an American, I could only have breakfast if I worked, so I spent an hour in the morning cleaning, sweeping out the lobby. Winnipeg was a dormitory to a small college. I met some European hippies who turned me on to some smooth blond hash, my first high since leaving the States. One of them said he was from London, but he had strong Asian features and long black hair. He borrowed a bar of soap and returned it covered with strands of his black hair embedded in the bar.

My most exciting nights were in Wawa, which was operating as an active archeological site. Canadians were welcome to stay up to a week if they worked on the dig, but alas, Americans were subject to the one-night rule, though I learned of a loophole. As long as I packed up all my gear and hung out on the trans-Can for a few hours, I could come back in and say I couldn't get a ride. They then allowed me to stay a second night rather than sleep in a ditch.

The hostelers shared quarters with the eggheads. There were a number of large tents, filled with cots. The best feature was a co-ed sauna that had been erected with a natural rock façade on three sides. It was like a small cave with a wooden door entrance. Everyone stripped and used the free towels to cover themselves. We sat and sweat for an hour at a time and then jumped into the ice-cold pool that was next to the sauna. Very European. At the pool, the towels came off, and we enjoyed the freedom and trust. I made love to a blonde from Norway who must have been forty years old. She treated me with great tenderness and taught me the art of the slow hand.

The food was outstanding: hot, fresh-cooked meals, tender beef and chicken, lots of fresh vegetables, and delicious spring-water to wash it all down. I received a lecture from a German who could not get over the fact that an American had picked french fries from his plate. They were in a diner while traveling together. He struggled with his English and said in a thick German accent, "He just reached over to…plate. We were in the middle of conversation, and…just reached over to…plate and took…fry. I would have given it him!"

"What did you do?" I asked.

"I slapped it! Out of hand!" He gestured as if smacking the hand down on the counter.

Near Lyleton, Manitoba, I got a ride from a Canadian rancher who owned a huge spread right on the border. He was on his way home and drove me for over a hundred miles and then offered to feed me. His wife welcomed me with open arms and prepared a feast. They were modest in informing me that 100 percent of what I was about to eat was homegrown, homemade. God-fearing people, she asked me to bow my head while she thanked the Lord for his generosity. Then we dug in: corn on the cob, mashed potatoes with gravy and onions, green beans, homemade bread, buckets of milk, and the most delicious, tender beef I had ever tasted, slaughtered just the weekend before. I cut the steak with a fork. Apple pie completed the meal, washed down with hot coffee and dead-serious conversation.

"There's a lot of responsibility with such a big spread," he said while gesturing out the window. The driveway was a full mile off the road. The ranch was furnished with harsh and aged wood furniture, much of it probably authentic antiques. Original portraits graced the walls. Everything was clean and spotless. "It might appear that we live simply. Sarah sews all our clothes, and she grows all the vegetables. But running the ranch is a big business. In addition to hiring all the help who work the cattle, I have to deal with accountants, bankers, brokers, and lawyers. We never had any children, never explored which one of us couldn't. We just accepted it with grace as God's decision." I was humbled at the purity of their beliefs and found myself confiding in them, the way I never could with my own parents.

After explaining my situation, I almost broke down in tears. "I don't know what to do."

He put his arm around me in a giant hug. "Well, son, I don't think the good lord cares much about our geography, but our governments sure do. What does that manual you're carrying around tell you to do?"

"It says to apply for landed immigration status. But I need to do that at the border, and I need to have some money to qualify."

"Well, I can lend you the money, son, as long as you promise to return it when you can." He drove me down to a small crossing and waited a few hours while I applied and made the passage. Then he dropped me off at the trans-Can. I no longer had to lie to get into the hostels. With nary a thought, I started hitching back East.

42

When you stop telling lies, what do you say? When you stop living lies, who can you be? What else is the aging process, if not a search for truth? As children, our imaginations dominate our being to the extent that we need someone else to look out for our daily needs. We are encouraged to play. We are rewarded when we lie. The more outrageous our claims, the bigger smiles and hugs they elicit. When does it change? How are we supposed to know?

When I arrived in Toronto, it was easy to find my way to Baldwin Street, to the Little America that had been so disparaged. I wanted to see it, not sure that I wanted to become part of it. I was, however, embraced, welcomed, valued, and appreciated for who I was, not for who I pretended to be. I was against the war to the extent that I had fled my country. I wasn't sure why. I couldn't explain it. I didn't need to. Others would argue about morality, abuse of power, racism, what have you. It didn't matter. I had my opinions, sure. I could even be persuasive.

But I could also be honest about by fears, not ashamed to name them. "I'm afraid to go to Vietnam. My brother was killed there. He came home in pieces. I still don't know why. Maybe if I understood why, I wouldn't be so afraid, but for the life of me I can't get it. Dominoes? Too fucking abstract. Communism? So what? I'm not that impressed with capitalism. Freedom? Give me a fucking break! I wasn't free to say I don't want to kill. Freedom to do what? To pay my fucking taxes, that's what!"

The coffee shops and bars were filled with these arguments. The draft dodgers were outnumbered by the deserters. Canadian society treated us no differently. We were Americans against the war, and we were criminals back home. This is what defined us. There were even a few Vietnam veterans who had turned against the war and wanted to live among us.

They had lived in the jungles, killed the gooks, eaten the monkeys and the tigers, and fucked the prostitutes. They had fathered *bui doi*, the dust of life, the halflings who would become outcasts wherever they went. And they had picked up habits. A world away, facing terrors we could only imagine, and they picked up the same habits we had. Grass: Vietnamese Black, Siamese Gold. Thai hash. Heroin: purer and cleaner than anything you'd find on a New York street corner. Acid: pure drops, no names, no labels. Tripping while bullets were flying. Blood and guts in 3-D, stranger than any hallucination.

They didn't get it either. The official accounts were full of lies. That much they were sure of. Body counts? Fake. Military discipline? A joke. Authority? You're on your own. Enemies? Everywhere. Who's more dangerous: the teenage girl with a grenade hidden in her blouse, or the lieutenant ordering you back to the front line? Guys shot off their own toes to get out. Others stepped on mines and lost their balls. Fifty thousand came back in plastic body bags. "Who the fuck are you to call me a coward for splitting?"

I could listen to their conspiracy theories all night. "Kissinger's a Nazi. Nixon's a grand dragon in the Ku Klux Klan. The Trilateral Commission wants to rule the world. The officers don't give a fuck about us. Ninety days in Officer Candidate School, and they have the right to throw our bodies at a fucking hill, a piece of dirt, a mound of shit? Have you ever stood waist-deep in a swamp for two days, scared to breathe? Leeches crawling up your fucking asshole, mosquitoes in your eyes, in your nose, in your mouth so you couldn't fucking breathe if you wanted to? So fucking cold that your lower half goes numb, and you can't feel your feet, and your dick disappears, but above the waist you're shivering, your teeth are chattering so loud you're afraid the gook sniper's gonna hear them and blow your fucking brains all over the swamp?"

No, the truth is way too strange to be bothered with lies. Everybody in Baldwin Street was facing their fears, finding their reasons. I was at home. I could relax. I could even get help. Christ, I could give fucking help. Slowly, at its own pace, self emerged. I could look in the mirror and see it there, hiding behind my eyes, trying to escape, trying to surface. Is this what you are afraid of? Seeing who you are? *Being* who you are? Discovering what you are and discovering that what you have been afraid of is this fear of discovery of what you are afraid of? Are you afraid of discovering your self? Or are you afraid that upon discovery, you will suddenly realize that you have not lived up to expectations? Whose fucking expectations, anyway?

All along I had thought that I was doing drugs to take a journey when in reality I was avoiding the journey. I wanted to stay the child, to live in fantasy, to imagine a self that was comfortable, happy in a closed world.

I had been in Toronto for less than a year when Cheryl came up for a long weekend. She had stopped smoking, enrolled in a community college. She was vibrant, exhilarating. Her laugh was electric, her smile contagious. I felt like a kid again, and I let my imagination roam. We made love as adults. As we slipped into an afternoon slumber, I held her close, tight. "I love you," I said. "I miss you. I need you." She hasn't left me since.

43

Cheryl came into the kitchen wrapped in a fluffy white terry-cloth robe. Her sweet smile barely poked through as she said, "Good morning."

"Morning," I said. "Look."

She took the newspaper and locked on the headline. Without saying a word, she read the story. "What about the vets?" she said. "This is not what we want. This is bullshit."

"I'm sorry, what?"

"Didn't you read the article?"

"Uh, no, I got stuck on the headline and started to worry about Pop."

She shook her head, laughing. "This is a pardon, not an amnesty. The government is admitting no wrongdoing. And it's only for you draft dodgers. It doesn't cover the deserters. They'll still have to go through a case-by-case analysis. This is such bullshit. It's like they're saying, 'Okay, boys, we know you're sorry, and we forgive you. You can come home now.' Fuck them." She'd gotten her Irish up and was so pissed that she turned beet red. "I better get down to the office. It's gonna be a long day."

I was so proud of her. For two years now, she had been working at the Toronto Anti-Draft Program, helping other American exiles, supporting the both of us while I tapped away at the typewriter trying to make sense of my life. I stood up and gave her a big hug. As she slipped into the shower, I went down the hall and turned the heat up, knowing that she hated stepping out into a cold bathroom. I listened to make sure the furnace kicked in, and just as I heard the whir of the fan, the phone rang. "Hello."

"Davey. Did you hear what President Carter did?"

"Yeah, Pop. It's on the front page of the *Globe and Mail*."

"So when are you coming home?"

I didn't realize just how much I had changed until that instant. I felt slightly anemic, especially in my legs. My legs felt weak, and they buckled imperceptibly. I tried to take a step, but I couldn't move. I looked out the window. The sun was higher now. A bird was twittering on the stark limb just outside the window. The ice crystal was dissipating, a thin line of water streaking down the windowpane. The depth of the silence on the phone line was offset by the cacophony around me: the birds' chirping, the icicles falling, the shower running, the fan whirring, the coffee perking, the refrigerator cooling—I heard them all, each of them indistinguishable from the others, so that the universe was abuzz. But they were all good noises. They were all comforting, clear, and clean. There were no helicopter blades, explosions, screams, gunshots, mortar firings, firecrackers, ash cans, cherry bombs, bottle rockets, eggs breaking, pumpkins shattering, cars braking, cigarette puffs, joint hits, coughing fits, bowls blown, death moans, needle punctures, punches, braking windows, car accidents, rock bands, television blares, radio static, phones ringing, beer belches, cops' threats, tears flowing, doubts screaming, crowds roaring, buses, subways, planes, motorcycles, air brakes, sirens, foghorns, mothers' pleas, or fathers' judgments.

"Davey, are you there, are you all right?"

"Yeah, Pop, I'm great."

"So, when are you coming home?"

"Pop, I am home."

"But—"

"No, Pop. I'm sorry. But this is home for me now. I feel safe here. I feel like I belong here. I don't do drugs; I don't drink too much. I don't have to lie; I don't have to pretend. I am welcome here. I belong here. Pop, I'm happy here. I'll visit you, and you can visit me. But I won't be moving back."

"You sound like your mind is made up."

"Yeah, Pop, it is. I love you, Pop."

"I know you do, son. I love you too."

"Pop, I finally figured out why Brian died."

"What'd you mean?"

"Brian died so that I could live."

"Of course he did, son, of course he did. Listen, your brother is here. Do you want to talk to him?"

"Sure."

"Hey, Davey, what's up?"

"Hey, Kevin. I am!"

When Cheryl got out of the shower, I was there to enfold her in a warm towel, fresh out of the dryer. "Umm, you're being awful nice today. Who was on the phone?"

"That was Pop and Kevin. Hey, guess what Kevin told me?"

"What?"

"He told me Schneid's is closing. Abe and Lynn are retiring and moving to Florida. Neither one of their kids wants the store.

They tried to sell it, but nobody wants it. They're just going to move out, and a real estate agency is going to move in."

"All things must pass," she said. "The end of an era."

"Listen, we've been together forever. We're doing pretty good, don't you think?"

"Yeah," she said, looking just a little worried.

I fell to one knee. She leaned over and kissed me, dripping water on me, laughing. "What're you doing?"

"Cheryl, will you marry me?"

"Uh, let me think about it. What's the rush?" Then she let out an unbridled scream of joy. "I thought you would never get around to this day!"

As I got up and twirled her about in my arms, I said, "Let's get married, girl. Let's have a baby. Shit, let's have two!"

ACKNOWLEDGMENTS

This book has been a long time coming, and I want to apologize if I miss any of my very early readers who suffered through my first, bloated manuscript almost fifteen years ago. I especially want to thank those of you who gave me detailed notes, even the ones who advised me to keep my day job: Kerry Bessey, Alan Centofranchi, Tara Hernan, Ron LoGiudice, Bill Morris, Debbie Morris, Beth Philmon, Gary Richman, and Terri Smith. I especially want to thank my family for their continuous support and honest feedback: Patrick Dempsey, Colleen Dempsey, Jeffery Payne, Regina Ballone, and most important, my best friend and partner for forty-five years, my wife, Janis.

Book cover design, illustration, and book design by Colleen Dempsey.

Please visit my website timfdempsey.com, through which you can contact me, or e-mail me at tim@timfdempsey.com.

Website design and support by Michael Rutledge.

Finally, I want to thank the folks at Kickstarter and CreateSpace, especially Victoria Wright, my editor, who have helped me realize my publishing dreams.

Made in the USA
Middletown, DE
31 January 2017